VENGEF

The third and final of t
gripping, gritty ganglanc
r

Vendetta. Payback. Justice.
Someone has to pay the price…

Jane's life is going well. She's happy and the business is going from strength to strength. Apart from one thing she desperately needs to complete her happiness, everything is good. Or it was, until slowly and surely things begin to happen which makes it clear something untoward is occurring.

A vendetta over an old score is putting Jane, her family and business at risk, but opinions as to who is behind this differs.

With suspicion pointing at anyone and everyone, it needs to be discovered who is manufacturing this never-ending stream of cleverly engineered payback before it is too late and everything she holds dear is ripped apart.

What readers are saying about *Vengeful Payback*:

- *"Impossible to put down…"*

- *"All three instalments would make a great movie…"*

- *"Amazing read…"*

- *"The interweaving of characters and their schemes throughout the plot was masterful…"*

- *"On the edge of your seat…"*

*** This book contains written depictions of graphic violence, sex and strong language. It also contains some themes that may be uncomfortable for certain readers.***

Also by Edie Baylis

Downfall Series

Until the End of Time (Downfall #1)
Escaping the Past (Downfall #2)
The Downfall Series Box Set

Retribution Series

An Old Score (Retribution #1)
Finders Keepers (Retribution #2)
The Final Take (Retribution #3)

Hunted Series

The Status Debt (Hunted #1)
The Family Legacy (Hunted #2)
The Target of Lies (Hunted #3)
The Hunted Series Box Set

Allegiance Series

Takeover (Allegiance #1)
Fallout (Allegiance #2)

VENGEFUL PAYBACK

DOWNFALL SERIES #3

EDIE BAYLIS

ATHAME press
- LONDON -

First published in Great Britain in 2018 by Athame Press.
This paperback edition published in 2022 by Athame Press.

Front cover photography: Yakobchuk Viacheslav/Shutterstock, Sascha Burkard/Shutterstock
Back cover: Magiclight/123rf

ISBN 978-1-9998110-4-4

Athame Press
Unit 13230 - PO Box 6945 – London – W1A 6US

Prologue

2001

PROUDLY TAKING JANE'S HAND as the organ cranked up, Seth looked down at her and smiled. He hadn't thought he would ever feel this happy, but today had proved him wrong.

His eyes ran over Jane as she smiled back at him, her hand squeezing his and he longed to kiss her. She looked perfect. The weather was perfect and his *life* was perfect.

As they made to walk back down the aisle through the packed church, now they were finally legally man and wife, Seth felt his heart may explode into millions of tiny shimmering, floating pieces.

Jane looked beautiful in the empire-line white wedding gown she wore, her sparkling tiara sitting atop the high-piled curls of raven hair on her head, leaving several loose waves cascading over her breasts and down to her waist. The diamond necklace he had given her as a wedding present sat perfectly around her neck and caught the light reflecting through the large stained glass windows of the old church they'd chosen for the ceremony.

Seth just couldn't keep the grin off his face. He knew he

looked good in his made to measure frock coat ensemble and crisp high-collared dress shirt. The exact cut of the jacket emphasised his wide shoulders in comparison with his narrow waist, but however good he felt, he had *nothing* on Jane.

He glanced once more at the necklace shooting its prisms of refracted light off its many facets before his gaze roamed lower over Jane's full breasts showcased to perfection in the low-cut sweetheart neckline of the dress. The band of large Swarovski crystals directly underneath her breasts which marked the empire cut of the gown accentuated the beautiful shape of her pregnancy under the soft flowing layers of satin and silk which gently cascaded over her large, but neat bump.

How he wanted to take her straight back to the honeymoon suite he'd booked in the country hotel and lock themselves away for ever, but he knew they had the reception to get through first. Plus, he'd got the rest of his life to spend with her.

There were only two months before their child was due to be born and Seth was ecstatic. Jane had fallen pregnant within the very first week of them rekindling their relationship and although it had been a complete surprise, it had been a great one. Everything was *so* meant to be.

He knew she'd have preferred to marry in a tight corset-style wedding dress, but when they'd received the doubly good news that not only was Jane free from licence and no longer on any form of probation or police radar and then learnt the police were no longer looking for him in relation to old crimes either, he realised they could safely assume their real names at last. With all this in mind he hadn't been willing to wait a *moment* longer to make Jane his once and for all and happily set about organising their church wedding for the second time – almost ten years since the first time he'd planned it.

On top of that after being handed the reins of the Glint club when Bill Benson retired, the business was going from strength to strength, even in the short time they'd been in charge, so things couldn't have been much more perfect.

Standing at the entrance to the church being showered in

confetti, Seth scooped Jane into his arms and gave her a long, passionate kiss, ignoring the myriad of flashbulbs going off around them.

He eyed Maggie standing in the crowd watching the proceedings carefully. He knew full well she wasn't over the moon about their reunion and even less happy about their marriage, not trusting that he wouldn't let Jane down. Seth smiled easily at her. She wasn't a bad girl – she was merely looking out for her friend, but she'd realise in time, like everyone else, that he wasn't going to repeat his mistakes this time around. Neither was Jane.

This time was for keeps and there would be no going back or breaking of promises. *Ever*. This time he would *deliver.*

'I love you Jane,' Seth murmured against Jane's breathless lips.

'And I love you,' Jane replied, having realised there was no point in fighting her feelings anymore. She stared up into the green eyes of the man she'd loved so fiercely for so very long and who had this time, so far, seemed to have stuck to every single thing he'd promised.

The only thing that could possibly have made her happiness complete would be to have had their daughter back from the system and standing next to them, but unfortunately that hadn't happened and it didn't look like it would but she hadn't given up yet.

Seth traced his finger along Jane's cheek and tilted her face back up to his. 'Thank you for making me the happiest man on earth,' he murmured.

Jane pressed herself up against him, her bump meaning she couldn't get as close to him as she'd have liked and smiled feeling a flurry of hard kicks from inside her.

ONE

2002

ANNA SLATER WAS NERVOUS. She'd been surprised to hear now Mandy was getting married she'd put her forward as her replacement. It wasn't so much she doubted her own ability. After all, she'd got a glowing track record of nannying since leaving college, but she was young and usually only the older ones got put forward for high-profile clients like this. However, it would be great to have Seth and Jane Wright on her CV.

It was all very well Mandy putting her forward, but it didn't mean she'd actually be called for an interview, but being as she'd been personally recommended…

From what Mandy had said, the Wright's home was amazing and if she got the job she'd be actually *living* there. She'd dreamt of a break like this. The only downside was that living close again would mean as well as her mother, her sister would expect to see her too. The last places she'd worked had been too far away to warrant regular visits.

Anna swallowed down her resentment. She'd been dumped with the burden of having to make it her life's work to ensure she was the polar opposite of her sister to help keep her mother sane.

They were a nice family, or at least, *had* been. It was Tina who had spoilt it. Ever since Anna could remember she'd ruined everything, using the death of their father as an excuse to spectacularly go off the rails.

She'd run away at thirteen and been hooked on all manner of things by fifteen. By the time she was sixteen, she'd buggered off for good and was working as a prostitute to fund her insatiable drug intake. Their mother had been beside herself waiting for that expected late night call from the police to inform her that her eldest daughter was dead. It hadn't happened, but Anna knew they'd all but been ostracised in their pleasant neighbourhood since her sister had made her choices.

Then when Tina had become so greedy for money, she'd risked everything by keeping her boyfriend's haul of imported heroin at her house. Unsurprisingly she'd got caught and surprise, surprise the boyfriend denied all involvement. Being as she was already known to the police for drugs and soliciting it hadn't taken too much effort to ensure Tina had got sent down and their mother's shame had been bottomless.

Anna had been determined to make up for her sister's shortfall by being a model student, getting good qualifications at college and working tirelessly since. Thanks to this she was now armed with plenty of glowing references, but still forever felt like she was working Tina's ever-increasing debt to the family off by softening her failings.

Anna had successfully orchestrated it so no one found out about her embarrassment of a sister, let alone be seen with her. How on earth could she be taken seriously if people knew she was related to a drug-addled ex-con whore?

Regardless of this, she still felt obliged to go and see Tina every so often, but it didn't mean she had to like her did it? Still, she had no intention of telling her if this new assignment came off for the Wright's. *Not in a million years.*

• • • •

JANE SCOOPED TOBY UP in her arms and planted a kiss on the top of his thick curly hair. 'See you later darling,' she said softly. 'I love you. Be good for Mandy now, won't you?'

Toby uttered a delightful string of babble and reached his chubby fingers out to grab at Jane's earring. Handing him back to Mandy, she smiled. 'I'm not sure when I'll be home, but hopefully it won't be too late.'

'Not a problem,' Mandy smiled, twirling Toby around in her arms. 'We've got plenty to do today haven't we little man?'

Jane pulled on her fitted black suit jacket and smiled. They had a beautiful home which Bill Benson had given them as part of the job, the business was running like clockwork and their association with the Millers had proved, as expected, extremely lucrative.

Walking down the stairs she grabbed the keys to her BMW and picked up her handbag. The only fly in the ointment was despite all of his efforts so far, Seth had failed to locate their first child, but Jason Miller had recommended another private investigator that was supposed to be the best of the best.

Miller had previously spoken about the results he'd got when previously tracing someone using this man and although Seth had been loath to discuss his private business regarding his daughter, he'd been forced to because they had drawn dead ends with everyone else they'd used.

Jane sighed deeply. Getting Grace back was more important than anything. Even though Seth had continually told her it wasn't her fault, she still felt responsible. After all, the prison authorities had taken the new-born from *her*, not him. It had been *her* who had signed away their daughter for adoption – not that she had much memory of that thanks to the cocktail of drugs they'd injected her with, but it had still been *her* who had done it.

Not a day went by when Jane didn't think about Grace and wonder how she was. She'd be six years old now and those reoccurring nightmares she'd had after her daughter was born had started again. *Except now they'd changed.*

For months after she'd had her first child taken from her she'd had the same horrible dream every night: she'd been forced to watch the prison doctor drowning her perfect baby in a bucket of water in front of her very eyes. After a while she'd even begun to suspect the dream might be true, being as the whole episode of what had really occurred still remained distinctly blurred. The same dream continued like a stuck record each night for the remainder of her prison sentence and she'd dreaded going to sleep.

Jane shuddered. Although the pain and loss had never gone away, the dream's occurrence had gradually lessened, but over the last few months it had returned with a vengeance.

The baby in a bucket had morphed into a beautiful little girl with raven hair and bright green eyes who looked miserable as sin. Sometimes she'd be subjected to the most appalling treatment at the hands of her adoptive parents. Other times it was abuse in a children's home where she was kept locked in an attic and on other occasions she'd be beaten or tortured.

Since having Toby shortly after their wedding it had brought it home even more that Grace was absent from their lives. Toby was treated like a prince and it broke Jane's heart to think that her daughter wasn't being treated well and wasn't where she belonged. *With them – her parents.*

• • • •

LACEY GARNER STARED blankly at her reflection in the small mirror propped on her dressing table and flinched hearing the sounds of someone stomping around downstairs. She glanced at the clock on her bedside table seeing she'd got just under an hour before her first punter was due.

Sighing, she ran her fingers through her shoulder-length dark blonde hair and scraped it back into a ponytail then touched up her lip gloss. *And this was supposed to be an improvement from living with her mother and Martin was it?*

She'd been so bloody stupid. She should have known that nothing in this world came without a huge fucking price tag, but she'd been so desperate and in need of someone to help her, she'd allowed herself to believe what had been said. Maybe because she'd *needed* to.

Lacey looked around the damp walls of the poxy bedroom she called hers. *It wasn't hers though was it? It was yet another cell where she could be used as a man's toy. She may as well have stayed where she was.*

Her mother's boyfriend had been pawing at her since he'd moved in when she was nine and by the time she was thirteen, his filthy hands groping over her pyjamas had progressed inside them, which had then moved on to having his way with her. She could still smell the stale beer and fags that were always on his breath.

She knew there had been no point in saying anything to her mother. The woman was always so drunk she rarely remembered she even had a daughter, let alone take on board what her pervert of a boyfriend was doing.

Lacey had become almost resigned to that way of life until one night last year had been the straw to break the camel's back. She'd returned from school after wasting as much time as possible aimlessly walking around the housing estate, to find her mother lying on her back with vomit splattered all down her ripped top, her saggy breasts exposed and a man she'd never seen before rutting between her legs.

She'd seen the needle on the coffee table and it didn't take much guessing to realise her mother was back on heroin. There were two other strangers sitting on the other sofa opposite and Martin stood eagerly watching wearing a big sneer. He'd leered at her, informing her she was up next. She'd seen the lust in those grotesque men's eyes as their gazes ran up and down her body and had known then that had been the end.

Lacey had slipped upstairs and shoved as much as possible in a holdall and wasting no time, opened her bedroom window and jumped down onto the flat roof below to make her way carefully down to the ground. From there, she'd run as fast as possible and caught the first bus into the city. There had been no turning back.

On her third day of sleeping in an underpass and literally starving hungry, Lacey had been surprised, but grateful when a woman approached her offering to buy her a cup of tea and a burger. Although she'd been wary of going off with the woman as she'd looked a bit drugged up, she hadn't been able to resist the offer of food and a hot drink.

Whilst Lacey hungrily devoured the burger and chips the woman had said she knew of a place which would gladly give shelter to young girls like her. She'd been too desperate to be overly suspicious and had stupidly followed the woman, who called herself Tina, back to a five-storey townhouse.

The woman she met next had appeared a little brash and the big man with his missing fingers and scarred face was intimidating, but despite appearances they were really friendly. *At first...*

Lacey had been too exhausted to ask any questions and had quickly flopped into the nice clean bed with its crisp sheets and fluffy cushions.

It was only two days later she realised she'd made a grave mistake when she'd learnt *exactly* what was expected of her in return for her board, but she'd been too shit scared to disappear. Besides, where would she have gone apart from home?

At least this place was slightly cleaner than her mother's shit-hole of a flat.

Two

SETH TAPPED THE ASH from his cigarette into the ashtray on the desk and flicked through the paperwork in front of him. He couldn't be bothered to deal with that now.

He glanced at his diary for the day before looking at Dan sitting opposite. When he'd been put in charge of the Glint, he'd given Dan more responsibility because he had the feeling that given the chance, the man would prove his worth and he'd done just that.

'So, what's today's plan?' Dan asked.

Seth pursed his lips. 'I've got a meeting with Jason Miller this afternoon. A couple of things we need to run through. Apparently, someone's been asking questions.'

Dan nodded. It was common for clubs to get potential suppliers testing the water about opportunities, but this wouldn't be something the Glint would entertain.

Phil, Bill Benson's son, Seth's friend and associate of old dealt with theirs and the Limelight's drug supply and he would be less that amused if it turned out someone was attempting to tread on his toes.

Things hadn't been the same between Seth and Phil since it had been discovered their mutual friend Digger had lied in his quest to keep Seth from Jane. It had turned out that Phil hadn't known of Digger's lies and believed Jane to be dead, but Digger's betrayal had led to Jane being incarcerated for longer and the loss of her child as well as keeping Seth from her.

Although Seth hadn't blamed Phil over this chain of events, it was Phil who couldn't handle the guilt and his men, rather than himself dealt with everything these days.

The door knocked suddenly and Jane stuck her head through the door. 'Morning boys!' she said brightly. 'Just letting you know I'll be calling that agency this morning.' She'd got the woman who Mandy had recommended over for an interview. Work was so busy. She needed to secure another live-in nanny and fast and she'd much prefer to go with recommendations rather than having to start from scratch.

'Ok, that's fine. How's Toby?' Seth had left before his little boy had got up.

'He's fine,' Jane smiled before disappearing once more.

Seth grinned as he turned back toward Dan and winked. 'Just got to talk Jane into having a few more kids now.'

He'd been in state of almost constant euphoria since he and Jane had got back together. Even though it hadn't been planned when she'd fallen pregnant within a couple of weeks he'd been overjoyed and it had hit him with an almost suffocating pleasure as her belly had swelled.

When they'd married and he'd watched her walking towards him up the aisle heavy with his child, his love had been crushing. The protectiveness and happiness he'd felt was overwhelming, but nowhere near as overwhelming as when his son came into the world especially as he'd missed the experience the first time around.

His heart was so full of love for his family he'd quite happily give her child after child like he'd always wanted. All he needed now was to secure their first child's return then both he and Jane would be complete.

Happily it seemed they were finally getting somewhere on that score. Although everyone he'd tried so far had failed to locate where Grace was, he *had* made inroads with where they stood legally.

The high-priced lawyer he'd brought on board several months ago had got a court to grant access to Jane's prison records and with a few well-timed payoffs to the right people, he'd got his hands on the paperwork concerning the removal of the new-born which the prison system had tried very hard to conceal.

Seth could now prove that Grace was taken from Jane illegally. The medical reports which had been lifted proved beyond any doubt that she'd been both sedated and tranquilised *four* times over the legal limit and it had been at this point which she'd been made to sign the paperwork.

There was speculation as to whether it was even Jane's signature on these damaging documents, but even if it was, whilst under the influence of a prison-administered overdose no court in the land would accept she had been physically or mentally able to undertake such a life-changing decision as to the permanent welfare of a child.

This combination gave them the much needed collateral to prove the removal of their daughter was not legal and therefore would be voided, giving them back their right of full custody. What was now needed was to locate Grace before she was actually adopted because if that happened, it would make things a *lot* harder or maybe even *impossible* to overturn.

Seth cracked his knuckles and smiled. Whatever happened he would get their daughter back one way or the other like he'd promised.

• • • •

TINA STARED BLANKLY at the dirty walls of her office at Elipse and aimlessly adjusted the photo of a topless woman hanging at a tilt on the wall in a black plastic frame. She walked slowly around her desk and sat down heavily on the chair.

Grabbing her blue handbag from the floor she pulled out a packet from the inside zipped pocket and eyed the small amount of heroin. There should be enough here for a couple of smokes. *Just.*

Should she smoke it now, or wait until later? Tina glanced at the time. *She'd wait until later.* She needed to speak to Eliza and Digger first and ask about a raise. She wanted more than she was getting, especially with what they expected her to do. It was no skin off her nose personally, but she knew damn well most people would expect a hell of a lot more.

The heroin debt she'd been racking up with Aiden Barber was getting out of control and she couldn't keep up with the repayments. She was bloody wriggling for cash and Aiden would stop giving her the gear on tick *real* soon if she didn't rectify the situation. *Fuck, fuck, FUCK.*

She'd phone Anna. It was about time she paid her a visit. Surely she could weigh her in a few quid? She was doing ok for herself after all, the snotty bitch. Her nose wrinkled up with ill-concealed annoyance. The way her sister looked down her nose at everyone like she was Lady-Fucking-Muck.

It was easy for Anna. It hadn't been her who'd ended up responsible for looking after a younger sister day and night whilst their bloody mother had wallowed in self-pity after their father had had the good sense to hang himself by a rope in the garage had it? No. It had been *her.*

Anna hadn't been the one to bear the pressure. She'd also escaped from being forever blamed for everything for the rest of time, hadn't she? Why? Because it had been *her* instead. *Again.*

It was *always* her.

Well, as far as Tina was concerned, Anna owed her - *big time*, so the very *least* she could do was to bung her a few quid now and then.

Even now each time she had the misfortune to see or speak to her Tina was still treated like a piece of shit by their mother. The horrible old bat wouldn't even lend her any more brass.

Maybe she wouldn't be so fucked up if her mother hadn't been so wrapped up in herself rather than thinking about her daughters.

Sighing in resignation, Tina got up from the desk. She didn't even know where Anna was. The cow hadn't visited her for at least two months, which of course meant she'd have to bite the bullet and phone their mother to ask of her sister's whereabouts.

Tina's mouth set in determination. She'd call her now whilst she was irritated enough to face the scathing comments and usual diatribe of blame spilling from the crusty old cow's mouth.

....

ELIZA SCOWLED AS SHE opened the paper. She glanced at the picture of Seth standing with his arm around Jane as they stood next to another well-appointed and locally respected couple at some poxy charity function.

The caption read:

> *'Mr and Mrs Seth Wright and Councillor Roberts with his wife Julia, attended the 46th banquet last month in aid of the Sunflowers Trust....'*

Eliza scanned the rest of the article:

> *'Owners of one of the city's most prestigious Gentlemen's club 'The Glint', Seth and Jane Wright, are well known for their generous charitable donations....'*

Eliza seethed, her teeth grating as her eyes ran over Jane's figure in the picture, resplendent in the tight velvet evening dress she wore. *As usual.*

Charitable fucking donations? Who were they trying to kid? Why did they have to get all this bloody recognition? If it hadn't been for Bill-fucking-Benson giving them the club because he'd gone mental after his missus had got topped, they'd still be exactly where they'd come from. *The fucking gutter.*

Eliza straightened down her hair extensions and pushed herself from her chair. Walking around the other side of her desk, she wrapped her arms around Digger's massive neck and planted a kiss on his stubbly face. She ran her finger down the thick puckered scar which stretched across the whole of the left hand side of his cheek and tried not to linger on his missing ear. Although completely healed, it was a permanent reminder of the punishment he'd received, courtesy of Phil and Seth for the lies he'd told. As were the missing fingers on his right hand.

In all truthfulness, Eliza knew Digger had been fortunate in walking away at all after what he'd done. The only reason he had was because of his long history with them. He'd also managed to truthfully convince them that when he'd lied about Jane being dead it had been a snap decision. He hadn't been in his right mind - his head was fucked. He'd immediately bitterly regretted it but had been unable to retract the statement. It had after all been down to *him* Jane ended up in the nick for so long and lost her kid to the authorities in the process.

Eliza scowled petulantly. It seemed Jane had made up for that since by having another kid in the interim so she couldn't be *that* bothered about the first one, could she? It was all bullshit put on for show anyhow. Jane didn't give a fuck about anyone but herself. She never had.

Psychos like Seth and Jane could pop out kids like peas whereas *she* couldn't have them. But that was set to change very, *very* soon. Her inability to have kids was would be her saviour and one thing was guaranteed. Jane and Seth would *not* be getting that child back.

On the flip side, Eliza knew she'd also been fortunate with how everything had turned out. It could have been *very* different. Trying to royally shaft Seth and Jane by threatening to expose them to Bill Benson had spectacularly backfired.

Unbeknownst to her they'd already levelled with him about their shared unsavoury past, but in her rush to snare Seth for herself she'd unwittingly attempted to screw Benson over as well.

She'd been hasty in opening her trap. If she'd have kept quiet, she'd have been fine. She'd already done a lot for Benson by serving Charlie and Ernie Carter up– admittedly it had been to save her own skin, but she'd still done it hadn't she? And Benson had known she'd needed compensation for that, hence her being offered to run Ernie's gaff, but after her balls up she'd been escorted from the city and banished like a dog.

Nothing though could have prepared Eliza to find herself having to start over again back at the bottom of the rubbish heap. And it really *had* been the bottom of the dump. The only good point was tempting Digger on board alongside her. Not that he'd had many options being as he'd also been shoved out. However, it hadn't been him who had been forced to ply his wares to unclean men on the back streets had it? No. It had been *her.*

She'd had do *something* about their grim situation because Digger had been rendered incapable for some time after Seth and Phil had caught up with him.

At least they'd been left alone since on the proviso their paths *never* crossed again. This was all very well, but banishing them had only fuelled the burning need to pick themselves back up with the sole incentive of hitting Seth and Jane where it hurt. *And that time was now.*

Thankfully after some time of working on her back Eliza had landed a client who had been so enamoured with her she'd fleeced enough cash from the stupid twat for some premises so *she* could be in charge again.

For sure Digger hadn't much liked her idea of concentrating on younger girls, but she'd needed to find a niche. She didn't have to particularly like it. That wasn't the point. There was a gaping market for it and she wanted the money that opening would bring. Business ideas weren't there to be *liked* – they were there to be *worked* and pull in the fucking cash.

Eliza smiled smugly. Digger wasn't complaining now, was he? The services they offered had ensured a very healthy bank balance and they'd got a lovely house nowhere near this dump of a brothel.

Besides they couldn't have remained living under Elipse's roof. Not if they wanted to succeed with their ultimate payback on Seth and Jane and both she and Digger wanted that more than *anything.* It was all now beginning to come together very nicely and she would not be stopping until she got exactly what she wanted.

On top of all that they also had a guy living on site and keeping tabs on things. Providing Steve Lomond had free reign over the girls then he was happy. Eliza had very little time for the man, but being as they could utilise him to aid them in various facets of their plans then it was worth putting up with his pig-ugly face and obnoxious perversions for that alone.

She'd had to really. They'd had very few people that they could trust or who were reliable as well as having half a brain. The one guy they had who fitted that bill could only do some of the things required. Aiden had been sent into the Limelight only this week to ask a few questions which she hoped would ruffle a few feathers and cause suspicion, but he'd had to abandon the job being as his brother worked there and a lot of the staff knew him. Her next port of call was to send Lomond because no one knew him.

'Fancy a break from work?' Eliza purred in Digger's remaining ear. She swivelled her body around in front of him so her deep cleavage was level with his eyes.

'Come here then,' Digger growled, pressing his mouth down onto her breasts.

Eliza smiled and straddled him on the chair, feeling his hardness growing as she wriggled on his lap. It was a bit of a pain he had all those fingers missing, but at least the ones on his left hand were still there, she thought smiling as his hand made its way into her knickers.

Yes, everything was going to plan nicely.

THREE

'THANK YOU FOR SEEING ME Mrs Wright,' Anna said nervously, taking the proffered seat in the beautifully furnished sitting room on arriving at the huge house.

'Call me Jane,' Jane said cheerily, taking the paperwork and sitting down on the other sofa. 'I'll just have a look though these.'

Anna studied the woman opposite her. Her eyes ran over Jane's slim but shapely figure encased perfectly in an elegant fitted cream dress. She was indeed beautiful - much more in real life than in the papers. She scrutinised Jane's heart-shaped face and full red lips in a perfect cupid's bow, her dark eyes framed with impossibly long lashes and the raven black waves of hair cascading down to her waist. The woman oozed class without a trace of ostentatiousness.

Anna's gaze continued around the room with its collection of eclectic furniture and shelves of books. A thick luxurious rug sat in the centre of the room atop the polished oak floorboards and a large chandelier was suspended from a heavy chain from the high ceiling. This room alone was bigger than the entire ground floor of her mother's house and she wondered silently whether she would get the chance to see any of the other rooms, betting they were all just as stunning. She hoped so and swallowed nervously. *She'd love this job and could very much handle living here.*

Mandy had told her Jane and Seth were really nice people and not to take too much heed of the stories she'd read about them. Anna would have been lying if she'd said she hadn't heard they were involved in all manner of gangland type activities and were as dangerous as hell, but on the flip side if they were *that* bad, surely they wouldn't be living somewhere like this or involved with influential people of the city, or featuring in the society and business pages of the paper half the time would they?

There had been a small part of Anna which had been half-expecting to walk into a room full of thugs clutching machine guns, wearing spats and trilbies like the people in that film *Bugsy Malone* she'd seen as a kid, but of course there was nothing like that at all and in the five minutes she'd been with Jane she'd seemed nothing apart from pleasant.

Ok, so they ran a Gentlemen's club, which apparently was a posh term for a strip club, but that was hardly a brothel was it!

Anna absentmindedly speculated what the husband was like. Maybe *he* was the psycho and Jane was the sweet naïve unsuspecting wife – again like in the films?

'So,' Jane said suddenly, shaking Anna from her thoughts. 'Your references are good and I have to say Mandy highly recommended you. You're young though. Twenty-three?'

'Yes, I'm twenty-three Mrs Wright, but I've worked consistently since I qualified. I've been both live-in and day nanny for several families – all for fairly long periods of time.'

'Call me Jane,' Jane repeated. 'Can't stand the formal stuff! So, what made you want to do this type of work?'

Anna smiled. 'I just love children. Always have. Being a live-in nanny means I can spend even more time with them.'

Jane nodded, taking in what the girl was saying.

'Sometimes it can get to the point where I almost feel like one of the family,' Anna continued.

'Yes, but you're *not* the child's mother are you!' Jane said sharply, acutely reminded these people were, when push came to shove, applying for the job of her child's stand-in mother and that stuck in her throat.

Reddening, Anna realised she'd somehow said something out of turn because she'd clearly seen a warning flash in the woman's eyes. 'I meant it's nice to work for a happy family.' she said quickly, attempting an apologetic smile.

'What of your family?' Jane questioned.

Anna's face fell slightly. *Oh no! Not the family question.* 'Well, I stay at my mother's when I finish an assignment in readiness for the next and I don't see my sister much. We're not close.'

Jane's expression softened. 'What about boyfriends?'

Anna shook her head. 'I'm not interested. It would be difficult to have a relationship with what I do. My work is the most important thing in my life, so boyfriends aren't something I give much thought to.'

Actually, they were. She'd thought for years about boyfriends because she'd never had one. She'd always been shy and nervous around the opposite sex so they'd always seen her as a bit of a standing joke. In fact, she'd never met a boy who had interested her enough to want to even go down that road. She didn't know whether it was because her sister had allowed all manner of old men and disgusting creatures to sleep with her for money which had put her off or what.

There had been one lad she'd gone to the cinema with when she was nineteen, but when he'd kissed her at the end of the evening, she'd felt embarrassed and unsure as to what she'd been supposed to do – especially when he'd pushed his tongue into her mouth. Either way he'd obviously been less than impressed because he hadn't asked to see her again.

On top of that she was far too shy for going out and mingling with people and so having a job where she could convince herself she was part of a family that she'd never had enabled her to pretend her dysfunctional *real* family didn't exist. Besides, children didn't judge or analyse her so it was perfect.

Jane smiled at Anna. That take on the boyfriends was what she'd wanted to hear. She wouldn't have random strangers traipsing through deflecting the nanny's attention from her child. *Or* perhaps overhearing something….

She looked at the girl in front of her. 'What's your availability?' Jane asked very aware of time frames. Mandy had three weeks left of her notice to serve, but if a suitable replacement was available before that time, she'd jump at the chance to leave

'I finished my previous assignment last week, so I'm available as soon as you want me to be,' Anna replied, aware she was sounding over eager, but at the end of the day, she *was*.

Jane smiled. 'Well, that's good. This job is for a full-time, live-in position. You'd get your bed and board and a full day and night off every week, but there isn't usually a set day for that. You're probably aware we have a lot of engagements we need to honour, but when we're here we like to spend time in the evenings with our son, so your time is your own those nights in addition. I appreciate it makes it difficult for you to plan anything, therefore it's quite a difficult assignment for most people because you'd have to work around our fluid schedule.'

Anna laughed. 'That's fine by me! I never have anything planned. You've probably guessed I'm shy so I don't tend to go out much.'

Jane frowned. 'Sometimes you'd need to accompany us to social engagements when Toby is there. Would that be a problem?'

Anna shook her head. 'No, apart from I doubt whether I'd have the sort of clothes suitable for the lovely places you go.' Realising she'd probably come across as sounding presumptuous, she blushed furiously. 'I-I mean I'm not exactly a virtue of fashion!'

Jane laughed openly, her face lighting up. 'You look ok to me!' She looked at Anna's smart two-piece suit and the pink roll-neck jumper underneath. 'Besides, we'd provide you an allowance for outfits for those occasions if you didn't have something you felt comfortable to wear so don't worry about that,' she grinned. 'Don't believe *everything* you read about us in the papers!'

Anna could have dug a hole and climbed in it. *She hadn't wanted to insinuate she read all the gossip.* 'Oh God, I-I didn't mean anything like that. I-I haven't heard anything bad. I...'

'Hey, relax!' Jane grinned. 'I'm winding you up!'

Anna breathed a sigh of relief and made a mental note to try not to take herself too seriously. She knew her nervousness invariably ended up becoming irritating and she didn't want to annoy this woman one iota. She really liked Jane Wright so far.

'Do you drive?' Jane asked.

'Yes, but I don't have a car right now,' Anna replied. 'I can always get one though.'

Jane nodded, pleased. 'We'd be looking at a six week trial period initially and we'll get you a car if needed, so that solves that problem. Is this something you think you'd be interested in?'

Anna smiled. *Did that mean she'd got the job?* 'Most definitely. It sounds fantastic. When would you like me to start?'

Jane frowned. 'There are things that haven't been discussed yet.'

Anna's face dropped. 'Yes, of course. I'm sorry. I'm jumping the gun, aren't I? I'm just keen, I...'

Jane held her hand up. 'Anna, you don't even know how much we're paying!' she smiled. 'If we're all happy after the trial period, the salary we're offering is fifty thousand a year, not including expenses. Does this sound reasonable?'

Anna nearly choked. *Fifty thousand? The most she'd earnt was eighteen.* 'Wow! That sounds *more* than reasonable Jane.'

Jane looked up hearing the front door slam. 'Excuse me a minute,' she said, rising from the sofa.

Jane had almost reached the sitting room door when Seth bounded into the room and without saying a word, pulled her tightly against him. Bringing his mouth down onto hers, his hands shifted her tight dress up over her thighs.

'God, I've missed you this afternoon,' he murmured.

'Seth!' Jane laughed. She pushed him away and pulled her dress back down. 'Being as you haven't noticed, we've got company.' She rolled her eyes at Anna. 'Anna, as you've probably guessed, this is my husband. Seth, this is Anna. She's going to be Toby's new nanny.'

Snapping his head around quickly, Seth's eyes locked on to the woman on the sofa and smiled widely. 'Hello Anna.'

Anna stared at the man as he crossed the room towards her, feeling her nerves quivering from inside. He was tall, extremely well built with a neatly trimmed beard, sharp jaw and the greenest eyes ever. His thick dark wavy hair was scraped back into a small ponytail at the base of his neck. Like Jane he was so much more attractive than in the photos she'd seen. *In fact, she'd go so far as to say he was beautiful.*

Stretching his hand out Seth grasped Anna's hand and shook it firmly. 'Pleased to meet you and welcome aboard.'

Anna hoped the furious blush she sensed creeping up her neck wasn't visible and her hand tingled with the electrical charge she felt from the man's touch.

'So,' Seth said, throwing his jacket haphazardly on the sofa and showing his well-muscled arms and torso through his fitted white shirt. He pulled his tie away from the collar and undid the top two buttons revealing a smattering of chest hair. 'Where are we at then?' He flopped himself down on the sofa and pulled Jane down next to him.

'We were *trying* to discuss hours and expectations,' Jane laughed.

'Yep, that's easy. Anna - you deal with Toby in the day and some evenings. The evenings we're in, we'll be with him. Nights though – if he wakes,' Seth smiled, '*you* deal.' He placed his hand on Jane's stomach and winked. 'Nights are *ours*. I want to continue the bloodline.'

Jane batted his hand away. 'He's a bloody nightmare. If he had his way, I'd have been barefoot and pregnant for years!'

Seth raised his eyebrows mockingly. 'Oh and you think that won't be how you're going to spend at least the next few years then? Except you'll have shoes of course!'

'Seth! You'll frighten her off!' Jane laughed, seeing Anna blush furiously. 'Look, you're embarrassing her.'

Anna smiled. 'Actually, it's nice you're so much in love.' *It was obvious. They were like the fairy tale. The complete and utter fairy tale in every way.*

Seth's face became serious. 'The only other thing is that sometimes sensitive business meetings occur from here, so we'd expect you to sign a full non-disclosure agreement.'

'W-What's that?' Anna stuttered, unsure what that meant.

Seth smiled in an attempt to put the nervous young girl at ease. 'It means that anything here, *stays* here. You speak to *no one* about us. Under any circumstances.'

Anna nodded nervously.

'You're undoubtedly aware the press like to print stuff about people whether it's right, wrong or indifferent and they'll go to any lengths to hunt people down to extract information which they'll twist around to make it as interesting as possible,' Seth said.

'What Seth's saying is anything that's printed about us won't have come from you right?' Jane's eyes glinted, hoping she was getting the message across.

'Not even for *any* amount of money,' Seth added. His eyes narrowed as he smiled thinly. 'Because if you did, we'd have to kill you.'

Anna laughed nervously. *At least they had a good sense of humour*. 'No, I'd never speak about anything that goes on here.'

'Right then, that's good,' Seth nodded. 'Have you met Toby yet?' Seeing Anna shake her head, he resumed a normal wide smile and got to his feet. 'I'll go and get him.'

FOUR

LOCKING HERSELF IN THE toilet Lacey pulled several pieces of toilet paper from the roll and meticulously laid it all around the seat. Satisfied she'd left no trace of the plastic seat uncovered, she sat down.

She felt tears beginning to escape from her eyes and desperately tried to hold them back. That bloody awful manager had booked yet another slot with her and was due any minute now. She hadn't even had chance to shower since the last client and she felt even more dirty and disgusting than usual. It didn't help this bloke was a nasty bastard who always hurt her. He got off on being exceptionally rough and she hated him.

When she'd asked Eliza if one of the other girls could sometimes deal with Steve Lomond's freebies rather than her, she'd got a swift slap around the face and was told in no uncertain terms that if Steve asked for a girl by name then that was who he would get.

Lacey glanced down at her knickers, hoping to spot a sign that her worst fears were not going to be confirmed, but there was still nothing. She was now two weeks late and was starting to believe that against probability the one time a condom had ever split had been unfortunate enough to have left a lasting reminder.

She'd ignored it - telling herself the chances were remote, but now it looked like it might have only gone and happened and she couldn't bear it. *Really* couldn't bear it. It was even worse being as the split condom had belonged to *him*.

A sudden sharp bang on the toilet door made Lacey's heart lurch in her chest.

'Oih! Hurry up in there. Steve's waiting,' Eliza's raucous voice screamed. 'Don't start telling me you're not feeling well or anything like that. Just get a fucking move on and make sure you're wearing your school uniform.' She knew Lacey was Lomond's favourite and it was more important than *ever* they kept him above everyone happy. As well as needing him to keep things running smoothly here, they also required his assistance with their other plans.

Lacey wiped the tears away from her cheeks with the back of her hand and quickly flushed the toilet. She'd made sure as requested she'd scrubbed her makeup off so Eliza and the punter would be happy. 'I'm coming now,' she said hollowly.

Standing up, she looked at herself in the mirror and felt sick as she adjusted her school tie over the overly tight cropped white shirt. The shirt wasn't hers, but the rest of the uniform was. She should still be wearing it, but in the right place. The school hadn't bothered trying to find out why she hadn't turned up for the last six months. Why would they? It wasn't like she was worth anything. She'd only got a couple of months to go before she officially left and then they couldn't do anything at all. Besides, it wasn't like they would see her. She was in the city for one and secondly, she'd only left this bloody building twice since being here.

The only time the girls were allowed out was when they were taken to that special doctor who also expected 'favours' to get their contraceptives and even then they were escorted. They were even escorted in an emergency.

There was a girl last month that a punter had gone crazy at because she'd cried. He'd paid ten grand for her virginity and she'd spoilt it for him apparently by crying, so he'd slashed her face up. And what had happened? Digger had driven her to an alley and dumped her, getting Aiden Barber to pretend she was his sister and call an ambulance. Aiden of course accompanied her to the hospital to make sure she said nothing apart from what had been agreed, which was that she'd been jumped on the way back from the Co-op.

Lacey shivered. She didn't like Aiden either. He might be nice looking and she knew a lot of the girls gave him freebies in exchange for a bag of gear, but she most definitely wasn't one of them.

Apparently now this girl was too 'ugly' to bother keeping, so Eliza had sold her on for a few quid to a bunch of Arabs from London. She'd disappeared a week later, still with all one hundred and four stitches in her face and that had been it.

Lacey felt like screaming. How the hell would she ever get out of here? She was no match for these people and knew damn well they'd find her if she escaped or breathed a word. She'd have to tell Eliza she might be pregnant though and knew she'd most likely get a beating, but if she was, she needed to get that pervert's baby out of her as soon as possible.

'Lacey!' screeched Eliza's rasping voice once more.

'I'm coming!' Lacey cried, taking a deep breath as she unbolted the door.

• • • •

'OH....' JANE GASPED, clutching at the sheets whilst Seth thrust gently but consistently from behind, his large hands holding her hips, his mouth on her neck and his breath hot in her ear.

She still sometimes felt like pinching herself about how much her relationship with the only man she'd ever loved had improved beyond her wildest dreams. She'd never *ever* believed she could be this happy and content. Had never thought it was possible. Seth had shown he was going to make it how it should have been from the start and unable to help herself, despite her misgivings on just how awful it had been and what they'd put each other through, she'd chanced it and had hit the jackpot. He'd delivered *everything* he'd promised and more.

Her body shuddered as Seth's nimble fingers teased her nipples into unbearable hardness whilst his steady pace grew faster. 'Wait!' she gasped, turning over even though it meant she'd temporarily lose him from within her.

Turning around to face him, Jane ran her tongue over Seth's lips, loving his taste and pressed her mouth onto his. Her fingers splayed over his muscular torso and pushing herself onto her knees, she traced her tongue around his nipples and in a line down the ridges of his stomach.

Seth's cock, thick and pulsing throbbed inches from her mouth and she flicked her tongue teasingly around the tip. Taking his hard shaft into her mouth, Jane casually worked him, his moans of need loud as she took him deep down her throat.

Feeling his lust nearing intolerable levels, Seth raised his pelvis higher. The effect his wife's lips and mouth had on him was always agonisingly pleasurable and he groaned with need.

'Jane, come sit on me. I want to look at you,' he panted and lifting her easily over him, smiled at her beautifully flushed face as with a gasp she eased onto his length.

He looked up at his wife as she began to ride him, her body resplendent in a tiny sheer baby-doll slip. The almost translucent material like spider web leaving every curve and part of her body tantalisingly visible.

Feeling Seth's cock thicken further, Jane began working him fast.

Seth watched Jane, her eyes closed and sweat beading on her brow as she moved harder and faster. He was so lucky. *So* fucking lucky. His life couldn't be much more perfect. Pulling the tie of Jane's slip, it fell around her hips and he greedily cupped her full breasts with his hands and gritted his teeth, trying to postpone his orgasm.

Feeling Seth twitch and expand again within her pushed Jane over the edge and her orgasm exploded around her, leaving her almost limp with gasping moans when his seed finally filled her.

Laying Jane gently to one side, Seth kissed her gently and trailed his mouth down her throat, over her breasts and down her stomach. He could feel the tight muscles of her abdomen under his lips and hoped it would only be a short time before it began swelling from another one of his children.

Knowing she'd happily take more, his mouth continued down. Spreading her legs, his tongue delved deep into her, his mouth sucking and her post-orgasmic moans reverted back to needy gasps. *He'd never get enough of this woman.*

He leisurely flicked his tongue around and in her, loving how she writhed below him, her hands bunching in his hair, her cries getting louder and felt the familiar ache as he quickly regained his hardness.

Pulling his mouth away, he moved his body up and with a contented sigh, pushed himself into Jane's willing and open flesh. Picking up a moderate pace, Seth rotated his hips and stared into Jane's eyes. *His life couldn't get any better.*

'Seth,' Jane gasped, her nails digging into Seth's muscular buttock and the pleasure rolling in waves from her core. 'I love you…'

Seth smiled hearing Jane's cries get louder and more desperate as rotating his hips he thrust deeper and felt her start to contract strongly around his cock. 'And I love you… The most beautiful one of all. Jane, you're my world.' *He'd got it all. Even after everything. All he'd ever wanted was his.*

• • • •

ANNA PAUSED OUTSIDE the bedroom door. Jiggling Toby in her arms, she smiled as he gurgled.

They were *still* at it then? She'd walked down the corridor over an hour ago with Toby to bring him to his parents, but after hearing Seth and Jane making love she'd quickly retreated. Judging by the noises she could hear the other side of the door they were definitely still going strong.

Smiling, she walked back down the long corridor again. *Was that what it was like then?* Flushing, Anna imagined what was happening behind those closed doors… In all truthfulness she didn't actually know and the way she was going, never would.

She'd been here a week now and was still getting her head around the layout of the house. It was like a rabbit warren with all the corridors and huge rooms. For the first few nights she'd been terrified she'd get lost.

So far everything had gone well and she was enjoying every bit. Her room – well, it was more like a suite than a room – consisted of a large bedroom with an en-suite bathroom and a separate lounge area, complete with a small kitchenette if she wanted some peace away from everybody else.

Her initial reaction was to eat in her room rather than face awkward dinnertimes at a table intruding on a family she didn't know, but she'd quickly realised that despite their wealth and extravagant lifestyle, Seth and Jane were unassuming and down to earth and she'd genuinely believed them when they'd said she was welcome to join them for dinner each night.

She'd made sure she gave them as much space as possible, even though it was tempting to be constantly around them. She couldn't explain it, but they both held an addictive ability to draw people to them.

Anna still hadn't seen anyone with a machine gun or a trilby, although there had been a couple of people around the house the last week who looked like plausible suspects from CrimeWatch, but that didn't mean anything. And little Toby was a treasure - a delightful little boy who lit her heart up every time she was with him. He was the most gorgeous creature. Jet black hair like his mother, but thick and curly like his father's. On top of that he had the cutest mouth and button nose, along with dark green eyes. He was just *adorable* and Anna felt like she could just eat him.

Jane and Seth, like Mandy had said, seemed lovely and a pleasure to work for. The only thing which made her a little uncomfortable was their unreserved displays of affection towards each other. Uncomfortable was probably the wrong word. It was more to do with that she'd never been around anyone who seemed genuinely happy together.

The second night of working for the Wrights she'd walked into the lounge to get a drink from the kitchen and to her horror Seth was taking Jane over the back of the sofa. Anna had almost died of embarrassment, but they'd just smiled at her as she'd muttered her apologies and rapidly shut the door.

Most days they kissed each other like it was their last day on earth. It was nice, but Anna was acutely aware all of this was stirring feelings in her of which she deemed highly inappropriate. She was also beginning to think about things she shouldn't be. She wanted to know what would make someone feel the way they did to make those type of noises. Those moans, groans and desperate cries of need…

She shifted Toby into her other arm as she stopped further along the corridor wondering where to go next, when she heard a door slam.

'Anna!' Seth's voice boomed.

Anna turned to see Seth walking towards her, bare-chested, his lounge pants hanging loosely from his hips. She forced her eyes not to linger on his muscly chest and the line of hair that ran from his naval disappearing into the low-slung jogging bottoms. Feeling the blush creeping up her neck, she tried not to stare at him. 'Oh, er, hi…'

Seth smiled and took Toby out of Anna's arms. 'Hello son,' he murmured, planting a kiss on Toby's curly head. 'Were you waiting for us?'

Anna blushed again and breathed in the smell of sweat and maleness coming from Seth. 'Well, I-I, er, went to knock a while ago but…'

Seth laughed. 'Ah yes, we had a bit of a lie in this morning didn't we darling?' His arm snaked around Jane who had joined him.

'I've come to say hello to my gorgeous boy,' Jane smiled, chucking Toby under the chin with her finger. 'Morning Anna.'

'Hello Jane. How are you this morning?' Anna said too

brightly, realising it was an absolutely stupid thing to say. From what she'd heard - both of them were *more* than alright.

Unable to help herself she found her eyes running over Jane's body. She may as well have been standing there naked. She could see straight through the sheer slip her boss wore and felt acutely aware she had a long way to go if she wanted a figure like that. She glanced down at her loose-fitting navy trouser suit and hip-length jumper that accentuated the overhang over her waistband.

'I'm feeling great Anna,' Jane smiled, running her hand down Seth's chest as she leaned against him. 'And looking forward to tonight. Don't forget you're accompanying us.'

Anna shook her head. 'No, of course I won't. I'm looking forward to it.' *Except she wasn't. She was dreading it. Completely dreading it.* Only a week in and she'd got to accompany Toby to a function Seth and Jane were attending.

Seth raised his son above his head and pulled a face at him, receiving a flurry of baby giggles in response then handed Toby back to Anna. 'Right you,' he grabbed Jane's hand. 'Come join me in the shower.' He playfully slapped her backside that was barely covered by the translucent material and winked at Anna. 'We may be a while...'

Anna watched as Seth and Jane walked back down the corridor and made herself refrain from following so she could listen as they made love again. *Christ! Was there something wrong with her?*

Shaking her head, she turned and walked downstairs. She had no idea what she would wear tonight and felt panic stir. Jane had asked if she'd got something suitable and Anna had stupidly insisted she had. What was she thinking? She doubted whether she had anything even *remotely* snazzy enough to be seen with that gorgeous pair, let alone anything suitable to accompany them to a private birthday event at a posh club.

She began to feel sweat form at the back of her neck. She was going to make a fool of herself, wasn't she? Show herself up for what she was. *Which was a fucking nobody.*

FIVE

TINA WAS GETTING IMPATIENT. She'd been sat outside the bathroom for five minutes and the stupid bitch still hadn't come out. 'Hurry up will you for Christ's sake!' she cried, banging her fist on the chipped door. 'How long does it fucking take to piss on a stick?'

She wished to God the silly girl hadn't even said anything to her. Why confide in her anyway? It wasn't like they were friends. It *had* meant however she'd been the one to tell Eliza it looked like the stupid cow had managed to get herself knocked up.

Tina rolled her eyes and scowled. She hated being the bloody go-between. All it had achieved was a torrent of abuse of Eliza's wrath then being sent down the chemist to get a test for the girl.

'Lacey!' Tina yelled, banging on the door again.

'I won't be a minute,' the muffled voice came from within.

Huffing petulantly, Tina paced irritably up and down the corridor. She hadn't got all night. She'd managed to get some gear from Aiden on the tick and wanted to go back to her room and top up her levels. Her teeth were starting to grate as it was. Even more so since her mother had slammed the phone down on her, the snotty bitch. At least she'd managed to get the message across that she needed Anna to get in contact and left her number. She'd have to weigh her in enough so she could clean her slate with Aiden. He'd stop giving her gear if she allowed the debt to get much higher and she couldn't be having that.

It was alright for Aiden though wasn't it? Thanks to his brother working with Jason Miller, he'd wangled getting in as his 'plus one' for some posh birthday bash later. Well lucky him. And what was she doing whilst everyone else seemed to be living it up? Babysitting some kid doing pregnancy tests!

Suddenly aware the bathroom door had opened, Tina swung around and stared at Lacey standing in the doorway. 'Well?' she barked.

Grey-faced, Lacey held the pregnancy test up in her shaking fingers, a single tear rolling down her cheek. The blue cross in the indicator panel showed the result quite clearly.

'For fuck's sake!' Tina snapped, snatching the test from Lacey's hand. 'Wouldn't want to be in your shoes when I tell Eliza.'

• • • •

ANNA DELICATELY SIPPED from her glass of white wine and continued whispering to Toby as he sat on her lap. At least he served as a distraction and something for her to concentrate on other than drowning in abject terror from being completely out of her comfort zone.

She wouldn't stay long. Toby had been invited along with Seth and Jane out of courtesy, but no one would expect a baby to be there late so she'd be able to retreat back to the house very shortly.

Anna glanced around the large room, opulent in dripping chandeliers and subdued lighting, velvet drapes and luxurious deep-filled seats. She'd never set foot in one of these type of clubs before. Actually, she didn't think she'd ever been in *any* type of club, let alone one like this. She tried to hide the enthrallment she felt from the host of designer dresses and jewellery worn by the women, betting even a pair of their earrings cost more than what she usually earnt in a year.

Anna glanced down at her dark green cotton dress and feeling even more out of place, pulled aimlessly at a loose thread on the cuff on her black jacket. She bit her lip and fought back the urge to cry with humiliation.

When they'd left tonight, Jane had made an effort to tell her how nice she looked, but Anna knew it was only said to make her feel less stupid. Jane must be mortified about having such a dowdy nanny. How she wished she'd taken up the offer of getting some decent clothes. This was so embarrassing and she was sure everyone was staring at her.

Reminding herself not to drink too much, Anna hurriedly placed her glass back on the table and jiggled Toby up and down. It was difficult not to consistently sip at the wine as a method of giving herself something to do. She hardly ever drank and the worst thing she could do was to get drunk on top of everything else.

Looking up she stared at Jane standing next to Seth, who looked resplendent in a tailored tuxedo, his arm protectively around her waist. Jane looked stunning. Her raven hair was piled up on the top of her head and secured with a diamond comb, leaving a handful of perfectly positioned waves cascading over her shoulders. She wore a beautiful floor-length deep red satin evening gown with a slight train, the soft shimmering material clinging sensuously to her body and emphasising her perfect figure as well as her flawless skin.

Anna had also been introduced to Jason and Linda Miller. She'd wished Linda a happy birthday, well aware the woman didn't know her from Adam and smiled through the embarrassment of being stared at blankly amid polite smiles. She could tell the pair of them were wondering why the hell the Wrights had employed someone whose fashion sense came from British Home Stores.

Feeling sweat gathering on the nape of her neck, Anna reached once more for her glass of wine. It wasn't helping that she'd stupidly decided to call her mother this afternoon out of duty, only to discover Tina had called asking her to get in touch. She'd had then had to go through half an hour of the same old story about how awful her sister was, along with the usual associated emotional blackmail.

Now she'd have to get in contact with Tina and that was the *last* thing she wanted. Sometimes she wished she could get a one-way ticket to the moon. Anna sighed, aware she'd now finished her third glass of wine.

'Anna?' Jane placed her hand on Anna's shoulder, making her jump.

Realising she'd been off with the fairies, Anna quickly swung around and looked into Jane's dark eyes. 'Sorry. Yes?'

'Photo!' Jane smiled, grabbing Anna's hand. 'Come on, up you get. The press want a photo and you and Toby should be in it.'

Anna felt nausea rush over her. 'Oh, not a photo! Surely not with me?' she blabbered. 'Why not just take Toby?'

Jane smiled. 'No, come on. You need to be in it too?'

'But I look…'

'Anna! You look fine,' Jane replied sternly. 'Now hurry up!'

Anna pushed herself nervously up from the table, horribly conscious the wine was having an effect on her legs and readjusted Toby into position on her hip. She carefully followed Jane over to where Seth was standing with Jason and Linda Miller. *This was worse than awful.*

Four or five press photographers gathered in a semi-circle in front of where the others stood against the curtained side door of the club's stage area where the name of the club was prestigiously emblazoned on the heavy velvet drape.

Jane took her position next to Seth, who placed his arm around her waist once more and the photographers beckoned Anna over to stand next to them.

Nervously shuffling into position, Anna forced a smile for the myriad of flashbulbs and Toby, photogenic as ever, grinned his gummy smile perfectly.

'Relax!' Jane whispered sideways into Anna's ear, evidently sensing her nervous discomfort.

Anna smiled gratefully, knowing she really must try to chill out. Jane's patience with her would only last so long.

Thankful once the photographs were complete, Anna scuttled back to her seat, noticing her glass of wine had been replenished. She'd really have to make her excuses soon. Besides, Toby was getting tired. She glanced up once more, her eyes finding Seth and Jane dancing closely to a slow number on the dance floor. Her body was pressed tightly up to him and she could see his mouth moving as he spoke in her ear, his hand caressing the small of her back.

She watched Seth's muscled legs move fluidly within the material of his expensive trousers and felt an unfamiliar stab of desire from inside her. Swallowing nervously, she tried to pick up her glass, but found she couldn't quite reach it. Anna attempted to shuffle forward in the chair without disturbing Toby who had begun to drop off in her arms, when a hand picked up her glass and passed it to her.

'Here you go,' a man smiled. 'I can see you've got your arms full.'

Surprised, Anna stared up at the blond-haired man and took the glass gratefully. 'Thank you,' she said nervously.

'Do you mind?' Aiden said, gesturing to the empty seat next to her.

'Not at all,' Anna said, secretly wishing there were no spare chairs. She was hopeless at conversations. *Everybody* knew that. She studied the man. He was tall, well-built and in his late twenties from what she could guess. He was also *very* attractive – apart from the edge of a tattoo on his neck poking out from under his collar. She didn't have much time for tattoos and wondered if the rest of his body were covered in them.

Knowing her eyes were tracing over the man's shirt and down to his waist, Anna felt a flush creep up her neck. *Dear God. What was the matter with her?* Twice now in the space of half an hour she'd felt herself get uncomfortably hot under the collar.

Aiden forced himself to smile. He'd only sat down because he was trying to avoid the attentions of a woman who'd made a beeline for him the minute he and Alan had arrived. He wasn't sure who she was, but did know she was old enough to be his bloody mother and could do without being stuck with her half the night.

When he'd seen this empty chair he'd been quick to move in on it, but this girl was about as interesting as a fly swat, so he wouldn't be hanging around. Not much of a looker either. He glanced around and saw the woman he'd been avoiding deep in conversation the other side of the room. *It was probably now safe to move off.*

Aiden raised himself to his feet. 'I'd best carry on mingling,' he said. 'Nice to meet you.'

Anna swallowed down her hurt, resigning herself that it was hardly surprising that the man had decided to disappear. She was so uninteresting he hadn't even asked her name. *No change there then.*

Grabbing her bag, Anna got up from the table, careful not to wake the now sleeping Toby. She'd go and let Jane know she was taking Toby home to bed.

• • • •

SETH TRIED TO IGNORE his erection and concentrated instead on Jane as she slept next to him. As much as he wanted to, he wouldn't wake her up purely so he could satisfy himself.

He sighed, glad the party was over. He hadn't enjoyed himself at all.

He'd got several things playing on his mind. Firstly, he'd had to thank Miller for giving him the info on his private investigator. He'd already spoken to Carl Mulligan and given him the details required to try and locate their daughter and the man said he'd be in touch as soon as he had some information.

Seth hadn't wanted to bring the subject up again with Miller, but regardless of anything else, the right thing to do was thank the man. If it meant they could get their daughter back it was worth it. *Anything was.*

Secondly, Miller had confirmed someone had been asking questions regarding the club's suppliers on Wednesday, but no one could say who this person was.

Seth's initial suspicions of it being something to do with the Cox Brothers had been unfounded. He'd already paid them a visit in person and it was safe to say they were *definitely* not the perpetrators. Even if they had been considering doing something along that vein at some point, they wouldn't be now. He glanced at the dressing table when he'd temporarily stashed the spare revolver on his return.

He frowned. He'd have to be *very* careful with what he was involved in. Although he'd taken a back seat with the hands-on side of things since Toby was born sometimes there was no option but to get involved. Like his lawyer said, *when* they'd located Grace and the case came to court, it was imperative there was *nothing* suspicious outstanding which could impact in gaining custody of their child.

Seth wrinkled his nose. He liked and respected Jason Miller and their joint dealings. Working together had proved *very* lucrative, but he was still a little uncomfortable with the man. He'd seen the way Miller had always looked at Jane and knew beyond *any* doubt the guy had a thing for her.

He was always asking after her, of which of course had been nothing less that polite but all the same, Seth could read between the lines. He knew Jason wouldn't hesitate for one second, given the chance, to take his place between Jane's legs.

Seth had done well keeping his jealousy under wraps like he promised Jane he would, but his outwardly controlled behaviour did not reflect how he felt inside and his rage burnt as fervently as it always had.

At the end of the day, Jane was *his* and his alone. He stared down at her perfect face, her long lashes casting spidery shadows on her flushed cheeks as she slept soundly. Even devoid of makeup she was the most beautiful creature he'd ever seen.

Letting out a soft murmur she turned slightly, her hand resting against his arm. Seth's arousal throbbed silently as he looked at her lips in and so wanted to press his mouth down onto them and taste her.

His eyes trailed down her naked body to her breasts and unable to help himself, his lips found her throat. *God, he loved her so much he felt he may burst.*

'Seth?' Jane murmured in a sleepy voice as she ran her hand through his thick wavy hair.

Lifting his head away from her, Seth smiled. 'Sorry beautiful. I couldn't stop myself from kissing you.'

Jane pulled Seth back towards her and sighed when his mouth found hers.

'I didn't want to wake you,' Seth whispered against Jane's lips. 'You're tired.'

Jane could feel Seth's hardness against her inner thigh and she moved so his hot tip pressed against her. 'I'm never too tired for you,' she smiled and yielded once more to his length.

Six

ELIZA HAD BEEN IRRITATED and angry to learn Lacey Garner had been so incompetent in allowing herself to get knocked up. *What the fuck was the point of her going to the trouble and expense of getting all the silly tarts contraception if they weren't going to use it properly?*

The stupid bitch had an allergic reaction to the contraceptive injection the first time she'd had it so Lacey's only alternative was condoms, but surely the thick cow must have put it on wrong for it to split? Eliza scowled. The girl was constantly chewing on her nails so she'd probably torn the fucking thing, the useless slag.

Eliza had been initially really angry, but after calming down, found to her surprise she wasn't anymore. Now she had a way to earn extra money because Digger had a rich foreign couple willing to pay a shedload of money for a kid so it couldn't have turned out better.

She pulled the brown envelope she'd received earlier from her handbag. She'd brought it with her just so she could keep looking at it.

Another wide smile broke across her face. The officially printed letter informed her and Digger that they had passed their adoption assessment. Admittedly Digger hadn't appreciated being scrutinised by social workers countless times, nor had he enjoyed having a police check or medical, but it was par for the course.

He'd just been fortunate his years of working with Seth and Phil had left no marks on his police record - aside from a few cautions, but they never counted for much anyway.

His injuries also hadn't been frowned upon. It had been easy to pass them off as resulting from a 'work accident,' which of course could be backed up by the hospital records as that had been the story they'd used at the time. Besides, his injuries wouldn't affect his ability to help care for the child, not that she suspected he'd be part of that once they'd got her. It wasn't his thing, but then neither was it hers. *That's what nannies were for was it not?*

Eliza though had been easy to check out – she had no blemishes on any record and her infertility only served as a plus point, making her a perfect contender for adoption. At least it had achieved something – apart from saving on contraception of course. Her only worry had been that her past and connection with the Elipse would be exposed, putting a *massive* kybosh on everything, but even that had slipped through the net.

To be honest, they probably hadn't even looked too closely. There were thousands of kids needing adoption so the authorities couldn't afford to be too picky. All that remained now was to be introduced to a potential child.

Eliza grinned smugly. There was only one child she was interested in and she'd made sure she'd discovered *exactly* where *that* kid was.

Eliza smiled. Taking a big gulp of her gin and tonic she smoothed her tight black top over her inflated cleavage and waited for Lacey to get to her office. She sighed impatiently. She'd sent Tina to fetch her a good ten minutes ago, so where the hell was she?

She cleared her throat irritably. Tina was another one. Actually having the cheek to ask for a pay rise! Who was she trying to kid? She got paid enough as it was. The greedy cow even insinuated people would demand more money for what they asked of her, but Eliza disagreed. People like Tina wouldn't usually be given the *chance* of a job, let alone whine they weren't being paid enough.

She'd laughed at Tina's complaints and stated that if she managed to triple the number of girls on site over the next three months then she'd get a raise. Failing that, she should shut the fuck up or get out. *Simple as that.*

LACEY GARNER WALKED timidly into Eliza's office and shut the door behind her. She stood uncomfortably, shifting uneasily from foot to foot.

'Sit down,' Eliza barked, gesturing towards a plastic chair the other side of her desk. She studied the young girl. 'Tina's informed me you're pregnant?'

Lacey's eyes remained fixed on her feet as she nodded silently. She knew Eliza and Digger's take on this. *Pregnancy equalled lost work which was unacceptable*. Luckily she had in no way shape or form any desire to remain so.

Eliza scrutinised Lacey's face, seeing her bottom lip trembling and felt like punching her. 'How did you manage that then?'

Lacey looked up quickly. 'I didn't *plan* it! A condom split. I didn't worry too much about it at the time as it was only the once.'

Eliza snorted. 'It only takes once though doesn't it? And condoms don't just split - especially the expensive ones I buy you. You must have done it on purpose. Trying to get out of working, were you?'

Lacey felt her eyes brim with angry tears. 'I did *not* do this on purpose. It's the *last* thing I want.'

Eliza eyed her suspiciously. 'How far along are you?'

Lacey shrugged despondently. 'I don't know exactly. A few weeks?' She'd missed her second period a week or so ago and had noticed her breasts had got disturbingly bigger. Her stomach was no longer flat, but there was nothing *really* obvious - for now at least, but she didn't think it would be too long before it was clear that monster's baby was growing inside her.

She couldn't wait until it was gone. The knowledge of being pregnant at sixteen was bad enough, but pregnant by *that man* sickened her further.

'I'm ready to go for the procedure as soon as there's an appointment,' Lacey said quickly.

Eliza raised her eyebrows. 'Procedure? What procedure?'

Lacey stared confused. 'The abortion of course. I know pregnancies mean lost work and I don't want that, so the quicker I can get this done the better.'

Eliza smiled nastily. 'Ah well, you'll be glad to know my attitude has softened on that subject somewhat.'

'What do you mean?'

'Well, it's been said I've been unfair in the past pushing girls to get rid, so in this instance I won't be doing that.'

Lacey looked horrified and a wave of nausea rose in her throat. 'But I want to get rid of it! I *need* to get rid of it!'

Eliza raised herself from her chair and slapped Lacey hard around the face. 'You ungrateful little whore! Some people can't have children and there's you bleating you want rid. How dare you!' She actually didn't give a flying fuck if people could have children or not - including herself, but it sounded better if she put it like that. It wouldn't then arouse any suspicion when her and Digger were granted custody of that kid.

Lacey raised her hand to her stinging face. 'B-but I *can't* have the baby. The father, he….'

'I don't give a fuck about the father. He's got nothing to do with it. Apart from the obvious of course!' Eliza laughed cruelly. 'Lacey you're having this baby.' She sat back down at the desk. 'I'll be honest. I was angry until I realised you've unwittingly given us an opportunity to make a few more quid.'

Lacey looked up at Eliza in horror. 'You're not suggesting I keep this baby purely to give some twisted blokes a kick?'

Eliza smiled. 'You really are stupid sometimes, sweetie, aren't you? That wasn't what I was suggesting, but now you've mentioned it, it could be another idea… I've heard some blokes get off on that sort of thing and with your makeup scrubbed off and a bit of downplay on your hair you could easily pass for twelve or thirteen. You'd be a knockout with the perverts.'

Lacey was speechless. She'd expected to get shouted at about the cost of an abortion, not informed she had to go through with the pregnancy. A wave of despair flooded over her and she began sobbing hard. 'Eliza, I can't. I really *can't*. I hate it. I don't want the baby. *Please!*'

Eliza grabbed Lacey's wrist and twisted it painfully. 'I'm not *suggesting* this – I'm *telling* you that's how it's going to be, so stop being so fucking childish, you selfish bitch. Besides, you won't be stuck with the kid. Believe me, I'm not forking out for *that*. It will be gone the minute it pops out because we have a buyer for it.'

Lacey felt sicker than she thought possible. 'And what if I won't do this?'

Eliza's eyes narrowed menacingly. 'I wouldn't advise that. You'd be stupid going against us.' She exchanged her expression for a patronising smile once the point had been made. 'You'll be pleased to hear you'll get a nice few quid for your inconvenience and of course we'll make sure you're looked after medically.'

Lacey sat motionless on the seat unsure of what to say or do.

Eliza clapped her hands together. 'Off you go now. You've got a client in half an hour.'

• • • •

STEVE LOMOND SAT happily in the bar at the Golden Lion and smiled when Digger placed a fresh pint on the table. Loosening his collar around his large neck, he lit a cigarette and smiled. He knew Eliza and Digger were relying on him for a lot of things recently. *He liked having control over people.*

Lomond studied Digger's large frame and watched him lower himself onto the opposite chair, taking a long drink from his pint. The man was a veritable mountain and even made *him* look small in comparison.

He tried not to stare too much at the thick scar running the length of Digger's face, nor the ear which had obviously been hacked off at some point. He'd also been unable to miss the guy's fingers on one hand were no longer resident. He frowned, inquisitive to know how this had happened to such a beast of a man. He didn't look the sort who would take any prisoners and was genuinely interested to know how he had befallen this fate. In fact, truth be known, there were a lot of things he was interested in.

Lomond rested his hands on his rotund belly and smiled. The gaff which Digger and Eliza ran was certainly a dump, but in all truthfulness it wasn't important. He'd fallen on his feet nicely here. Somewhere to live with the added mega-bonus of a selection of young flesh on tap, courtesy of Digger and Eliza's generosity. *What more could he ask for?*

One in particular was his favourite and he made sure he had a good go with her as often as possible. He'd book Lacey at the very least once a week and sometimes more if time allowed. Yes, that was *definitely* a perk. Plus more young ones were being sourced every week, but none had taken his fancy as much as her.

Lomond repositioned himself slightly in his chair feeling an erection forming with the thought of sinking his teeth into her pert young breasts. Christ, how he enjoyed making the stupid bitch beg. The best was when he fucked her so hard she cried, whilst pretending she wasn't.

He didn't even mind he was being asked to go on sojourns into posh strip clubs to start the cat off amongst the pigeons, although he didn't understand all the ins and outs as to why, but the more things he did for Eliza and Digger, the more indebted they became and soon he'd have a handy bit of leverage.

That Aiden bloke who worked alongside irritated him and although it hadn't been part of his original plan, Steve realised if he played his cards right, he could side-line him, then get his hands on his heroin dealings. He smiled. *He'd got it all planned. Fuck. He'd make a bastard mint from this.*

Lomond smiled happily at his pint. *It was all going very well indeed.*

Digger looked up, a thin trickle of sweat making its way down between his shoulder blades. 'I think our enquiries are having the desired effect Steve, so well done for that.'

When he'd caught up with Aiden this afternoon, he'd said his brother Alan had confirmed Lomond's visit to the Limelight on Wednesday had caused the required reaction compared to his attempted effort. It had created ruction within the top ranks too. So much so that Seth Wright had been present with Miller this morning.

Digger took another slug of his pint and folded his arms across his chest. He fixed his gaze on Steve Lomond. 'There's something else I need you to get onto as a matter of urgency.'

Lomond grinned exposing his blackened teeth. 'No problem. What is it that you need me to do?'

Digger frowned. Eliza had been so happy after receiving that letter earlier and he hadn't liked to ruin her day by dropping a nuclear bomb on her joy about what Aiden's brother had heard Miller and Wright discussing.

He shoved a cigarette in his mouth. 'I need you to arrange a meeting with Seth Wright and masquerade as a private investigator who goes by the name of Carl Mulligan.'

Eliza would go loco when she learnt what had occurred. They needed to act quickly he knew that, but firstly he needed a damage limitation plan in place to soften the blow when he broke the news.

Seven

TINA WOKE SUDDENLY and immediately wished she hadn't. Last night had been one of her rare nights off and she had gone slightly over the top. Her head felt like it had been filled with concrete and someone had smashed all of her teeth in with a plank of wood during the night.

She groped blindly at the rickety bedside table and with a sinking feeling the memory of finishing the last of her gear seeped into her mind. Slight panic radiated as she remembered how much was outstanding on Aiden's slate. *If she couldn't get something together in the next hour or so for a fix she'd be well and truly in the crap.*

She glanced towards the thin blue curtains gingerly held up with drawing pins and surmised it must be fairly early. Was she supposed to be doing anything? *Christ, she was even unsure of the fucking day!*

Pushing herself up against the ripped vinyl headboard, Tina glanced at the man lying face down the other side of her bed and scowled. She eyed the pair of stained tracksuit bottoms and the faded grey hoody in a heap on the floor and sighed. *For God's sake.* Her eyes traced over his skinny frame and shrugged. She had no idea who he was but it hardly mattered.

Forcing her aching body from the bed Tina unsteadily grabbed the man's clothes from the floor, her nose wrinkling up when a blast of body odour assaulted her nostrils. She rifled through his pockets hoping to come across a wrap or two of something, but there was nothing.

As withdrawal tremors begin to make themselves known, Tina knew she'd have to locate Aiden very soon and plead to his better nature to allow her further credit. She had to get some money from somewhere. She'd spent virtually the whole of last week on the lookout for potential candidates to up Eliza's numbers. She *had* to get more girls on the books. She needed that raise. It was the only way she would survive.

Despite the long hours trawling around her usual haunts of bus and train stations, subways and shopping centres, for once she'd failed to even pull in *one* girl. Not only was she desperate for the cash, but also paranoid she'd get sacked on top.

Swigging the last inch of warm flat cider from a two-litre bottle Tina stared despondently at the damp wall of her room. She'd still heard nothing from Anna the snobby little slag. *Absolutely jack shit.*

Would she actually have to physically go to her bloody mother's house and get Anna's whereabouts out of her? It was getting very close to the point where she'd quite happily break into the old bat's house and sell what remained of her crummy furniture to get some money together.

Ignoring the greasy skinny man in her bed who was beginning to make sounds of regaining consciousness she quickly slipped from the room.

Walking into the girls' kitchen and noticing not *one of* the lazy tarts had yet bothered surfacing, Tina pushed the overflowing ashtray to one side of the table and ignored what looked like a small pile of congealed baked beans stuck to the top of the scratched tabletop.

She glanced around for something to drink and saw some cheap supermarket-own lager on the floor in a carrier bag. Helping herself to a can she sat down at the table and rolled a cigarette in her shaking fingers. Lighting it she hoped it wouldn't make her feel any sicker than she already did.

Tina pulled the local paper across the table and aimlessly flicked through the dog-eared pages, scanning the endless boring articles. Leafing through, she stopped suddenly at the entertainment, business and society pages. *No way! Was that ANNA?*

Tina focused her eyes as best as she could on the photo swimming in front of her eyes. *Yes, it was definitely her. OH MY GOD!* The picture was taken at that posh club Aiden got invited to the other week *and* she was pictured with none other than the notorious Seth and Jane Wright.

She squinted at the photographer's caption:

> *'...A fabulous night was had by hundreds at the Limelight club for Linda Miller's birthday. Linda, pictured with her husband Jason, celebrated in style along with Seth and Jane Wright and their gorgeous son, Toby - accompanied by his nanny, Miss Anna Slater...'*

So that was what Anna was doing? *Nanny for the Wrights*? Tina smiled happily. The lucky bitch had fallen on her feet this time, hadn't she? Everybody knew how bloody rich the Wright's were. For God's sake - she herself had been forced to listen to Eliza banging on about the pair of them for what seemed like centuries. About how fucking lucky and sorted they were. About how they'd only got where they were today at *her* expense and that the pair of them owed her *big time*. Oh yes, she'd heard it *countless* times.

This was good. It appeared there may well be a God after all. Tina smiled conspiringly to herself. Now Anna definitely couldn't give her that old welly she had no cash. The Wrights wouldn't be paying her peanuts to look after their precious son that was for certain. She grinned. She'd be having some of that - unless her darling sister wanted her to arrive at her place of work on a regular basis in front of her posh employers that was....

Yes, she'd get a nice regular sum from her snotty sister for this one.

Tina glanced at the clock hanging on the kitchen wall. Eliza would be surfacing soon and she'd insist on a meeting. The woman would be *most* interested in hearing what she'd got to say.

• • • •

MAGGIE WATCHED JANE slip her feet into a stunning pair of designer toe-post sandals with the daintiest of kitten heels. The deep gold leather set off the slight tan she sported.

The shop assistant kneeling at Jane's feet ensured the shoe fitted perfectly and smiled graciously. 'Would you like to stand up for me now Mrs Wright and have a little walk around to see how they feel? Beautiful choice I must say,' she gushed.

Maggie fought back a giggle watching Jane roll her eyes at the assistant's bowing and scraping, knowing full well she'd never get used to being waited on.

Jane took two steps forward in the sandals before stopping and kicking them off. 'Yep, these will do nicely thanks,' she said quickly.

'Does Madam not want to try on some other colours? Perhaps a colour for different outfits? We have a dark purple pair which would go *just right* with the dress I saw you wearing in the paper last month.'

Jane gritted her teeth. 'No thank you. Just these will be fine.' Putting her hand in her bag she retrieved her purse and pulled her bank card from it.

The woman almost curtseyed and taking the card, thanked Jane profusely. 'If you'd like to come to the till when you're ready?'

As the assistant wandered off to box up the shoes, Maggie looked at Jane. 'So how much are they?'

Jane shrugged. 'Haven't a clue!'

Maggie laughed. 'How bloody funny! How times have changed!'

'Tell me about it!' Jane grinned. 'It's worth it just for the amusement value. If only they knew eh?'

Maggie smiled. It was true. It wasn't *that* long ago that store detectives frequently followed them around any shop they went in. Apparently, they looked the 'type' who would steal. Now Seth and Jane were one of the most well-respected and connected couples in the city, people fell over themselves to be involved with them. What they didn't know was that Seth and Jane were exactly the same as they'd always been.

She'd been extremely worried when Jane had returned to Seth. She'd been convinced their relationship would be as damaging, dangerous and toxic as it was previously. She hadn't believed for one minute Seth would do things properly this time. How many times had she heard him promise Jane that? This time though he'd delivered what he'd promised and even though she'd spent the last two years on edge waiting for the shit to hit the fan, it hadn't. Both Seth and Jane were happy. In fact, *so* happy sometimes Maggie thought she must be hallucinating the entire thing.

Obviously they were still very much embroiled with the firm, the club and all the unsavoury dealings that went on within, but from everything she'd seen these days they both had a lower involvement with incriminating activities. Maggie was exceptionally glad about that being as she had been less than enamoured when Dan had been given a proper job with the firm, graduating quickly into Seth's right hand man.

It had done her a favour though. After Dan's money started rolling in, she'd made the decision to quit work completely. Dan had supported her fully as he knew it would help her nerves immeasurably and it had. Now she was so much more relaxed and happily spent most days pottering around the lovely house they'd purchased.

After collecting the shoes from the till, Maggie enviously eyed Jane's figure in a clingy blue top, tight black trousers and knee-high stiletto boots as she followed her to the department store's restaurant where they each ordered a sandwich and glass of wine.

Jane sipped at her drink. She'd had *that* dream again last night. She'd watched Grace being slapped around and left alone in the dark with nothing to eat. She'd been a horrified silent observer watching her daughter sob in anguish in a corner of the cold, bare room.

She'd woken up, barely able to breathe – her own sobs stuck deep in her throat and it had taken a few minutes to get her bearing enough to confirm it had only been a dream.

Jane had spent the rest of the night lying awake staring at the ceiling and thinking about her first born. *What if the dreams were trying to tell her something? What if it was true and it was happening somewhere right now?*

The need to get her daughter back was gradually suffocating her and the gnawing feeling was getting worse. She hadn't said anything to Seth when he'd woken. What was the point? She knew he'd got people on the case.

EIGHT

'FUCK ME TINA, YOU'VE put the icing on the cake here,' Eliza said happily as she poured herself the fourth gin and tonic of the afternoon. *What an amazing piece of bloody luck*!

Tina grinned, more than pleased her news had gleaned such a positive response. 'So, what do you want me to do then?'

Eliza rolled her eyes. 'Well, I would have thought that was obvious to most people,' she snapped. 'The first thing is to get in touch with your fucking sister.'

Tina stared at Eliza, not happy she was still speaking to her like a piece of shit even though she clearly wanted what she could offer. 'I have tried but I'll try again.'

'Not just *try* again Tina. You'll *do* it. I want to hear you've seen her by the end of the week,' Eliza said getting irritated. *Couldn't the stupid tart see how important this was?*

Tina studied her dirty fingernails unsure how she would get Anna to meet her by then when she hadn't even acknowledged her message. 'Ok, but what do I do when she does?'

Eliza sighed loudly for effect. 'Do whatever you need to get her to feed you the ins and outs of the Wright's lives,' she said sternly fixing her stare on Tina's glazed eyes.

She grabbed Tina's wrist painfully and pulled her arm across the table. 'Listen. You said you needed extra brass so if you pull this off properly, I'll ensure you're generously rewarded.' Eliza's eyes narrowed as she leaned closer. 'But I'll tell you now if you fuck it up, I'll personally make sure you're ruined in every way possible as well as in ways you couldn't possibly imagine.'

Having made it very clear what was expected, Eliza loosened her grip on Tina's arm and lounged back in her chair. 'Now get the hell out of here. You've got work to do!'

• • • •

LACEY RETCHED INTO THE toilet for the fourth time. She knew she was pissing the others off by locking herself in the bathroom, but she didn't care. She needed to be somewhere where no one could see her.

It wasn't morning sickness which was plaguing her. It was *fear*. Pure, unadulterated and all-consuming fear. She felt like a medical experiment completely out of control of her own body and the excruciating vileness of what was expected of her was eating away at her like a cancer.

Even though for as many years as she could remember her life had been unbearable, it was *nothing* in comparison to how she felt now. For the first time ever she'd been seriously contemplating ending it all, but even that was unobtainable as she was never allowed out of this place. *She couldn't even go and buy any pills.*

Feeling another surge of bile stinging her throat, Lacey hung back over the toilet bowl and let the tears flow freely down her face. *She wished she was dead. Stone cold fucking dead. Nothing could be worse than this.*

She could barely even face going in the shower anymore. Couldn't stand having to brush her hand over her stomach whilst washing in case she felt that *thing* growing inside her. That monster's thing...

She hated him. She hated it and she hated herself. He'd had his usual session with her today and seeing his blackened teeth and fat paunch hanging down as he leered at her made her feel even worse. She'd wanted to scratch his eyes out.

Eliza had made it very clear she wasn't in any way to inform Steve Lomond he was the father, but Lacey had no intention of doing that. She would get rid of this baby one way or the other. *She had to.*

Nausea threatened once more and without time to question what she was about to do, she punched herself as hard as possible in the stomach. Once, twice, three times. *Come on! It had to go. PLEASE!*

Angry tears coursed down Lacey's face, realising she was unable to punch hard enough to warrant any form of injury. She was hardly the strongest girl out there. Refusing to give up hope and fuelled with desperation and anger she ran back out to the corridor. She'd an idea. *It was worth a try.*

Standing at the top of the steep wooden staircase down to the third floor landing, Lacey's breathing came in ragged bursts as she gulped in large mouthfuls of air and her jaw set in determination.

Clasping her hands behind her back and promising herself that under no circumstances would she move them, she found herself hesitating. *Stop fucking around. Do it Lacey. DO IT!*

After a quick check behind to make sure no one was watching and before she could continue procrastinating, Lacey allowed herself to topple forward.

She hit the wooden stairs on her front, the impact knocking the wind out of her and pain seared across the width of her stomach as she crashed down the remainder of the steps.

Finally coming to a stop on the threadbare runner of the third floor landing, Lacey lay retching and desperately gasping for breath. The pain in both her stomach and ribs was intense and through her laboured breathing, she smiled, quietly confident that would have done the trick.

• • • •

SETH GLARED AT JANE as she pushed her food around her dinner plate. 'I asked you not to bother with that appointment,

Jane, didn't I?'

Jane glowered back at Seth, ignoring Anna fidgeting uncomfortably on the chair the other end of the table. 'Yes you did,' she spat. *She didn't really want to discuss this in front of Anna, but he was giving her little choice.* 'But I've told you before you should be more bothered about getting Grace back before thinking about *more* kids!'

Seth slammed his fork down on the table in anger. 'Bothered? Of course I'm fucking bothered! What you do you think I've been doing?'

'Well whatever you've been doing hasn't resulted in anything has it?' Jane sneered. Overtired, the images from last night's dream still vivid in her mind's eye weren't helping her overall mood. 'Otherwise, where is she?'

'For fuck's sake, Jane. Everything I do is for you or us.' Seth waved his arms around theatrically. 'What's wrong with wanting more children?'

'Nothing!' Jane screamed, standing up. 'Apart from the fact it's not *you* who has to have them is it? Being as I'm so busy with the club and everything else, do you really think we can take on more right now? Has it ever crossed your mind that perhaps I might want to look after our children *myself* rather than pay someone else to take my place?' She glanced at Anna.

Anna smiled nervously and leaving her dinner, got up from the table, quickly scooping Toby out of his highchair. 'We'll go and have a look at some books for a while shall we Tobes?' she said quietly before hurrying out of the room.

'See what you've done now? Making Anna uncomfortable. Saying all that shit in front of her. What's wrong with you?' Seth screamed.

'Nothing's wrong with *me* Seth. I'm far too busy trying to avoid having more babies when we don't even know where one of them is and we barely see the one we *do* have,' Jane spat, her eyes narrowing. 'Hence why I'm going to the bloody appointment.'

Seth ran his hand through his hair. 'While you're at it why

don't you have a hysterectomy instead of a replacement IUD? *That* way there'd be no risk of being unfortunate enough to get pregnant again! Maybe you'd like to let me know what you've decided *afterwards* yeah?'

Picking up her plate Jane launched it across the kitchen, the china exploding into several pieces as it hit the quarry tiled floor. 'I might as fucking well, Seth, being as you seem to have lost interest in getting our daughter back! All you care about is replacing her with more!'

Seth stood up, his race red with rage. 'You know that's not true. I've told you I've been doing *everything* I can possibly do regarding that.'

'Yeah, of course you have,' Jane bitched.

Seth sighed and tried to rein in his temper. He didn't want to get angry. 'We've been through all of this before and know that's not how it is.' He stepped around the table. Touching Jane's arm, he attempted to pull her towards him. 'Come on, let's not row. We don't argue anymore remember?'

Jane yanked her arm away feeling tears pricking the back of her eyes. 'Get off me Seth and leave me alone. Go back to the club, will you? You're always there anyway.'

Seth scowled, his patience evaporating. He grabbed his car keys. 'Fine. I'll do that.'

• • • •

ANNA HAD BEEN GRATEFUL when after Seth had left Jane had entered the sitting room and scooped Toby out of her arms, telling her to go and have a couple of hours break. She'd been glad to get out of the house. In the month she'd worked there she hadn't ever heard Seth and Jane argue until tonight. It had been more than uncomfortable.

It was evident Jane resented not having as much time as she'd like with Toby. Maybe *she* was doing something wrong? She couldn't think what it might be, but that didn't mean there wasn't something. Jane had always complimented her on the things she did and the way she was with Toby, but now she was beginning to wonder.

Anna felt horribly insecure. She really enjoyed working for the Wrights and loved Toby to bits. The thought of being told her services were no longer required filled her with dread.

Picking up her bag, Anna left the house deciding she'd take a nice walk. It was a pleasant evening and still light, so she'd have a stroll to get some fresh air, sure that everything would resolve itself by the time she returned.

Anna was already feeling revitalised by the time she reached the bottom of the long gravelled driveway. That was until she saw Tina sitting on the wall at the end of the drive.

'Hello Anna,' Tina smiled, exposing her yellowing teeth.

'T-Tina? W-What the hell are you doing here?' Anna glanced back up the driveway in the hope that no one could see her sister from the house. 'How did you know I was here?'

Tina laughed. 'It's not that difficult little sis. Especially when you pose for the press with your well-known employers! It's common knowledge they live in probably the poshest house this side of the city!'

Anna grabbed Tina's elbow and steered her away from the driveway.

Tina put on a mock-hurt expression. 'Aren't you going to invite me in and introduce me? You're not ashamed of your big sister, are you?'

Anna swallowed hard. *Was she kidding?* She took in Tina's grubby pink hooded top and skin-tight low-slung jeans hanging pathetically on her bony hips. She looked every inch the drug-addled mess she was. 'You can't just turn up here and no, I'm not inviting you in. For God's sake Tina, this is my *work*.'

Tina's eyes narrowed, already finding it difficult to remain pleasant where this conceited bitch who was somehow related to her was concerned. 'Still high and mighty I see, dear Anna,' she said sarcastically. 'Maybe if you hadn't ignored the message I sent to you via our darling mother then I wouldn't have been forced to come and find you.'

'I haven't spoken to mum for a while,' Anna lied. 'I've been busy since starting this new job.'

Tina scowled, knowing full well Anna was far too nice where their mother was concerned to forget the obligatory weekly phone call or visit. 'I need to speak to you. Is there somewhere we can go instead then?' she asked.

'I haven't really got time Tina. I'm sorry. There's been a few problems here tonight, so I should go back in.' Anna had been looking forward to a walk, but would much rather put up with the uncomfortable atmosphere in the house rather than be caught talking to Tina. Christ, if Jane or Seth saw her with someone like this she'd most likely be out of a job, or at the very least have to answer questions that she'd worked very hard to distance herself from.

Tina was less than convinced. She couldn't afford to be fobbed off with excuses. *Certainly not at the moment.* 'Well you seemed to be on a mission the way you were walking down the driveway.'

'Yes, well, I…' Anna faltered, knowing full well Tina didn't believe her lies. 'If you've come round to ask for money yo…'

'I'm in debt,' Tina interrupted. 'I've got problems – big ones and I need your help. Straight up, I'm *begging* you. I wouldn't have come otherwise.' She looked down at the floor, attempting to appear as contrite as possible and hoping her sister would buy it. With effort she forced a lone tear from her eye. '*Please* Anna?'

Anna stared at her sister, betting despite all of this spiel it was probably some magnified sob-story in return for a lump of money to fuel her ever-increasing bloody drug habit.

She scrutinised Tina's face. 'Ok, but I can't stay long. We can't hang around here though. Follow me.' Anna grabbed Tina's arm. 'There's a small park not far from here where we can talk.'

NINE

'WHAT DO YOU MEAN he's not available?' Digger roared, his face flushing red with rage. 'What the fuck do we pay him for if he's not around when we need him? Tell me that?'

'Don't be having a go at me,' Eliza spat, her anger rising. *As if this wasn't bad enough without him having a dig.* She'd been over the moon last night when Tina had got back, informing her she'd made contact with her sister and already made inroads, but her good mood had quickly evaporated when she'd arrived at the office this morning to learn Lacey was bleeding and had had some form of accident.

'He's out of the country for two days on a conference,' Eliza said. That was all she knew when she'd tried to get hold of Dr Gopal first thing.

'A likely fucking story,' Digger raged. 'More likely the greasy bastard's holed up with a bunch of tarts somewhere. That's more his fucking style. Why the hell are we bothering with him?'

'You know full well why. He doesn't ask bloody questions, does he? It doesn't change the fact we need to get Lacey seen by *someone* and quickly.' Eliza could already feel tendrils of fear radiating up her spine with the prospect of her money-making idea going down the pan. If Lacey lost this baby then all her plans would have been for zilch.

'What sort of fucking accident did the silly cow have?' Digger asked.

'How should I know?' Eliza screeched. 'Fell out of bed or something. She's got a bruise across her stomach and is bleeding like I said. Does it fucking matter how? What the hell are we going to do?'

Digger sighed. 'She'll have to go to the hospital.'

'How can she? You know there'll be lots of questions and I wouldn't put it past the sly bitch to drop us in it. She's not happy with my plans for her as it is.'

Digger snorted. 'She'll say fuck all. She'll have to go to hospital if you want to make sure she's alright.'

Eliza could feel panic rising and her mind raced as she watched Digger pick up the phone and press a button.

'Aiden?' Digger growled. 'Get up here now.'

'What are you doing? You haven't got time to talk to Aiden!' Eliza blabbered.

'Shut the fuck up Eliza and go and get the girl.'

• • • •

'SO,' DIGGER SAID slowly and calmly. 'You're Lacey's boyfriend ok?' Seeing Aiden nod, he continued. 'You're also the father of the child and therefore need to act suitably upset. Demand she be scanned and that they do whatever they need to ensure both her and the kid are ok.'

He looked towards Lacey who perched gingerly on the edge of a chair, her arm wrapped tightly across her stomach and her face grey with pain. 'Tell me what happened and what you're going to tell the hospital.'

'I-I fell down the stairs whilst going to get a drink in the middle of the night. I felt a bit dizzy and must have slipped,' Lacey lied, her voice monotonous.

'You stupid bitch!' Eliza screamed. 'Don't you realise how important this is?'

'I-I thought I would be ok. It didn't seem too bad. It was only this morning that I began bleeding.' Lacey hoped the joy she'd felt when waking in agony and seeing sheets covered in blood wasn't showing on her face. *It was going to be ok. She knew she had to be losing that freak's baby.*

'If you're losing this fucking kid because of your stupidity you're going to pay. Do you understand?' Eliza spat. Seeing Lacey nod, she grabbed a makeup bag. 'Now put your goddamn head up. I need to put some slap on you. Make you look a bit older.'

Digger scribbled on a piece of paper and handed it to Lacey. 'These are the details you need to memorise on the way to hospital. Do you think you can at least do *that* properly?'

Lacey glanced at the paper which consisted of a name, address and date of birth - none of which were hers. 'But what if they check?'

'What if they do? They'll find the details tally up completely.'

'B-But….'

'But nothing. They belong to a girl two years older than you who used to work for us. As far as everyone else is concerned your name is Sandra, you're eighteen and live at 10 Portman Street. Now memorise it.' Digger looked up. 'That goes for *you* as well Aiden.'

'Not a problem,' Aiden said. He didn't know what was going on, but being as there was two hundred quid in this for him, he didn't much care. *Whatever floated their boat.*

'Right then. Get going the pair of you. Don't let her out of your sight Aiden,' Eliza snapped. 'And remember what we told you Lacey. Fuck this up and you'll sorely regret it in more ways than you think possible.'

Digger waited until Aiden had left the room and then turned to Eliza. He could see she was all but hyperventilating with stress and knew this wasn't the ideal time, but it had to be done.

'Seth Wright has contacted a private investigator to find Grace again. A bloody top one this time too.'

Eliza eyes snapped on to his. 'You *WHAT?*' This couldn't be happening. Not now. She'd already got in contact with Social Services specifying the area she wanted a child from and had put together a massive list of factors required, knowing it would narrow the available choice dramatically. If her plan worked there should only be a handful of children who fitted her very specific requirements and if she was *really* lucky there might only be one who matched. *The right one.*

If the social were alerted that the birth parents were requesting information and digging around then any adoption attempts on the girl would be put on hold until the birth parents request could be dealt with. *She couldn't have that. She wouldn't. She hadn't got this far for it not to pull off now.*

Digger put his hand on Eliza's arm. 'Don't panic. It's in hand.'

'What you do mean it's in hand? How the fuck can it be in hand? Shit Digger, this will *ruin* everything. We're *this* close,' Eliza wailed.

'I know and like I said, don't panic. I'll stop Seth and Jane getting to the investigator,' Digger said calmly.

'And how do you propose to do that?' Eliza screamed, snatching the piece of paper from Digger's hand. 'Carl Mulligan? Oh Jesus! Even *I've* heard of him. He's shit hot! Come on – it will take him less than thirty seconds to find Grace he's that good. Even that one we used found her – admittedly it was difficult, but he still did in the end.'

Digger smiled. 'I told you… It's in hand.'

Eliza's eyes narrowed. 'Wait… Either way we need to up our game here. If whatever your plan is doesn't work then we can still fuck this up. We have to make sure Seth publicly loses his rag or gets copped for something dodgy – anything to make him out as an unfit parent which will screw up any hope in hell he's got of getting custody of that kid.'

'Exactly!' Digger grinned. 'You worry too much Eliza. There's *always* a way around everything.'

• • • •

'I'LL BE BACK LATER,' Jane said, glancing out from the small lead-light hall window at the drizzle outside. Pulling her jacket from the coat stand she grabbed her clutch bag from the hall table.

'Say bye to Mummy, Toby,' Anna said holding Toby against her hip and moving his pudgy little hand in a wave.

Forcing a smile Jane shut the door behind her unable to even bring herself to cuddle her darling son. The guilt raged as she moved towards her car. *What sort of mother was she?* She was exhausted. Another sleepless night courtesy of the argument her and Seth had had until God knows when and then that dream had plagued her again throughout the rest of the night. How *dare* Seth moan about her having her contraception replaced. She wouldn't even consider having more children until they'd got Grace back.

The fact the lawyer had said involvement with the wrong side of the law would completely scupper their chances made things worse. If they located Grace and then after all that they couldn't get her back because of what they did it would finish her. Jane couldn't think about that possibility.

Anna let out a slow release of breath hearing the BMW's engine roar into life and retraced her steps back down the long hallway to the kitchen. She secured Toby in his highchair and walked to the fridge to prepare an afternoon snack for him.

She fought the urge to sit down at the table and burst out crying. Seth had left without saying a word this morning, so things between him and Jane were obviously still strained.

Anna hadn't actually expected things to be any better judging by the slamming doors and raised voices she'd heard well into the early hours of the morning. It had been audible even from the other end of the house and it was an impressively *large* house.

It wasn't like she could sleep anyway. There wasn't any chance of that. Handing Toby a small plate of carrot sticks to get his teething gums around, Anna gave in to her needs and sat at the table, putting her head in her hands. *What on earth was she going to do?*

She knew her sister would go to most ends to try to get more money out of people, but what she was asking would ruin *everything* and if she didn't submit to Tina's demands then she dreaded to think what would happen.

Anna took a deep intake of breath to try to override the rising panic. She'd rather be giving her sister money any day of the week than what she'd asked for. It put her in a horrible quandary. Ok, so she'd handed over £250 last night, but she'd expected that. That was *normal*. What she *hadn't* expected was to be asked for information about her employers.

The minute they'd sat on a bench in the park Tina had burst into tears. Clutching onto Anna's arm she'd sobbed about her massive drug debt. 'They said I could pay it off by getting information they need on the Wrights for an old score,' she'd said.

'Why would *you* be expected to be able to get this information?' Anna had asked, not fathoming as to why anyone would think Tina could glean such knowledge.

Tina had then become angry. Her voice had been heavy with hiccupping sobs. *The question was would this ploy work? It had to.* 'It's *you*, isn't it, Anna? *You*. You're the one that's dumped me in it. It's *always* you. They saw that fucking picture in the paper of you posing with them at that posh bash. Someone recognised you from one of the few times you've bothered to see how I am and word got around.'

Anna hadn't been sure what to think. It had all sounded rather far-fetched. She frowned. She'd landed such a good position and she didn't want to betray the Wrights for their kindness by snooping on them. *She didn't like it.*

'I'm sorry Tina, I'm not prepared to do this to save your neck. *You* chose your way of life and the people you mix with. You'll have to live with it,' she'd said as sternly as possible.

Tina had then begun screaming and shouting. *Work it, work it...* 'But it's only because of *you* that I'm in this position. If I don't get the information they need it'll cause me big problems,'

Tina had sobbed, fresh tears rolling down her face. *My, she should have been an actress!*

Anna had quickly become annoyed from too many years of listening to her sister's lies and bullshit. 'Sorry Tina, I'm not doing it. Seth and Jane have been nothing but good to me.'

Tina's 'woe-is-me' act had disappeared as quickly as it had manifested. 'Don't know why you're even that bothered about them anyway, but you're leaving me with no choice,' she'd spat, her eyes narrowing. 'If you don't do what I say then I'll fuck your life up. I'll personally tell the Wright's who I am. I'll turn up *every* day with drugs for you and do whatever I have to do to ruin your career you bitch! You think the Wrights would want you around their darling son then?'

Anna's stomach sunk. *She wouldn't?* Sadly she knew full well Tina would have no problem whatsoever following through with her blackmail and threats.

'And don't forget Anna – imagine what it would do to Mum? Having her golden child's name publicly sullied like her sister's? Or worse still… They could turn on *her*… You want that on your fucking conscience too, do you?' Tina had sneered.

That had been what clinched it. Anna couldn't cope with her mother being hurt mentally or physically when she could have stopped it. Besides, all of this stemmed from her connection. *She knew she should have refused that bloody photograph. Oh God… What the hell was she going to do?*

Anna sighed and angrily swiped her hair away from her face. She had no choice. She'd have to do what Tina wanted.

TEN

DAN EYED SETH ACROSS the desk in his office. He could see the shadows under his eyes and had been able to tell from the moment he'd walked in that he wasn't in a good mood.

'Any news as to who this guy is or where he's from?' Dan asked.

Seth ran his fingers through his hair and knocked the contents of his glass of whisky down in one. 'Do you think if I knew that we'd be sitting here right now?' he snapped irritably.

Dan held his hands up. 'Ok ok, stupid question,' he said in a bid to placate the situation.

Seth took a deep breath and tried to compose himself. 'Barry and Martin have been doing some digging this past week.' He pulled out a sheaf of paper from his desk drawer and flicked through some of the pages. 'We've got some names and addresses of these scouts who could have been doing the questioning. We need to find out if any are involved.'

Dan nodded, taking the piece of paper from Seth and running his eyes over the names. 'I recognise this one,' he said frowning. *Neil Batchelor*. The name rang a bell but he couldn't quite put his finger on where from. 'When's Barry and Martin lined up to do that?'

Seth sparked up a cigarette and blew out the smoke slowly. 'They're not. *We* are.'

'Us?' Dan was surprised. Although Seth had reduced his hands-on dealings, he knew those hands were a lot dirtier than they were supposed to be. The man just couldn't help himself.

Dan swallowed. Each time Seth went down this road he had to be careful to keep it away from Maggie. As far as she was concerned Seth had retired from that side of the business and so, by proxy, had he. She would certainly not be happy to learn these episodes were more frequent than she thought. Furthermore, from what Seth had said about his daughter, he had more reason than *ever* to keep his nose clean.

He watched the smile spreading over Seth's face and immediately felt even more uncomfortable. *He knew that look too well.* 'You're deadly serious about doing this yourself aren't you?' Dan said, already knowing what the response would be.

'Yeah, why not?' Seth grinned. *He needed to take his irritation out on someone after all.*

'Is that a good idea?' Dan asked gingerly.

Seth slammed his fist down on the table. 'If you're going to question me then go home!' he barked.

Dan sighed inwardly. 'Don't be like that mate.' *He'd just have to make very sure Maggie didn't find out he'd been part of it.*

'I need to know who these people are. I'm not having whoever this cunt is taking the piss and I want to find out *exactly* who it is who feels they can take me on,' Seth growled. He stood up from his desk and paced around the room. He felt like he was out of control in all facets of his life and he didn't like it. He needed control of *something*.

Dan eyed Seth closely. 'Is everything ok?' he asked seeing Seth look at his watch once more.

'Yes, fine. Why?' Seth said, glancing out of the window absently.

'You just seem on edge. Aside from all this we're still friends at the end of the day and you can always tell me if something's up.'

Feeling a little guilty, Seth turned and walked back to the desk. 'Jane has an appointment which I don't agree with that's all. Nothing for you to worry about.'

Dan remained silent. He knew better than to press the issue. Whatever it was had definitely caused Seth to want to take his frustration out on others – that much was clear.

• • • •

LACEY FELT LIKE she was tripping out. She'd managed to do exactly what Eliza and Digger required from her. She'd memorised the information needed to stick to the story. Aiden was so convincing in his part he could have won an Oscar and no one had seemed suspicious, so at least that was one thing Eliza would be pleased about. She'd also be pleased that the baby was fine.

Lacey's heart had been racing waiting to go in for the scan. She'd been twitching with anticipation of hearing: '…no heartbeat…' She knew it sounded heartless, but she *couldn't* have this baby. *She just couldn't.*

Her eyes had moved around the waiting room, looking for possible escape exits she could run out of to get away from this madness and somehow get her life back. Even if it meant she had to live in an underpass, there were two things which were certain: one was she *would* get away from this life – away from Digger and Eliza and two – she would *not* have this baby. Christ, she'd rather be dead.

Another door had opened and Lacey's eyes had met with a beautiful dark-haired woman. She eyed her gorgeous designer clothes, her hair and immaculate face. She was a real stunner. It was that woman from the papers – *Jane Wright.*

Slightly star-struck, Lacey had felt special when the woman had smiled at her, but her happiness hadn't lasted long. Within five minutes her mind had been 'put at rest' to learn her baby was unharmed. *She'd been 'very lucky' apparently.*

She'd felt like screaming. Aiden had done an award-winning

performance of crying with happiness and trying to snog her face off as she'd lay on the bed, when all she'd wanted to do was curl up into a ball and wait to get hit by a train.

'I would date your baby at around fourteen weeks,' the woman had said sweetly.

Feeling nausea rising, Lacey forced a smile before readjusting her clothes and blindly leaving the room.

Aiden had waited to collect the scan picture but unfortunately had been quick to catch up with her. She stole a look at him as he walked beside her, insisting she held his hand to make it look convincing.

Feeling panic rise up her spine, Lacey's breath became shallower and the hospital corridors closed in like a narrowing tunnel. Bright lights flashed at the back of her eyes and her skin became clammy. Unable to help herself, she stumbled against Aiden, clinging onto his arm with her hand over her mouth.

'What are you doing?' Aiden cried, holding Lacey steady as she clung to him. 'Lacey? What's the matter?'

'I'm going to faint!' Lacey mumbled, her eyes darting around.

'Let me get a nurse,' Aiden said, looking around for anyone in uniform.

'No, NO!' Lacey cried. 'They might admit me.' She spotted the Ladies toilets a couple of yards away. 'I'll go in there. I just need to be sick and have five minutes.'

Aiden paused, well aware he'd been instructed not to let her out of his sight. He looked at Lacey's ghostly pale face and clammy skin. She wasn't putting it on and the last thing he wanted was for her to spew down his new Adidas top.

He quickly steered her to the toilets. 'Go on then. I'll wait over there for you,' he nodded towards a group of grey plastic chairs bolted to the floor by the window.

• • • •

JANE WAS WASHING HER hands in the sink when the grey-faced teenager bolted through the door and lurched towards a washbasin. She watched as the girl heaved violently into the white porcelain.

Jane faltered, unsure what to do. She watched the girl as her dry retching continued and could see she was unsteady on her feet. If she wasn't careful she'd hit the deck at any moment or at the very least, chin the washbasin. Furthermore, she'd seen the girl's eyes. It was the same one from the waiting room and she'd experienced more than enough over the years to read behind the lines to know this wasn't illness the girl was suffering with. *It was fear.*

Jane decided she'd take the matter into her own hands. Glancing at Maggie, who raised her eyebrows questioningly she approached the girl.

Holding the girl firmly around the waist to steady her, Jane rubbed her back. 'Sweetheart, you need to calm down.' She needed to get this girl to steady her breathing. It was verging on hyperventilation. 'Breathe. Deep breaths. You're not going to be sick. Come on now. Calm it down.'

Lacey wasn't sure whether it was the tone of the woman's voice or because she was being physically supported with what seemed like genuine concern, but she felt the last few months of emotion and despair rising up from her feet like a volcano.

With a large intake of breath, she allowed herself to be steered to an area past the hand dryers that contained a long shelf, a mirror and two chairs. Like a little child she was guided onto one of the plastic chairs. She rested her head on her knees and tried to regulate her gasping breaths.

'What's the matter with her?' Maggie asked. She didn't want to get involved in somebody else's drama. She'd had more than enough of her own over the years, as had Jane and she had no idea why Jane had felt the need to go to the aid of this complete stranger.

'Not sure,' Jane muttered, 'but something's not right.' She didn't like this. She knew it wasn't her problem, but she couldn't just walk away. *This girl was in the shit big time.*

'Come on. She's fine now,' Maggie said, touching Jane's

arm. 'It's not our business. We should go.'

'You have a short memory Maggie,' Jane muttered quietly. 'How would you have felt if I'd have walked away from *you* when you'd needed me?'

Maggie quickly stood to one side thoroughly put to rights. She wrung her hands together. It was true. Jane had never abandoned her - whatever the cost, but she had a new life now. Looking at the skinny girl in front of her, it seemed she was more akin to a time from Jane's past, rather than where she was at present.

Sensing the girl was calming down, Jane gently placed her hands either side of the girl's face and tilted her head up. 'Now, tell me what's going on?'

Lacey's eyes met Jane's for the second time that day and her breath caught in her throat. *It was Jane Wright again.* 'Oh!' she gasped. 'It's *you*! You're from tha…'

'It doesn't matter who I am,' Jane interrupted. 'Let's go and get a coffee and you can tell me what's happened.'

Lacey's eyes widened with fear and she grasped Jane's hands. 'I-I *can't*! If I go out there, he'll see me and then I'll have to go with him.'

Jane frowned and glanced up at Maggie. *She'd been correct in thinking something wasn't quite the ticket.* 'Who'll see you?'

Lacey's eyes darted from Jane to Maggie and back to Jane again. *Could she trust them?* Her mind was all over the place, but her life was over whichever way she looked at it, so what did she have to lose? She quickly came to the conclusion she would place her trust in this woman. The worst that could happen would be what would happen anyway.

Everything was worth risking if it meant the *slightest* chance of being able to somehow get out of this unbearable situation.

'I-I….' Lacey hesitated, the words she'd longed to unburden herself from sticking in her throat.

'Am I right in presuming you're pregnant?' Jane asked. Seeing the girl hesitantly nod, she frowned. 'And who will see you? That bloke you were with? Is he the father?'

'No,' Lacey said dully. 'I'd rather he was though…'

'So, what's the problem? Are you scared of something?'

Lacey couldn't help herself. Bursting out crying, she leant forward into Jane. Clinging on she began sobbing in earnest, the whole story quickly spilling from her in a torrent.

Jane listened as the girl spewed out the horrific details of what she'd been put through and what was planned for her. Stroking the young girl's hair as she shook like a leaf, she glanced at Maggie who stood motionless looking equally horrified.

Letting the girl's sobbing die down to muffled hiccupping sobs, Jane held her gently at arms' length so that she could look into her face. 'Right, you listen to me.'

Once she was sure she'd got the girl's full attention, Jane continued. 'You're coming with me. You won't be going back to that place.' She tried to ignore the shocked look plastered across Maggie's face. She had to do this. There was no way she could allow it. No way could she go back to her happy life knowing she'd left this girl to return to a hellhole. *It was fucking wrong and she wouldn't allow it.*

Lacey's mouth hung open in shock. 'Coming with *you*? Really? Do you mean it?' Her face resumed its haunted expression. 'But they'll find me.'

Jane smiled through gritted teeth. 'They can *try,* but they'd have to get through me first and that isn't easy,' she said resolutely. 'Maggie, I need you to deflect that person out there. The one masquerading as her boyfriend.'

Maggie's eyes darted around nervously. She looked at Lacey. 'Where is he and what's his name?'

'Aiden. His name's Aiden and he's sitting in the chairs opposite these toilets. What are you going to do? Please don't make me go to the police!' Lacey stammered, feeling panic rising once again.

'I don't do the police so don't you worry about that,' Jane snapped. 'Maggie, find this Aiden. Look suitably flustered and panicked. Turn it on big time. Tell him his girlfriend's collapsed and that he needs to get someone.'

Maggie stared horrified. 'But what shall I do if he tries to get in here?'

'For fuck's sake. You *know* what to do,' Jane cried. 'Give him some spiel. Drag him down the corridor to find someone. Act freaked out.' Opening her bag, she fished out a headscarf and wrapped it loosely around Lacey's head and shoulders. She then slipped her jacket off and handed it to the girl. 'Put this on.'

Jane looked back at Maggie. 'Go! We'll give you thirty seconds and then we're coming out. Make sure you've got him away in the opposite direction. Once you've gibbered some crap to a member of staff and he's ensconced with them, they'll be dashing back here. At this point slip off in the other direction, find the nearest exit and make your way as quickly as possible to the main road. Keep walking and I'll come and find you in the car.'

Looking nervous, Maggie nodded and with a final glance at Jane and the trembling young girl she dashed from the toilets.

ELEVEN

ELIZA STARED AT THE clock and took a long swig from her glass of gin. 'Where are they?' she snapped irritably, scowling as Digger flicked through the paper seemingly without a care in the world. 'Are you even listening to me?'

Looking up, Digger smiled causing the scarring across his face to pucker. 'Chill babe. They'll be back soon.' *Why did women always have this uncanny knack of over dramatizing just about everything?*

'But they've been gone *hours*!' Eliza whined.

'For God's sake, Eliza. Have you forgotten what waiting times are like in hospitals? It's only been a couple of hours.'

'*Four* actually,' she snapped, frowning at the chipped edge of one of her false nails.

Digger laughed. 'Four then. Maybe she's had to have some tests?'

Eliza sat up straight. 'Well if that's the case it must mean something's wrong.'

'Oh, for Christ's sake!' Digger muttered and ran his hand over his shaved head, his patience wearing thin. 'It doesn't mean anything of the sort. Aiden's with her. He'll have it in hand. If there had been a problem don't you think he'd have called?'

Eliza opened her mouth to fire a suitably venomous retort in Digger's direction when the door to her office burst open. Swinging her head around in shock, she stared at Aiden standing in front of them, red-faced and out of breath. 'Aiden! Where the fuck have you been?' she screeched.

Aiden leant on her desk with both hands, desperately trying to catch his breath. 'I got back as fast as I could. I had to make sure before I left,' he panted.

Eliza glanced at Digger. 'Make sure of what? What's going on? Where's Lacey? Is everything alright?'

Aiden resembled a rabbit caught in the headlights and looked towards Digger in the vague hope of some support against the barrage of Eliza's questioning.

Digger stood up from behind his desk and held his hand up. 'Whoa! Slow down Eliza! Give the poor guy chance.' He turned towards Aiden. 'Right mate, what's the score?'

Aiden took in a deep breath, thankful to get a full lungful of air. 'I looked everywhere. I just don't know how she could have vanished.'

A cold rush of ice raced up Eliza's spine. 'Are you telling me Lacey isn't with you?' she asked slowly, desperately trying to contain her voice from turning into an ear-splitting screech.

Aiden nodded slowly, unable to meet either Eliza's or Digger's accusatory glares.

'You've lost her, haven't you?' Digger growled, getting impatient. *Enough beating around the bush.*

Without waiting for an answer, Eliza darted around the desk, her large fake breasts bouncing like beach balls. 'You fucking idiot!' she yelled, slapping Aiden hard around the face. 'Where the fuck is she?'

'Eliza!' Digger shouted warningly and grabbed her around the waist, effortlessly pulling her away. 'Let's all just calm down.' He nodded towards a chair, gesturing for Aiden to sit in it.

Aiden raised his hand to his face to touch the stinging red mark left by Eliza's hand and sat down automatically even though all he wanted to do was to get as far away from them as possible. *He'd known he would get in serious shit for this.* 'We stuck to the story you gave us and no one asked any questions,' he said, trying to keep his voice steady rather than disintegrating into babbling. 'Lacey was more in awe of that Jane Wright woman.'

Eliza scowled. *What was Jane doing there? Pregnant again, was she?* 'Right, but?'

Aiden rummaged in his pocket and pulled out the creased scan picture. Glancing at it he held it up to Eliza. 'Everything's fine. The baby's unharmed,' he smiled.

Ripping the photograph from Aiden's hand, Eliza scrunched it up and threw it on the floor. 'What does that matter if Lacey's disappeared?' she yelled.

Digger intervened once more. 'Calm Eliza!' he muttered. 'What happened then?'

'We were walking down the corridor and Lacey started going all funny,' Aiden glanced up at Digger. 'She wasn't putting it on I swear. She was sweaty and looked grey - like she was going to pass out. She said she needed to be sick and went into the toilets while I waited outside.'

'And she disappeared from the toilets?' Eliza snapped.

Aiden nodded. 'Yes…. Well, she must have. I don't know how. I was waiting opposite watching the door, but she didn't come out.'

Eliza rolled her eyes. 'Did you not think to get a nurse when she said she felt ill?'

'I suggested that, but Lacey was worried they might ask questions and she had a point. She said she just needed to throw up and splash some water on her face.'

Digger frowned. 'So, when she didn't come out did you go in?'

Aiden shook his head. 'She'd only been in there a few minutes when a woman came racing out straight over to me. Asking me if I was Aiden and saying my girlfriend had collapsed. She said we needed to get a nurse, so I rushed up the corridor with this woman. Right freaked out she was. When me and the nurse went back to the toilets, they were empty. Lacey had gone.'

Eliza sighed. 'And this woman? The one who told you Lacey had collapsed?'

Aiden frowned. 'I don't know. I turned around and she'd disappeared.'

'Classic,' Digger grunted. 'What happened then?'

'I ran to the exit, but could see no sign of Lacey, nor the woman that fetched me. The nurses put a call over the tannoy and I was told to hang around in case Lacey showed up, but after a while I left.'

Eliza scowled. 'It's possible she may have been carted off by a nurse whilst you'd gone to fetch one. Someone may have found her.'

'I was gone less than a minute or two,' Aiden argued.

'It's still feasible,' Eliza repeated, clutching at straws.

'Or more likely the bitch did a runner,' Digger mumbled.

'But she was in a right state,' Aiden cried. 'She could barely walk. There's no way she was putting that on.'

'You'd be surprised what women can fake!' Digger hissed accusingly.

Ignoring the bait, Eliza concentrated hard. Lacey *was* in a state physically. She'd barely eaten for weeks and didn't look like she'd be capable of sprinting out of the hospital.

'It was obviously a set up,' Digger grumbled.

'With who? Lacey doesn't know anyone and wouldn't *dare* approach a random person. She's not stupid!' Eliza was getting riled. *There had to be a rational explanation. Surely?* 'You should have searched the wards until you found her, you stupid bastard. She must be in there somewhere.'

'I-I didn't know what else to do.'

'Right, you might as well fuck off then,' Eliza screamed. 'You've done enough damage. Don't expect to be paid for this either.'

Digger jerked his head towards the door, giving Aiden his

signal to leave – pronto. After the man had gratefully beat a sharp exit he turned towards Eliza. 'So now what?'

Eliza topped up her glass from the gin bottle. 'Have you got any ideas?' Eliza snarled, her eyes narrowing into slits. 'We've got a lot of money riding on this and we need to find the fucking stupid cow.'

'The bitch has done a runner. It's fucking obvious!' Digger growled. 'God knows how and who with though.'

• • • •

DAN SAT UNCOMFORTABLY in the passenger seat as they sped along and glanced at Seth whose eyes were fixed on the road. He hoped this guy would be in, otherwise he knew he'd be trailing around the rest of the night until Seth had spilt some blood to get the frustration out of his system.

Whilst Seth was in a good mood and things were running smoothly at work and home he kept out of the shitty side of things, but anytime something irritated or stressed him he quickly reverted back to the Seth he'd always been. *The dangerous one.*

'Here we are.' Seth screeched to a halt outside a small semi-detached house behind a row of tatty looking shops. 'Let's not stay long otherwise my wheels will probably go missing!'

Leaning over, Seth double checked the address on the list. 'Yep, this is the one. Neil Batchelor.' He removed his handgun from under the driver's seat and pulling a magazine from his overcoat's inside pocket, rapidly secured the clip.

Dan eyed the pistol. 'You're planning on using *that*?' he asked, worried.

Seth raised an eyebrow and smiled wryly. 'Depends if this bloke makes it easy for himself.' He could see the expression on Dan's face and guessed he wasn't pleased about the choice to pay calls personally, but he didn't care. He needed the answers and wouldn't sit here doing nothing. Whether Dan liked it or not it was important he showed his face with the strong arm side of things occasionally.

That was the only reason he'd got where he was after all and Dan would do well to remember that when he felt he'd rather take the 'comfy seat' approach. Although he didn't mind sitting behind a desk and calling the shots, he didn't want anyone to forget *exactly* who he was. *He was Seth Wright.*

Placing his handgun in his waistband, Seth got out of the car and confidently strolled up the garden path with Dan following behind. He banged loudly on the door and tapped his shoe impatiently on the stone doorstep as the hallway light came on.

The door opened and a man stood with a can of lager in his hand wearing an annoyed expression. 'Yes?'

'Neil Batchelor?' Seth didn't offer an explanation as to his presence and waited calmly with a steely glare, until the man in front of him realised who was on his doorstep.

As the penny dropped, the man's mouth hung open and the extent of his mistake seeped into his brain. 'Mr Wright!' he gibbered. 'Jesus! What are you doing here? I-I mean, what can I help you with?' *Fuck. Fuck. Fucking shit fuck. This was not good.*

Trying not to smile at the man's obvious panic, Seth casually stepped over the threshold and calmly pushed past into the hallway. 'Mind if we come in?' he asked belatedly.

'Y-Yes of course. Please come in,' the man stuttered, well aware Seth already had. Glancing out of the doorway and up and down the road, he quietly shut the door.

Dan stood behind the man as he hovered in the hallway, unsure what to do or say. He *knew* he'd recognised that name. *Neil Batchelor. He'd definitely seen this guy before.*

'Can I get you guys a drink?' Neil asked, nervously holding up his can. 'Lager?'

Seth shook his head. 'No thanks. This is only a quick visit. I was hoping you could help us with something. Can we go in here?' he nodded towards a room off the hallway.

'Of course,' Neil replied and pushed the door open, ushering both men in.

Seth walked into the man's lounge, making sure he didn't

trip over the threadbare carpet which had rolled up at the edges and gathered in ridges. He glanced at the illuminated fish tank in the corner containing a collection of brightly coloured fish, a loud water filter and a host of garish plastic plants shoved into the grit at the base of the tank. 'Nice fish....' he muttered.

'Thanks,' Neil said attempting to smile, aware there must be some point to this visit which most probably didn't include complimenting his tropical fish. He didn't know what it was, but suspected he wasn't going to like it.

Dan stood silently watching the hint of a smile playing at the corner of Seth's mouth and braced himself for the kick-off.

'If you like fish there's another tank in the kitchen if you'd li...'

'I don't actually like fish at all,' Seth interrupted. 'But I would like it if you'd be kind enough to tell me who sent you to ask questions at Jason Miller's club?'

'Jason Miller's club?' Neil repeated, taken off guard.

'Yes, Jason Miller's club – The Limelight? You went in to poke around regarding his suppliers.' Seth paused. 'Now I think I'm correct in surmising *you* aren't a potential supplier?' He made a point of looking slowly around the shabby room. 'But I suspect you know who is, or at the very least, who asked you to do the digging?'

Dan frowned. *That was it.* That was where he knew this bloke from. When he himself had been involved in gopher work for firms like Benson's this Neil guy used to do the same for the Millers. Like many, he'd been on the periphery, but had definitely been one of Miller's runners. *Why would he be attempting to make inroads into Miller's club for someone else?*

Seth stepped towards Neil, the tell-tale glint bright in his eyes. With the speed of lightening he reached out and gripped the man around the throat. 'Now I suggest you tell me what you know.'

Neil's eyes bulged as he fruitlessly attempted to prise Seth's hand away from his windpipe. 'I don't know what you're talking about!' he spluttered. 'I haven't been in Miller's club for *ages*!'

Seth's fist connected perfectly with the man's nose, instantly exploding it and sending him crashing to the floor. 'That's not true is it? You were seen in there, now let's see…' He pulled out a piece of paper from his pocket and scanned down the list. 'One day last week I think...'

Seth dropped to his haunches whilst Neil rolled around on the floor trying to stem the bleeding from his broken nose. He pinned the man down. 'Did that jog your memory at all?'

'I-I, er…' Neil's eyes darted around the room.

'Well?' Seth roared, lifting the man's head from the carpet by his collar. 'Who sent you?' On receiving no response, he slammed Neil's skull down hard onto the floor.

Dan stood stock still and winced hearing the sound of the man's head smack on the deck. He'd let Seth deal with this until he got the nod. He knew better than to step in until he was explicitly asked to.

'Ok, OK. I did go there on Tuesday,' Neil gibbered. 'It was only to see a few of the lads I used to work with.'

Seth sneered. 'What do you mean *used to work with*? Think I'm stupid, do you?'

'No!' Neil panicked further. *He'd heard Alan Barber's brother had for some reason been asking around, but he couldn't drop Alan in the shit about that. Alan was a decent guy, even if his brother wasn't.* 'Seriously, I don't know anything about the questions. I heard someone mention they'd been approached, but I don't know who by. I didn't see him. Just some young guy.'

'And who was this *young guy* exactly?'

'I really don't know. Honestly!' Neil bleated feeling Seth's fingers pressing deeper around his neck. 'You know how it works – people send people, who send people…'

'Yeah, I know that, but I like to do things myself personally sometimes as you can see… So, I'll ask you again – who was doing the asking?'

Dan felt it time to add what he knew. 'This bloke actually did work for Miller so he might be telling the truth.'

Seth glanced up. 'Did he now…' *Was this an inside job or*

something? Was Jason Miller setting him up? Was he the one on the take – making it look like an outside firm? 'You work for Miller?'

'I used to,' Neil spat. 'I got binned off two years ago.'

'This guy was one of the peripheral runners Seth. I remember him,' Dan added.

Seth nodded. Dan should know. He was one of the outsiders back in the day himself. It made sense he'd know the others on the circuit.

'He stopped being used because his loyalty was questioned,' Dan continued. Neil Batchelor had become far too attached to the brown stuff for anyone's liking. This had made him non-choosy as to whom he sold his services to and that wasn't appreciated.

Seth was bored. Getting to his feet he pulled his heavy overcoat to one side and drew out the gun from his waistband. With legs slightly apart he pointed the barrel casually in the man's face. 'Last chance dick head. Who are you doing the running for?'

'No!' Neil wailed, flailing around in a pointless attempt to outwit the gun's barrel which trailed his every move like a magnet.

He started crying when Seth made a big show of cocking the gun. A horrible pathetic sight as he lay in a heap, his smashed nose bubbling with bloody snot. 'It wasn't me! I only heard a guy did some digging,' he sobbed.

'And what did you 'hear' his name was?' Seth sneered, slipping off his overcoat. *Miller told him the guy asking the questions happened on the Wednesday, not the Tuesday... Fuck it – this bloke was irritating him.*

'I don't know!' Neil screamed wild-eyed. 'I *swear*!'

'His *name* Neil? The runner's name?'

Neil frowned, the sweat pouring from his face. 'I-I don't know.... I can't think....'

Sighing, Seth suddenly fired the gun into Neil's left kneecap and Dan tried not to jump back in surprise.

Dropping back down onto his haunches next to the writhing, screaming man, Seth shook him hard. 'Suggest you shut your noise unless you want to attract undue attention. You don't want any more grief on your back, do you?' He smiled savagely, enjoying the familiar feeling of adrenaline rushing through his veins. 'Now your concentration is fully on me – last time - tell me who this guy you *heard* asking questions is – his name and what he looks like?'

Neil clenched his teeth to control the urge to continue screaming as the pain from his shattered kneecap wracked through him. 'He's young – in his twenties with blond short hair. Tall and slim.'

'Name?' Seth growled and pressed the heel of his shoe down on Neil's kneecap.

Howling, Neil began retching.

'Concentrate, you cunt!' Seth roared. 'His *name*? The blond guy's fucking name?'

Gasping in loud gulps of air, Neil sobbed openly. 'I-I'm not sure. Adam? Or Aaron… Definitely began with A.'

Removing his foot, Seth smiled. 'Thanks Neil. That will do for now. We'll be back if we need more. In the meantime, if you think of anything you know where to find us…'

Scowling at the blood splattered over his white shirt sleeves, Seth placed his handgun back in his waistband and shrugged on his overcoat. 'I trust you won't feel the need to mention this to anyone?'

Watching Neil shake his head frantically as he rolled about on the carpet, Seth smiled. Nodding to Dan, they quietly left the house.

TWELVE

ANNA HAD BEEN SHOCKED when Jane returned late this afternoon. She'd been accompanied by that Maggie woman, who she'd seen several times before and a young girl, who she most certainly hadn't *ever* seen.

The girl looked awful. Judging by her red eyes she'd been crying and also looked ill. She was as nervous as anything and Anna had no idea where this young frightened girl had come from. She'd tried to say hello but was promptly cut short and told to go and run a bath for the guest.

Anna wasn't in the best frame of mind herself. Tina was clamouring for information, but she hadn't found or overheard anything of much interest. She had to at least try otherwise her career would be over, not to mention her mother's mental state if that happened.

Anna ate her dinner with Toby at the kitchen table and for once his happy little face didn't do anything to cheer her up. She looked at the large bouquet of flowers on the table and for the fourth time since they'd arrived earlier, wished that for once in her life someone would do something like that for her.

Feeling very despondent, Anna pushed her uneaten dinner to one side and walked to the fridge. Jane was still upstairs with the mystery girl and there was no sign of Seth either. She pulled out the two plates of sandwiches she'd made and with Toby in one arm, made her way up the stairs.

After putting Toby to bed, Anna walked to the guest room and hearing Jane's voice coming from the other side of the door, gingerly tapped upon it.

'Yes?' Jane snapped.

Anna hesitantly opened the door and slowly walked into the room. The young girl was sitting on the bed, her hair wrapped in a fluffy white towel and she was wearing one of Seth's T-shirts that was long enough to wear as a night shirt.

Anna smiled nervously as she set the two plates of sandwiches down at the end of the bed. 'Sorry to bother you. I thought you might be hungry.'

Jane forced a smile. 'Thanks Anna.'

Anna stood only for a couple more seconds before realising the heavy silence translated that she shouldn't be loitering. Retreating from the room, she pulled the door closed, but remained outside and pressed up against the door.

'You need to eat something Lacey,' Jane said.

'I'm not hungry,' came a small voice in reply.

'I realise that, but the worst is now over.'

'It isn't though is it! It can't be over until *this* is gone.'

The young girl's voice was thick with anger and Anna frowned, trying to decipher what 'this' meant. She heard Jane sigh.

'I know sweetheart, but don't you worry. It's all in hand. We'll get this sorted before the end of the week, I promise.'

'What about your husband?'

Jane laughed. 'Don't you worry about him. He'll back me up. If you want to get rid of the baby, I'll help you and Seth will also make sure they won't find you, ok?'

Anna jumped out of her skin when a door slammed downstairs. Footsteps were fast coming up the stairs. *It must be Seth! She couldn't be caught eavesdropping!*

Quickly retreating from outside the guest room, Anna moved

as rapidly as possible along the corridor, realising with dread she hadn't time to reach her room before Seth rounded the corner. Flattening herself behind a jutting wall she held her breath.

Hearing Seth's footsteps moving along in the opposite direction she risked peeping out from behind the wall. He stood outside his study in his overcoat and Anna frowned, wondering why he'd come upstairs without hanging it in the normal place on the wooden coat stand in the hall.

Anna got her answer when he shrugged off the coat and then quickly walked into the study. She swallowed hard, her throat felt like something was stuck at the back of it. Seth's arms and hands were covered in dried blood and his crisp white shirt was equally splattered.

Looking towards the room where Jane was holed up with the girl and sensing no one was about to open the door, Anna carefully walked up the corridor towards the study. Her brain was screaming to just go to her room and pretend she'd seen nothing, but she had to know why Seth was covered in blood. Or was this the first instance she'd seen with her own eyes of the sort of things the couple she worked for were involved in? *She had to find out. It might shut Tina up for a while.*

Ignoring the rapid beating of her heart pounding relentlessly in her chest, Anna reached the study and peered through the crack of the ajar door. Seth stood behind his carved wooden desk. She watched him pull a handgun from the waistband of his trousers and remove the magazine. Checking the contents, he replaced the clip back in the gun and flicking a catch down, opened the filing cabinet.

Hurriedly putting the gun inside, Seth locked the drawer and stood still, his expression stern, but pensive. He wiped the back of his hand across his forehead and sighed as he inspected the blood staining his hands, arm and shirt.

Not daring to move and drawn to the presence of the man she was silently watching, Anna's breath hitched as she watched Seth unbutton his shirt and slip it off. She stared at the rippling muscles adorning his arms and torso and felt her heart quicken further.

Reaching down, Seth picked up a leather holdall and stuffed the dirty shirt inside. Anna's eyes travelled down the ridges on his stomach and followed the line of dark hair running from his navel to disappear behind the top of his trousers that sat on his hips.

She watched entranced as he strode over to the washbasin and began scrubbing at his hands and arms.

As Seth stood with his wide back to her, his muscles well-defined and rippling, Anna wondered what it would be like to touch them. Shaking her head to rid herself of these inappropriate thoughts she realised she needed to get back to her own room as soon as possible before her presence was discovered.

• • • •

SETH POURED A GLASS of whisky and sat down at the desk. Taking a long drink from the crystal tumbler, he leaned back in the chair and sighed. He needed to piece together what the information he'd got from that Batchelor guy meant. He'd no idea who this Aaron, Adam or whatever he was called was. Nor whom he was connected with, but he'd work it out. Presuming of course that twat was levelling with him. If he wasn't, then he'd be paying for it. Tonight had been a mere taster of what he'd do to the bastard if he was messing about.

The prospect of this whole thing being an inside job from Miller was still floating uncomfortably around in his brain. He couldn't get it out of his head. Was this arrangement Miller had with him an elaborate set up to cut him and the Glint out of the running so that the Millers would have the monopoly?

Seth shook his head in annoyance. He was being paranoid. That Batchelor guy worked for the Millers a few years ago of which Dan had confirmed. He wasn't connected now - Dan would have known if he was. No, he was being stupid. This mistrust of Jason Miller's interest in his wife was colouring his view and he needed to remain rational. Plus, Batchelor had visited on the Tuesday and Miller said the questions had been reported on a *Wednesday*.

Seth lit a cigarette and took a deep pull, savouring the smoke curling in his lungs. He hadn't seen Jane either and his mind had been distracted whilst he'd been dealing with Batchelor. He hated arguing with her. He'd have this drink and get his adrenaline levels back to normal, then he'd go and find her to put things right.

Sensing movement outside his study, Seth's gaze moved towards the door. 'Jane? Babe? Is that you?' He was surprised when Anna poked her head around the door.

'Good evening Mr Wright. It's only me. I was just about to check on Toby.' She cleared her throat in embarrassment. 'I'm sorry. I didn't mean to disturb you…' She had to at least *pretend* she was shocked by the sight of him half-dressed rather than making it obvious she'd watched and dare she say, *relished* seeing him strip down to his waist.

Seth grinned seeing Anna's flushed red face. 'Don't worry Anna,' he beckoned her into the room. 'Come in.'

Anna nervously stepped into the study and stood uncomfortably wondering what to do. *What happened if he suddenly decided to shoot her? She'd seen the gun with her own eyes.* For the first time since she'd been in the Wright's house, tendrils of fear crept into her brain.

'Blimey Anna, stand down! I don't bite!' Seth laughed, pouring a small measure of whisky into a second tumbler. 'Here, have this.' He gestured to a seat the other side of the desk. 'Don't worry, I haven't got my cock out! You're safe with me!' He laughed heartily watching Anna's blush spread furiously across her chest. 'How's my boy been today?'

Glad for the change of the subject, Anna took a sip of the whisky and enjoyed the feel of the spirit as it warmed the back of her throat. A wide smile spread across her face as it always did with the thought of that dear little boy. 'Oh, he's been an absolute darling like usual.'

'Good day then?' Seth asked, stretching his long legs out to the side of the desk.

Anna forced herself not to look and instead concentrated on Seth's face, noticing he'd got dimples hidden under his closely cut beard when he smiled. *Stop it Anna*, she admonished herself. She needed to change the subject. 'Beautiful flowers you sent to Mrs Wright.'

Seth's eyes narrowed. 'Flowers? What flowers?'

Anna hesitated, realising she'd somehow said the wrong thing. 'Oh, erm… flowers arrived this afternoon. I thought…. I mean, I presumed that….'

Seth frowned. *Who was sending Jane flowers? It certainly hadn't been him.*

Anna cleared her throat and quickly stood up. 'I'd better get on. I was on my way to check on T..'

'I thought I heard you come back Seth,' Jane said, walking into the room and stopped, seeing Seth shirtless and Anna with a drink in her hand. She raised an eyebrow. 'I didn't realise you were busy…'

Anna blushed deeper. 'I was on my way to check on Toby and I was just saying hello.' She smiled nervously and made her way out of the room as quickly as possible.

• • • •

JANE WAS BUSY removing her makeup in the en-suite bathroom when Seth came in and stood behind her. 'I need to talk to you about something,' she said.

'And I need to talk to you too, but for now….' A soft smile played on Seth's lips as he looked at his wife. Reaching around he pulled at the tie around her satin robe.

Jane met Seth's eyes in the reflection of the mirror as her robe slipped from her shoulders and fell in a heap upon the tiled floor exposing her nakedness to his gaze. She took in his powerful shoulders standing a foot above hers and felt his need pressing against the small of her back. As he ran his hands lightly down her arms she closed her eyes, feeling her nipples puckering into hard points at his touch.

'Jane...' Seth murmured, scooping her hair out of the way so he could trail a line of kisses down her neck. 'I'm sorry about what I said last night and for disappearing this morning.' His hands gently ran over her breasts. 'You're right. Let's get Grace back before we think about having any more kids.'

Turning herself around to face him, Jane slowly traced her finger down his chest, over his hard stomach and heard him take a sharp intake of breath as she unzipped his trousers and wrapped her hand firmly around his length.

She moved her hand down his cock and as his mouth searched for hers, she smiled. 'That's all I was saying Seth, but I'm not saying never ok?'

Seth grinned widely and lifted Jane on to the marble sink surround. Her eyes were half-closed as his hands massaged her breasts hardening her nipples further. His eyes ran over her body as he stood between her thighs. 'Christ, I love you,' he whispered and slid into her. *He'd ask about the flowers later.*

THIRTEEN

ELIZA WAS TRYING TO enjoy Digger's tongue working her frantically. He'd taken the initiative by pushing her backwards onto her desk and burying his head between her legs, but it just wasn't working. She normally loved impromptu stuff like this, but just had too much stuff on her mind today to relax.

'What are we going to do?' she whined.

Stopping, Digger irritably raised his head and looked at her. 'For God's sake Eliza, you've got to accept the little bitch has done a runner. She's *gone*!' he snapped huffily. Christ, it didn't say much for him if all she could think about was the girls when he was desperately trying to make her come.

Wiping his hand across his mouth, Digger got to his feet. 'Listen, it's not the end of the world. We've got *more* than enough stuff to be getting on with without this kid thing,' he reasoned. 'Do you not realise we're *this* close to fucking Seth and Jane up once and for all? That was the fucking plan to start with before all this business with that stupid cow started wasn't it?'

Eliza pulled her skirt down and slipped from the desk. 'Don't you think I know that, but are you that thick-skulled you've forgotten you've lined up a buyer for Lacey's kid? That stands to net us some good coin!' She pouted heavily. 'It will bring in *thousands* extra Digger. I thought you agreed it was a good idea?'

Digger sighed. *It wasn't a good idea. It never had been.* In all honesty he'd only gone along with it because she'd wanted to do it. 'Yes babe, it was,' he lied, pulling Eliza into his arms. 'But only in as much as it was available. Now it's not I can't see the point in worrying about it.'

He stroked her hair. 'Listen, you tried your best to locate her and she definitely wasn't still in the hospital under any name, so she's ok and somewhere. Let it go. You're not thinking rationally.'

Eliza pursed her lips. 'I think Jane Wright's behind this. She was at the hospital that day and what happens if Lacey tells someone?'

Digger sneered. 'Why would it be anything to do with Jane? Besides, Lacey won't say a word. She knows what would happen if she did.' *She'd sorely pay for it.*

Eliza folded her arms, accepting Digger was probably right. However, she'd still be keeping her ears open because if she caught wind of Lacey's whereabouts, she'd make sure she was returned. It was always a risk when one went AWOL, but she still wanted it checked out. 'I want you to make sure for definite the bitch isn't at the Wrights.'

Digger sighed. 'Ok, but I'm not having anyone waste *days* on it.' He picked up the telephone. 'Aiden? Get yourself up here.'

Eliza stared at Digger. 'What the hell are you calling him in for? Don't you think he's done enough damage? He can't be fucking trusted!' she snapped.

'Don't be stupid woman! The hospital incident was out of his control. He's alright Aiden is.'

Eliza arched one of her overly-plucked brows. 'You could have fooled me…'

'As well as checking out what you've asked, I have another job for him to do at the Limelight. His inroad in there courtesy of his brother is invaluable!'

Eliza smiled. She loved Digger. Well – at least as much as she could love anyone these days she supposed and he was good at keeping her mind on track on the occasions when it drifted off at a tangent. 'Ok, maybe you're right. As it happens I have another idea for Aiden too, but forget about that for the time being. I have some great news. Social Services have called me,' she raised her eyebrow suggestively. 'Guess what? Due to my *very* specific criteria in a child they can unfortunately only match us with two children…'

'Right and?' Digger muttered uninterested.

'Well…' she grinned, perching back seductively on his lap and wrapping her arms around his neck. 'The Wrights' kid is one of them!'

A broad grin broke out over Digger's face. 'Excellent! When do we get her then?'

Eliza laughed. 'Oh Digs, I wish it was that simple! We've got to meet both the kids first!'

'Whatever for? We know which one we want!' Digger grunted irritably. *He hadn't got time for this old welly. Taking the kid was one thing, but having to play happy families with it plus another completely irrelevant one was another.*

Eliza sighed heavily. 'We've got to at least show some interest in both kids otherwise it will look suspicious. I've got to set up a meeting for it. It'll be at our house and you need to be there too.'

Digger nodded glumly, hoping he wouldn't be expected to act like a doting wannabe father or something. *He wouldn't have a bloody clue.*

Eliza was closely watching Digger's expression. 'I hope you'll make an effort. You know how important this is.'

'Yes, I know,' Digger mumbled. *It didn't mean that he was looking forward to it.* 'We'll discuss this later. Aiden will be here any moment.'

• • • •

AIDEN FELT UNCOMFORTABLE doing anything which might cause his brother trouble.

'But it's not about involving Alan, Aiden. We just want to ensure you remain in close contact with him so you can get easy access,' Eliza smiled.

Digger grinned. 'As well as needing you to give one of the bar staff a slap, don't forget it's the Wrights we're primarily after and we want your help with that by getting friendly with their au-pair.'

'Their *au-pair*?' Aiden asked, surprised. *He liked the sound of that. Weren't au pairs always young blondes with big tits?*

Eliza pulled a newspaper cutting from the drawer. 'It's unlikely, but have you seen this woman before?' She unfolded the picture taken at Jason Miller's club. 'You went to this as your brother's guest, didn't you?'

Aiden looked at the picture. *Oh God – it was that dull woman he'd sat next to for all of five minutes...* 'Actually, I do know her,' he said, pointing to Anna. 'Well, I don't *know* her, but we spoke for a few minutes that night.'

Digger smiled. 'That's good because *she's* the au pair.'

Aiden's face dropped. 'What? You want me to go out with *her*?'

'What's wrong with her?' Eliza screeched. 'We're not asking you to fucking marry the woman! Just get to know her. Make her like you. Get into her pants and make her scream with pleasure!'

Eliza had heard Aiden was useful in the sack. She eyed him up and down. *She wouldn't mind a go with him herself, truth be told.* 'Make this Anna desperate for you. Treat her nice and pretend you're mad for her. Make her come and her legs shake! That way you'll get info out of her and also get into the Wright's house thereby giving us an upper hand,' she winked running a sharply tipped nail the length of his thigh.

Aiden scowled. He had no wish to get anything out of this Anna. *Even that.*

Eliza's face turned hard. 'Listen,' she hissed. 'I think you fucking owe us for losing Lacey, don't you?'

That statement alone quickly reminded Aiden that episode would be used against him for ever by the looks of it. He nodded slowly. 'Ok. Give me the address and I'll see what I can do.'

'You can't just go round there you moron! You'll have to arrange to accidentally bump into her,' Digger added. 'She's Tina's sister, by the way and she's meeting her this afternoon. Why don't you just happen to be walking past once she's left Tina?'

Tina's sister? It gets worse! Aiden looked up, resigned to his fate. 'Alright, I'll go and speak to Tina and see what the plan is.' He needed to catch up with Tina anyhow. He knew she'd been avoiding him because she owed him and he was losing his patience with her.

Digger smiled happily as he left the office. Everything was starting to fall into place quite nicely. He would have Seth this time and he'd do *anything* to attain that. It had *never* been an option to swallow what Seth and Phil had done. He'd just let them believe that and bided his time in the interim.

• • • •

SETH EYED JANE as they pulled up in the parking lot outside the Italian restaurant. He'd been shocked this morning to find some scrawny timid-looking stranger sitting at his kitchen table nibbling toast.

Anna hadn't looked surprised. She seemed already party to the visitor and it was just him who wasn't. He'd pulled Jane from the room and she'd given him a brief run down, but he needed to know more. A random stranger was in his house, around his child and he didn't know the *first* thing about her, but then it seemed, neither did Jane.

Seth had been even more shocked when Jane recounted what the girl had said. *How did she know the girl was telling the truth?* For all they knew she could be one of the many glue-sniffing little tarts who'd got knocked up by their boyfriends and was spewing out some far-fetched sob story to get attention and of course, *money*.

Seth scowled. *He needed more information*. 'Jane, if you're getting involved in shit like this then you need to be sure she's telling the truth. Who are these people who've been making her do this?'

If what the girl said was true then he'd make it his personal mission to destroy them. How could he not take people out that were pulling stuff like that? It was *disgusting*! If anyone did that to his daughter....

A vein in Seth's temple throbbed as the sinister thought crept into his mind. For all he knew something horribly sinister *could* be planned for the daughter they'd lost, but hopefully he'd have more luck locating her with this new PI.

Gritting his teeth, he felt his eyes involuntarily fall to Jane. *If anyone hurt his children or his wife, he'd....*

'I don't know who they are Seth,' Jane had said. 'Lacey was too emotionally drained to answer questions last night. Whoever it is though has put the fear of God into her. She was adamant she wouldn't give details, but believe you me, I intend to find the fuckers!' she snarled.

'I don't think you'll be dealing with them, do you?' Seth frowned. 'I don't want you putting yourself or Toby at risk. I won't have you becoming a target by getting involved with whatever's going on here.'

'Oh Seth, we'll *always* be targets now and again with what we do, you know that. Besides, you haven't filled me in with what's happening with the clubs.' She raised an eyebrow. 'Or why you had blood on you last night....'

Laughing at Seth's expression, Jane smiled. 'You think I haven't known you long enough to see when you've done something – even if you've tried to conceal it?'

Seth grinned. 'Not much to say really. Just delivered a friendly warning babe that's all...'

'Well as long as it's nothing that could stick. We don't need anyone on our case remember?' Jane opened her handbag revealing the pistol concealed inside. 'On the flip side, I have to admit *I'm* carrying again. Like you said – something's going down here – from your side, rather than mine and we don't want to be sitting ducks, do we?'

'For God's sake Jane! I said I'm dealing with it didn't I?'

'Yes,' Jane agreed, stroking his hand. 'You did and *I'm* dealing with what's going on with Lacey, so let me find out more info and then we'll talk. After she's had the abortion tomorrow it will be easier for her to spill the beans.'

Seth sat back in shock. 'The *what*?'

'I've arranged an abortion for her.' Jane stuck her chin out in defiance. 'Don't you *dare* tell me that's wrong, Seth. I told you she was pregnant by one of those bastards who get off on young flesh. The tossers who run the place were forcing her to keep the child and then sell it on! It's fucking *disgusting*. You can't expect me not to help her.'

Seth nodded. 'No, I don't. I don't expect that at all.' The whole thing sickened him and he could already feel his blood boiling. He just wished he knew for *certain* the girl was telling the truth. 'Believe me Jane. If this is true, then the minute we find out who these wankers are I'll personally ensure they're removed.'

Jane smiled. Unclipping her seat belt, she stretched over and kissed Seth hard on the lips. 'Thank you. Now hadn't we better go in and meet the Millers for lunch?'

Seth raised one eyebrow. 'And you're *sure* it wasn't him that sent you those flowers?'

Jane sighed theatrically. 'Yes, I'm sure. Why on earth would Jason be sending me two dozen red roses? Come on! It was obviously a delivery mistake – lucky me eh?'

She turned away and opened the passenger seat door. Seth had grilled her about those flowers last night. It was true she didn't have a clue as to who had sent them or why, but it wasn't true that it was a mistake with the delivery. They'd definitely been meant for her because the attached card had read:

Jane,
Let me know when we can finally be together. I'm waiting.

Always
J
xx

Luckily, she'd found the card and got rid of it before Seth had seen it. He'd only grill her and she didn't want to give him a reason to do that. Neither did she want to tell him about the phone calls.

Three silent calls she'd received last night, near on one after the other. The caller hadn't said a thing – all she'd heard was heavy breathing. It was probably a prank. These things happened, but what with everything going on at the moment – both at the clubs and with the girl, she knew Seth was on edge and didn't want to give him reasons to keep her under guard, or constantly trailed around on the off chance someone was trying to get to them.

Someone was trying to stir the shit, but she had no clue as to who or why. As for the crap on the card which had come with the flowers, it was utter rubbish. She was *Seth's* and certainly no one else's.

• • • •

'SO, WHAT DO you know?' Tina asked, greedily pulling on one of the cigarettes Anna had bought for her.

Anna stirred the spoon around in the chipped mug and glanced out of the stained window in the café where she'd arranged to meet her sister. 'Not a lot.' She was really uncomfortable with this whole arrangement.

Tina folded her arms across her chest. 'You'd best find something because I got grabbed around the throat last night, so things had better happen soon otherwise I'll be forced to start taking action...'

Anna felt sweat begin to bead on her brow. *Tina was deadly serious. She was going to fuck her life up, wasn't she?* She stared at the steaming mug of tea in front of her. 'Well there's a couple of things…' she faltered.

Tina sat forward at the table. 'Yes, go on,' she prompted.

'When Seth returned last night, he was covered in blood. He didn't see me, but I saw *him*.' Anna lowered her voice further. 'I peered through the door and he pulled a gun from his trousers and locked it in his cabinet. Then he took his shirt off, put it in a bag and washed his arms.'

'Bet you enjoyed looking at him without his shirt on, didn't you?' Tina pushed, seeing Anna blush. 'He's fucking *hot*!'

'Don't be silly, he's my boss!' she exclaimed. Seth might be her employer, but Tina was right on one thing and that was he was *extremely* attractive. 'He then heard me outside and invited me in for a drink.'

Tina looked surprised. 'Fuck me Anna, this is getting better by the second. He invited you in for a drink? Half-naked? Fuck!'

Anna sighed. 'It wasn't like that, but I ballsed up when I said the flowers he'd sent Jane were nice. Judging by his reaction he obviously hadn't sent them and I think I may have caused a problem.'

Tina smirked. 'Oh, so Jane's been a naughty girl, has she?' She knew Eliza had sent the flowers with a message designed to cause an issue and would be glad to hear it had succeeded. 'Did they have a card with them?'

Anna looked up. 'Card? How do I know?'

Tina sighed loudly. 'Oh, for Christ's sake, Anna. *Look*. Look for the fucking card! If it's not there - find it! Check the bins, whatever. Maybe Jane threw it away if she's hiding an affair?'

'She's not having an affair! They're crazy for each other,'

Tina sneered. 'I expect that's what they *want* you to think. Rich people *always* mess about. Find the card and place it something Seth will find it.'

Anna frowned. 'I don't really want to do something like that.' She didn't like this. She didn't want to be party to such underhand behaviour. Seth and Jane had given her a job and treated her well. They'd been nothing apart from nice to her.

Tina scowled. *Come on Anna.* 'Don't forget what will happen if you don't. Besides, you don't know what these people are *really* like. Just because outwardly they seem ok and are being nice to you at the moment….' Her eyes narrowed. *She had to think quickly.*

Raising her hands to her mouth suddenly in shock, Tina gasped. 'Oh my God, Anna! I've just realised something. You said Seth came in with a gun *last night*? Are you *sure* it was last night?'

Anna nodded timidly, rapidly wishing she'd kept this gun thing to herself. 'Yes, it was definitely last night.' It was hardly likely she'd have forgotten when it had happened. That had been the first time, apart from in films, that she'd ever seen a *real* gun.

'Now it makes sense….' Tina continued, forcing a realistic expression of anguish across her face. 'I heard earlier that this guy called Dennis – a single father with poorly children - he was shot last night. The Wrights have been threatening him for ages. *That* must have been why Seth had the gun and was covered in blood. Fucking hell Anna, it was *Seth* that did it don't you see? I *told* you, didn't I? How much more proof do you need? Imagine what he's going to do to *you* when he thinks you're using drugs around his kid…'

Anna paled and felt her hands begin to tremble. *This was fast turning into a nightmare!*

'You *really* need to be delivering what I need to clear my debt,' Tina said, her eyes cold.

Ok, so it was all bullshit. Dennis didn't have disabled kids. In fact, she didn't even know anyone called Dennis. Whoever Seth Wright had really shot, Tina didn't know or care. *She needed to get this cash. She'd thought Aiden was going to knock her teeth out last night.* 'So, will you find this card from the flowers and put it somewhere Seth will find it or not?'

Anna felt so nauseous she felt she might throw up. *What choice did she have? It appeared she really was working for and living with psychos.* 'But what if there's no card?'

'There'll be a card. *All* flowers come with a card!'

Anna's shoulders slumped despondently. *She'd never been sent flowers so wouldn't know.* 'Ok.'

Tina grinned widely exposing her yellowing teeth. 'And you need to get that shirt - the one covered in blood and then bring it to me.'

Anna's eyes widened. 'How on earth am I supposed to do that?' she squeaked.

'That's *your* problem, but if you know what's good for you, you'd better get a move on.'

FOURTEEN

JANE GLANCED AT THE clock in the waiting room. Lacey had been gone for over an hour, so shouldn't be much longer.

Jane had exhausted the supply of magazines available on the coffee table and she raised her eyebrow seeing the only one she hadn't flicked through was a copy of *Anglers Weekly*.

She was trying not to focus her gaze on any of the other waiting women – after all it was obvious what they were all there for, although some of the women were undoubtedly the mothers of their younger companions: the daughters who had embarrassedly managed to get pregnant.

Jane watched them all sneaking furtive glances at each other hoping there was no one they knew in order to save the humiliation of their or their daughter's predicament within the elite circles they liked to be part of. She snorted with the hypocrisy. This lot might have loads of money, drive the best cars and hob nob with the well-connected, but when push came to shove, everyone from all walks of life had the same issues to face from time to time.

Jane had specifically arranged Lacey's procedure to be carried out in a private clinic out of the city for two reasons: one, so there was no chance of Lacey bumping into anyone who may know her, or know *of* her and two, less chance that she herself would. The last thing she wanted was gossip floating around about her being seen in an abortion clinic. The press would *love* that.

Jane's mind wandered off to how Toby was doing. Anna hadn't been herself lately. The girl seemed preoccupied and more nervous than usual and hadn't even been able to look her in the face this morning.

She frowned, hoping Anna wasn't planning on leaving. Maybe the best thing to do would be to have a chat with her and see if she was finding everything ok. If Anna had anything that was bothering her or if she was unhappy with something, then now was the time to say, rather than later.

Interrupted from her thoughts by a door opening, Jane looked up as a woman wearing the clinic's uniform approached.

'Mrs Wright? Lacey's in the recovery room so you can come through and see her now.'

Jane got to her feet and followed the woman through the door. Lacey lay on the bed looking pale, shaken and very small. She walked over and took her hand. 'How are you feeling?'

Lacey nervously checked to make sure the woman had left the room. Satisfied they were alone she winced as she propped herself up. 'Has it gone?' she asked quietly.

'Yes love,' Jane answered softly. 'It's all done.'

'Are you sure?' Lacey questioned, panic clear in her voice.

Jane nodded. 'The baby's gone Lacey, I promise.' She'd checked with the nurse as they'd walked down the corridor to confirm everything had been successfully carried out. 'You'll be a bit sore and bleed for a couple more days I expect, but everything went well. You'll be back to normal before you know it!'

Tears of relief seeped from Lacey's eyes as Jane's words sunk in.

'Are you ok?' Jane asked.

'I will be now. I don't know how to thank you for doing this for me.'

Jane smiled. 'You can start by telling me how all of this happened.' Watching Lacey's face drop in disappointment she continued. 'You really do need to tell me everything and I mean *everything*.' She needed to know what she was dealing with so this girl and any others were not exposed to further harm by whoever was running this sick gig.

• • • •

ELIZA SMILED AT the little girl clinging shyly behind the social worker in the doorway to her lounge.

'And this is Emily,' the social worker said brightly. 'She's been really looking forward to meeting you, haven't you Emily. We hope *this* time you'll find each other a good match...'

With the silence weighing heavily in the room, Eliza felt her muscles aching from fixing the wide beaming smile across her face.

Only the other day they'd been introduced to the other girl – the one they weren't interested in. Although the kid was kind of sweet in a fragile, sad sort of way, it was irrelevant because she was of no use to them. Eliza had stated that she and the child just hadn't 'clicked'.

Despite the social worker's pushing to give it a little more time before making a firm decision, Eliza had made it clear her feelings were final. She'd needed access to the *right* kid sooner rather than later and hadn't time to ponce around to anyone's feelings.

Eliza still hadn't seen the girl hiding behind the social worker and tried not to make it obvious she was attempting to peer around the woman's large thighs to get a glimpse of the girl who seemed hell bent on remaining obscured from view.

She had to ensure this was Jane's kid. It made no difference if she was called Emily these days rather than Grace – that happened a lot with kids like her. That had been part of what had made tracking her down so difficult. All the credentials about birthplace, age etc. added up, but she needed to see for herself. Surely there would be some resemblance to her biological parents? Jane and Seth's faces were indelibly etched in her mind so she'd spot any true likeness a mile off.

Eliza glanced at Digger noticing he looked extremely uncomfortable. *He needed to get a grip. She couldn't pull off this doting 'We-Want-To-Be-Your-New-Parents' thing if he sat there with a face like a slapped arse, could she?*

'Hello sweetheart!' Eliza said in the sickliest sweet voice she could conjure up. 'I'm Eliza and this is Di… erm… Sam.' She ignored Digger's death stares. *She'd had to use his real name as she could hardly introduce him as Digger, could she?*

'Do you want to come over here to sit by us and tell us a little about yourself Emily? We'd love to get to know you,' Eliza continued, subtly wiping her sweaty hands down her knee-length smart skirt. *Come on! I need to see your face kid!*

The social worked pulled the little girl forward slightly. 'Come on Emily. These nice people have invited us around especially to meet you.' She glanced at Eliza. 'She's a bit shy.'

The little girl reluctantly stepped forward and stood awkwardly, her small hand clutching a doll.

Eliza couldn't hide the audible intake of breath when she cast her eyes on the child in front of her. Her gaze locked on the girl's curly raven hair, emerald eyes and exquisitely pretty heart-shaped face. She studied the pouting rosebud mouth and swallowed hard. *Christ! This was definitely Seth and Jane's child no mistake. The kid had won the jackpot with her looks by inheriting all of her parents' best bits.*

She stole a quick glance at Digger who looked equally astounded with what they were looking at.

'My, don't you look pretty!' Eliza said brightly. 'I love your dress!' She hadn't even noticed what dress the kid was wearing, but she'd had to say something.

The child beamed from the compliment and her whole face lit up. 'It's my best one!' she cried happily, the shyness slowly evaporating.

Eliza patted the sofa. 'Come and tell me about your dress then.'

The child ran over to the sofa, jumping onto it and Eliza stifled the urge not to scream at the kid to mind her shoes on the cream leather.

'Will I be living with you now?' she asked boldly, staring at Eliza with intense eyes like Jane's, just with Seth's colouring.

Momentarily taken off guard by the look in the child's eyes, Eliza's mouth flapped up and down silently.

'Emily!' the social worker interrupted. 'You know you're not supposed to ask questions like that.'

'No, it's ok,' Eliza said, waving her hand dismissively. She turned towards the child. 'We'd very much like it if you decided you wanted to live here, wouldn't we Di… erm, Sam.'

'Yeah,' Digger grunted, unable to get his head around this. God, having this kid here would be far too close to having a bizarre combined version of Seth and Jane in his house.

'I think perhaps the next thing to do is arrange a day where you three can spend more time together getting to know each other properly,' the social worker beamed. 'Would you like that Emily?'

The little girl nodded enthusiastically. 'Yes please!'

Eliza smiled widely. 'That's great. Let's arrange it now.' *Maybe then they could fuck off and get back to Elipse. This afternoon she'd have to break the news to Lomond that Lacey had gone AWOL and he wouldn't be happy.*

• • • •

ANNA WAS IN COMPLETELY unchartered waters in more ways than one. Toby was having his afternoon nap so she'd taken the opportunity to have a bit of time in her room.

After she'd left the café, she'd been shocked when she'd literally bumped into a man.

'Hello! Anna isn't it?' the man had asked. 'Do you remember me?'

It had taken her a few seconds to place the good-looking tall blond man she'd met at that awful function the other week. She hadn't even thought he'd known her name he'd been that desperate to get away from her before. Shyly she'd smiled, unsure what to say or do with this unusual turn of events.

'I'm Aiden by the way. I'm sure you don't remember my name or even me! You must get chatted up by everyone!' he'd said smiling, exposing a row of straight white teeth.

Anna had blushed. *Hardly. She never got chatted up by anyone, let alone the nice looking ones...* 'Yes, yes of course I remember you. How are you?' she'd asked timidly, frantically trying to disguise her nerves whilst remembering the art of conversation.

'All the better now I've seen you. I can't believe I've been so lucky as to run in to you like this,' Aiden had gushed. 'I've been trying to get into contact with you since the Miller's party.'

'You have?' Anna had asked perplexed, her eyes running over his muscled arms. 'Why?'

'Well I was hoping you'd let me take you out for a drink?'

'*Me*?' Anna had squeaked. 'Well, erm...'

'Please say you will,' Aiden had moved closer, his tall frame towering above Anna.

Feeling heady from the scent of his aftershave wafting over her and knowing her face had heated, Anna had hoped her uncontrollable habit of blushing wasn't too obvious. 'I-I don't get much time off,' she'd answered, annoyed at her quick rebuff.

Aiden had looked disappointed. 'Oh, if...'

'But...' Anna had quickly interrupted before she'd lost her nerve, 'I get some evenings off when my bosses are at home. The only problem is I'm never sure when that will be.'

Aiden had smiled widely once more. 'That's ok. Here.' He'd pulled out a scrap of paper and handed it to her. 'Here's my number. As soon as you find out when you're free, call me and we'll meet up.'

'I-I don't get much notice,' she'd stammered, still unable to believe a man like this was asking her for a date.

'That doesn't matter. I'll happily drop whatever I'm doing if it means I can take you out. Call me anytime – last minute, whatever and I'll be there.'

Anna had smiled and held her breath waiting for him to say he'd been joking, but he hadn't.

'Right, I'd best be off. I don't want to hold you up. Really looking forward to seeing you Anna,' Aiden had said, reaching out and gently touching her face with his fingertips.

Anna had remained rooted to the spot and watched Aiden continue down the road. She'd raised her hand to her face and touched the place where he'd put his fingers, leaving a searing heat. Only when he'd disappeared around the corner did she trust herself to walk on, surprised her shaking legs still held her up.

It had all been unexpected and she hadn't a *clue* what to do next. As she'd walked, she'd glanced in a shop window and caught her reflection. *She needed an image revamp. How could she expect someone like Aiden to take her seriously looking the way she did?*

On impulse, Anna had determinedly walked into the nearest boutique, convinced the slim and fashionable shop assistants had been scrutinising her whilst she'd attempted to casually browse the myriad racks of clothes.

Anna stared at the bag of clothes she'd purchased. She hadn't tried them on in the shop. She'd been too embarrassed and desperate to get away from the badly concealed whispers, giggles and smirks aimed at her.

Slowly untying the carrier bag, she fished out a short stretchy skirt and two low-cut tops and looked at them in horror. They were very nice and all that, but as well as being *extortionately* expensive, they weren't *her* sort of clothes.

Picking up a dark halter-neck top boasting a deep plunge neckline, Anna held it up gingerly against her. *She'd never have the confidence to wear something like this would she? But didn't this sort of stuff make men desire women?*

The thought of having a man want her in *that* way was alien. *Especially a man like Aiden.* She'd no idea how to attract a man's attention and even less of an idea what she'd actually do if she did.

Slipping her pink blouse off, Anna nervously put on the

black halter neck and eyed herself in the mirror. Astounded by the reflection of her large breasts pushed up to create a deep and generous cleavage, she gasped. *Could she really wear something like this?*

Hesitatingly she slipped her black trousers off and pulled on the skirt. She didn't believe she had anywhere near the sort of figure to be able to wear this type of clothes. *However...*

Anna looked back in the mirror once more and risked a slight smile at what she saw. Her mind moved towards imagining what Aiden would look like naked and a shiver ran through her. *How it would feel to touch him. To touch his....*

What would it feel like if he did to her what she'd heard Seth doing to Jane?

Sensing a throbbing twinge between her legs, Anna frowned. This had to be wrong. She needed to stop this and concentrate on what she needed to do keep her job.

And were her employers so vicious to have shot that poor man Dennis? *Could it possibly be true? It had to be. She'd seen it with her own eyes. Well, virtually...*

Anna sighed. She had no idea how she'd hold her nerve to call Aiden, let alone meet up with him. Still he seemed eager. Didn't people say life worked in mysterious ways? And to think she'd been moaning about having to go that party! Perhaps her life was finally beginning to liven up?

Anna glanced at the clock and realised she'd been locked in her room far too long. She needed to find that card and put it somewhere before Jane or Seth came back, plus she needed to locate that shirt.

She was in no way happy about doing something which could cause a problem to people who had been nothing but good to her. She'd just have to swallow the overall uncomfortableness of the whole situation because if she wasn't careful, she'd lose her job and screw up her mother's life even more.

Tina was a bitch and this was horrible!

• • • •

STEVE LOMOND SCOWLED listening to Eliza's response. 'What do you mean she's not available?' He'd booked another session with his favourite only to be told she wasn't about. 'I hope she isn't busy servicing someone else? You know I take fucking preference. That was our agreement was it not Eliza?'

Eliza refrained from scowling at the ugly fat bastard opposite and instead leaned provocatively against her desk, knowing it accentuated the cleavage of her over-pumped chest. 'Of *course* I haven't, Steve,' she purred. 'Lacey's not well that's all. She's got the shits and I didn't think you'd want that as part of your session.'

Both her and Digger had agreed Lomond was not to be told of Lacey's disappearance being as he had a thing for her. *At least not yet*. Not whilst there was still a chance they could locate the bitch and bring her back to get on with her bloody job. They didn't want anything to put him off what he was doing for them. *His part in their plan was imperative.*

Lomond smiled exposing his rotten teeth. 'Oh, I don't know... She's such a darling I think I'd forgive her even if she cakked on me!'

He leaned across the desk and squeezed Eliza's breast painfully with his meaty hand, well aware she was attempting to sugar-coat his disappointment. 'You're too fucking old for my tastes, so you can put *those* away.' *He knew he could push the limits right now because they owed him.*

Eliza scowled. *The fucking prick!* She had no time for this greasy fat jumped-up twat at the best of times, but they needed his help even if it meant having to put up with his sarcastic and rude comments. *Once this was over she'd make sure he was offloaded.*

'Do any of the other girls take your fancy?' she asked, forcing her voice to remain amicable.

Lomond sniffed in disapproval. 'Not particularly, but if Lacey's not back on form in a day or so then I'll have no choice but to get shat on. I'd rather that than any of the rest of them that you've got.'

Eliza swallowed nervously. *This wasn't great.* She'd hoped she could at least tempt him with one of the others. A lot of them were, or at least *looked* young enough to suit his tastes, but apparently not. It seemed he'd got himself fixated with Lacey, which made it even more galling that she'd done a bloody runner. Not only had the bitch fucked up her plan of some easy extra cash, but she'd also binned off the needs of a bloke who had the power to help her in her personal vendetta. She had to find Lacey and get her back. *Pronto.*

'I've got a bit of news regarding Wright,' Eliza said, hoping to steer the focus of the conversation away from his obsession with the only girl she couldn't provide.

'Oh yeah?' Lomond leant forward to help himself to a glass full of whisky from the decanter on Eliza's desk.

Trying not to stare at the ultra-large measure the man poured from her best whisky, Eliza smiled. 'Tina's silly bitch of a sister works for the Wrights. It couldn't be better. She'll be getting gen we couldn't possibly hope to glean from outside, not to mention putting in place certain *things* I'm orchestrating.' Eliza paused, pleased to see she had Steve Lomond's full attention.

'Aiden as well as you are working on the case from outside to upset the apple cart,' she continued.

'So, what have you got so far?' Lomond asked, taking a long gulp of the whisky.

'Well...' she smiled. 'We've learnt Seth Wright has been getting his own hands dirty again and got his guns of out mothballs,' Eliza said gleefully, hoping Lomond would be impressed with her findings. 'We're not sure yet as to who was the recipient of this, but we're working on finding out.'

Lomond looked thoughtful. 'That's interesting and fits what I've been informed of. A runner who'd previously worked for Miller has been put out of action by getting a kneecap blown off.'

'By Seth by any chance?' Eliza questioned.

'I don't know, but the guy has been grilled about who was sticking their nose into Miller's club. They were very insistent in trying to discover who I was...'

'And did he spill?' Eliza asked warily.

'No. He doesn't even know it was me! He hasn't a clue! It sounds like he's fitting someone else up, so I take that as red. People don't tend to be stupid enough to lie to me.'

Eliza hoped Lomond wasn't aiming that last comment at her. 'It makes sense that Seth was the perp. Just his style and we know from Tina's sister he was covered in blood and carrying.'

Lomond nodded. 'I'm surprised you haven't heard about it yourself,' he jibed.

Eliza grimaced. *So was she.* Why wasn't anyone doing their fucking job around here and keeping her informed? The fact this twat was telling her made it look like she was a bastard amateur. It certainly wasn't the impression she wanted to give. *Especially to him.*

Eliza scornfully watched Lomond top up his glass yet again. *For fuck's sake. That stuff cost a fortune.*

Lomond smiled widely. 'I've changed my mind. You might as well grab me one of those other girls Eliza. I'll waste half an hour until your other half gets back to take me out for a few drinks.'

• • • •

SETH REPLACED THE HANDSET on the cradle and stared at the phone for a few seconds longer. He hated answering the phone only to get it put down when he'd spoken. That sort of stuff never failed to get on his tits. He *hated* bloody cold callers.

If he was in need of double glazing or a new kitchen, did these people not think he'd phone somewhere up himself rather than wait on the off chance some random person might happen to call offering what he needed? It was ludicrous and even more ludicrous their sales tactics included not *speaking* when he answered.

Seth glanced at the coat stand. *Jane and that girl still not back yet?* They'd better hurry up because he needed to go to the Glint tonight and he wanted Jane to accompany him.

He felt they should show their face in the actual club for an evening. Not just him – he wandered through there enough as it was, but *together*. Jane was very much part of the Glint and lately she'd been so busy she hadn't spent much time on the shop floor. They spent half their time at functions these days and he fancied a nice drink with his wife in *their* club.

He wanted to show her off as much as he could. Jane got more beautiful every day that passed. Every year that went by subtracted nothing from his desire for her and he never got tired of being seen with her on his arm. Walking with his wife everyone seeing them, knowing she belonged to *him*. This alone gave him more satisfaction than he'd dare to admit out loud. Seth smiled. Every minute he questioned his good fortune and that would *never* change, not with Jane by his side.

Seth glanced at the antique grandfather clock standing proudly in the tall hallway. *Surely they would be back soon?* He wanted to know if she'd managed to get the promised information from Lacey and furthermore what she intended to do going forward. He hoped she didn't suggest the girl remain here indefinitely. He didn't mind her staying for a while, but certainly not for any great length of time. *It was out of the question.*

Seth made his way down the hallway, walked into the kitchen and stared at the fridge. *Sod it. He'd have a quick beer or two whilst he waited.*

Opening the fridge, he pulled the door, but it got stuck and glanced down at the floor, seeing a scrunched up piece of paper. Tutting, he picked it up. *Wasn't that what bins were for?*

Glancing at it as he moved towards the bin, Seth's eyes focused on Jane's name at the top of the crumpled card. Frowning, he straightened it out and began to read.

FIFTEEN

JANE FIRED THE ENGINE on her BMW and sped off down the drive. She needed to put some space between her and Seth for an hour or so.

She could see why he was angry, but she didn't have an explanation she could give him to appease the situation. *Two days* she'd put up with his attitude and after he'd returned after disappearing for a full twenty-four hours with no explanation, he'd barely said two words to her. She'd told him *countless* times what he'd read in that card was untrue, but also knew she couldn't prove it.

When Seth hadn't returned last night, Jane had felt physically sick. It had only been Lacey's presence which had enabled her to keep her mind slightly off the situation and stopped her going crazy.

She'd tossed and turned half the night and in the morning, when she'd woken exhausted, finding his side of the bed still empty, she'd locked herself in the dressing room and stared at herself in the large mirror.

The image of Seth being surrounded by beautiful slim strippers pawing him wasn't the greatest confidence booster. It wasn't exactly a secret people found Seth attractive and if he wanted to hurt her in that way, she was sure he'd have no problem finding hordes of takers. Based on the anger he'd displayed towards her, the club would have been *exactly* where he'd gone.

Reaching the end of the drive, Jane glanced to the left and saw a dark blue saloon. *That was the same car which had been parked there before….*

She hadn't thought too much of it earlier even though it was unusual to see anyone hanging around, but seeing the same vehicle again rang alarm bells.

Jane squinted as best as she could to try and work out who was in the driver's seat, but thanks to the car's tinted windows and because it was twilight she couldn't see any details of the person at all.

Not liking the situation, she rapidly pulled out of the drive and accelerated up the road, checking her mirror to see if the car tailed her.

• • • •

'I'LL JUST FINISH THIS fag and then I'll be off bro,' Aiden said as Alan stood up from his seat in the staff break room at the Limelight. 'I've got some prep to do before tomorrow's meeting.'

Alan stubbed his cigarette out in the ashtray and slapped his brother on the back. 'No worries. We'll meet up for a proper drink next week, shall we? Isn't it about time you got a free car from your place considering all these meetings you have to go to? From what you've said you never seem to be in the showroom these days.'

Aiden grinned. 'I know. That's why I keep saying there's no point trying to catch me at work because I'm always on the road! Give me a call soon, yeah?'

Keeping the smile fixed on his face until his brother had left, Aiden sighed. It wasn't that he was always on the road at all. The truth was he hadn't worked at the car salesroom for over a year since he'd started working for Digger, but he couldn't tell Alan that.

If Alan knew where he worked then he'd ask questions which would put them both in a bad position. He loved his brother and didn't want to jeopardise him in any way.

It was especially awkward now Digger and Eliza wanted him as well as Lomond to stir things up at the Limelight. As to exactly why, Aiden wasn't sure and most certainly hadn't been made privy to that information. Without insulting the man who paid him, it wasn't like Digger was in the same league as the Wrights and Millers of this world.

Aiden glanced at his watch. *She should be here any second.* Digger had made it clear which woman he should target and he'd been instructed to give the girl a slap, making out it was to do with wanting information about the club's coke suppliers. He wasn't happy about what he had to do, but he couldn't afford to have a conscience. As long as Alan didn't get dragged into the crossfire, he didn't much care.

Hearing a door open Aiden quickly pulled the balaclava from his pocket and slipped it over his face.

When Billie-Jo walked into the small break room seeing the man in the balaclava lurch towards her, her mouth hung open to form a perfect 'O'.

Wasting no time, Aiden clamped his hand over the girl's mouth and pushed her out of the door back into the small corridor. Shoving her against the wall, he pressed his weight up against her. 'Tell me who you arranged the delivery with today?' he hissed. 'If you call for help, I'll fucking kill you.'

The girl's frightened eyes darted around in abject terror as she shook her head vehemently.

Aiden stared at the girl. *Damn, she was pretty.* He could feel her large breasts against his chest and the sensation of her soft body crushed into his aroused him.

Forcing his concentration back to the job in hand rather than the growing hardness in his jeans, Aiden removed his hand from her mouth, whilst keeping the other gripped tightly around her neck. 'Tell me what you know…'

'I-I don't know anything!' she whimpered, terrified. 'What delivery?'

Aiden's irritation escalated. *Did the silly cow think because she was a pretty one she could deflect him?* 'Don't play dumb,' he snarled. 'Tell me who did the delivery. What firm supplies this place and the Glint club?'

Billie-Jo began to cry. 'I-I swear I don't know what you're talking about! The beer delivery? It's the usual brewery.'

Aiden's teeth set on edge. Digger wouldn't be happy if he didn't get the point over well and good. Angrily his free hand painfully squeezed the girl's right breast, before trailing up the inside of her thigh. 'Do I have to *force* you to tell me?'

'P-Please don't do that,' the girl sobbed, tears rolling down her face. 'I've got a boyfriend. Well, fiancé actually.'

'How nice,' Aiden sneered. 'Like I care. Now, who does this fucking delivery? Last chance, bitch!' He glanced towards the door, knowing he needed to be quick because someone else would undoubtedly be due in for a break soon.

'I-I don't know anything about the deliveries,' the girl insisted. 'Honestly. Now let me go!'

'Have it your own way,' Aiden said, pulling a blade from his pocket. *He'd have to make this look good at least.*

'No, NO!' the girl cried, her voice alarmingly loud.

'Shut up bitch!' Aiden shouted, swiping at her face.

It was only when Billie-Jo went silent, standing frozen in shock did Aiden see exactly what he'd done. *He needed to get out of there fast.* 'Let that be a message to your boss!' he muttered. 'He'll know who it's from…'

Watching as the girl slumped against the wall and slid slowly to the floor, Aiden pulled open the outer door, rapidly removed the balaclava and headed out towards the lobby.

Disappearing into the night, Aiden lit a cigarette and hastily made his way back to his car. Shrugging with indifference over what had just occurred, he fished his keys from his pocket. *Time to meet Anna.*

• • • •

MAGGIE HADN'T BEEN altogether surprised to see Jane on the doorstep. Obviously upset, she'd ushered her in and sat her down at the kitchen table.

'So, who were the flowers from?' Maggie asked.

Jane looked up in surprise. 'Not you as well! How did y..'

'We had Seth ranting about it last night,' Dan explained with a touch of irritation in his voice.

Jane breathed a sigh of relief. *He'd been here rather than the club.* 'I don't know who they're from.' Watching Dan raise an eyebrow, her eyes narrowed defensively. 'So, *you* think I'm lying too?' she snapped.

'We didn't say that did we?'

'You didn't have to,' Jane remarked sullenly.

Maggie glanced at Dan. 'But why did you try to throw the card away?'

Jane angrily helped herself to a glass of vodka. 'In answer to your question, I threw the card away because I knew it would cause problems. I didn't have an explanation for it, but I *swear* I don't know who sent them. All of that shit in the card is lies and I don't know how it made its way out of the bin either!'

Dan cleared his throat. 'Seth think it's Miller.'

'That's insane! We're just friends,' Jane muttered.

'Don't you think it's a bit strange what was written on the card?' Maggie asked. In all honesty she'd be lying if the thought as to the truthfulness of it hadn't crossed her mind. Although it was a long time ago, Jane hadn't a great track record where her fidelity to Seth was concerned.

Jane sipped at her drink and sparked up a cigarette. She frowned, her mind working overtime. 'Someone's setting me up.'

'Who would do that? And why?' Dan asked, unable to think of anyone who would have reason to go to that trouble or what it would achieve. *It made no sense.*

'I even threw the bloody flowers away after all of this. They were nice as well,' Jane said, attempting some humour in the ridiculous situation.

'It's not funny though Jane is it? You know what Seth's like,' Maggie said.

'He's not as bad as he used to be,' Jane muttered, noticing the disbelieving looks which passed between Maggie and Dan. 'And I got a phone call this morning.'

'Who from?'

'I don't know. I didn't recognise the voice.'

Dan frowned. 'What did they say?'

Jane stared at the table. 'It was a man. He said he saw me at the restaurant and would expose my so-called affair with Jason.'

'What? The Italian restaurant the other day? Seth was with you, wasn't he?' Maggie said.

Jane clocked the silent looks exchanged between Maggie and Dan and slammed her hand down angrily on the table. 'What the hell's going on? Do you really think any of this shit is true? It's a bloody set up! That much is obvious!'

'No of course not babe,' Maggie muttered feeling uncomfortable. 'Could this be anything to do with Lacey?'

Jane looked up, startled. '*Lacey*? Why would it be anything to do with her?'

'You could have trod on someone's toes by getting involved. The boyfriend perhaps?'

Jane frowned. *It was ridiculous.* 'Maybe I should fill Jason in about what's been going on.'

Maggie glanced nervously at Dan. 'Seth wanted to go and have it out with Jason last night. Thankfully Dan talked him down. The mood he was in I think he might have killed him.'

'It made things worse that you concealed the note,' Dan pointed out as Jane sighed irritably.

Jane finished her glass of vodka and held it out to Maggie for a refill. 'I know… I didn't think. I just didn't want to put any thoughts like that in his head. Probably because I knew it wasn't true!' she paused. 'There's something else though…. I think I might be being followed…'

Dan looked up. '*Followed*?' Even with the incidents they'd had at the clubs, trying to set Jane up on a personal level didn't make sense.

'Watched. Followed. I don't know. I also don't know who by before you ask. A car at the bottom of our drive has been there twice now and no, I haven't told Seth yet.' Jane watched as yet again, Dan exchanged glances with Maggie. 'Do you think I'm making this up or something?'

Not getting an immediate answer pushed Jane's patience too far. Standing up she grabbed her bag from the table. 'Forget it yeah? You believe what you want. I'll see myself out.'

SIXTEEN

LACEY NOW FELT a hundred percent better both physically and mentally. She felt like a thousand ton weight had been lifted from her shoulders since the abortion.

The only fly in the ointment was Jane had been none too pleased she wouldn't divulge any further information as to who had put her in this position and yesterday had said if she wasn't honest about it, she'd have to leave.

Lacey was in a state of panic about that. This was the first time in *years* that she'd felt safe and she didn't want that to change. She'd do *anything* to ensure she could stay. Even if it was only for a month or so until she'd figured out what to do, but Jane had been adamant.

Lacey wrung her hands together. Jane didn't know Digger and Eliza and had no idea just how crazy they were. If she breathed a word, they'd hunt her down and kill her. Jane probably didn't believe that was possible, but *she* did. She *knew* it.

As much as she'd like to be able to tell Jane everything, she'd been too indoctrinated with threats for the last God knows how long and Jane didn't understand that. Look at the place she lived in and what they had. No, she'd have to think of a way to try and remain here.

She'd considered approaching Jane again tonight, but her and Seth had been arguing and only Seth was in. He'd even given Anna the night off, so Lacey had sat in her room most of the evening.

She pushed herself to the edge of the bed. She'd go and speak to Seth about her staying. *Maybe she could convince him*?

• • • •

SETH STARED IRRITABLY at the pile of paperwork. Picking up an envelope he turned it around in his hands then ran his fingers through his thick hair. He glanced at the clock. It had been three hours since Jane had flounced out of the house in tears and he was getting concerned.

He shouldn't have accused her of having an affair with Jason Miller. Realistically he knew she hadn't gone behind his back.

Seth poured himself another large measure of whisky and stared at it. Jane hadn't given him any reason to doubt her since they'd got back together, but Miller definitely had a fascination with her. What with everything else that had been going on he'd begun to suspect that she might be right and it *was* a set up.

But who would do this and why? Apart from Miller of course... Maybe he was staging this elaborate set up? Perhaps Miller wanted both the monopoly of the clubs and his wife?

Shaking his head to dislodge these raging thoughts, Seth frowned. His initial urge had been to steam round to Miller's and rip his throat out, but admitted he wasn't good with trusting people. After all, even his closest friends had shafted him in the past.

Topping up his glass once more, Seth focused his eyes back on the envelope. It did him no good going over and over the myriad betrayals he'd had pulled on him. He wouldn't act on his suspicions until he knew for a fact Miller was behind it. He just hoped that he was wrong. He'd kill anyone who tried to hurt his family. *That was a fact.*

He placed the glass back on the desk and took a deep breath.

When Jane got back, they'd talk, but if she didn't return soon, he'd have to go and find her. The thought of her wandering around somewhere upset made his blood run cold. Especially if there really *was* someone trying to cause trouble.

Seth's mind turned to the phone call he'd received earlier from Carl Mulligan, the latest private investigator. He'd got some information so they'd arranged a meeting for tomorrow. He hoped it would be what they'd been waiting for. Either way he wouldn't mention it to Jane until he knew the score. He didn't want to get her hopes up if this one, like all the others, amounted to a dead end.

Before Seth could come to any concrete conclusion the sound of a knock on his study door startled him. Looking up, he was surprised to see Lacey standing in the doorway.

'Sorry to disturb you Mr Wright,' Lacey said timidly.

Seth smiled. 'It's not a problem. You're not disturbing me. What can I do for you? And call me Seth.' He beckoned the girl into the room noticing she was distinctly nervous. He could hardly be surprised. Understandably she had little trust in men, or *anyone* for that matter, so it was his call to put her at ease – at least as much as he could.

Seeing the girl standing uncomfortably two feet from his desk surreptitiously glancing around his study, Seth smiled once more and gestured towards the seat the other side of his desk. 'Come and sit down and tell me what's bothering you?'

Seth topped up his glass as Lacey sat on the chair. 'I'd offer you a drink, but I've only got whisky,' he laughed, hoping his easy tone of voice would relax her.

'T-That's ok with me,' Lacey said quietly. 'I-I mean I'd like a whisky if that's ok?'

Seth frowned. She was only sixteen. Still she'd been through enough to warrant one he supposed. 'Ok,' he smiled. 'Just a small one.' Grabbing a second glass, he poured a measure from the decanter and handed it to Lacey.

'Mr Wright, I mean Seth… I need to speak to you,' Lacey said, determination evident in her voice.

Seth leant back in the chair and folded his arms. 'I'm listening.'

Lacey cleared her throat. 'Jane said that if I didn't tell you about when and how my, erm, situation happened then I'd have to leave. She said you'd agreed with her.'

Seth nodded. 'I see and yes, I do agree with her. It doesn't mean we *want* you to leave though.' He thought for a moment. *He had to be careful how he worded this.* 'Lacey, what you've been through isn't acceptable under any circumstances and we need to ensure it doesn't happen again to anyone. My wife has risked a lot doing what she did for you.'

'I know and I'm grateful, it's ju…'

Seth held his hand up. 'I haven't finished. Like I said, Jane's risked a lot getting involved in something that isn't her business to and she could be risking some form of comeback. We all could – hence why we've asked you to be honest.'

Lacey remained silent, her eyes cast down to the floor.

Seth decided to try another approach. 'While you're under our roof and being as we've become involved in this to help you the least you can do is to tell us what you know.' He raised an eyebrow. *This was a gamble.* 'Or we might start presuming you weren't being straight with us at all and that your pregnancy was the result of a boyfriend. Perhaps you just didn't want to tell your parents?'

Lacey's head shot up, her eyes brimming with tears. 'So, you think I'm lying? You think I'm lying about everything do you? I knew it!' she wailed.

Seth sighed. 'No sweetheart, I didn't say that. I said it makes us wonder why you won't tell us the whole truth.'

Tears fell freely from Lacey's eyes and rolled steadily down her cheeks.

Watching the young girl in front of him sobbing openly, Seth began to feel bad for even suspecting what she'd said hadn't been kosher. 'Now come on, don't get upset. I just need to know. It's important. If these people are doing what you say, then they know you've disappeared and will be looking for you.' He paused, sensing he'd got her full attention. 'We want to know what to look out for so we can protect you and I also need to ensure there are no retaliations on my wife. I do not want *anything* happening to her as payback.'

Lacey laughed hollowly. 'They won't want her. She's too old.'

Seth frowned. 'Thirty-two's not old Lacey.'

'I know that!' Lacey spat. 'But to *them* it is.'

'Are you saying they only deal with children?' Seth pushed, his skin crawling at the thought.

Lacey shook her head. 'Not *children*, children. At least not as far as I know. It's younger girls - mainly around sixteen – some a bit older, but they'd use even *younger* ones if they could. Jane must have told you everything I told her about the place.'

Seth nodded. 'She did, but I want to know the name of this place and of the people that run it.'

'I-I can't. They'll find me and kill me for definite. They'd know it came from me.'

'So how do they get these girls to work for them? How did you start working there?'

Lacey stared bleakly at the floor as Seth got up from his desk and walked around the other side. He put his hands on the girl's shoulders, feeling her trembling beneath his fingers. 'You can talk to me Lacey. Just tell me how *you* wound up there.'

'I-I ran away from home. I had to. I was sleeping rough and then I met this woman. She seemed ok and bought me some food. Said she knew someone who'd give me somewhere to stay.'

'And you went?'

'I didn't have much to lose by then,' Lacey muttered.

'And what was this woman called?' Seth asked.

'I'm not sure,' Lacey lied. Seth's hands on her shoulders make her feel safe. She didn't want him to release this reassuring hold.

'Yes you are. What's her name?' Seth pressed, sternness in his voice.

'T-Tina,' Lacey stammered. *It didn't matter giving her name out, surely?*

'Surname?'

'I've no idea,' Lacey answered truthfully.

'And she's the woman who runs it?'

'No, that's someone else. She just works there.'

'As a prostitute?'

Lacey shuddered, acknowledging that's how she would have to describe her past. 'No. She's the one who finds the girls. She looks round stations, parks etc. for likely ones. At least that's what I understand of it.'

'Ok, so you now need to tell me who runs this shit-hole of a fucking place. Come on girl! I need to sort this out for you and all the other girls,' Seth barked, his patience wearing thin. He didn't have time to sit through counselling sessions. He needed the info sooner rather than later so he could deal and deal *now*.

'I can't say anything else,' Lacey repeated, the shutters slamming down. She'd already said too much and now the man was losing his temper. *Like all men did.* Tears fell from her eyes once more.

Looking up into Seth's hard green eyes, Lacey grabbed his arms. 'Please Seth. *Please* don't make me go just because I can't tell you.'

'It's not that you can't tell me. You *won't*.' He tried to smile. 'I know you don't trust me, but you need to Lacey.'

'Just *please* don't make me go!' Lacey sobbed. 'I'll do anything.' She wanted to tell Seth and Jane about Eliza and Digger, but her ingrained fear was too strong. If she kept quiet she might be able to get on with her life without having to look over her shoulder for the rest of it.

Lacey looked back into Seth's handsome face. 'You have no idea what you and Jane have done for me. I'm so grateful, really. I don't want you think I'm not. I'd do anything to thank you.'

'You don't need to thank us,' Seth said.

'Oh, but I do…. I'd do *anything* to make you believe I'm thankful and not being untruthful,' Lacey cried, throwing herself against Seth's chest.

'Well you know what I'd like you to tell us…'

'That's the only thing I *can't* do,' Lacey whispered, a glimmer of an idea forming in her desperate mind. *He was a man.* Her hand dropped from where it lay against Seth's chest and she took his hand.

She pulled Seth's hand onto her left breast, whilst her other hand ran down his thigh to his crotch. 'I can *show* you how grateful I am though,' she whispered.

Yanking his hand away in horror, Seth recoiled, his shock immediately replaced with anger. 'What the fuck are you doing you stupid bitch?' he roared. 'You think I want *that*? From *you*? You think I want *that* from a kid? How fucking *dare* you!'

Lacey stood frozen in terror, realising she'd misjudged the situation horribly. *She'd been wrong. Seth Wright wasn't like the other men.* 'I-I'm sorry! I thought….'

'Whatever you thought, you thought fucking wrong!' Seth spat. Grabbing Lacey's arm, he marched her to the study door. 'I suggest you get yourself out of my sight and *never* try something like that again!'

Seventeen

AIDEN KEPT HIS LINE of concentration on Anna rather than the girl who was smiling in his direction from the bar. He'd already eyed the barmaid's slender figure encased in a tiny red dress and knew that if he could choose, he'd go for her rather than the woman sitting opposite fiddling uncomfortably with her handbag clasp. *Still, he had a job to do, so needs must.*

Consoling himself with giving the red-dressed girl a wink whilst Anna wasn't looking, Aiden attempted to steer her into some form of conversation, but it was hard.

He'd been surprised to hear from Anna earlier. He'd presumed he'd a lot more work to do before she'd pluck up her enough confidence to phone him but it seemed, thanks to the Wright's unexpected argument, she'd been given the night off.

He'd also been surprised when she'd walked into the pub where they'd agreed to meet, wearing something he wouldn't have thought she'd have had the balls to wear. Admittedly she didn't look the best in a short skirt with those chunky thighs of hers and that distinct muffin-top, but he'd not been disappointed by the large and ample amount of cleavage on show, courtesy of her low halter neck top.

He glanced at Anna again. She'd already had two glasses of

wine, but they had done zilch to help her painfully stilted conversation. It was *him* who was keeping it flowing whilst she sat there looking thoroughly frightened – like she was about to get caught sneaking off to smoke fags during a school trip.

The whole point was to get her talking wasn't it? He slowly realised this would be more of a long-term project than he'd anticipated.

Plastering on a winning smile, Aiden sparked up a cigarette and nodded towards Anna's empty glass. 'Hope you don't mind me smoking?' he asked belatedly, not caring whether she minded or not. 'I'll get a bottle this time, shall I?'

Anna shook her head. 'I'd better not. I should be getting back. It's almost 10.' She knew coming here had been a bad idea. Aiden thought she was boring, didn't he? She'd seen him looking at the barmaid whilst she'd sat here like a mute lemon. She couldn't even have a conversation for God's sake and she needed to question why her life was always so lacking in anything remotely interesting? Aiden would never want to see her again after this. *A total disaster.*

Aiden grabbed Anna's hand. Seeing her jump, he tried not to laugh. 'Ok if you don't want a bottle, have another glass. It's not late and you're entitled to a proper night off with the amount of work you do.' *For fuck's sake. She wanted to go at 10 o'clock? After two drinks?*

Bolstered by the feel of Aiden's hand on hers, Anna fought against the instinctive urge to pull her hand away, reminding herself that it was *normal* for someone to do things like that if they were interested. Maybe he did like her if he was trying to convince her to stay? Perhaps he liked her enough to see through the crippling shyness she'd been saddled with most of her life? She hoped so because, dare she say it, she liked him. *Really* liked him. Look how handsome he was and he was sat with *her*.

'Go on then,' Anna smiled. 'Just one more.'

Grinning, Aiden sauntered to the bar and Anna found herself watching the way his muscular legs moved. A pang of jealousy washed over her when she saw the way the barmaid openly flirted with him.

Anna took in the woman's pretty face and figure and sighed. She'd never be able to compete with women like that and furthermore, wouldn't know *how* to. Would she ever get over the impediment of being in a rut of paranoia? *Oh God. It was so humiliating and more to the point – impossible.*

Watching Aiden make his way back over clutching a bottle of wine, Anna forced herself to maintain a calm expression.

'I know you said you didn't want a bottle, but I thought I'd get you one anyhow. You don't have to drink it,' Aiden grinned.

'Thanks,' Anna smiled. The way she felt at the moment she could happily drink five bottles, but wouldn't. *After all, she was far too sensible to do anything out of character like that wasn't she?*

• • • •

JASON MILLER HAD BEEN surprised but pleased to be informed Jane Wright was waiting in the lobby downstairs requesting to see him.

It had already been a long night. There had been a problem an hour ago of which he'd yet to be filled in about, but it appeared to now be sorted. He glanced at the clock. Not even midnight. Tonight he'd been planning on leaving well before the place closed because Linda had been moaning about his late nights and he'd promised to make an effort to knock off early sometimes.

He got up from behind his desk. He'd normally have got a member of staff to bring visitors up, but for Jane he'd make an exception.

Reaching the corridor, Jason opened the thick door leading into the lobby and immediately saw Jane sitting on one of the leather sofas. 'Jane!' he cried, smiling widely as he strode across the carpeted entrance. Placing his hands on her shoulders, he kissed her on the cheek. 'How nice to see you. Please come up to my office.'

Jason held the door open to allow Jane to pass through

before him and couldn't help but eye her shapely legs as she walked in front of him. He ushered her into his office and gestured towards the sofa at the far end of the room rather than sitting formally at his desk. He'd already detected worry in her eyes and even though she'd done a good job of concealing it, he'd thought a more relaxed seating arrangement was in order.

He watched Jane slip off her coat and place it on the back of the sofa and his eyes ran over her body in its fitted dress. 'Drink?' Jason opened the door of a glass-fronted cabinet hosting a fine selection of wines and spirits.

'Gin and tonic please,' Jane smiled.

Pouring both the drinks, Jason joined Jane on the sofa. 'So,' he smiled, forcing his mind to clear the thoughts he experienced every time he was within her proximity. 'Is everything ok?'

Jane held his gaze. 'I don't think so.'

Jason sat forward slightly and frowned. *If there was an issue why was Seth not here?* 'And what's that?'

Jane took a sip from her glass wishing she didn't need to have this conversation. 'You didn't send me flowers by any chance, did you?'

Jason sat back surprised. *Flowers?* 'No, I didn't. Should I have done? I can get some delivered to you if you'd like?' he laughed.

Jane forced a smile. 'No, I thought not. Listen, I'm being serious. Someone's trying to cause problems.'

'What do you mean?' Jason frowned. 'What sort of problems?'

'I had a bunch of flowers delivered.'

Jason grinned. 'My wife would love it if she got flowers, but don't tell me – they weren't from Seth right and he's got jealous?'

Jane didn't smile, she just looked worried. 'Yes – made out to have come from you….'

'Me?' he said, a grin on his face. 'Why me?'

'It's not funny Jase!' Jane snapped. 'The card was signed 'J'.'

Jason smiled. 'Jane, I didn't send the flowers!' he said incredulously. 'Even as a joke!'

Jane looked at the floor and nodded. 'I know, but I had to ask. It didn't help that I threw away the card. I knew it would cause problems. The issue was it then miraculously reappeared where he could find it. I've been getting phone calls too.'

'What?' Jason cried.

'I know, I know. It's complete bullshit.' Jane placed her hand on Jason's knee and lowered her voice. 'Someone's watching the house too.'

'Does Seth know about all of this?'

'Obviously he knows about the flowers. He found the card and went mad. He's convinced we've been having an affair…' Jane looked sadly at Jason. 'He doesn't know about the calls or the car.'

Jason grimaced. *The last thing he wanted was Seth Wright convinced he was having an affair with Jane.* 'And the rest? You're *sure* that's what happened?' he asked quietly.

'Why wouldn't I be? Of *course* I'm sure!' Jane snapped.

'You need to tell him everything. I'll talk to him as well. I can't believe he'd think I'd do that.' Jason folded his arms. 'Listen Jane, I won't lie. I think you're beautiful as well as clever and well – put it this way, if it wasn't treading on anyone's toes…'

Jane blushed. 'Jase that's not helpful…'

'Maybe not,' he smiled. 'Just being truthful. I'm sure it's not as serious as you think. It's probably something and nothing. A disgruntled punter from one of our clubs perhaps?'

Jane's eyes narrowed. 'You think I'm being melodramatic?'

'I didn't say that. I'm saying if it's serious we'll get to the bottom of it.' He raised himself to his feet. 'Now get yourself home and tell Seth what you've told me.'

• • • •

LACEY'S FEET WERE HURTING. She wished she'd put her flat boots on, but in her haste to get her things together she'd stupidly worn the ones with heels. She'd no idea how long she'd get away with sitting in McDonalds before they kicked her out, but it was the only place she could think of that was open at 1 in the morning, short of places in the city centre and she didn't want to go there. She'd stay here for the rest of the night if she could get away with it.

She sipped slowly from her second coffee and tried to keep her eyes from meeting the gaze of any of the drunk or plain weird people who had a penchant for hanging around during the small hours. It seemed everyone was staring at her and the last thing she wanted was grief.

Lacey felt tears sting the backs of her eyes. *What was she going to do now? She'd ruined everything. Stupid, stupid bitch that she was.*

What had she been thinking? She'd realised far too late that not every man was as twisted as the ones she'd been unfortunate enough to be surrounded by in the past. She felt like kicking herself - both for her stupid presumptions and because she'd have been better off telling Seth and Jane the truth about Eliza and Digger.

All she'd done was insult the man who'd been the first to be kind to her without wanting sexual favours in return as well as opening herself up to be more of a target if Eliza and Digger caught up with her. If she'd told Seth and Jane the truth then at least she'd be under their protection, but it was too late now.

After being forcibly ejected from Seth's study, Lacey had spent a good solid hour face down on her bed, her body racked with sobs from a combination of self-pity, humiliation and downright anger. When she'd heard Jane return, she'd decided to speak to them both. She'd wholeheartedly apologise and tell them *every bit* of information she knew about Eliza and Digger to prove she'd been telling the truth.

Walking down the stairs, Lacey had heard them talking and instinctively listened to their conversation from outside of the door.

'I'm not having this shit any more Jane,' Seth had roared. 'I couldn't get any more information out of the stupid cow and then when she started begging us to let her stay, she only fucking offered herself up to me!'

Lacey had been able to hear the anger dripping from Seth's voice. The rage had almost penetrated through the wooden door that she'd had her ear against.

'It was quite clearly bullshit from the off,' he'd raged. 'You put yourself at risk for her and then she pulls a fucking stunt like that? Thinking I'd go with little more than a child! Like I'm some kind of sicko? Well I won't have her in my house any longer.'

Lacey had frozen in horror against the door as the extent of exactly how much she'd ruined her own chances sank in.

'She's going Jane. I'll drag her out of this house myself if you don't arrange somewhere else for her in the morning,' Seth continued.

Eyes blurred with tears, Lacey hadn't stopped to hear any more of the painful conversation that she herself had caused and had run back to her room. There she'd hurriedly slung her possessions into a bag and within fifteen minutes she'd been on her way.

EIGHTEEN

SETH'S NOSE BURIED ITSELF in Jane's skin as his lips trailed a hot line down the nape of her neck, inhaling the intoxicating scent only she had.

Jane clutched at the sheet as he gently upped his pace from behind and he smiled feeling her begin to contract around him as he brought her to climax. He loved sleepy morning sex. Knowing she'd released, he allowed the building orgasm rising within him to peak and groaned as the last drop spilt from him.

Sighing contentedly, he wrapped his arms tighter around Jane and let his hands trace slowly over her hardened nipples. They hadn't had much sleep at all. After his outburst last night, she'd told him she'd been to see Miller. He hadn't liked that, but liked what she'd said about someone watching the house even less. He'd get one of the boys permanently outside to watch the place.

Jane turned over onto her back and smiled at Seth as he pressed his lips down on her neck. She stroked his hair. 'Seth, I know you're cross about what Lacey did, but I really don't think we should make her leave. She wouldn't have meant to insult you. It's what's always been expected from her. We'll be putting her in danger if we make her go.'

Seth raised his head slightly unwilling to take his lips from Jane's smooth skin.

'We should give her the benefit of the doubt. We'll find out in the end who put her through this,' Jane continued.

Seth propped himself up on his elbows. 'I didn't appreciate what she did. It made me feel like shit Jane, but if you really want her to stay, then I won't argue with you.'

Jane smiled. 'Thanks.'

'Now,' Seth smiled, grabbing Jane's arm. 'Come over here Mrs Wright. I'm ready for you again.' He nodded towards his regained erection.

'You'll have to wait,' she laughed, kissing him. 'I'm going to speak to Lacey and tell her everything's settled.'

Seth jokingly pulled a sulky face as he sat up in bed and ran his hand down his hardness. 'You sure I can't tempt you?' he winked.

'You've *always* tempted me…' Jane laughed. 'However, right now I'm going to put her mind at rest and then go and see Toby.'

• • • •

ANNA KNEW THE NEWS wouldn't go down well and was toying whether she should knock Jane's bedroom door.

'Morning Anna,' Jane said brightly walking down the hallway in a silk robe. 'And hello gorgeous!' Scooping Toby from Anna's arms she snuggled the little boy against her and smothered his curly head in kisses, gaining a torrent of delighted baby giggles.

'I was just about to come and see you,' Anna said quietly. She could do without having to deal with this in all truth. She'd been late back herself last night and her head was fragile.

She'd hadn't been that drunk, but drunk enough to make her feel less than ok this morning. She'd have had to be drunk to have the confidence to let Aiden kiss her at the bottom of the driveway. She must have been doing *something* right because his kisses had been frantic and hungry. He'd pressed her against the wall and Anna had distinctly felt a hardness pushing against her stomach as he'd leaned against her.

As well as giddy from the alcohol, she was giddy with the knowledge that she'd made a man want her. *That had been a new experience.* She'd been breathless, hot and overwhelmed as Aiden's tongue had explored her mouth, his hands running over her back, her legs and then onto her breasts.

She'd been so carried away and intoxicated by the feelings that she'd clearly engendered in this man, she'd been close to allowing him to free her breasts and allow his fingers to push inside her knickers. *To touch her.*

Startled by the sudden sound of someone approaching along the path Anna had hurriedly pulled away and much to Aiden's disappointment, quickly made her excuses and returned to the house. Not before she'd sneaked a look at his tell-tale bulge of arousal. *For her.*

Walking on air she'd entered the house and hastily retreated to her room, terrified Jane or Seth would see her and ask her where she'd been. It had been almost 1am by the time she'd got back. To think she'd been adamant she wasn't interested in boyfriends! She'd contentedly fallen asleep with a smile on her face and an unrequited aching between her legs.

On waking up this morning Anna had blearily got showered, still unable to completely wipe the smile from her face. That was until she'd taken Lacey her usual cup of tea, only to find her missing. Her stuff had gone and there was a note on the bedside table:

> *Dear Jane and Seth,*
> *Sorry for what I did. I really am and can't apologise enough. I need to thank you for all you have done, but I overheard your conversation last night and know you'll never forgive me, so thought it only right that I leave.*
> *Much love and thank you from the bottom of my heart.*
> *Lacey*
> *xx*

With a horrible realisation, Anna knew it must have been Lacey who had been on the path last night and if she hadn't been so wrapped up with Aiden, she'd have seen her and might have been able to stop her.

'What do you mean, gone?' Jane cried, ashen-faced.

'She left this note,' Anna handed Jane the small piece of paper.

Jane scanned the contents. 'And you're *sure* she's gone?'

'As sure as I can be,' Anna replied. 'All her clothes and stuff are missing. She must have gone last night. Maybe even before I got back.' *There was NO WAY she'd admit she'd witnessed it or could perhaps have stopped it.*

'Oh shit!' Jane spat and handed Toby back to Anna. Turning on her heels she moved as quickly as possible towards the bedroom. 'SETH!'

• • • •

SITTING OPPOSITE ANNA in the café Tina smiled, purposefully attempting to act more pleasant. *That had been Eliza's idea.* She'd said Anna would be more receptive if she did.

Anna had been dreading meeting up with Tina like they'd planned, but needed to make sure she did everything in her power to keep her job and her mother sane. And of course, from a purely selfish point of view she'd wanted to call Aiden to see if he fancied meeting up this afternoon. She'd barely been able to think of anything else but *him* since the other night.

All of this was completely new to her, but she found as well as being fluttery and nervous, she retained the fuzzy warm feeling inside that someone liked her. *Really* liked her.

'So,' Tina said, taking a sip of her tea. 'Have you got it?' *She needed to get Seth's shirt.*

Broken from her thoughts, Anna looked up. 'Why are you even bothering to have a conversation when all you're interested in is blackmailing me?'

Congenially ignoring Anna's pathetic attempt at sarcasm, Tina smiled. 'You're still my sister Anna...'

Anna stopped herself from raising her eyebrows. *As if Tina gave a fig about anything she felt!*

Sensing the expression on her sister's face, Tina swallowed the urge to smash the chipped mug she was holding into Anna's mouth. *She was obviously going to have to work her first, the miserable bitch.* 'You look different,' she smiled, looking her sister up and down appraisingly.

'Don't know why!' Anna replied sullenly.

Snotty bitch! 'You just look great!' Tina lied. 'I mean, really you do. It's the clothes! Did you not see those blokes over there perving on you when we came in?'

Anna couldn't help the small hint of a smile that formed on her lips. She *had* noticed them looking at her breasts in her new top. She'd thought they were taking the rise out of her at first, but gradually realised that men *had* actually been giving her the time of day recently. And she was secretly enjoying this belated attention from the opposite sex. Not that she'd admit it to Tina of all people.

'You got a bloke or something?' Tina pressed.

Much to her horror, Anna felt the blush rise up from her chest to her face.

'My baby sis got herself a bloke at last?' Tina raised her hands to her mouth theatrically. 'Oh, come on Anna! I know we don't see eye to eye, but I *am* your sister.' *Come on! I'll pretend I like you, just give me the fucking shirt.*

Anna frowned. *Don't see eye to eye?* That was a bit of an understatement wasn't it? Still, she was *dying* to tell someone – even if that someone was Tina.

Tina raised her hands in mock resignation. She knew full well Aiden was working his magic on Anna and from the dreamy look on her sister's face it seemed it was working. 'Listen, it's about time you found yourself a nice man,' she continued. 'All these years you've been working and you've done *so* well.'

'Well enough to be blackmailed obviously.' Anna was unable to stop her retort.

Tina feigned a suitably hurt expression. 'It won't be for ever. Do you think I'd do this if I had any other choice? I fucked up. My life's hardly good is it?'

Anna stared at her sister and against her better judgment felt sorry for her.

Tina was on a roll. She'd seen the wavering doubt behind Anna's eyes and knew she was showing signs of softening her attitude. 'If you've met someone then I want to know who the lucky man is!' she smiled.

Lucky my arse, Tina thought bitchily. Aiden had already filled them in about his 'fun-filled' night with Anna. 'Like talking to a cardboard cut-out,' he'd said and that 'kissing her was like dabbling in necrophilia!' He'd had to run though scenes from pornos in his mind to make his cock suitably hard to look like he meant business apparently. He'd had them all in stitches over it during the meeting yesterday.

Anna, desperate to say something even if it was to her piece-of-shit blackmailing sister, leant across the table and lowered her voice barely above a whisper. 'Well, there is *one* guy….'

'Yes…?' Tina said, hoping her attempt at eager interest was believable. 'Who then? Don't keep me in suspense.' *Like I don't know already…*

'After we met up the other week, I bumped into this guy I'd met at the Miller's party,' Anna continued.

'What that posh party?' Tina whispered. *Of course, Anna couldn't resist the temptation to name drop. Make herself look important.*

Anna nodded. 'He was walking past after I left you. I couldn't believe it! We got talking and he asked me out for a drink!'

Tina watched the smile on Anna's face almost splitting it in half. 'You like him then?' She saw Anna look down at the floor shyly and giggle. *God how old was she again? This was downright embarrassing!* 'I take that as a yes and that the feeling's mutual?'

Anna couldn't help herself and grabbed Tina's hand over the table. 'Oh my God Tina, he's *really* into me. His name's Aiden. He was kissing me – like really hard. Like how you see on the films, you know and well, I could feel his… you know, his…'

Trying not to laugh, Tina pretended to look shocked. 'You mean you touched him?'

'No! I could feel it, but I didn't touch it. It was pressing against me. His, you know, his…'

'His *cock*?' Tina said loudly.

Bright red, Anna glanced around the café, cringing with the thought that someone might have overheard. 'Sssshh!'

'Oh, don't worry about it! So, did he have a big dick then?' Tina said equally loudly, revelling in Anna's embarrassment.

'I-It felt *massive*, but I-I…'

Tina leant forward and dropped her voice. 'So, have you got it?'

'Got what?' Anna asked confused.

Tina managed to retain her neutral expression. 'The shirt. Seth Wright's shirt. The one you told me about?' she hissed.

'Oh yes,' Anna said, suitably distracted by discussing the wonderful man who liked her. 'Why do you want it anyway?'

Tina shrugged. 'It may be useful at some point.' She guessed Eliza wanted it for some kind of insurance – for what she wasn't sure, but it hardly mattered.

Anna handed the carrier bag over the table. 'I hope they don't notice its missing…' Her heart had been in her mouth when she'd sneaked into Seth's study to retrieve the shirt from the holdall she'd seen him put it in. She'd kept it under her bed ever since in constant fear it would be discovered and if that happened, she hadn't the first clue how she could have gone about explaining why she'd taken it.

Tina snatched the bag and quickly stuffed it into her grubby rucksack. 'Nah, he's probably got so many shirts he won't notice in a month of Sundays! Anyway, forget about that – this Aiden – are you going to fuck him then or what?' she asked, knowing full well her sister would expect at least a five year engagement and a wedding before that happened.

'Of course not! I've only seen him once!' Anna exclaimed, horrified.

'Oh, lighten up. If he's nice and you like him then what have you got to lose?'

Anna looked thoughtful. 'Quite a lot judging by what happens to some people.'

Tina's eyes narrowed as she tried to deduce whether Anna was having a veiled dig. 'What do you mean?'

'There's this girl who's been staying at the Wright's. Jane helped her escape from her boyfriend and this weird place which had some form of hold over her. She's only young and was pregnant, but….'

Tina's skin prickled slightly and she sat up attentively. 'Really and who was this then?' *It couldn't be could it?*

NINETEEN

ELIZA STARED AT THE monitor split into eight different sections that was positioned on her desk. Pressing a button on the keyboard, the split screen morphed into one larger display and she peered closer. *What the fuck was the girl playing at?*

Squinting harder, Eliza frowned as she watched the girl on the screen. Her nose wrinkled up focusing on the man's large white stomach overflowing like a blancmange onto the bed. A thick trail of dribble hung from one side of his mouth as he panted, his hips bucking as much as they could, given his immense weight, whilst the girl knelt by his side, giving the most boring version of oral sex she'd ever seen.

'Look at this Digger,' Eliza muttered, gesturing towards the screen. 'The stupid bitch has barely got the tip of this bloke's withered cock in her trap! Where's the deep throat they pay for?'

Walking over Digger stared at the image on the screen, agreeing the girl was definitely not putting her back into it, but shrugged. 'He seems to be enjoying himself.'

'That's not the point!' Eliza snapped. 'We don't want a reputation of shoddy service, do we? I'll be calling her up here this afternoon. See how she explains herself when faced with the evidence.'

'Are these contraptions purely to prove a fucking point to these slags? Is that the *only* reason we've shelled out for the bloody things?' Digger asked. He'd never been in favour of this CCTV system in the first place and had said so, but Eliza had gone and had it installed anyway. He'd got back this morning only to find the damn thing up and recording. Now it seemed he was doomed to be stuck with constant streams of fat bastards getting sucked off or screwed all day long.

At least something was going right though. The stunt they'd arranged at Miller's club last night was sure to cause problems. Digger made a mental note to get Aiden to follow up with another casual meet with his brother, but would have to leave it a few days yet. They didn't want to arouse any suspicion.

On a separate note, Steve Lomond had done alright. In fact, he'd come up trumps. He'd cancelled the agreement Seth Wright had with Carl Mulligan by calling his office. Posing as Seth Wright himself, Lomond had insisted on speaking to Mulligan rather than pass the message via his dim-witted secretary. He'd had the foresight to realise if he did that there was a high chance Mulligan would have wanted to call Wright to discuss the sudden change of heart regarding the lucrative assignment of finding his daughter.

By pretending he was the man himself, Mulligan had had no choice but to swallow it without question. Then masquerading as Mulligan, Lomond had called Seth Wright, telling him he'd got some information. He'd arranged a meeting this very day.

Digger smiled. *That guy had some brass neck. What a top job! He couldn't have done it better himself!*

There should be no complications with getting their hands *legally* on the Wright's kid the way this was going. They'd got another day lined up with the brat coming up, which was a pain in the arse, but knowing achieving this would rip Seth's fucking heart out made up for anything else. Just the mere thought of his final destruction was what gave him the drive to get up every day.

Digger turned back to Eliza seeing she was still staring at the

CCTV monitor.

'Digger, this system isn't just for filming the girls. I thought if we play our cards right it won't be too long before people will come in who will be worth blackmailing.' Eliza pouted, pressing a button and the view changed to the reception desk, the front door and the car park. 'Plus, we have *these* views too which are always useful.'

Digger peered at the screen once more. 'Fucking hell Eliza! You've had all those put in too? How much did it all cost?'

Eliza wrapped her body around Digger's and pushed herself up against him. She ran her hand up his thigh and over his crotch. 'It'll pay for itself babe, you'll see.' *Ok, so she'd got most of it free in exchange for giving the installation engineer a personal seeing to, but Digger didn't have to know that.*

Feeling himself start to harden as Eliza continued palming his groin, Digger smiled and slipped his good hand inside her bra. 'I guess it would be useful, yes.'

'Sorry to bother you,' Tina yelled, bursting into the office. 'I've got some important news.'

Irritably pulling away from Eliza, Digger glared at Tina. 'For God's sake Tina! What is it now?'

Eliza rearranged her top and shot daggers at the woman who had rudely interrupted her soiree. 'Fuck off, will you?'

Tina stood her ground. 'Trust me, you'll want to hear this and I'll be wanting payment for what I'm about to tell you.'

Eliza stepped forward, her rage boiling with the blatant cheek of the heroin-riddled cow.

Sensing what was about to happen, Tina realised she'd better act fact unless she wanted a slap. 'I know what's happened to Lacey!' she blurted.

Eliza froze in shock and then rapidly sat down. 'Tell us everything you know. *Now* Tina.'

Satisfied she'd got their full attention, Tina sat casually in the opposite chair and smirked. 'Lacey's been living with Jane and Seth Wright.'

'*What?*' Eliza screeched. 'How?' *She knew it. She'd always suspected Jane had something to do with the disappearance and she'd been bloody right.*

Tina sat back and paused, immensely enjoying that for once she had complete control. 'I don't know entirely. Anna said Jane 'rescued' Lacey from her 'boyfriend' and a place that had a 'hold' over her.'

Eliza paled. *Did Seth and Jane know it was them? Fuck. Fuck. FUCK! This would ruin everything.* 'Well, where is she? What did she say?' Eliza gabbled. 'Do they know about us?'

Tina read the thoughts speeding through Eliza's mind and raised her hand knowing she was risking pushing this situation. 'What's in it for me?'

Digger sat forward aggressively in his chair. 'Are you trying to blackmail us, you cunt?'

Tina sneered. *She couldn't lose here. They needed her.*

Eliza grabbed Digger's arm, her nails biting into his skin. 'Don't start. We need this information.'

Digger gritted his teeth. 'What do you want Tina?'

Tina smiled sweetly. 'Two hundred quid and some H.'

'Done!' Eliza said quickly. *She'd been expecting the skank to ask for a lot more than that.*

'Get on with it then,' Digger snapped irritably.

'Jane got Lacey out of the hospital. Took her back to theirs and that's where she stayed. *That's* how she disappeared,' Tina stated calmly, eking out every morsel of information she'd gained for as long as possible.

Eliza ran her hand through her auburn hair extensions, growling in irritation when her nails caught painfully on a knot. 'I don't believe this. So, it was *her*? For fuck's sake! After all the shite Jane Wright's pulled over the years and she *still* plays the fucking martyr?' *God, she really needed to get that adoption finished and total that bitch's sanity for good.*

'As far as I know, or rather as far as my *sister* knows, Lacey wouldn't give them any information about you.'

'At least we taught the little slag something,' Digger sniped, his blood boiling. *So, Seth Wright had got one over on him once again had he?*

Eliza rubbed her hands together. 'Well this is great news. If Lacey's at the Wrights it won't be difficult to get her, even though she must be keeping a low profile. We've had the house watched for the last week as it is.'

She scowled. *Aiden obviously hadn't done a very good job of watching anything!* 'Now we know she's there, she'll have to come out at some point. I'd better make a list of people I need to call.'

Tina sat patiently, not yet wanting to spoil Eliza's disillusionment. 'Can I have the money and gear then?'

'Have you seen the girl? Did your sister say how she's doing? Lomond will be pleased to have her back on the scene. I can't wait to tell him th…'

'She's had an abortion…' Tina said quickly.

Eliza stopped in her tracks and exchanged glances with Digger. 'She's had *what*?'

'An abortion…' Tina repeated. 'Jane Wright organised it a couple of weeks ago. There's no baby anymore.'

Eliza's teeth grated together. Picking up a glass from the desk, she threw it against the wall in rage.

Tina jumped back in shock as tiny splinters of glass shattered around the room.

'Eliza!' Digger roared. 'Keep a lid on yourself!'

'Keep a lid on myself?' Eliza screeched. 'Are you kidding me? That bitch arranged for my girl to get rid of the baby behind my back and I'm supposed to be alright about that am I?'

Tina raised her eyebrows. *Anyone would think Lacey was Eliza's daughter the way she was going on.*

'The fucking whore! She'll pay for this.' Eliza paced up and down the room.

Digger folded his arms and tried to bring the situation down. 'Ok, well we can't do anything about the baby so let's just concentrate on getting the girl here and back to work. If you're right and she's kept her gob shut then it won't be too hard.'

Tina grimaced. *They were going to like this next piece of*

information even less. 'She's no longer at the Wright's.' She screwed her eyes shut in anticipation of another glass being launched across the office, but there was nothing.

'Where is she then?' Digger asked worrying calmly.

Tina glanced at Eliza who was staring glassy-eyed at the desk, anger bubbling from her in waves. 'That's the problem. No one knows. Even the Wrights don't. They were going to kick her out after she tried to get it on with Seth and wouldn't give you two up.'

'She tried it on with him?' Digger asked incredulously. *The little whore! Not the innocent like she pretended to be, was she?*

Tina nodded. 'Anna overheard their conversation. Lacey must have heard it too because the next morning she'd gone…'

'And no one knows where she is?' Eliza asked, her voice now steady and calm.

'Not from what Anna said, no. She's got no reason to lie to me,' Tina confirmed.

'Right,' Eliza picked up a pen from the desk. 'We'll make sure *we're* the ones who find her. Starting now.'

'Oh and you may want this…' Tina grinned, handing over the bag containing the blood-stained shirt.

'Thanks,' Eliza muttered, shoving it in her desk.

Tina stood up from her seat, glad the conversation was over. 'Gear and money?'

Eliza smiled. 'You can have it when we find the slag. Now fuck off Tina.'

• • • •

SETH NERVOUSLY GLANCED at his watch. *Half an hour before Mulligan was due.*

Opening a drawer in his desk he pulled out his calendar, pleased to see he had no further appointments today. Pulling at his collar he pushed his finger under the edge, hoping it would ease the tightness in his throat, but realised the constriction he was experiencing was not to do with his shirt and everything to do with being on edge.

Jane was in a right state over Lacey's disappearance, sure something was going to happen to her. She'd wanted him to go out today and find the girl, but he'd refused. How could he spend the day doing that? This meeting he'd got with Mulligan was ten thousand times more important than Lacey.

Seth had left this morning with Jane adamant she'd scour the city for the girl herself. He ran his hand through his hair. This was all getting too much. He'd tried to call her twice since arriving at the club, but it had gone to voicemail and he didn't like it. He didn't want his wife wandering around looking for someone who could potentially have people after her with an axe to grind. She'd have gone anyway. He'd never been able to stop her once she'd got her mind set on something.

Seth sighed. At least Martin and Barry were on shifts watching the house which was one less worry for him to have to deal with. His concern had only increased when an hour ago Jason Miller had arrived. He'd expected it to be awkward due to all the shit with the flowers, but it turned out Miller had a lot more than that to be concerned about. And therefore of course, by proxy, so did he.

He learnt that last night at the Limelight one of the barmaids had been slashed. Cut to ribbons she was by all accounts. One of her eyeballs had been virtually hanging out and the inside of her mouth had been exposed where the bastard had cut her from her eye down to the corner of her lips.

Seth felt his anger rise once again in his veins. There was no need for that sort of shit. That poor girl would be disfigured for life. He knew which barmaid it was when Miller described her. Pretty little thing - due to get married next month. He also knew the woman had no knowledge whatsoever about the suppliers. Very few of the staff did.

The bastard had obviously got his inside knowledge wrong as he was convinced she knew the details about the coke supply and was hiding them, although he obviously knew a certain amount of inside information to be aware no one else was in the area where he was waiting.

The man had been long gone before the girl was discovered by another barmaid. Miller had said although he knew there had been trouble, he hadn't been aware it was so serious, or what it was regarding until a long time afterwards. The staff had done the right thing by playing it down to the rest of the punters and had managed to get the girl out of there and to hospital without any customers catching a glimpse of her ruined face. This decision to keep it quiet had been wrongly interpreted by some of the staff, meaning that Miller had also been kept out of the loop until it was too late.

Seth gritted his teeth. It was when Miller had said the bastard said he'd know who the message was from which had really got his goat. He'd been insinuating that *he'd* been behind the attack. Christ, someone was really trying to do him up like a kipper. It was obvious, to him at least, that he and Miller were being played off against each other.

Jason hadn't bought this theory, dismissing it as fantastical. Seth rolled his shoulders to try and relieve some tension. *But was it fantastical? He certainly hadn't any other ideas as to why these things were occurring to engender suspicion between the two camps.*

What had made Seth's blood run even colder was when Miller let slip that Jane had been in the club shortly after this incident had occurred. *It could have been her the man attacked...*

This whole thing had *more* than underlined to Seth, if not Jason Miller that they needed to get to the bottom of who was behind this shit. Obviously, Seth's frightening tactics on that Neil Batchelor bloke would definitely have been reported back to whoever was behind it – that was presuming it was connected? Whichever unknown was the organ grinder here was without a doubt serious in their intentions.

Seth's head was swimming. There were too many unsavoury things going on and he was unsure which one to deal with first. He'd wanted to get on the case straight away, but couldn't. He wouldn't cancel this meeting with Mulligan for anything.

Knocked from his mental turmoil by his desk phone ringing,

Seth quickly picked up the receiver and listened to the voice on the other end. 'Yes, that's fine. Send him up.'

Replacing the phone back onto its cradle, Seth sat back in his chair and took a deep breath. *Fuck, he was nervous. Extremely nervous.* He stretched his neck to ease the tight muscles. He needed to get this over with and hear what the score was.

The office door tapped lightly and Steve Lomond was ushered into the room.

Seth stood up. 'Carl Mulligan?' He shook the man's hand warmly and gestured for him to sit down, studying him as he did so.

The man looked nothing like what he'd expected – this bloke looked like a thug. The sort that always had his fingers in someone else's deal. Seth tried to hide the distaste he experienced whilst eyeing the man standing in front of him.

Apart from his repulsive physical looks, there was an aura radiating from the man which made him feel inexplicably queasy.

Seth mentally reprimanded himself. Was he judging the guy because he didn't like the way he looked? How unfair was he being? When all else was said and done, Mulligan may resemble the remains of a pig that had been half-devoured by a hideous tropical disease, but according to Jason Miller he was one of the best private investigators in the field and his services cost a pretty penny, so he'd bypass his unfortunate look.

Seth forced himself not to show just how over anxious and nervous he was. He'd been trying not to get his hopes up over this, but had still been unable to quite manage it. 'A drink Carl?'

Steve Lomond smiled. It had been relatively easy to concoct this one together. All it had taken was a bit of searching around record offices to locate a kid who had the same birthday as Grace Wright and who also had been put into care. Once he'd got that it had been simple to track down where these people lived.

The handy guy he knew, who was a dab hand at forgery, hadn't had too much of a hard time putting together some legal-looking paperwork, that should, in the face of Seth Wright wanting to see documentary proof of his discovery, hold up to scrutiny.

Lomond stared at Seth. Looking at the eagerness on this clown's face, he thought it unlikely he'd be questioning any validity of his findings. After all, Carl Mulligan had an *extremely* good reputation. He'd already written down a list of details that should shut the prick up nicely anyhow.

He slowly passed a piece of paper across the desk to Seth. 'Mr Wright, I'm pleased to tell you that we've found your daughter,' Lomond grinned.

TWENTY

LACEY FELT COMPLETELY DRAINED. She was exhausted beyond comprehension. Forcing herself to prop her body up onto her elbow, she reached over to the small table next to her bed and grabbed the plastic bottle of water. Unscrewing the top with shaking fingers, she took a gulp of the tepid liquid then sank back down on to the pillow.

Lying on her back, she stared blankly at the magnolia ceiling through her sore eyes. Her lethargy was all-consuming and she felt unable to even summon up enough strength to go downstairs and have something to eat. She wasn't hungry anyway and certainly hadn't wanted to talk. In fact, she wasn't *anything*. She'd cried all the tears she owned and now there were none left.

Lacey stared at the daylight coming through the thin curtain hanging at the window and absentmindedly wondered what time it was. The last forty-eight hours were little more than a vacant void and she had very little recollection of anything that had happened. She'd hardly slept – if at all. She couldn't be sure. She couldn't be sure she'd been awake either. She'd been existing in a strange limbo – hovering between everything, but being part of nothing. Completely disassociated from reality.

She'd be the first to acknowledge far too much had pent up

over the years and a crash was long overdue. However, reality was gaining focus and she wanted to ensure she grasped hold of it, grateful she'd managed to reach this place before crashing into oblivion.

Lacey ran her tongue along her teeth. *Urgh. They felt disgusting*. She would have to brush them today without fail. It was time to join the land of the living.

After leaving Seth and Jane's she'd tumbled into a pit of panic when sitting in the café with absolutely nowhere to go. She'd been so angry with herself for ruining the chance she'd been given she'd hardly noticed a girl approach.

'Looking for somewhere to stay babe?' the girl had asked.

It hadn't taken long for a scout for someone like Eliza to hit on her. The initial flood of panic caused her to look around, half-expecting Eliza and Digger to have caught up with her, but this had been quickly replaced by determination.

She wasn't sure how she'd summoned up the energy or the power from within herself to manage to manifest this unexpected surge of defiance, but she had. Digger and Eliza had *not* been there and it would have been all too easy to go with that girl. It would have meant she'd have had a roof over her head and after all, she knew how to play the game. But it had become blindingly apparent, like an epiphany that she would *never* allow herself to be treated like that again.

Jane and Seth had showed her it didn't have to be that way and she wouldn't screw up twice. Maybe soon – once she'd got herself sorted out, she might pluck up the courage to go and see them and apologise face to face.

Calmly telling the girl she wasn't interested, Lacey had walked away from the solace of the café into the night. Repeating that sentence like a mantra she'd blindly wandered around the entire night, fighting off propositions from drunks and junkies who appeared like rats from the sewers and continued to swallow down the panic.

All she'd had to do was to make it through *one* night and then she'd be able to try her first port of call. By 8.30 the next morning she had.

Refusing to be disheartened when the Women's Refuge said they couldn't take her, Lacey had however taken their advice. At least one part of it. She hadn't bothered approaching the council. Because of her age it was likely she'd get taken into the care system and that she could not cope with.

With her strength and resolve falling fast and the ever-present impending panic level creeping higher and higher with each minute that passed, she'd made the last journey and there she'd found her salvation.

Pegasus Place was perfect. The large town house had been converted into what could only be described as a bright, colourful and *clean* hostel for young women. No men were allowed and *no one* with any ongoing connection to anything unsavoury were either. There was a strict 'zero drugs' policy in place and no access to anyone who thought it acceptable to sell themselves. This place was solely for young women who wanted to better their lives and get out of the rut which society had dumped them with.

Lacey had explained her story – or at least the parts she felt able to tell to the pretty blonde woman in her mid-thirties. She'd been fully expecting to be let down gently, but to her utter surprise, Sylvia had smiled and explained one of their girls had felt ready to move on only that morning and they had an unexpected free bed if she wanted it.

Bursting into tears of relief, Lacey had been shown to her new room. It was tiny, but clean and it was *hers*.

Sylvia had knocked on her door several times to see if she was ok when she hadn't surfaced, but could quickly see she'd been having a meltdown and understood this was needed before she could pick herself back up.

Lacey pushed herself up and moved to the edge of the bed. She forced away the tendrils of fear which were still hanging on to her for grim death and taking a deep breath, stood up. She'd take a shower and then go and see what to do next.

This time would be different.

• • • •

'JASON, I'M TELLING YOU it was horribly embarrassing,' Linda continued, her voice grating like nails down a blackboard.

Jason Miller had desperately tried to feign interest for *ages* as his wife described the 'interesting' things going on in everyone else's lives in great detail. He hated she assumed he actually wanted to know what her and her mind-numbingly boring friends talked about on their daily lunch dates.

He could feel his eyes beginning to droop and attempted to concentrate on a tuft of Linda's left eyebrow which had, without her knowledge, broken free of the weird glue-like substance she slapped on her face every day in the never-ending pursuit of eternal youth. He knew he was zoning out, but was powerless to stop himself. He also knew it was only a matter of time before she noticed.

Jason realised Linda had suddenly stopped talking and try as he might, had *no idea* what she'd said for at least the last ten minutes. Judging by the expression in her eyes she'd already worked this out for herself.

'You're not even listening, are you?' she squawked.

'Sorry,' Jason muttered. 'I was just thinking about something.' Not that he'd be able to tell her that a member of his staff had been disfigured on his premises and he had no idea who had done it, or why. Well, he had his suspicions. *Seth bloody Wright*. Seth wanted the Limelight – it was obvious and the twat was too stupid to realise he'd been rumbled.

One thing was for sure and that was this needed to be handled carefully. He had to keep Seth on side until he'd got proof. Make him believe he hadn't been sussed.

'Surely *nothing* can be more important that this? Especially when it involves people you're involved with?' Linda snapped. 'I'm appalled you're associated with people that like. It will ruin my reputation Jason.'

'Whoa! Hang on a minute!' Jason said his attention now on his wife. 'What on earth are you talking about?' *God, he could do without this. What now? Had Sandra McBride's nails caught in the door or something equally earth-shattering?*

'I can see you're rolling your eyes at me,' Linda sniped, studying him.

Jason sighed, aware he probably was and tried to look like he cared.

'You need to be more aware of what's going on around you Jason. These sorts of things might not bother you, but they damn well bother *me*!'

Jason placed his drink down on the table as calmly as he could. 'Are you going to enlighten me or what?'

'I already did, but you weren't listening like I suspected,' Linda snapped, making a big show of reaching under the restaurant table for her handbag in the pretence she would leave him to sit there on his own. Not that she ever went through with it. She just liked making him *think* she would.

'Come on Linda,' Jason said sweetly, grabbing her hand. 'I'm sorry. I've got a few staff issues in the club at the moment. Now tell me what's upset you.'

Placated with his apology, Linda replaced her handbag and leaned forward. 'Jane Wright's had an abortion…'

'An *abortion*?' Jason cried in surprise. 'What are you talking about?'

'Keep your voice down!' Linda hissed. 'I've had it on good authority. Although it's only a matter of time before it becomes common knowledge, we don't want the press asking for our opinion about it before we have to, do we?' She slugged at her white wine, looking pained. 'I didn't even know she was pregnant. It's not right. Who'd get rid of their own child? It's disgusting.'

'But…' Jason tried to speak, but Linda was on a roll.

'I've heard the press are running a story in tomorrow's papers. Sandra told me out of courtesy. Her daughter's husband works for that paper and he told her. They've got photos and everything.'

Jason frowned. 'And when was this supposed to have

happened? This abortion?'

'Just over a week ago apparently. Like I said, they've got photos.'

'Photos?'

'Yes. I saw them. It's *definitely* her. Someone was in a clinic the other side of town – you know that posh one? I can't say who, but they took the photos there. Jane's waiting to go in to have it done. You can see that from her expression. You should see her face – she looks *very* worried.'

Jason couldn't help himself and started laughing.

'What on earth's funny about any of this? It's not funny! *Three* of the ladies today asked me how I felt being associated with someone who would do that. The press will want my opinion.'

'Not that it's any of your or your friends' business as to who chooses to have an abortion or why, as far as I know Jane's not even pregnant,' Jason said slowly. 'And you won't be giving the press your comment on *anything*!'

'Wh... How do you kn…'

'Whether she has or hasn't, it's not up to *you* to have an opinion,' Jason interrupted. He rolled his eyes. *Did people really have nothing better to do that make this sort of shit up?*

Linda's eyebrows knitted together accusingly. 'It's been hinted it wasn't even Seth's…'

Jason paled. *Was this to do with whoever was trying to stir trouble with those flowers or was it part of Seth's set up? That would mean it would be pinned on him next. Holy shit.*

'And why did you see her last night? I thought you were at the club?' Linda snapped jealously.

'It was at the club. She popped in…' Jason said dismissively. There was no way he'd tell Linda why Jane had come to see him. She was jealous enough as it was and always had been. Linda was ten years older than him and had been forever paranoid he'd go off with a woman more of his own age. Especially a stunningly beautiful one. *Like Jane…*

'I bet you were pleased about that!' Linda sniped,

determined to have a dig.

'So, what was the other thing you were worried about?' he asked, trying to deflect her from the subject of Jane. Christ, if she found out about this business with the flowers and the affair accusations, he didn't think she'd ever let him live it down.

'Jason, you need to stop associating with Seth Wright if this sort of stuff is going around…' Linda said mysteriously, enjoying toying with the information.

'Oh, for God's sake Linda!' Jason snapped. *He really wasn't in the mood for this today.*

'It's hardly surprising she wanted rid of a baby if she's been having an affair. She clearly doesn't know who the father is.'

'*Linda!*' Jason cried. 'Be careful with what you're fucking saying.'

'As should *you*!' Linda hissed through gritted teeth. 'If it's true, then your name *and* mine will be mud by association.'

Jason stared at her in disbelief for several more seconds. He hadn't heard anything so ridiculous. Sniffing in contempt, he picked up his glass from the table and quickly downed what remained of his drink. Raising his hand, he summoned the waiter for their bill.

'What are you doing?' Linda asked. She'd quite fancied a piece of that nice-looking chocolate cake and Jason had said he'd be free all afternoon, so why was he asking for the bill?

'I'm leaving. Stay if you like, but I'm not listening to any more of your shit.' Getting up, he pulled out his wallet and threw a handful of twenties on the table before walking away.

• • • •

JANE COULD HARDLY believe what she was hearing and her heart crashed at a crazy pace in her chest. She felt light-headed and was glad she was sitting down. 'Are you *serious*?'

Smiling, Seth grabbed Jane's hand and squeezed it. He couldn't quite believe it himself and thought he'd done a sterling job of keeping it to himself all the way to the restaurant. It was only when he'd managed to bag their favourite table – a private one in a secluded alcove had he filled Jane in with the news. 'I'm deadly serious. Our daughter's fine and living in St Ives.'

Jane was gobsmacked. She hadn't been in the mood to go for dinner because she'd been out most of the day asking questions to anybody and everybody who may possibly have seen Lacey, but had drawn a complete blank.

When Seth had returned saying they were going out, her initial reaction was to refuse, however he'd been insistent so she'd given in. Now she was very glad she had.

A warm glow filled Jane to the brim and she felt almost drunk on happiness rather than from the two bottles of champagne they'd shared. 'Oh Seth,' she exclaimed. 'This is absolutely wonderful news. Are you *sure*?'

Seth smiled at his beaming wife. He would love to photograph the expression on her face. The joy radiating from her was intense. 'I'm completely sure. I knew Mulligan had some info, but I wanted to know what that was before I said anything. I didn't want to get your hopes up in case it was a dead end. There's been loads remember?'

It was true – they'd both been on tenterhooks so many times over the last year and a half with promises of information and leads which had come to nothing. She'd started to believe they'd *never* find their daughter, but now they had. 'Oh my God, this is just so perfect. But St Ives…. That's *miles* away!' Jane cried.

'It doesn't matter. She's safe and we know where she is.'

Jane grabbed Seth's hand. 'When can we go? Tomorrow?'

'We can't just turn up!'

'Why not?' Jane snapped. Grace was *their* daughter. They had every right to go and see her.

'We need to do this properly,' Seth said getting up from his seat and moving to sit next to Jane on the high-backed padded settle. He kissed her softly on the lips and then smiled. 'We can start the ball rolling with the courts now. Now finish your champagne. I'm taking you home.'

Twenty One

STEVE LOMOND COULD FEEL his erection straining painfully against his trousers when he backhanded the girl for the third time, his chunky sovereign ring imprinting on her face.

His narrow squinty eyes stared at the frightened girl. 'You'd best not be about to cry on me you little bitch. I know you love the rough play really, don't you?'

Selena stood naked in front of the fully-dressed fat manager and tried to smile. 'Yes.' She'd overheard him being discussed several times by some of the other girls and they all said the same thing. *Get doped up before going with him. It hurts less.*

She had to do it straight. There was *no way* she'd get herself on that gear.

'Did you say you enjoyed it?' Lomond growled, flecks of spit spraying from his mouth as he relished the girl's cheekbone already blackening. 'It don't look much like it to me!'

'No, I love it. I really do!' Selena said dully, wincing as the grotesque man groped roughly between her legs, painfully shoving two of his thick calloused fingers inside her.

'Good, good….' he murmured, jabbing his fingers as deep as he could. *They needed it rough these tarts. With their tight cunts and their pathetic faces. Pretending not to like it when they did.*

Oh yes, they loved it – they all wanted cock. With his spare hand, he reached out and twisted the girl's nipple painfully.

'OW!' Selina screeched. *She hadn't expected that too.* 'You're hurting me!'

Lomond's eyes narrowed, his anger at this ungrateful bitch intensifying. 'You said you liked it!' he growled, unzipping his flies. He needed to release his cock. It would burst trapped in there.

He irritably struggled to free his engorged member from his trousers. 'Turn around!' he snarled, running his hand down his length.

Selena glanced around frightened, not used to having to turn her back – especially with a psycho like this. No wonder everyone resented Lacey for doing a runner and landing all the others having to take turns with this bastard. However, she could hardly blame the girl.

She didn't know what had happened with Lacey, but it had caused no end of problems. Eliza and Digger were controlling with what the girls were and weren't allowed to do, even more now than usual, especially with those cameras which had been put in. They'd all received threatening lectures about what would happen if they even *thought* about wandering off.

Selena didn't have the first clue where Lacey had gone, but hoped she'd continue to evade those two from catching up with her and bringing her back to this sicko.

Selena flung her hand out as she was suddenly and unexpectedly launched forward over the end of the bed. She gasped with pain as the brass footboard slammed into her hip bones and before she'd even had chance to take stock of what was going on, howled in agony as Steve Lomond forced himself hard into her rear end.

• • • •

JANE RECLINED BACK in the lounger and tried to let the lush leafy artificial foliage and tropical ambient temperature of the poolside relax her. It was Maggie's idea to have an afternoon out with just the two of them at the spa and although she'd been reticent after what she'd learnt this morning, she was glad she'd come because Maggie was a well-practised soundboard for her to get her frustration off her chest.

Jane readjusted the large crocodile clip holding her wet hair away from her face and repositioned herself slightly on the lounger so that it was easier for her to lean over and reach the drink on the marble-topped table between them.

Maggie watched Jane slowly sipping from her gin and tonic and absentmindedly swirled the ice around the glass with the gold-coloured mixer. She glanced around at the staff poised around the edges of the pool room ready for the slightest glance or nod from any of the customers so they could rush to take their orders.

They'd already had four waitresses in the last five minutes asking if there was anything they needed. Or rather, if there was anything *Jane* needed. She hoped no one else came over for a while because she knew Jane's irritation level was heightening with each intrusion.

Maggie knew Jane needed to get whatever was going on off her chest and realised the constant interruption from people wanting to speak to the infamous *Mrs Wright* wasn't helping. Of course, neither had the paper running that stupid story the other day. It was obvious everyone was trying to work out if the rumours about the abortion were true or not.

Maggie had to take her hat off to Jane. If it had been *her,* she'd had locked herself away and cried for months, let alone deal with the bombshell she'd been dealt with regarding her daughter.

'You're going to have to explain to me what's going on here Jane, I'm really confused,' Maggie said. The last thing she'd heard when Jane had called her up over the moon the other day was that their daughter had been located. She also knew from what Jane had said, the removal of the child had been illegal and now it was just a case of crossing the 'T's' and dotting the 'I's'.

Jane looked pensive. 'I'm worried when it gets to court,

something we're not expecting will be dumped on us.'

Maggie frowned. 'The prison stuff is done and dusted isn't it?' she lowered her voice. 'It won't affect this – they've told you that. And both of you have stepped back from the dodgy things... you know, personal involvement with, you know...'

Jane raised her eyebrows. Yes, it was true they were a lot less personally involved with violence these days, but she also knew Seth still rolled his sleeves up a lot more than Maggie was clearly aware of. Even *she* probably didn't know some of it.

What with all this hassle brewing with the clubs and the strange events that had happened Jane felt someone was intent on sparking some form of reaction from one or both of them and the way it was going, it probably would. If that happened at this point in time it would surely spell disaster now they were finally able to move forward with getting their daughter back where she belonged.

Besides, it wasn't like she could tell Maggie that. Jane had already guessed Dan would have made out they had somehow all morphed into being holier-than-thou because otherwise she'd only fret.

'I'm sure something will rear its ugly head...' Jane muttered.

'Grace is *your* daughter. They *have* to return her to you!' Maggie exclaimed. 'She should never have been taken in the first place!'

Jane scowled. *Did Maggie not think she knew that?* The whole thing was ridiculous and in all honesty it was starting to get on top of her. The solicitor had even said the other day during their last phone conversation that having an au pair would not go down well in court. Apparently, this was looked upon as equal to not having time to look after the children someone already had without taking on more.

Just thinking about it made Jane's hackles rise. They may be busy, but only because they were trying to ensure things could be kept together. Regardless of the amount of time they had, Grace was *their* daughter and she should be with *them*.

'Apparently our child is now called Patty,' Jane spat.

'*Patty*?'

'Her name's Grace not fucking *Patty*!' Jane seethed. 'That's her legal name now it seems.' *That had really got to her when Seth had showed her what Mulligan had found.*

She hated it. *Fucking hated it.* She'd named her daughter Grace and was being told that someone, not satisfied with purely taking her daughter, had taken her fucking name as well.

Seth wasn't so bothered. *Well he wouldn't be, would he?* 'Seth said it's just a name and wasn't that important,' Jane barked angrily. Well her name was important. To her at least

'Well, if it's a case of not getting involved in anything untoward, why don't you both just step away from the Glint? Or get rid of it?' Maggie said dismissively.

She was aware Seth was most likely doing a lot more than either Dan or Jane mentioned. *Leopards didn't change every one of their spots after all...*

Jane's eyebrows shot up. 'Are you for real? Get rid of the club? What the hell would we do instead?' She almost laughed. *Maggie genuinely didn't have a clue about real life, did she?* 'I'm sure Dan wouldn't be best pleased either. I think it would just be *you*!'

'Why? Whether you realise it or not, Dan's job's very stressful...'

'Are you having a laugh?' Jane raged, getting irritated. 'What the hell would *you* know about it? What would *you* do for spending money Maggie if Dan wasn't bringing in the coin you've come to expect so that you can potter around the fucking house all day? Ever thought about *that*?'

Maggie refused to rise to Jane's hurtful remarks. She knew she was angry and stressed and didn't mean it. If doing something meant Jane getting her daughter back then she'd gladly support her in whichever way she could, even if that meant losing out financially.

'I was merely making a suggestion,' Maggie said quietly.

'Oh my God!' Jane yelled. 'Have you any idea how irrational you sound, you stupid bitch? What the fuck would you know anyway? You haven't a clue!'

Maggie reached out and touched Jane's arm. 'I didn't mean it like that and for the record, I'm sure Seth didn't mean anything by what he said about Grace's name not being important either.'

'I WANT MY DAUGHTER BACK!' Jane shouted, hot tears forming at the back of her eyes.

Maggie glanced up, noticing everyone was now looking in their direction. 'Shh babe. Keep your voice down. You don't want them all to know what's going on, do you?'

'What does it fucking matter? Everyone seems to have an opinion whether I like it or not!' Jane yelled and pushed herself up from the lounger. She grabbed her gin and tonic. 'LOOK AT ME EVERYONE!' she shouted. 'I'm the one who apparently kills babies!'

'*Jane!*' Maggie hissed, horrified. *What the hell was she playing at?*

'Oh and look! Yes, that's right. I'm drinking ALCOHOL! Aren't I dreadful? I don't deserve to be a mother, do I?' Jane screeched. 'Fuck you! Fuck the LOT of you!'

Throwing the glass to the floor, Jane watched it smash over the tiles before stalking away from the poolside to a stunned silence.

• • • •

'WHO WAS THAT big fat man?' Emily asked, tugging at Eliza's skirt as she hurried to keep up with her striding along the corridor.

Eliza slapped the little hand off her. *She didn't want sticky grubby mitts all over her clobber.* 'Don't worry about him,' she snapped. 'It's no one important. Now hurry up. I've got things I need to get on with.'

Eliza irritably pushed her hair away from her face. She'd been planning getting her lips plumped up again today, but then that bloody social worker had called, reminding her about their day with Emily. She'd only gone and forgotten about it hadn't she.

Racing back to the house, Eliza had luckily made it back just in time before the kid had showed up and she'd had to lay it on thick about how excited her and *Sam* were about spending the day with Emily…

Well no they weren't. There was too much going on.

Blathering on about baking and doing jigsaws together, Eliza had breathed a sigh of relief when the social worker had finally left and she'd wasted no time in shoving the kid in the car so she could get back to Elipse to make sure everything was running as it should be. But then she'd been stuck with the kid following her around the whole time and it was getting on her tits.

Glancing at the child trailing her like a puppy, Eliza ushered her into the office and quickly slammed the door. 'Sit over there,' she muttered to Emily whilst glancing at the CCTV monitors.

'What are they doing?' Emily asked, peering at one of the screens displaying a girl riding a punter hard.

'Oh, just playing,' Eliza snapped, hastily pressing the 'off' button. *For fuck's sake – this was just not working out well at all.*

'Can we do a jigsaw now?' Emily said, her little rosebud mouth pouting.

Eliza glared at her. *The kid was a spit of Jane and it was unnerving.* 'No, we fucking well can't! Does it look like I do jigsaws?'

Emily's mouth formed an 'O'. 'It's naughty to swear!' she said horrified.

'Shut up!' Eliza barked, handing the child a copy of The Sun. 'Go over there and leave me be so I can think. You're making my head hurt!'

Eliza poured herself a large vodka and slugged it down in one. *The sooner these formalities were done and dusted the better. Then she could get on with hiring a nanny to look after the bloody kid.*

She just had to remember to make sure the kid understood that if she didn't want anything 'horrible' to happen to anyone she liked, including her poxy doll, then it was *very* important to tell that *nice* social worker of hers how much of a wonderful time she'd had at the house today. They hadn't been here at all either. That was a definite no-no and something the kid needed to get into her thick skull.

• • • •

TINA HAD FELT A little bad when she'd made the first of the phone calls, but by the time she'd completed the third one she didn't.

It had been Jane Wright who'd answered the telephone on each occasion. She couldn't tell how successful she'd been in her quest, but knew she'd at least hit a nerve. *Especially with the last call.*

Tina took a gulp straight from the bottle of vodka she'd managed to nick earlier from Tesco and wiped the back of her hand across her mouth.

'Who *is* this?' Jane had angrily demanded during the third call. Tina had ensured the first two had remained annoyingly silent.

'Is your husband there?' Tina had asked.

'Who wants to know?'

Tina had been able to imagine the irritation on Jane Wright's face. She was one of those people who hated not being in full control of any given situation – that much was obvious.

'If he's not there *again* it may be worth finding out exactly where he is…' Tina had said mysteriously.

Jane had not responded with any comment, purposely intending not to rise to the bait.

Tina had been unperturbed. 'Maybe you should ask if he knows where Lacey is….' Tina had said slyly, knowing Jane would not have divulged Lacey's previous presence in their house to anyone. Neither was it common knowledge the girl had gone. Only thanks to Anna was anyone else privy to this inside information, therefore it was a prime subject to use. *Eliza had been right. It would get Jane thinking.*

'*Who*?' Jane has asked after a slight hesitation.

'Maybe then you'll find out where your husband goes on his late nights…' Tina had said quickly before replacing the handset.

She'd left the phone box content she'd done well. She hadn't needed to say any more. It had been just enough to get that trumped-up snobby bitch's mind ticking.

Twenty Two

JASON MILLER STUDIED the frown on Seth's face as he stared in concentration at the numbers laid out on the desk in front of him and saw a nerve twitch sporadically in his neck. His eyes ran down over Seth's crisp white shirt which he'd rolled up to the elbows showing his muscled forearms.

His eyes became fixed on the thick gold wedding band on Seth's left hand that was splayed over a sheet of paper. Jason frowned seeing bruising and a couple of small cuts on his other hand and he sighed quietly to himself.

Last night Linda had made sure he'd listened to the latest speculation going around in her circles about Jane's alleged abortion. Apart from the possibility of the child not being Seth's, it had been hinted he was becoming fly with his fists on his wife too.

Jason found it difficult to believe this man could be knocking Jane around, but saying that, a *lot* of things which wouldn't normally have crossed his mind as a possibility had done recently where Seth Wright was concerned.

The way he felt at the moment meant he was unsure about *everything*. Equally worrying was what Linda had done. He still couldn't quite believe she'd been so stupid and could gladly kill her for putting him in such a position.

The photograph which had gone to press about Jane and the 'abortion' had sparked a lot of controversy. As it was, he'd had a call himself yesterday afternoon asking for his opinion and to comment on the story. He'd derived great pleasure in refusing to say a word.

Jason expected Seth had received calls too, but he hadn't liked to ask. In fact, he hadn't even mentioned the article, but he'd have to now, courtesy of Linda. *What on earth had she been thinking?*

His bloody wife had only given the press more unsubstantiated fuel, thereby enabling them to speculate and insinuate Seth was slapping Jane around. Now this article was in today's paper:

Maybe Mr 'Wright' isn't right after all

Linda Miller, wife of Jason Miller - owner of the influential Limelight club, stated 'although I'm unsure as to the validity of Jane Wright ending a pregnancy, I wouldn't be surprised - what with rumours of an affair...'

Jason and Linda are close friends and business associates of the Wrights and Mrs Miller has expressed to us her upset and disappointment she felt hearing things were far from alright in the Wright's marriage.

'Jane sought out my husband late one night at the club. I don't know why, but it's obvious something's wrong....' Mrs Miller continued.

When asked whether Mr Wright had resurrected his well-known violence and was using it against his wife, Mrs Miller interestingly refused to answer one way or the other, but her response suggested she was aware of an issue:

'I cannot possibly comment on that, but neither I, nor my husband will continue an affiliation with anyone capable of domestic violence...' she stated.

We have attempted to get a statement from both Jane and Seth Wright, but neither were available for comment. We hope this isn't the beginning of an unhappy ending for one of city's favourite and well-respected couples.

Reported by James Hill

Jason glanced at Seth again, fairly confident he couldn't have yet seen the story. He'd have to show him of course, but had no idea how he could excuse what Linda had done. The stupid cow. She'd all but publicly accused Seth of beating his wife up.

Seth looked up from the paperwork, feeling the tension in the room. He knew Jason was toying with bringing up the subject of the newspaper article and didn't envy the position the man's wife had put him in, but admitted he'd purposefully not mentioned it because he'd wanted to see if Jason had the balls.

He'd seen the article himself first thing. It was, of course, complete rubbish, however he hadn't failed to notice the furtive glances he'd received this morning.

'Is everything alright?' Seth asked, giving Jason the opening he clearly required.

Jason pulled out a copy of the newspaper. 'Not really.... Have you seen this?' He passed the paper over the desk to Seth. 'All I can say is that I'm really sorry. I've no idea what she was thinking.'

Seth waved the paper away. 'I've already seen it.'

Jason couldn't hide his surprise. He'd been sure Seth would have ranted about the injustice of it all. 'Really? And you're not angry?'

'Not angry? Of *course* I'm fucking angry!' Seth barked. 'I just want to know what you're going to do about it?'

'I'll speak to Linda tonight,' Jason said.

'I didn't mean Linda,' Seth replied coldly. He didn't doubt Jason would have words with his past-her-best wife, as would *he* at some point, but she wasn't the one who needed to take priority as far as he was concerned.

'Who do you mean then?' Jason asked frowning. 'Oh no Seth, you can't go after the reporter. We've got too much going on at the moment to draw more attention to us.'

'To draw attention to *you*, you mean?' Seth snapped spikily. It was alright for *his* name to be dragged through the mud, but not Miller's? It was *his* firm sticking their necks out and doing the digging and working on who was behind the troublemakers whilst Jason and his bunch sat back. Probably because it was Miller himself staging this shit. Every day that passed this theory became more plausible.

'Please Seth, don't make waves with the press. I doubt whether they'll publish anything else and it will blow over soon. Besides, no one would believe that shit about you anyway,' Jason had contested.

Seth watched Jason's face, knowing damn well from what he'd seen so far people *were* questioning the validity of what had been printed. He'd also seen the flicker of emotion behind Jason's eyes that he'd tried to hide and realised sadly that *he* was questioning the truth too. In fact, everything Seth suspected Miller was involved in regarding possibly setting him up, this could well be part of it. Miller could have urged Linda to get involved so he could play the 'concerned' business partner whilst gathering more ammo.

Feeling both saddened and angry about the whole thing, Seth forced a smile. 'Ok, we'll talk about dealing with this properly some other time, but the press shouldn't be printing shit like that. Jane's not happy and neither am I. I trust you'll be setting Linda straight.'

He didn't give a rat's arse what was said to Linda and neither did he care if he rocked the boat with the press. Furthermore, regardless of Miller's involvement, if he genuinely thought he'd let a reporter twat print that shit without being brought to rights, then he was well and truly losing the plot, but he'd let him think otherwise.

• • • •

ANNA TRIED HER BEST to keep up with Toby's demands, but felt like going back to bed. She had no idea how she'd managed to even get up this morning, let alone coped with a baby. *God, what had she been thinking last night?*

She didn't think she'd had that much to drink, but she must have done judging by the way she felt and what she'd done…

She hadn't had chance to fully decide how she felt about her newly acquired status, except being as she was questioning it, she guessed perhaps the honest answer was that she wasn't fully enamoured, but it was too late to regret it now.

She'd thought she'd have felt somehow 'different' after losing her virginity, but she didn't. She still felt like Anna, except dare she say, disappointed - both in the act itself and her own attitude which had led to it. She just wasn't like that and couldn't quite believe she'd been so forward.

She was very glad that Aiden had the foresight to let himself out first thing this morning. If the Wrights realised she'd brought a man into their house, then she'd lose her job for sure. *She'd broken her own rules as well at theirs.*

Anna had begun to think Aiden had stood her up when, last night he still hadn't arrived half an hour after they'd arranged to meet for a drink. She'd been just about to leave when he'd rushed through the door full of apologies.

She hadn't dared complain about his lateness – after all she knew she was lucky in the first place to have a man like *that* interested in her.

As the evening wore on, Anna had felt a little tipsy by her fourth glass of wine in quick succession, but after she'd finished her fifth it was as if she'd morphed into a different person.

Anna chucked Toby under the chin and smiled. It was difficult not to, what with his gorgeous, perfect little face. She felt terrible. Not just physically, but mentally.

She shifted on the chair slightly, trying to find a more comfortable position that might ease the burning throbbing pain still present between her legs. As it was, the first thing she'd had to do this morning was to strip the bed and get her sheets in the washer hoping the blood stains would come out.

'Morning,' Jane said unexpectedly walking into the kitchen

and making Anna jump.

'Morning,' Anna mumbled, watching Jane pad across the tiles to give Toby a kiss on the top of his curly head. She looked tired. Tired and miserable. 'Are you ok?' she asked timidly, wishing she could ask her opinion about last night's experience and whether it was normal not to enjoy it, but that was obviously out of the question.

'Yes, I'm ok. Why do you ask?' Jane said accusingly.

Anna quickly averted her eyes. 'No reason,' she hesitated. 'You just seem a bit upset.'

Jane stared at Anna, saying nothing for a minute or two almost as if she wasn't quite there.

Never able to deal with silences, Anna fidgeted in her chair.

'Are you happy working here Anna?' Jane asked suddenly.

Anna looked up sharply. 'Happy? Yes of course I am. I love being here!' she exclaimed. *What on earth had prompted that? Did Jane know about Aiden or found out she'd been snooping?*

Jane frowned slightly. 'You haven't seemed yourself lately. Is something making you uncomfortable or is someone bothering you?'

'No. Nobody's making me uncomfortable.' Anna watched Jane frown for the second time.

Jane stared at Anna. 'I think I'll go and have a bath,' she snapped.

Anna watched Jane walk from the room. She knew she'd spoken out of turn last night. When Aiden had told her of the rumours going around about Seth being heavy handed with Jane, Anna had been surprised and said although they'd been arguing lately, she'd seen no physical violence but *had* heard an awful lot of shouting, slamming and smashing of things. And no, she couldn't be *entirely* sure there had been no violence from Seth's part. Now she began to feel it would have been better not to have had an opinion at all. She should have just kept her mouth shut.

• • • •

SETH GRITTED HIS TEETH as he pushed down on the

accelerator. It had only taken the one phone call to get the required information. He drummed his fingers impatiently on the steering wheel and glared out of the window, eyes narrowed on the traffic lights willing them to change. If his information was correct, he'd only got a small window to achieve what was needed. He glanced at his watch. It was cutting it fine but he should just about make it.

Turning the corner, he screeched into a parking bay on the road and quickly hopped out of the car. Shrugging on his coat, he made his way rapidly towards the station.

Seth moved into one of the archways littered with old cans, used needles and other detritus and waited patiently, hearing the wheels of the train grinding to a halt on the track above. He took in a deep breath, happy he'd got into position just in time.

Flattening himself against the wall, he stood silently and watched the thin straggle of people disembarking the late train. He hadn't thought there would be too many getting off at this time of night during the week and he'd been right.

Seth paused. Light drizzling rain was visible via the illumination of the street light the other side of the road. He had to gauge this correctly and hoped the guy he wanted wasn't too close to anyone else, otherwise his plan would be thoroughly thwarted.

Tracing the outline of the baseball bat through the deep inside pocket of his dark wool overcoat, a small smile pulled at the corners of Seth's mouth. This had to come together. He needed to ensure there would be *no* further instances of what had occurred.

From his concealed place under the dark and extremely smelly arch he heard the unmistakable clatter of feet advancing down the metal steps of the foot bridge from the opposite platform. With finely tuned hearing, Seth estimated around ten people had disembarked from the train and that they were fairly widely spaced apart. Based on the information he'd got from the telephone call earlier there was a good chance the person he wanted was the last in line.

James Hill had boarded the 11.15 train into carriage G. From the direction the train was travelling, that carriage would be positioned furthest along the platform, meaning Hill should be the last one off.

Seth silently watched several passengers from the train pass the mouth of the archway. *None of them were James Hill.*

He hadn't enlisted Dan in this. He knew the man felt he should be stepping away from personal involvement with anything messy. As for Jane, she'd go batshit if she found out. She'd been too angry and throwing blame around about everything last night to have a rational conversation about it. *Besides, talking about stuff didn't change what needed to be done.*

Senses on full alert, Seth stiffened as a lone figure passed the archway mouth. *There's the fucker.*

Stepping out from the archway, quickly clocking whether there was anyone in the vicinity, he was glad to see the view clear from both ways. 'Excuse me!'

The man slowed and hesitatingly looked around questioningly.

Not wishing his face to be illuminated in the dim glow of the street light, Seth ensured he remained well within the shadow of the archway overhang. 'Was that the last train coming in tonight do you know mate?' He watched the man's face relax as he realised he wasn't being questioned by a random glue sniffer or money cadger and stepped forward to answer.

Wasting no time, Seth grabbed the man and dragged him backwards into the darkness of the archway. Frozen in shock, not a sound escaped from his mouth as he was roughly pinned up against the slimy wall.

'James Hill?' Seth growled, his voice low and menacing. 'I presume you recognise who I am?'

James Hill remained mute with fear, his eyes darting around desperately as he realised *exactly* whose hands were wrapped tightly around his windpipe.

Seth smiled viciously. 'That's right – I'm Seth Wright...

You know, the one that beats his wife up?'

'I-I…' James stuttered, unsure as to what his response should, or *could* be. 'Well… did you?' he whispered. He knew this question would not go down well but his journalistic instincts were too ingrained to help himself.

Red mist descended in Seth's brain and his vicious smile turned into a rabid snarl. 'You fucking what? *What* did you say?' Yanking the man towards him, he threw him full force against the opposite archway wall. He knew he should keep a lid on his temper, but it was no use. *How could he when this poncing shite was asking questions like that? Seriously?* 'No, I fucking did not and you will officially retract your bastard inference by printing an article apologising for your gross mistake!'

Winded, James looked up at Seth. Standing a good five inches taller, the glint in his eyes was feral. *Just do what he says, James. Do whatever the fuck he wants. The guy's a nutter.*

Before he could stop himself, James' mouth overtook his brain. 'In that case you'll need to give me an interview,' he garbled.

Seth bared his teeth. 'Aside from Linda Miller, who else did you speak to?'

Suddenly confident, James Hill raised his eyebrows. *This bloke was a meat head. He was all talk.* 'Oh, come on! Surely even *you* know I can't divulge *that*!'

Seth stared at the man in disbelief. *Was he taking the piss? He had to be! Did he have no control anymore or what? Did people think he could be messed with?*

Pulling the baseball bat from his coat, he grabbed the man around the throat once more. 'You think this is a joke, do you? Think it's fucking *funny*?'

Belatedly realising he'd horribly misjudged his reasoning, James raised his hands needing to quickly acquiesce. 'Ok, ok. What do you want me to do?'

Seth smiled, his resolve decided. *He didn't care what anyone else thought. This fucker needed sorting.* 'Don't worry about it. It doesn't matter. I've changed my mind because I don't believe you'd do the right thing even if you had the option.'

James' eyes widened in terror as Seth raised the bat. 'No! Wait! I…'

Unwilling to give the man any further leeway, Seth brought the wooden bat down hard on the man's skull, watching with satisfaction as he rapidly crumpled to the ground. *Thought he could take the mick, did he?*

Seth could have left it there. After all, he'd only been planning on delivering a warning, but unable to control his ire over being questioned and messed around by this piss taker, he raised the bat again.

Leaning over James Hill's unconscious body, Seth eyed the visible crack already made in the man's skull and brought the weapon down full force. He now needed to finish it.

Twenty Three

LACEY FELT LIKE PINCHING herself. She'd been fortunate. She was still waiting to wake up and find it had all been a dream, but she hadn't. *It was definitely real.*

She glanced around the shop and inhaled the comforting smell of the books surrounding her and smiled widely.

Jennie – a girl she'd clicked with at Pegasus Place, had been offered this job in the independent bookshop because she'd been cleaning there for some time when the position became available. She was happy doing her bit of cleaning and didn't want additional responsibility as her head was still not in the right place, so instead she'd suggested Helen, the shop owner, took on Lacey instead.

Lacey really liked Jennie and had been overjoyed to find a friend. *A genuine friend.* Jennie had been living at the hostel for six months after getting off drugs and away from abusive parents. She'd remained completely clean, thanks to the hostel's support. She was doing really well with rebuilding her life. At nineteen she was older than Lacey, but they got on really well.

Lacey still hadn't felt able to confide to her friend in detail about her story, instead giving a vague account of being forced into prostitution. It wouldn't have helped spilling the beans about

Eliza and Digger, nor about that vile fat bastard and the baby…

The less she thought about that gave her the best chance of moving on and that was what she was determined to do.

Lacey looked down the list of books earmarked to order and cross-referenced them against the book catalogue. The shop had closed its doors to the public an hour ago, but she'd been happy to stay behind to make a start on the new listings. In fact, she'd wanted to. The more time she could spend with her beloved books, the better.

She glanced at the clock. As long as she was back by 7pm Sylvia wouldn't worry. Although Pegasus Place didn't have a curfew, Sylvia wanted the girls, at least for the first few weeks of finding their feet and regaining their confidence, to be back by 7 or let her know when they would be back.

She'd felt comforted by this request. It made her feel like someone cared. Tidying up the paperwork and books covering her desk in the small back room, Lacey picked her handbag up from the floor. She grabbed her jacket and walked through to the main part of the shop.

'I'm off now Helen,' she smiled, knowing the owner of the bookstore would be there for hours yet, side-tracked with wading through the new book arrivals.

'Ok Lacey. Have a good evening. See you in the morning,' Helen replied and watched as Lacey let herself out of the shop door.

• • • •

JANE SAT UP IN bed and stared unseeing at the magazine she was unsuccessfully trying to read. Angrily throwing it on the floor, she blinked back the tears.

After finally getting herself together this morning she'd gone to the Glint in an attempt to try and get some work done to take her mind off last night's telephone calls. If anything, this had been a big mistake because she'd become immediately aware of the uncomfortable atmosphere hanging heavily from the moment she'd stepped over the threshold.

Feeling exceedingly frustrated over the whole situation she'd stormed up to the office, only to find Seth absent. Dan had been there and had tried to hide his surprise on seeing her, which had only fuelled Jane's irritation.

'What's going on Dan?' she'd asked.

'Don't know what you mean?'

'Where's Seth?' Jane had asked.

'Gone to see Miller,' Dan had muttered, looking down at a sheaf of paperwork.

Jane's eyes narrowed. *Seth hadn't mentioned a meeting with Jason Miller.* She'd watched Dan cover something on the desk with another sheet of paper.

'What are you hiding?' she'd snapped.

Dan had held his hands up in submission. 'Blimey Jane, what's got into you this morning? I'm not hiding anything. Why would I do that?'

Unconvinced, Jane had stared at him for a short while before trying to convince herself she'd been imagining it. 'I'd best look at last month's takings,' she'd said, opening a desk drawer.

'Oh, I've done those,' Dan had smiled.

Jane had found herself getting angrier. 'Do I not help run this gaff anymore Dan? Am I not fucking needed or something? What's going on? Everyone's acting strange.'

'Come on Jane. No one's acting strange. I only did it because I thought it would help!' Dan laughed.

Jane had stood up quickly, grabbed her bag and had begun to walk from the room. 'I guess I'll just go paint my nails like women are supposed to do, shall I? Maybe the atmosphere will return to normal once I've gone?'

'Don't be like that!' Dan had pleaded. 'I….'

Jane hadn't bothered hanging around to hear the rest of his excuses.

She picked up the glass of vodka from her bedside table and slugged it down. *Why was she not being kept informed? Everyone doing her job for her? And where the fuck was Seth?*

She glared at the bedroom clock. It was gone midnight and

he still wasn't back. *Something was wrong. She could feel it in her bones.*

Getting back in bed, Jane sighed. The thing was, she wasn't imagining it. She hadn't dreamt the phone calls last night, nor the ones received tonight.

When the phone had rung, she'd immediately thought it was Seth. Angrily picking up the handset, she'd barked into it. 'Are you coming back tonight or what?'

Much to her horror, the same voice which had spoken last night had laughed, clearly enjoying her wrath. 'Oh dear. Mislaid your husband again, have you?' The voice was sarcastic. 'Don't you know where he is? Didn't you listen to what I told you?'

Jane had slammed the phone down. She'd even gone so far as to pull the connection from the wall socket so she didn't have to listen to the grating voice if the phone rang again.

Whether she wanted to admit it or not, she'd begun to suspect Seth *was* doing the dirty on her, but who with? Could the caller be right? Had it been with Lacey? Was it *still* with Lacey?

Jane felt thoroughly nauseous. A sixteen year old that *she'd* brought into their home…

She picked the glass up from the bedside table and threw it against the wall. As it smashed into pieces, Jane flicked the light off and lay down to stare sightlessly into the dark.

• • • •

DAN PUSHED MAGGIE'S thighs further apart. He was immensely enjoying the delicious moaning sounds she was making whilst she grasped at his hair. He relished the anticipation of the promised prize. That was before the front door starting banging.

'Dan!' Maggie panted. 'There's someone at the door.'

Determined to ignore it Dan continued despite the noise becoming louder.

'*Dan!* You'll have to answer it,' Maggie insisted.

Frustrated, Dan glanced at the small round clock balanced on the bedside table. *Quarter past bloody midnight? Was whoever was at the door trying to wind him up?*

'Hurry up!' Maggie urged, nudging Dan as the knocking continued. 'It must be important!'

'Important my arse!' Dan grumbled, forcing himself out of bed and pulled on a pair of tracksuit bottoms to conceal his fast deflating erection. *For fuck's sake.*

He begrudgingly dragged himself down the stairs and flicked the hallway light on. Fumbling with the chain across the lock, he yanked the door open, his displeasure evident by the large scowl plastered across his face.

'Dan,' Seth muttered, quickly pushing past into the house.

Shutting the door rapidly behind him, Dan was momentarily confused. 'Seth? What are you doing here?'

'I need to use your shower mate. Do you mind?' Seth mumbled. He hadn't known what else to do. Things had inevitably got messy. He hadn't planned for that and admitted his temper had got the better of him. There was little point in worrying about it now. *Not that he was....*

The only thing he was concerned about was stressing Jane out. She didn't need anything else playing on her mind and had left strict instructions to all at the Glint this morning that under *no* circumstances should anything be mentioned to her about that latest article in the bloody paper.

Regardless of right, wrong or indifferent, Seth didn't want *anything* to upset Jane. He'd protect her from everything at *any* cost and if she thought he'd caused more issues by getting rid of that prick reporter, then that would have the opposite effect of what he wanted. He knew Dan didn't agree with it either. It was easier all round if *no one* knew the ins and outs.

Seth glanced at Dan, who still hadn't said a word. 'Dan? Did you hear me? Alright if I grab a shower?'

Dan hastily pulled himself to his senses rather than staring at the blood splattered down Seth's coat, shirt and liberally caking his hands. 'What the....'

'Take this,' Seth muttered, shrugging off his coat and

bundling it into Dan's arms. 'Bag it up and make sure you get rid as a priority tomorrow. Fucking burnt it ok?' He stared at Dan. 'Alright if I go up? Where's Maggie? She asleep?'

Dan grabbed Seth's arm as he made to take the stairs. 'Seth, what's going on?'

Seth peered up the staircase, then turned back to face Dan. 'I can't say, or rather I *won't*.' His voice remained a low whisper. 'If you don't know anything, you can't be implicated. Trust me.'

Dan frowned. 'What have you done? You need to tell me!' How was he expected to cover or do anything if the man wouldn't level with him? It wasn't right and he needed to know. 'Seth, you n…'

'Dan,' Seth smiled coldly. 'Just don't ask. You don't need to know. *Really*. If Maggie's awake, tell her the same yeah?'

Dan stared at Seth as he loped up the stairs. Hearing the shower start to run, he placed the coat in a bin bag and then trailed upstairs himself. Maggie would be nosing around any second and he needed to get there first.

TWENTY FOUR

JANE AWOKE TO FIND Seth nuzzling into the back of her neck.

'I know it's late baby, but I've missed you,' Seth murmured, his lips trailing along her shoulder.

'Mmm,' Jane stirred, happily feeling his hard body pressing against hers. His hands slipped underneath her satin negligee, one running over her rapidly hardening nipples and the other finding its way into her knickers. Feeling desire immediately ignite at his slightest touch, she heated further when she moved, feeling his rock-hard erection pulsing.

She breathed in deeply, taking in the scent only *he* had.

What the? Flowers...?

Jane stiffened as her memory returned. Quickly opening one eye she focused on the clock. 3 am. *The phone calls and now smelling of perfume....?*

Seth groaned in frustration as Jane turned away from him. He propped himself up on his elbows and lowered his mouth onto her nipple. 'How do you want me babe?' he murmured, his hand tracing down her body and back between her legs.

Jane fought the raging desire she felt as Seth's fingers expertly distracted her mind from the knowledge she'd discovered. His mouth worked her nipples into unbearably hard points of heat and she felt herself surrender. That was until another blast of flowery scent from his hair rapidly reminded her of the suspicions. *He'd had a shower, but not here. Where had he showered and why?*

Pushing Seth's hand and head away, Jane pushed herself up to a sitting position and quickly pulled on her robe. 'Have you been showering?' she asked as calmly as possible. 'You smell of flowers.'

'Oh baby!' Seth groaned, his hand running down his erection as he knelt back on the bed. 'Not now eh? I need you.' He opened his arms. 'Come on and sit on me. Whatever you want.'

'Seth, why have you been showering?' Jane pushed.

Seth ran his hand through his hair irritably. 'What the fuck are you going on about Jane?' *Shit. He thought that shower gel smelt a bit perfumy. It must have been Maggie's. He shouldn't have used it.* 'I haven't had a shower!' he lied.

'I can smell perfume Seth…'

Seth sighed dramatically and pushed himself to the side of the bed. 'You're tired honey. Let's just go to sleep.'

'I don't want to go to fucking sleep! I know what I can smell!' she raged. 'Are you screwing someone else?'

Seth nearly choked. '*What*? What the hell are you talking about?'

Jane jumped out of bed. Yanking the door open so hard it slammed back on the wall she stormed from the bedroom with Seth close on her tail.

'Jane! What's going on?' he shouted, hastily pulling his robe around himself as he followed her towards the study.

'As if you didn't know!' she snapped. She slapped the light switch on. 'You keep disappearing and for the second night in a row I've had phone calls telling me you're with someone else…'

'*What*?' Seth stared astonished. *This was crazy!*

'You then turn up at 3 in the morning having obviously just come out of someone else's shower! What the fuck do you want me to think?'

'Jane, I swear! It's not what you think. I promise you,' Seth pleaded. *Surely she couldn't think he'd cheat on her? Not Jane?*

'Who have you been seeing? Who are you sleeping with?' Jane asked, fighting off the tears threatening to spill from her eyes and hating herself for acting like a jealous harridan. *Seth was the jealous one, not her.*

'God Jane!' Seth cried. 'No one! I've been seeing or sleeping with no one. Just you.' He moved forwards to touch her, but she batted his hands away.

'Don't fucking touch me, Seth Wright. Is it Lacey?' she screamed.

Seth paled. 'WHAT?' *Surely he couldn't have heard that correctly?*

'That's why you wanted me to kick her out is it? In case I caught you at it? But you can't keep away, can you? You've been to see her. I've been told.'

Seth's eyes narrowed. 'I can't believe you're saying this! You're accusing me of shagging a fucking sixteen year old?' His disbelief was heavily laced with both hurt and anger. 'You're probably making this shit up to try and get me to admit to your crazy fucking paranoid stories!'

'How *dare* you!' Jane screamed, stepping forward and slapping him hard around the face. 'It's not me who's been fucking school kids is it?'

'You *what*? You bitch!' Seth raged, raising a hand to his stinging cheek. 'What the hell is wrong with you? Do you not remember how angry I was when the silly cow tried it on with me?'

'Yeah, that was very convenient wasn't it? Except she didn't try it on with you, did she? *You* seduced her and she's still getting it from you by all accounts!'

'Shut the fuck up Jane!' Seth raged. *This had gone far enough*. 'You'll wake Toby. Is that what you want?'

'You should have perhaps thought of that before,' Jane seethed. 'Now Toby will know what a cunt his father is.'

'*Enough,* Jane!' Seth yelled, picking up a clock from the

desk and launching it at the wall. Barging past Jane in rage, he sent her crashing into the desk.

'SHIT!' he cried, grey-faced reaching for Jane. 'I'm sorry baby. I didn't mean to do that. Are you alright?'

Sobbing, Jane pulled herself to her feet and ran from the study. 'Get the fuck away from me Seth.'

• • • •

ANNA RAN BACK TOWARDS her bedroom and closed the door behind her. Breathlessly she leaned up against the door in an effort to control her racing heart.

She moved towards the bed and quickly picked up the phone, dialling the number with shaking fingers.

'What is it?' Aiden mumbled into the receiver. He glanced across the bed at the barmaid with whom he'd spent half the night thoroughly enjoying. Now the phone had interrupted what little sleep he was able to get.

'Aiden is that you?'

Aiden frowned. 'Anna?' *Oh no. what the hell did she want? Four times she'd called since he'd slept with her and now she was stalking him in the middle of the night too?*

'I don't know what to do!' Anna whispered. 'You know what you said about those Seth Wright rumours? Well him and Jane have been screaming and shouting for ages again, but from what I've just heard, I think he's just hit her.'

Aiden paused. 'Are you sure?'

Anna had barely been able to believe it herself. After listening to the raised voices which had initially woken her up, she'd gone to see if Toby had been disturbed too, when she'd realised Seth and Jane's argument had moved from the bedroom into the study.

From what she'd heard, it looked like Seth was sleeping with that young girl who'd disappeared. Then she'd heard that big crashing sound.

Daring to peep through the crack of the door, Anna had clearly seen Jane crumpled against the desk with Seth moving towards her.

'Aiden. What should I do?'

Aiden grinned. *This was a perfect opportunity...* 'Is it still going on now?'

'Jane's locked herself back in the bedroom and as I speak it sounds like Seth's breaking the door down,' Anna hissed, hearing the unmistakable sound of someone kicking hard against wood.

'Anna, he's got to be stopped. Leave it with me.'

'What are you going to do?' Anna whispered. *From what Tina had said it was plausible the Wrights could turn on her next.*

'Don't worry. Nothing to implicate you. Trust me Anna, I'll deal with this.'

Putting the phone down, Aiden smiled widely as he dialled Eliza's number. Even if she was cross being woken up, she wouldn't be for long. He'd get plenty of brownie points for giving her the golden opportunity of putting an anonymous call into the police against Seth Wright.

• • • •

MAGGIE STARED AT Jane's pale face as she sat on the hospital bed getting more and more impatient. She glanced at the clock on the sterile white walls of the cubicle. *5 am.*

Jane had called an hour ago to say Seth had been arrested. Maggie had rushed over within five minutes whilst Dan had gone to the police station. She'd fought through the throngs of press still clustered around the bottom of the driveway and although Martin had done his best to move them on, the police had clearly stated because the photographers were now outside the property boundary there wasn't a lot they could do because they weren't trespassing.

When Maggie had entered the house, Jane was being questioned by two female officers. The dark discolouration of a large bruise was already clearly visible at the top of her arm. She'd been screaming at them that Seth hadn't attacked her, but the police had insisted she get checked out at the hospital.

Jane had been shepherded from the house leaving a wide-eyed and frightened Anna on the doorstep literally holding the baby. One of the officers had insisted on accompanying them to hospital. This meant Maggie hadn't been able to get any information as to what had *really* happened.

'It'll be fine,' Maggie soothed, clutching on to Jane's hand. 'You'll see.' *She hoped to hell she was right. That bastard, Seth. He'd done it again, hadn't he? He'd lost the plot and fucked everything up. Again.*

Jane glanced at the nurse as she filled in the paperwork. 'There's nothing wrong with me. I'm *fine*!'

The nurse smiled. 'Of course you are dear...'

Jane gripped Maggie's hand. 'Where's Seth?' she hissed. 'He can't get charged! It will fuck our case up!'

Maggie sighed. *Seth had definitely been arrested for attacking his wife. What a fucking mess.* She had no idea what was going on. As it was, Dan had been vague when she'd discovered Seth showering in their bathroom in the middle of the night and now a couple of hours later – *this.*

The nurse patted Jane's hand and looked at her. 'Mrs Wright, if your home is untenable, we can get you support and help. Like a refuge. You don't have to be on your own with th…'

'My home life is just fine, thank you!' Jane snapped, watching the nurse give one of those knowing looks reserved for people not wanting to admit the truth. She felt like screaming. She wasn't a victim of domestic violence! It had been an accident. *The only thing Seth seemed to be guilty of was screwing around and if that were true, she'd brain him herself.*

'Well, just so you know – help is there,' the nurse smiled.

Maggie eyed Jane hoping she'd keep her temper in check. 'Are the police still here?' She knew they'd be hanging around waiting to take a statement.

The nurse nodded. 'I'll send them in.'

Waiting until the woman had left the room, Maggie quickly

turned to Jane. '*Did* he hit you?'

Jane shook her head and her eyes narrowed. 'Of course he fucking didn't! It's worse… I think he's been sleeping with that Lacey. And if he has, then after killing him, I'll find her and wring her fucking neck.'

Twenty Five

ELIZA PEERED INTO her compact mirror and smacked her lips together to ensure an even coverage of bright magenta lipstick.

She looked over at Aiden from the opposite side of the desk and smiled. Aiden was proving to be worth his weight in gold. Without his connection to Anna she wouldn't have been privy to the inside information enabling her to put in that well-timed call to the police and of course to the press.

Eliza grinned viciously. Judging by the phone call Aiden had received from a panic-stricken Anna last night about the argument it seemed that, as planned, thanks to Tina's ongoing phone call campaign, Lacey was being accused of being the recipient of Seth's illicit affections. *It was all going very nicely to plan and this was only the start...*

She smiled widely, her whitened teeth bright in the morning light and turned once more to the front page of the paper. The large colour photograph showed Seth handcuffed and bare-chested being dragged by a whole host of police officers down his driveway. The anger in his eyes was evident and he wore a ferocious snarl which only heightened her attraction for him.

Even after everything he'd done to her in the past, Eliza had never been able to quash the desire she had for the man. Not that she'd go down that road again after he'd screwed her life up, but her body reacted without her consent every time she thought of him. This physical attraction, combined with genuine hatred was rather confusing.

Aiden watched Eliza staring at the photograph. 'Bloody good shot isn't it?' he laughed.

Eliza nodded. 'I see your girlfriend's photo-bombed the pictures.'

Aiden raised his eyebrows and walked behind Eliza to stare at the paper from over her shoulder. Now she'd pointed it out he could see Anna's head poking around a door from within the house. *She looked like a ghost.* 'Silly cow!' he muttered. 'And she's *not* my girlfriend.'

Eliza spun around in the chair and crossed her legs slowly in front of him, knowing his line of sight would be conveniently down her large cleavage. 'Thought you'd have enjoyed breaking the girl in?' she quipped.

In fact, they'd all found it highly amusing that Aiden had been tasked with getting info out of Tina's frigid, highly virginal sister. However, it hadn't taken him long to get her to fall for his charm and deflower her. Eliza could however sense his reluctance to continue the rendezvous with the boring bitch, but it was *imperative* he did.

'Sacks of spuds aren't exactly my idea of a fun night!' Aiden moaned. 'And she keeps phoning me.'

'Well that's good. If she hadn't phoned you last night, I'd never have been in the position to make that call, would I?' Eliza looked at Aiden from underneath her thick false eyelashes, knowing he was looking *exactly* where she'd wanted him to.

'So, what's your idea of fun…?' Her gaze ran over the swallow tattoo on his neck, down his muscular torso to his small waist. He was a nice looker and even though she was a good few years older, she'd bet he'd thought about her. *After all most people did.* She smiled sweetly. 'I just want you to know we're *very* grateful…'

Aiden swallowed nervously. *Was Eliza making a play for him?* She was tasty enough and he wouldn't mind getting his hands on those massive bazookas of hers. He watched her run her tongue over her full bottom lip. 'I much prefer my women to be more adventurous in the sack than Anna,' he said, aware there was a husky tone to his voice.

Eliza uncrossed her legs giving Aiden a glimpse of her red lacy knickers. 'I'm afraid you'll have to put up with the lack of excitement where she's concerned for some time yet….'

Aiden felt his groin throb when Eliza moved her hand slowly up to the zip holding her black top together.

'Maybe I can alleviate some of your disappointment,' Eliza purred, pulling the zip down, immediately freeing her large enhanced breasts. *Plus get you to do more stuff I need.*

Digger had spent so much time with that bloody Lomond bastard lately she'd barely had any servicing and this whole situation with Seth and Jane getting screwed over had turned her on. Besides, she needed to keep Aiden in her debt and what better way than to show him what delights she could offer his cock?

Aiden stared greedily at the large mounds visible in front of him and forced himself not to reach out and take then into his hands. A quiet groan escaped involuntarily from his mouth. He'd always been a sucker for big tits and this preference had not waned. But what should he do? He didn't want to make the first move in case she was setting him up. And what if Digger came back?

Before he could make a decision it was taken out of his hands when Eliza quickly unzipped his jeans and his cock sprang out, hard and resplendent.

'Nice specimen….' Eliza purred, guiding his shaft between her huge breasts.

As Eliza squashed her ample assets around his length, Aiden moaned and watched her lick her lips, knowing she was about to take him into her mouth.

• • • •

'IT'S A BIT LIKE looking for a needle in a haystack Steve,' Digger remarked whilst they cruised along the road. He glanced at the man sitting in the drivers' seat and saw the resolute expression etched across his face. He realised with a sinking feeling that it was pretty obvious Lomond wasn't going to be talked down. He sighed. He had no choice but to go along with it, just make damn sure he policed the situation. It was madness going out looking for Lacey Garner personally. Absolute *madness*. He'd have to ensure this twat didn't do anything to draw attention to either of them.

Lomond glanced angrily in Digger's direction. 'If you and your wife had got your fucking fingers out before now by getting the girl back then we wouldn't be doing this would we?'

'We haven't given up on finding Lacey. In fact, Eliza's putting in place another plan today.' Digger wasn't sure what Eliza had in mind, if anything, but he had to say *something* to placate the situation. 'It's all going well regarding the Millers and Wrights though don't you think?' he continued, hoping the change of subject would veer Lomond's mind away from this ridiculous pursuit. 'Eliza's cleverly engineered can of worms is definitely causing them to suspect each other.'

Lomond glanced at Digger again. All he'd been able to think about was this girl. He wanted her back. *That* was what he wanted to take priority, not the club or the extra money it was bringing him.

He'd surprised himself, but he knew what he wanted and this was it. He wasn't used to not getting what he desired and *demanded* he received it.

Lomond slammed his meaty hand down on the steering wheel. 'Listen, I've helped you and your poxy business more than enough already Digger. You and Eliza need to remember that. You *owe* me, got it? I can easily take everything away as quickly as I put it in. It shouldn't be *me* having to look for the girl anyway! *You* should have already done this. It's not fucking difficult. You know what I want and you need to deliver!'

Digger tried not to let the unease he felt show. *The man was obsessed with that girl.* Why couldn't he just get on with the other ones they'd put up for him? Still, he needed to keep him on side. Eliza would go mental if Lomond refused to do what they wanted. Whether he liked it or not, they *needed* him.

He gritted his teeth. 'I agree. You shouldn't have to go to this trouble. Let me put some more balls in motion and leave it to us. I'll get the results I promise.'

'You said that last time…'

'I know and we *have* looked for Lacey I can assure you of that, but I don't think we realised the extent of how much you wanted her so let us change that.'

Digger despised having to grovel, but he *had* to get the guy to back off otherwise he'd cause them no end of issues. They weren't exactly an innocuous pair and would gain attention, especially if they went round questioning girls in the back streets. *God. It didn't bear thinking about the repercussions that could bring.*

'I'll get my guys back on this straight away and I *guarantee* we'll find her in a few days.' Digger could feel the sweat trickling down his thick neck. He hadn't the first clue what else they could do aside from what they'd already done, but Eliza had better come up with something. And fast.

Lomond scowled. 'I *always* get what I want Digger.'

Digger nodded. *He didn't doubt it.* 'And you shall have it. Let's turn the car around and go for a drink somewhere and then I'll get the plan in place.'

Steve Lomond scowled. 'Ok, but on your head be it. If she isn't back by the end of the week, I'll ruin you. I'll go to Wright and tell him what I know. Do you understand?'

Digger smiled. 'Loud and clear.'

• • • •

DAN WATCHED JASON MILLER carefully as he scanned the contents of the paper for the fourth time. He couldn't read much into what was going through the man's mind, but based on the concentration and pensive expression over his face, it was unlikely to be a cut and dried conversation.

He'd gone to the Limelight as soon as he thought it feasible for Miller to have arrived for the day and straight away it had been obvious there was unrest with his staff. Since the unprovoked attack on Billie-Jo, there had been general suspicion between all the workers, purely because it still hadn't been uncovered as to who had disfigured the poor woman.

Fingers were being pointed left, right and centre because there were no unaccounted people there that day who could have entered the location where the attack happened, apart from the staff of which, until that point had all been above suspicion. Since then everyone had been questioning their own judgement and the air of unease hung thick.

After the first press release involving Linda Miller's insinuations further questions had been raised by the troops. Not that anyone had come directly to Miller and said it, but the man wasn't stupid and knew they must have been talking amongst themselves. *Questioning his involvement with a man who was giving his wife a slap*.

Jason folded up the paper and passed it across the desk to Dan. 'I presume you've seen the latest?'

Taking the paper, Dan nodded. He'd seen it first thing this morning after he'd left the brief to do his work in the police station. He'd been planning on going home to freshen up, but the minute he'd seen the article he'd made the decision to go and see Miller.

Jason watched Dan stare mutely at the paper. 'It's now starting to look bad on me. To be involved with someone who's been *formally* picked up for these offences isn't good.'

'I appreciate that, but Seth hasn't been *charged*,' Dan argued, fixing his concentration back on the paper. The papers had done a sterling job. The story had of course made the front page, carrying impossible to refute photos of a handcuffed Seth being carted off.

Violent Attack Concerns for Businesswoman

Amid speculation last week, it is now undisputed there are serious problems within Seth and Jane Wright's marriage.

Mr Wright was arrested late last night at his home after an anonymous caller reported a domestic violence incident to the police.

On arriving at the scene, officers found Mr Wright to be extremely angry, as well as difficult to control and Jane Wright very upset. Damage within some of the rooms in the Wright's house was concurrent with a violent incident.

Sergeant Barrow, present at the incident, stated: 'I can confirm after a reported incident by a member of the public, Mr Wright has been arrested on suspicion of an assault against his wife...'

When asked about the outcome of the arrest Sgt Barrow added '...it's too early at this stage to comment...'

Jane Wright, recently surrounded by rumours of a termination following an alleged affair, was taken to hospital following the violent attack. At the time of going to press it is not known as to the welfare of Mrs Wright. The hospital has declined to comment.

The reason for Mr Wright's assault on his wife is, at this stage, unknown, but an anonymous source stated '...the Wrights have been having difficulties for some time...' This backs up the statement from Linda Miller – wife of Jason Miller and business associate of Seth Wright. Our anonymous source added '...lately there have been plenty of loud arguments which have been concerning...'

The source declined to be specific over the subject of the arguments, but hinted there were accusations Mr Wright has been having an alleged affair with a much younger woman.

This latest incident points that unfortunately if Mr Wright doesn't curb his behaviour he will, if he hasn't already, soon lose the respect of this city.

In the meantime, we would all like to extend our good wishes to Mrs Wright and hope she makes a speedy recovery.

Reported by Luke Chapman

'How's Jane?' Jason said, trying to ignore Jane's alleged affair had been mentioned in the papers again.

'She's ok and has refuted the domestic violence claims – probably because there *wasn't* any!' Dan said quickly. Seth had been beside himself with the thought that he'd accidentally hurt Jane, but hadn't helped his situation by refusing to cooperate with the police, even with the brief present until Dan had got an update.

'You need to get to the bottom of it all Dan. And quick,' Jason looked up sternly with hooded eyes. 'My father has worked extremely hard to earn the reputation the Millers have in this city and it's going to take a lot of damage limitation to reduce the impact of this on me and my club,' he said.

Dan nodded mutely, unsure as to what he could say in Seth's defence. He knew Seth was capable of a lot worse violence than the general public was aware of and realised Miller was more than aware of this, but he should know Seth would never turn on Jane.

'Are you telling me you think this is true?' Dan questioned.

Jason Miller frowned and pushed a glass of whisky across the desk. 'It's irrelevant what I think personally - it's a matter of business. The general consensus is leaning towards something going on that's not good with the Wrights. Seth's been a loose cannon lately as you well know.'

Dan nodded and took the proffered glass. Recently Seth had been taking matters into his own hands a lot more, plus there was that incident from last night – turning up for a shower covered in blood which he *still* didn't know the story on. Although hearing breaking news on the radio this morning about the brutal murder of one of the paper's own reporters had given him food for thought…

He frowned. James Hill had written the last article that had been published about Seth and Jane and now he was dead.

Thankfully at this precise moment in time the police had no suspects or motive for the crime, but on the same vein, he had no intention of bringing Miller's attention to that one.

'Whatever I think Dan, this photo…' Jason prodded the newspaper, 'is irrefutable evidence Seth was arrested. Whatever the truth behind it, it's what people *perceive* isn't it?'

Dan swigged his whisky. *Jason was right. It would take one hell of a damage reversal exercise to rectify this.*

'And,' Jason continued. 'I won't associate with anything or anyone who could damage my business.'

Dan looked up quickly. 'Are you saying you're pulling your partnership?'

Jason sighed and leant back in his chair. 'I don't know what to do at this precise moment. Either way I look at it it's caused me grief which I'm not happy about.' He accepted the whole root of this story had stemmed from his own bloody wife in the first place, so didn't want to make too much of a rash judgement, but it was true. He couldn't and *wouldn't* let all the work he and his father had achieved be erased by Seth Wright. If that meant binning him off, then that was indeed what he'd do.

Jason stared at Dan. 'I'll have a think and after that I'll make my decision.'

Dan nodded. Finishing his whisky, he stood up. 'I'd best get back down the police station. Seth should be released shortly.'

Jason shook Dan's hand. 'Oh and Dan – tell Seth to give the Limelight a wide berth for a while – just until all of this shit has died down.'

Dan walked despondently from the room. Jason's final statement made it seem like he'd already made his decision.

Twenty Six

DAN EYED SETH WARILY whilst he topped up his whisky. Since being released from the station he'd been consistently drinking. It hadn't been hard to get the charges dropped without Jane giving a statement. However, Seth had not taken it well. *He hadn't taken it well in the slightest.*

Seth's mind was ticking over at ten to the dozen. He realised he'd drank well over the level to enable proper function and also knew Dan was watching his every move. Furthermore, he knew the man was itching to ask him about the elephant in the room and was pointlessly trying to gauge when would be the best time to broach the subject and how best to word it.

Seth's teeth clenched. It didn't matter *when* Dan asked or how. He'd still ask and there wasn't a best way to do it. Using all of his concentration to ignore the beady eyes fixed on him as he reached for the whisky bottle again, he sighed.

He needed to see Jane. He'd been advised to stay away for twenty-four hours to put some breathing space between them, but this was not sitting well. It wouldn't help. He *needed* to see her. He'd got to get it through to her that he hadn't been unfaithful. He *never* had and neither would he.

He didn't know what bothered him more: that Jane thought

he'd cheat, or that he'd go with someone little more than a kid. *Both, truth be told.*

Seth put the crystal tumbler to his lips, the alcohol taking its toll as he clumsily missed his mouth and slopped whisky down the front of his shirt. *Christ he was drunk.*

And what was all that about with the phone calls Jane kept receiving? The ones where someone was telling her he was having an affair? These phone calls never happened when he was there. And what about the people watching the house? Neither Martin nor Barry had seen anyone the whole time they'd been posted outside, apart from some bloke who had apparently walked Anna home one night. *That he'd be following up on.*

Seth reached clumsily over the desk for the whisky yet again, his eyebrows knitting together. *Furthermore, who'd called the police last night? None of it made any sense.*

Dan watched Seth's mind working overtime, his fingers stumbling with the screw-top cap of the whisky bottle and his jaw clenched in frustration. 'Seth, don't drink any more. You'll be no use.'

Seth laughed. A thin, hollow sound. 'Seems I'm a nuisance to *everyone* at the moment.'

Dan sighed. The last thing he needed was Seth on a drunken self-pity trip. Whether he liked it or not, he'd have to fill him in about Miller, but doing it when the man was drunk was not a good idea. *Saying that, what choice did he have*? 'Seth, you n…'

'Who called the cops?' Seth said, his steely gaze fixated on Dan.

'I've no idea, but it definitely looks like someone's out to set you up.'

Seth's eyes narrowed. 'Is there something you'd like to tell me?'

Dan sat back in his chair and raised his eyebrows. 'Are you suggesting it's *me*?'

Seth quickly stood up and much to his annoyance, staggered slightly. 'Don't get fly with me pal!' he slurred. 'I'm asking you a fucking question and I'm not in the mood for lip.'

Dan clenched his fists in frustration and fought the urge to tell Seth to fuck himself. 'It's *not* me if that's what you want to know and for the record, it's not Maggie either. Did you not notice we've put ourselves in the firing line thanks to you coming round caked in God knows whose blood. You haven't even had the decency to level with me about that and you think we'd phone the bloody cops? Seth, if I thought you'd hit Jane, I'd floor you my fucking self regardless of what you are and don't think I wouldn't.'

Seth stared at Dan and his face morphed into a scowl. *Floor him, would he? If he ever hit Jane, he'd floor himself!* He despised that it had been put about that he'd lay a finger on his beautiful wife. It was bad enough he'd accidently knocked her into that desk, but he'd *never* have hit her. All he cared about and all he'd *ever* cared about was that she and the children were safe.

'You need to take a look closer to home as to who could be stirring. Your au pair for a start?'

Calming down slightly, Seth shook his head. 'It couldn't be Anna. She hasn't got it in her. She wouldn't say boo to a goose, plus she wouldn't be that stupid!'

'How come the press were conveniently there too? It *had* to be a tip off. Whoever phoned the cops also phoned the press. It's someone with an agenda.'

Seth sat down heavily on his seat and grabbed the whisky.

Dan snatched the bottle out of his hands. 'Stop this Seth and fucking concentrate!' he barked.

Seth looked up sharply, feeling the urge to lamp Dan for his cheek, but refrained. He knew the man was speaking the truth. He needed to get this sorted. *All of it.*

'We need to find out who's betraying you and feeding this shit around.'

'Aside from Linda fucking Miller you mean?' Seth spat. *The bitch. It was probably her that called the cops. But there was no way she'd have known Jane and he were arguing. Could it be Anna after all?*

Dan inhaled deeply. *Now was the time.* 'Linda Miller isn't worth wasting your energy on, but Jason is…. He wants out….'

'*What?*' Seth slammed his fist down on the table. 'Why is that may I ask? Didn't he have the bollocks to tell me himself, the spineless bastard!'

• • • •

AIDEN MIGHT HAVE known there would be a catch. During his unexpected tryst with Eliza the other day he'd found himself eagerly agreeing to make more inroads looking for Lacey.

Eliza had made him feel special by firstly pointing out that he was being trusted to be responsible for finding Lacey and then in the same breath, she'd casually reminded him that it was due to *his* failings in the first place that the girl had escaped.

The trouble was, once Eliza had sunk herself onto his rigid shaft and begun working him like a machine, he'd have agreed to anything. *And now he was trapped.*

He knew full well she'd got one over on him with bells on. Now not only did she have the leverage to blackmail him because he knew she'd have no problem informing Digger of his 'indiscretions'. He'd done it all to himself because his need for gratification was, as usual, all consuming.

Aiden scowled as he pulled into the multi-storey car park. He glanced at the girl sitting in the passenger seat who hadn't said two words since she'd got into the car.

'Where are we going?' Selena asked. She had no idea why she'd been told to accompany Aiden into town, apart from locating Lacey Garner. The story Aiden had given her certainly hadn't matched what she'd heard from the other girls, but then again it was none of her business.

'I don't know,' Aiden answered. 'We'll have to scout around. Ask as many people as you can who look the sort who may have seen or been in contact with her.' He fished a photo of Lacey from his pocket. 'Here, take this. Say you're her sister or something. Something *believable.*'

Selina stared at the picture of the pretty girl with haunted eyes. 'Is she in trouble?' She didn't want to get involved with anything which could cause more issues. There was undoubtedly a very good reason why the girl had done a runner – Steve Lomond for one - and she didn't want to be party in bringing her back to *that.*

'Eliza's got a soft spot for her,' Aiden lied. 'She's heard on the grapevine she may be danger, so wants to locate her. Whether you believe it or not, this is for Lacey's benefit and if you try to impede what Eliza wants, I promise it won't be good,' he said, the unmistakeable threat heavy in his voice.

Nodding and although utterly unconvinced, Selena opened the car door and stepped out.

• • • •

'DAN!' MAGGIE HISSED as she pulled the kitchen door closed and dragged him halfway up the hallway. 'Are you out of your mind? We can't keep doing this.'

Dan opened his mouth to respond, but Maggie silenced him by putting her finger on his lips. 'I *mean* it! It's ridiculous.' She nodded towards the closed door. 'I told you before I wouldn't get involved with anything suspect and you're involving me. You're also involving *yourself* and I won't have it!'

'Keep your voice down,' Dan muttered, glancing up the hallway. 'He'll hear you.'

'I don't care!' Maggie said, her voice rising. 'I'll tell him myself if I have to. None of this is right and *we'll* be the ones implicated with whatever's going on here if we're not careful.' She raised her eyebrows. 'Let's face it…. *You* don't know do you?'

Dan's silence confirmed Maggie's suspicions and made her determination stronger. She had no idea what was going down and realised Dan kept a lot of it from her, but now it was obvious he was in the dark as well as her. She didn't like it. Seth's behaviour was getting much too reminiscent of the old days and she was feeling that all-encompassing cold dread every time he was on the scene which didn't bode well.

Jane had been acting erratic lately too and Maggie was sadly coming to the conclusion that it looked like it may all come round full circle. She desperately hoped not, but wasn't willing to risk Dan or herself being dragged into their shit.

'Regardless of anything else, they can't see getting back involved in this sort of shit. If it hits the fan, like it invariably will in the end, it will completely scupper getting their daughter back,' Maggie hissed. 'Being as they seem blind to that, *we're* not so it's up to *us* to stop them – for *their* sakes.'

Dan looked exasperated. 'What the hell am I supposed to do then Mags?'

Maggie rolled her eyes. 'For Christ's sake, Dan. He's got to go.'

'The man's getting it from all sides here. I can't abandon him too. Everyone's got it in for him and trying to set him up.'

'But *are* they?' Maggie spat. 'Have you questioned as to whether any of it *is* true Dan? You're forgetting I know him of old. I know what both him *and* Jane are capable of and I think you forget that sometimes. Believe me, I wish I could forget it but I can't.'

Dan stared at Maggie unsure what to say or even what he *could* say. The truth as to how she felt was coming out now. *Things were getting complicated.*

'I *knew* it would end up like this. I *never* fully believed Seth wouldn't start doing this sort of shit again. I've always said th…'

'That I was a psycho and always would be? That Jane should have left me and kept it that way? Yes, I know full well how you feel, Maggie,' Seth interrupted, making his presence known as he leant unsteadily against the door jamb.

'Seth, I…. Maggie wasn't saying th…' Dan blustered.

'Shut it Dan. I might be drunk, but I'm not fucking deaf!' Seth roared.

Maggie paled and tried to ignore the daggers Dan was glaring at her. 'We're just worried about you Seth, that's all,' she said quietly, her determination to sort the situation reversing like a getaway car. 'You'll mess up your court case and I'm worried.'

Seth sneered. 'Like hell you are. Why the fuck are you trying to make things worse? Don't you care about Jane? What do you think will happen if I keep getting set up?' he slurred. 'Don't you think that's important even if you don't give a rat's arse about me?'

Maggie folded her arms, finding a small burst of inner resolve. 'It's not that I don't care about you Seth. I do, but you shouldn't expect us to do things like this for you all the time.'

'All the time?' Seth raised one eyebrow and stumbled slightly as he moved forward. 'It's only been the once Maggie. Tell you what, I'll get out of your hair shall I? Perhaps go home and give Jane another kicking and wait to be arrested again along with everything else. That's if she hasn't already divorced me for fucking sixteen year olds!' he yelled sarcastically.

'Now you're being ridiculous!' Maggie yelled.

'Then tell me what the fuck's so important you're having problems dealing with this, will you?'

'I just don't need all this shit again ok?' Maggie screamed. Turning on her heels she ran upstairs, tears flowing down her face.

• • • •

IT HAD BEEN A long walk home, but Seth knew he needed both the time and the fresh air to sober up and sort his head out. He'd not had much choice but to leave Dan and Maggie's if he'd wanted to remain being anything near a decent person once Maggie had had once of her meltdowns. *Furthermore, what the hell was he doing standing there drunk when he should be at home with his wife?*

Fuck these people trying to cause issues. They weren't important and he'd deal with them, but the priority was Jane. These things she thought were going on: phone calls and these wild accusations… *Was she cracking up? Was all of this pressure about Grace too much?*

The hackles on Seth's neck tingled with anger at the lost time and their lost child. He shoved his hands further down in his pockets as he continued slowly along the road, his unsteadiness improving the more he walked.

It wouldn't surprise him if these bouts of paranoia Jane was getting stemmed partly from the emotional turmoil she was feeling over their daughter, along with the impact of finding out where she was. He knew it was hitting her hard and what Maggie had told him about Jane's behaviour recently in the spa was a good example of her beginning to lose it.

Rounding the corner of his road Seth spotted Barry's car not far from his driveway. Approaching the dark saloon, he tapped on the window and shrugged his shoulders questioningly. Seeing Barry shake his bullish head signifying there had been no movement or watchers to the house, Seth nodded and continued.

He smiled as his boots crunched noisily up the gravel pathway. He couldn't wait to see Jane. Every time he was away from her it was painful. It was imperative she listened to him and believed he wasn't guilty of her suspicions. He *had* to make her realise it was her mind playing tricks.

The vendetta to do with the club was a different story however and it was only a matter of time before he'd prove this was down to Miller. He had to show Jane the rest of this stuff was unfounded.

Letting himself in through the front door the house was in darkness, apart from a light in the kitchen. Seth's eyes narrowed. *Just one thing he needed to do first.*

• • • •

ANNA ALMOST DROPPED her glass of water on the kitchen floor when suddenly feeling a presence like a buzzing charge, realised someone was in the room.

Swinging around, she was astounded to see Seth two feet behind her, regarding her with steely eyes. She hadn't heard one sound to signal his arrival, yet here he was – almost upon her.

With her heart pounding, Anna attempted to replace the shock plastered across her face with a smile and opened her mouth to speak, but stopped realising Seth's expression and demeanour hinted that things were *far* from alright. She faltered, unsure of what to do or say. Her nervousness was glaringly obvious.

Looking at what she could see behind Seth's green eyes, Anna felt an invisible ice-cold finger of fear tap her on the shoulder. Overriding the constricted feeling in her throat, she managed to force her words out. 'Mr Wright,' she squeaked. 'You're back!'

Seth smiled thinly and took a step towards her. 'Yes, it seems I am…'

Aware she was now trapped between Seth and the work surface, Anna couldn't pull her eyes away from him and stood stiff with fear waiting for him to speak. In the close proximity between them she could smell spirits on Seth's breath and could see he'd been drinking. *Whisky at a guess and a hell of a lot of it.*

Her eyes darted across the room, realising there really was no way to get past this man without physically pushing him out of the way and that was not a plausible route to take.

'So,' Seth drawled. 'Was it *you* who enlightened the police last night?'

Seth's voice coming unexpectedly after such a long silence startled Anna further and the question's subject worried her even more. *Shit! What the hell did she do now?* 'M-Me?' she stammered meekly.

'Yes, *you*!' Seth growled, placing one hand on the work surface to the left of her, trapping her further into position. His body was now only six inches from hers and she forced herself to look into his eyes, more than aware of his over-dominant position.

Anna quickly lowered her eyes to the floor. 'I-I didn't call the police on you Mr Wright. I wouldn't do that.' *Well it was true. She might have called Aiden and told him what was happening, but she'd only done that because she'd been terrified and hadn't known what else to do.*

She'd been as surprised as they had when the police arrived. She wouldn't have called Aiden if she'd known he would do that, but he was most likely trying to protect her. He seemed good like that.

Seth's mouth formed into a grimace. 'Why else would they have turned up in the middle of an argument if it wasn't you Anna? Tell me that! There may be several people who'd love to set me up, but it would be an amazing coincidence if someone outside of the house happened to *guess* the best time for the cops to arrive….' He smiled savagely, baring his straight white teeth. 'How do you explain that?'

Anna stared at the floor, knowing she was acting guilty as sin, which of course in a way she was.

Seth gripped Anna's face with his hand and pulled it firmly up so she was forced to meet his eyes. 'Well?'

'I-It wasn't me who phoned either of them Mr Wright,' she repeated, hoping against hope he'd buy it.

Seth studied Anna's face. He *knew* she wasn't being straight. She knew *something* about it and he felt like giving her a slap. 'I'll find out you know,' he sneered, the faint hint of a smile across his full mouth as he released his grip. 'Ok, so try this one… It had to be *you* who spoke to the press.'

Fighting the urge to touch where Seth's hand had gripped her face, Anna knew there was little point denying that one. 'T-They cornered me and I panicked. I didn't say all that stuff though, I swear. They've twisted it around.' She'd seen the newspaper and had been horrified. It was obvious she'd been the source. Who else could have been interviewed at the scene with 'inside' knowledge?

In all honesty she'd been so frightened and confused she couldn't remember what she'd said to that pushy reporter, but regardless, the most insinuating parts of her statement had been twisted around and bolted together.

'I-I'm sorry if what they've quoted me as saying has made things worse. He just kept firing questions at me and wouldn't let me back into the house. I needed to get to Toby.'

Seth scowled. *Another reporter he'd have to pay a fucking visit to then?* He walked over to the fridge, grabbed a can of lager and leant back against the work surface, studying Anna.

Anna stood unmoving. *Could she go now?* ‘I-I’m glad you’re back and it’s all sorted out anyway,’ she muttered, attempting to take a step towards the door.

Pushing quickly away from where he leant, Seth easily blocked Anna’s path. ‘Just one last thing… Who the fuck brought you home the other week? What’s his name and has he been in my fucking house?’

Twenty Seven

SELENA KEPT WALKING. This was the third day in a row she'd gone around town for hours in what, as far as she was concerned, was a near impossible task.

On the upside, despite the pain from her blistered feet, she'd quite willingly spend the rest of time looking for Lacey Garner if it got her out of having to service Steve Lomond. *Or any of the others for that matter*.

She turned into a small street leading to a marketplace. Seeing a café that looked still to be open, she smiled. She'd just grab a quick drink. Her mouth was parched and she needed to rest her feet for a couple of minutes. Surely she was allowed a break?

She pushed open the door and gratefully flopped into an empty plastic chair. Ordering a diet coke, she glanced around the café. She smiled watching two women over the opposite side attempting to hold down a conversation in between having Playmobil figures shoved in their faces for the thousandth time that day.

Selena glanced at the girl sitting at the next table, noticing she was also looking at the two women and inwardly smiling in sympathy. As their eyes met, Selena smiled shyly. It would be so nice to have friends like a normal person her age, but of course that was impossible.

'Rather them than me....' the girl muttered.

Selena grinned. 'I agree! Have you just finished work?'

The girl smiled back. 'Just about to start actually.' Seeing the confusion on the young girl's face, she laughed. 'I'm a cleaner. I start at half five.'

'Have you been doing that long?'

'A few months. I quite like it actually. It's at the book shop down the road. Hadley's. Do you know it?'

Selena shook her head. 'No, I don't.' Remembering she had to maintain a story when talking to others she got her brain in gear, swallowing down the resentment that she could never be herself. 'I'm not from around here. I've been to visit my cousin.' She nodded her thanks as the waitress deposited her drink on the table.

'I'm Jennie by the way,' the girl said.

Selena smiled. 'I'm Jill,' she lied. 'My cousin's friend has gone missing. She fell out with her folks and took off a couple of weeks ago. No one's seen her since.' She bit her lip in fake concern. 'Her mother's going crazy. It's a nightmare.'

Jennie raised her hand to her mouth. 'What's she going to do?'

'I have no idea. Hey, I don't suppose *you've* seen her, have you?' Selena said. *It was a long shot but worth a try....*

Jennie smiled. 'I doubt it. I don't see or know many people.'

Selena fished out the photograph of Lacey from her handbag. 'The least I can do is ask. My cousin's going spare worrying about her.'

Jennie took the photograph and glanced at it. *Was that Lacey?* The girl in the picture had different hair and was wearing heavy blue eye makeup, but still looked very similar. 'Oh my God! I think I *do* know her!'

'You do?' Selena nearly choked in surprise. 'Where is she?'

'What's this girl's name?' Jennie asked flabbergasted.

'Her name's Lacey, but she could be calling herself

something else being as she took off. She's supposed to be starting a scholarship at that sixth form college – you know – Sacred Hearts – in a few weeks and now she's throwing it all away over a silly argument.'

Jennie stared. *Sacred Hearts?* That was the very expensive private college and the fees there were extortionate. *So Lacey wasn't who she made out herself to be?* She'd *thought* she'd been vague when they'd shared their histories. That was because Lacey's had all been lies.

Jennie felt winded with hurt and humiliation. *How stupid she'd been*. She'd been brutally honest about the shit life she'd had, whilst Lacey had been *pretending* she'd had a tough time when really she'd had a privileged upbringing. *And she'd taken up a place at the hostel, the selfish bitch?*

Anger radiated from Jennie. 'Yes, I know her. Well, I don't know her much at all,' she snapped. *That was quite obvious.* 'She works in the shop where I clean.'

'Do you know where she lives?' Selena asked hurriedly.

Jennie got up from the table, not in the mood to answer further questions. The sense of betrayal she felt towards the girl she'd begun to think of as a good friend was painful. 'I need to go. I'm going to be late.'

'But can you ju...'

'Look, I don't know anything else alright?' Without looking back, Jennie quickly left the café.

• • • •

JANE HAD PICKED up everything she'd needed from the shops so began making her way back to the car, stopping momentarily to buy a newspaper. Standing in the shop she quickly flicked through the pages, pleased to see the photographs she and Seth had posed for taking prominent positions.

They were quite nice. She ran her finger along Seth's jaw in the image as she scrutinised the pictures. It had been her idea. She'd felt it would be beneficial for Seth if together they publicly laid the speculation about their marriage being in crisis to rest and quashed the domestic violence rumours by posing for a series of pictures.

The photographer had been exceptionally good, capturing *exactly* what she'd been hoping to convey. One of the pictures showed them relaxing on the sofa: Seth was reclining back with one arm around her laughing and she had her feet up on his lap, staring at him adoringly.

On another, he was standing behind her in the garden, his shirt open at the neck and his sleeves rolled up to his elbows. His lips were on her neck and his hands caressed her shoulders.

The article had simply stated: '*It's plain to see there is nothing whatsoever amiss in the Wright's marriage*'.

Jane smiled. For once the press had done something worthwhile. She hurried along the road, eager to get home so they could get on the road. It would be a long drive.

Passing the large front window of an up-market coffee house Jane saw Jason and Linda Miller sitting at a table. She paused. They were deep in conversation. *Probably discussing how they could turn Seth over again...*

Anger bubbling, Jane yanked open the door and ignoring the waiter poised to seat newcomers, pushed past leaving him staring after her in confusion.

She strode unhesitatingly through the zig-zag of tables, well aware most eyes were on her. Without a second's hesitation she walked straight to the Miller's table and slammed her bag in the centre of it. 'I can't begin to tell you how disappointed I am in you,' she hissed.

Seeing the shock flood Jason's face, Jane knew she'd caught him off guard. 'I find it difficult to understand why you'd believe ludicrous bullshit rumours contrived by sad, jealous bitches over what you know personally to be fact Jason.' Jane shot Linda a pointed look, noticing the woman was unable to raise her eyes from the floor, like it held the embodiment of Christ.

Jason turned a deep shade of red, sensing everyone in the coffee shop was looking at them. Half of them, if not *all* could hear too. 'Jane... this isn't the time or the place...'

Jane laughed loudly and placed her hands on her hips. 'Everywhere is an inappropriate time and place where *you're* concerned being as you lack the bollocks to say anything to the people your actions affect! You'd rather send messages through the grapevine.' She glared at Linda again. 'I'm surprised being as you usually have no problem with discussing people's business regardless of whether it's right or wrong.'

'It was nothing personal. I had to make a decision based on th...'

'*You* had to make a decision?' Jane interrupted Jason. 'How *dare* you disrespect my husband! By glibly jacking off your association is as good as publicly announcing he's guilty!'

Jason frowned. 'I said nothing of the sort!'

'As good as, Jason. As good as.' Jane interjected, prodding Linda hard in the shoulder. 'As for *you*....'

'Jane,' Linda began in her nasally put on upper-class voice. 'You're blowing this out of proportion bec...'

'Blowing it out of proportion?' Jane shouted. 'It's acceptable to fabricate stories that destroy people is it?' She leant down level with Linda's ear and lowered her voice. 'I strongly suggest you keep your plastic fucking mouth shut and never take it upon yourself to speak shite about my family again.'

Jane enjoyed watching Linda pale with every word she uttered. 'I'd quite happily slap those fucking lies from your head if it wasn't so crowded in here, but if I hear *one* more piece of vicious shit from you,' she turned to Jason, '*or* you, then rest assured I will!'

She grabbed her bag from the table and turned away from Linda, glad that she could see the woman's hands shaking. 'As far as I'm concerned Jason, any friendship we've ever had is *done*. No one disrespects me, my husband or my family. Do you understand?'

Without waiting for an answer, Jane turned and walked straight out of the coffee house, turning on her flashbulb-worthy smile for the benefit of the host of spectators as she left.

Twenty Eight

JANE KNEW SETH WAS scrutinising her from his position in the hotel bedroom. She could feel his eyes burning into her without even looking. She still wasn't comfortable with what had been going on.

When he'd come in the other night still drunk, her first instinct had been to start screaming and throw him out and it had got even worse when he'd started suggesting her paranoia was because of Grace.

Paranoia? She wasn't imagining the things that had been happening. He was trying to make out she was crazy!

Jane frowned. Whether she liked it or not it she had to agree that a vendetta over the clubs wouldn't include the sorts of things she'd had happen, but why had no one else witnessed what she'd experienced? *It was all too confusing.*

Jane accepted Seth hadn't been playing away. She'd already felt bad she'd been gullible enough to believe the bullshit that caller had spouted.

Seth had promised he'd get to the bottom of what was going on, but first he'd wanted to take her away. *They were going to go and see Grace.*

In the car on the long drive down Jane knew Seth had been

trying to get her to open up, but she'd been locked inside herself. The elation about seeing her daughter again had been replaced with anxiety. How would she keep herself at a distance when she got the proof she was expecting: that her daughter was unhappy and mistreated? How was she expected to walk away at the end? *How would she cope with any of it?*

The answer was that she couldn't. Although Seth had made her promise they wouldn't approach the girl and needed to do things properly, she wasn't looking forward to seeing first-hand what horrors her daughter had been exposed to because of them. *It would rip her right to the core and she knew it.*

Seth watched the expressions passing across Jane's face in the mirror's reflection and knew her mind was working overtime. He stared transfixed as Jane eased her loose silky light-blue top over her head. Standing with her back to him, she brushed her long raven hair in the mirror, the matching pale blue bra and knickers setting off her light tan perfectly.

His eyes roamed over her breasts spilling from the silken and lace cups of the bra to the remains of the still visible bruise on her upper arm and another pang of guilt for inadvertently hurting her flooded him.

Trying to distract himself from the erection throbbing mercilessly as he stared at the women he loved so dearly, Seth looked around the room. The hotel he'd booked last minute was very nice indeed with its four-poster bed and sumptuous linen. It had been a long drive to get down to St Ives, but it was something they needed to do – Jane especially. At least she now believed he hadn't slept with Lacey. The rest he could deal with, but for now, being here and doing what Jane needed was his priority.

Seth's eyes moved back to his wife. *She was the most gorgeous creature on the planet.* Unable to help himself he wrapped his hand around his length, desperate to feel some release. 'Come here…' he groaned.

Jane turned from the mirror and smiled mischievously.

'Hurry up woman!' Seth growled and kneeled up, his

erection proud. 'Have you not seen this? Can you not see what you do to me?'

He'd wanted her from the second he'd seen her. Always had and always would. That she could believe he'd ever want anyone other than her physically hurt. There was absolutely *nothing* to dilute the overwhelming love, lust and utter want he had for this woman. Grabbing Jane's hand, he pulled her onto the bed and peeled off her knickers.

'Seth,' Jane moaned, the physical need for her husband betrayed the anger and hurt of the past few days.

Seth pulled Jane to the edge of the bed. 'Now, you stay right there,' he instructed, dropping to the floor. Quickly delving his tongue into her, he probed and sucked, pleased to hear her moan with pleasure.

Jane began pushing herself against Seth's mouth and groaning, steadily moved her hips.

Seth lapped and sucked, his tongue dancing rhythmically on Jane's clitoris. He wanted to be inside her. He'd *live* inside her if it were possible. He increased his speed – loving her taste, loving the way she felt on his tongue and she pulled at his hair, her breathing coming in short, gasping pants.

Bucking her hips, Jane came hard, the waves of her rushing climax consuming her. Whilst she was still contracting with the after throes of orgasm, Seth pulled her closer to the edge of the bed and pushed his fingers into her, making swirling thrusting movements whilst his other hand ran steadily down his rock-hard cock.

Seth watched Jane writhe below him, her eyes half-closed and unable to hold out any longer, entered her. Feeling the effect of her velvety wetness as he pushed into her easily yielding flesh, he moaned as he filled her. Groaning with need, he thrust deep.

'I'm going to come again!' Jane cried, feeling another orgasm rapidly approach.

'Come babe,' Seth growled, feeling her tightening around his cock. 'I love you Jane and I'll make you come hard all night.'

Jane abandoned herself to the crescendo of sensations for the second time. There was nothing she could do about all of the 'what ifs' of the coming day, so there was little point in worrying about it.

She'd worry about it tomorrow.

• • • •

TINA TRIED HER BEST to concentrate on what Aiden was talking about, but she was rattling for a hit and wondered when it might be good timing to slip into the conversation about more credit. She tried to stop her teeth from grinding, but knew they would, regardless of what she wanted and in the heavy silence of the small room she hoped he couldn't hear it.

She was getting more and more pissed off. Eliza *still* hadn't delivered on the deal she'd promised in return for information because there was still no Lacey.

It was all really unfair. Without *her*, Eliza would have jack shit and wouldn't have been able to achieve half of what she'd managed to pull off so far. To top it all, she'd got that desperate for cash yesterday she'd forced herself to pay her mother another visit to see if she could cadge a loan.

Again, all the old witch had been interested in was asking about Anna. Christ, at this rate the chances of her paying off her debt was disappearing quicker than piss in a festival toilet.

'Well? What do you think?' Aiden said, abruptly jolting Tina from her thoughts.

'Sorry. I was just thinking about something,' Tina muttered quickly.

'I hope it was useful as I haven't got all day!' Aiden snapped. He wasn't in the best of moods. Against his better judgement he'd had to service Eliza again this morning and it had been an *extremely* close call. Only moments after he'd done his flies back up had Digger lumbered into the office. Eliza might not be getting as much attention as she needed from the man, but Aiden valued his prize jewels, which would not remain attached if that man got wind of what was going on.

Aiden had been able to tell by the expression on Eliza's heavily made-up face that she found this 'sailing close to the wind' game they'd been playing lately exciting, but *he* didn't. Wasn't it bad enough that he'd got a call from Anna last night and he'd been less than happy over what he'd learnt? Now this drug-addled bitch Tina was giving him the run around – staring off into space like a fucking zombie. *He didn't have time for this crap.*

'What was the question again?' Tina mumbled.

Aiden sighed and slammed his fist down on the desk. 'For fuck's sake! I've already told you your fucking sister was questioned and all but threatened by Seth-fucking-Wright. He'd heard she's got some kind of 'boyfriend'…' He wiped droplets of spittle that had sprayed from his mouth in rage off his chin. 'Everything and I mean *everything* will go tits up if he puts two and two together. Namely I'll be fucking DEAD!'

Tina forced herself to recall what he'd said previously. 'So, she told him you'd been to the house?'

Aiden ran his fingers through his blond hair. 'Well not exactly. She told him I'd walked her home. Said I was a friend… Thankfully she had the sense to deny I'd been inside, thank God!'

'Holy shit!' Tina cried. *This was all they needed.*

'He asked for my name, but Anna gave him a false one,' Aiden added. He'd nearly had a coronary until Anna swore down she hadn't given Seth Wright his name. It wouldn't have taken long to be found if that had been the case.

Tina frowned. 'I'm surprised Anna had the nous to do that. She doesn't know you're involved in any of this does she?'

Aiden shook his head. 'Of course not. Do you think I'm stupid? The only reason Anna didn't shop me was to save her *own* neck,' he spat. 'Boyfriends or visitors aren't allowed and she doesn't want her lies discovered.'

'Sounds like she's finally learning something!' Tina laughed, attempting to joke.

'It was done purely from panic,' Aiden scoffed. 'Your

sister's a fucking liability Tina. The only things she knows about is what you're doing – again all lies, but it won't be long before she realises you're involved with me. She's the sort who'll start flapping her gums. Can we not bin her off before it's too late?'

'No!' Tina wailed. 'It's the only way I can get the info so Eliza will pay me. You want your fucking money for my debt, don't you? Without Anna I'd be fucked! And your involvement with her gets you brownie points so what's the problem? Besides she believes what I've been telling her. She won't risk losing her job or upsetting our mother.'

Aiden almost laughed before shaking his head in despair. 'Yes, I do want my fucking money, but we need to move quicker than this. Eliza will be in a good mood when I tell her Selena's discovery of the location of Lacey Garner, but until we can get that confirmed it's still up in the air.'

Tina laughed. 'In the meantime, get our mother topped, then I'll tell Anna Seth bumped off the old bat! After all the shit I've fed her she'll believe that no questions asked. You'd get all your money back in one go that way too.' She leant back in the chair smugly. 'Oh it would be *so* funny! I don't think I'd be able to keep a straight face if I saw her receive *that* news.'

'You're bloody mad you are,' Aiden snorted jovially. 'I thought you were serious for a minute then!'

Tina stared at Aiden as she leaned forward towards the desk, all mirth now absent from her face. 'I *am* serious Aiden. I'd be quite happy if the old bitch was removed. It would save me a whole lot of grief and I'd be able to finally get some fucking money out of the selfish cow.'

Aiden studied Tina carefully. *She was serious the twisted slag.* He scratched his chin slowly. 'You'd need to think about that very carefully Tina…'

'I've been thinking of nothing else most of my life,' Tina replied dully.

Twenty Nine

LACEY TRIED TO CONCENTRATE on where she was putting the books on the shelves, but couldn't get her mind into gear. She had no idea what had happened during the last twenty-four hours to elicit such a change, but it had most certainly occurred and she didn't know what to do about it.

She'd been looking forward to seeing Jennie last night, however when she'd got back to Pegasus Place, she wasn't in the communal lounge like they'd arranged.

Lacey had waited patiently for half an hour, thinking she must have got held up, before eventually deciding she'd go and try her room.

She'd gently knocked on Jennie's bedroom door. Receiving no answer, she'd knocked once more. 'Jennie, it's Lacey. Are you ok?' she'd called, concerned her friend might be ill.

'Go away!'

Momentarily confused, Lacey had stared at the white wooden door for several seconds before knocking again. 'Jennie?'

The door had flung open taking Lacey completely off guard. Jennie stood in the doorway, her rage twisted with rage. 'What the fuck do you want?' she'd spat.

Lacey had been shocked. 'Jennie? What's happened? Are you ok?'

'I'm ok, yeah *I'm* ok, but *you* aren't!' Jennie yelled, her eyes blazing.

'W-What are you talking about?' Lacey had been thoroughly confused.

Jennie had laughed nastily and prodded Lacey hard in the chest. 'Had your laugh have you, you stuck up bitch!'

Lacey had continued to stare blankly at Jennie, unable to answer through shock alone.

'Pretending you don't know? Your little game's been found out and you and your posh mates won't be having any more fucking laughs at *my* expense!'

'Laughs? What do you mean?' *What on earth was she talking about?* 'I don't understand.'

'Go on. Fuck off. Go back to Mummy and Daddy and your mates at Sacred Hearts, you selfish cow! How *dare* you take a place here pretending your life's fucked up,' Jennie had screamed.

When the door had slammed in Lacey's face, she'd shakily made her way slowly down to her own room before bursting into tears of shock. It made no sense…. *Mummy and Daddy? Sacred Hearts? What was Sacred Hearts?*

Lacey had been sure it must have been a misunderstanding and that it would all come to light by the morning, but she'd been wrong. Whatever had been eating at Jennie hadn't been rectified, because judging by the reception she'd received from the other girls this morning Lacey realised Jennie must have filled them in on whatever she was supposed to have done because *everyone* had blanked her. Apart from one girl who'd spat at her when she'd left to go to work.

Lacey felt heartbroken. She'd been alienated and had no idea why. Now she'd lost her only friend.

Suddenly realising she'd got company, Lacey turned from the History shelf and promptly dropped two of the new books she'd been about to shelve on the floor. Cursing under her breath she looked up, seeing a young girl perusing one of the shelves.

Remembering she was paid to be of help to customers rather than wallow in her own self-pity, Lacey forced herself to get it together. 'Are you alright over there? Do you need any help?'

Selena looked around and tried to remember what she was supposed to say if she was spoken to. She'd only come in to get a proper look at the girl to make sure they got the right one.

She fidgeted nervously. Aiden would be doing his nut. She'd promised to only be a couple of minutes. *It wasn't like she wanted a conversation.*

Although she'd only had a glimpse of Lacey once or twice at Elipse there was still a possibility the girl might recognise her, especially if she hung around too long, but she couldn't return without confirming this girl was the right one.

Remembering she'd been asked a question, Selena stumbled over her words. 'I, erm…. No. Well, I *was* looking for a book on Cross-stitch….' *Cross-stitch?* She cringed. *Why on earth had she said that? Why hadn't she just said horror fiction or something?*

'I'm not sure if we have anything like that,' Lacey said, stepping out from behind the bookcase. 'We mainly do fiction here, but I'll have a look for you.' She studied the nervous girl. 'Don't I know you from somewhere?'

'I don't think so,' Selena garbled, panic descending upon her like a landslide. *Fuck! She needed to get out of here.* This was *definitely* without any doubt Lacey Garner and if she got wind she was from Elipse then everything would be buggered up.

Selena moved towards the door and Lacey frowned as she searched for the requested book. 'I won't be a moment.' *There was something strange going on here. Was this girl a shoplifter? Was she trying to distract her?*

'I'd better go, but thanks for your help.' Selena muttered, sweating profusely.

'What about your book?' Lacey questioned, her eyebrow raised in curiosity.

'Oh, erm, I'll have to come back. I'll miss my bus else,' Selena jabbered, quickly disappearing out of the door.

• • • •

JANE SAT IN THE passenger seat of Seth's Mercedes and fiddled nervously with her nails. She'd had very little sleep and hadn't been able to even manage more than one bite from the lavish breakfast that had been ordered to the hotel room first thing this morning.

She knew she'd been getting on Seth's nerves pacing around, but she just couldn't sit still and wait for the time to pass. She'd been waiting *years* for this moment.

Finally, after what seemed like centuries they'd got into the car and on the road and had made good time in finding the school where they'd been told their daughter attended. It was situated a few miles from St Ives and was a quintessential village school: a tiny building, housing around fifty children within its Victorian walls. It also boasted a neat playground, surrounded by old ornate wrought iron railings.

'Mulligan gave me a photo of Grace's adoptive mother,' Seth began after they'd parked up, reaching into his pocket. 'It came through as we left yesterday. I meant to show you last night. It means we'll be able to work out who our daughter is depending who she runs to.'

'I'll know our daughter the *second* I lay eyes on her,' Jane snapped, snatching the photograph from Seth's hand. A woman with a pleasant face stared back at her. She studied it closely, putting the woman in her early forties with a chin-length mid-brown bob, kind eyes and a large smile. 'And this is her *mother* is it?' Jane snarled. *Where was the dead-eyed addict she'd expected?*

'Mulligan couldn't get his hands on any photos of Grace,' Seth explained. 'I did ask.'

'Like I said, I don't need a photograph. I'll *know* her!'

Seth sighed. He knew Jane was finding this difficult and began to question whether this had been a good idea. So far it seemed detrimental rather than helpful, which was the last thing he'd wanted.

Jane's stomach was in her mouth as she kept her eyes trained on the door of the school. She eyed the group of happy mothers waiting patiently for their children to come through the door and swallowed the lump in her throat. *She too was waiting for her child. The one who didn't know she was her mother.*

Seth studied Jane's face out of the corner of his eye without moving his concentration from the woman on the photograph at the school gate. He knew Jane was coiled like a spring. He squeezed her hand.

Jane's heart was beating at ten to the dozen and she couldn't wait to get the proof to back up the theory she'd clung desperately to all of these years. She'd easily be able to detect the visible misery on her daughter's face the moment she saw her. The minute she had this confirmation she'd be out of the car like a shot. No one would be able to stop her. *Even Seth.*

She'd give the bitch putting her daughter through hell and masquerading as Grace's mother a damn fine fucking kicking to within an inch of her life. And she didn't care if she had an audience.

Even though Jane had been absent Grace's entire life, she knew she'd have that unbreakable bond which existed between blood that nothing could take away. She'd get her daughter back where she belonged.

Hearing the church bell opposite chime signalling the quarter hour, adrenaline pumped harder in Jane's veins, her breathing shallow. Her neck craned forward when the school doors opened and a stream of children erupted from the old building. Her eyes frantically searched each young girl's face as they rushed towards their waiting parents.

Jane suddenly clutched Seth's hand. 'There Seth!' she cried. Her eyes locked onto the small girl beaming with happiness as she ran towards the woman on the photograph. *Hang on a moment...*

Jane leant further forward, her hand poised on the car door handle and squinted to get a better view. *That child wasn't her daughter.* 'Seth,' she muttered, the words all but sticking in her throat as her heart plummeted directly down to the pits of despair. 'That's not Grace. That's not her…'

'What do you mean? Of course it's her!' Seth watched the dark-haired child run towards the woman on the photograph and smiled involuntarily seeing the joy plastered over both his daughter's and the woman's face as she picked her up, planting kisses all over her face.

'That's NOT our daughter!' Jane screamed. She pulled at the door handle, but Seth's hand shot across and held her like a vice. 'Get off me Seth!' she cried.

'Don't do this Jane,' Seth warned, aware she'd been about to bolt from the car.

'Get the fuck off! That's not our Grace!' Jane roared, fighting against him. *She had to get out. She needed to make sure she was right.*

'JANE!' Seth yelled, aware people were walking past their car to get in their own. 'Control yourself!'

Jane slowly relinquished her struggling and flopped back in the seat as the child and the woman walked towards them. With her heart in her mouth she took another clear look at the girl who was now mere *feet* away.

A single tear rolled down her cheek. 'That child is *not* my daughter…' Jane whispered against the glass of the passenger seat window. 'Your man was wrong…'

Seth ran his hand through his hair. *Wrong? How could Mulligan have been wrong? It wasn't possible…*

• • • •

'DID YOU HAVE TO bring the bloody kid?' Aiden grumbled staring at the baby in the pushchair.

Anna waved a toy bunny rabbit in Toby's direction and smiled as he giggled at the distraction, reaching out for the toy with his chubby fingers. 'What do you mean?' she asked, turning to stare at Aiden. 'Of course I had to bring him. It's my job, not my day off. I'm taking him for his usual afternoon stroll. This was the best I could do when you phoned asking to see me.'

She was disappointed. She'd felt things were going off the boil with Aiden – from his side at least and now his comment confirmed her opinion. He hadn't been very attentive and had been looking for reasons why he couldn't see her each time she suggested meeting up. Now he'd called her asking to see her today. *Was it to dump her?*

'Do you not want to see me anymore?' Anna asked timidly. *She knew he wanted to dump her.* Systemic trembling began all over her body as she painstakingly waited for the answer she didn't want to hear.

So much for her plans of a *proper* relationship. He was the one – she knew it. She'd given herself to him, which was a big deal - to her at least and she'd thought he'd felt the same, but he didn't. *Of course he didn't. Why would he?*

Aiden realised he needed to pull himself together and up his game. He'd been so focused on how much he hated having to mollycoddle this stupid cow, he'd forgotten he was supposed to be in love with her.

However ridiculous the whole thing was and however much it pissed him off, he had no choice. He'd have to do a better job and quickly. From what she'd just said it sounded like he'd been horribly unconvincing and that wouldn't go down well at all with his puppet masters.

He scowled. *Fucking Puppet Masters.* That was about right. It was *exactly* how he felt and knew he'd only got himself to blame. Still, he needed to get on with it and not lose sight of what he was supposed to be achieving. Especially with what was planned for later, which – if it all went to plan – might mean he could afford to step back from his involvement with Eliza. He might even be able to afford to leave the Elipse altogether.

Things were moving fast. *Too fast.* But he had no choice and even less say in any of it. Sometimes he wished he wasn't involved in at all. If Seth Wright ever found out in any way, shape or form about his part in any of this, then his days were numbered. *Probably in single figures....*

Taking a deep breath, Aiden turned to Anna and smiled,

gently brushing a lock of her brown hair away from her face. 'Oh baby, of *course* I still want to see you. I'm sorry if I've made you feel that way. That's the *last* thing I want.'

Seeing Anna's face crumple with relief, Aiden smiled and forced himself to take the baby out of her arms to bounce him on his knee. *Bloody kids! He hated them.*

'I'm sorry if I've been distracted, I really am. It's just things have been really hard at work the last few weeks.' Aiden looked towards the floor, forcing a suitably sorrowful expression. 'I think I may be about to lose my car sales job.'

Anna's hand flew up to her face. 'Oh my God! Why didn't you say?'

'Because I didn't want to worry you,' he murmured, hoping he was pulling this feeble excuse off. He'd barely mentioned *any* job purposefully so as to not put himself in a precarious position. Anna had no idea he worked with Tina and he needed it to stay that way.

'But Aiden, I....'

'Shh....' Aiden said, placing his finger on Anna's lips. Moving Toby over on to his other knee, he pressed his lips gently against hers. 'I'll make it up to you, I promise.'

'When can we see each other next?' she asked. '*Properly* I mean.'

Handing Toby back to Anna, Aiden hid the scowl as he eyed a trail of dribble across his new jeans. 'Well, I've got things to do tonight, but we could arrange something over the next day or two? When's your next day off?'

Busy tonight, was he? Anna thought jealously. *Probably seeing another woman who was far more interesting.* 'I can't have any time off until Seth and Jane get back,' Anna said miserably, strapping Toby back securely into his pushchair.

'Back?' Aiden raised his eyebrows. 'Where have they gone?' *He didn't know they were away.* This scuppered tonight's plans. *Christ. It was a good job he'd seen Anna. Had all of this gone through tonight he'd be hard pushed making her believe what was going to happen was down to Seth.*

Anna shrugged. 'I'm not sure where they've gone. Down south, I think. Why?'

Aiden forced himself to look interested. 'No reason, just wondered that's all. It's just weird I suppose – my girlfriend working for celebrities.' *There. She'd like that.*

Anna warmed hearing Aiden refer to her as his 'girlfriend'. 'They're not really celebrities.'

Aiden laughed. 'They are in this city and in our sort of circles.'

'*Our* circles? What sort of circles are they?'

Aiden could have kicked himself for slipping up so grotesquely. 'I meant just in the city that's all....'

Anna frowned. 'I would hardly say we were part of *their* sort of circles. With the things *they* do....' She wanted no part of what it seemed she now knew Seth and Jane Wright were capable of.

Aiden studied Anna's face. *Maybe now was time to have a bit of a dig around?* 'I know you were shaken up with what happened before with Seth but...'

'It's worse than that,' Anna interrupted. 'You've no idea. There's a lot more going on with that man than you realise.'

Aiden knitted his fingers through Anna's and smiled. 'Like what baby?' *The stories were obviously getting to her. This was good.*

Anna shook her head. Although she trusted Aiden, she didn't want to broadcast that her sister was blackmailing her or what she'd heard Seth and Jane had done to that poor man with the disabled children in case it led back to her and made things worse. 'I can't say, but they're not nice people. I realise that now.'

She studied a group of daisies on the grass in front of the park bench they were sitting on. She'd thought of nothing else for the past few days since Jane and Seth had argued and had felt more and more uncomfortable around them. She'd little choice but to find another job, but couldn't just up and leave because she needed the money. However, she would have to start looking for another position. She needed to be true to herself and she just wasn't happy working for that sort.

Aiden realised that now wasn't the time to push further. 'Well if they're away, why don't I come round and keep you company?'

Anna looked up surprised. 'I thought you had things to do?'

Aiden brought his lips back down onto Anna's. 'Nothing that's more important than you....' He may as well get a bit more into her good books if he had the chance and if the other job was off the cards for the time being.

Anna smiled, loving the feeling of warmth which trickled down from where his lips had been right into the core of her being. 'You know I'm not supposed to have anyone in the house. It was a close call before and Seth was suspicious.'

Aiden grinned. 'We'll just have to be careful then won't we! What they don't know can't hurt them. Or us...'

THIRTY

'FOR FUCK'S SAKE DIGGER!' Eliza snapped, her patience wearing thin. 'How many more times do I have to tell you? We need to go and get her back. *Now!*'

Digger scowled, trying not to look at the CCTV screen Eliza was watching which showed a girl in Room Nine riding a punter's face like a bicycle.

As the girl sat on the man's face looking like she was all but suffocating him, the man – a heavy-set guy, naked apart from a pair of frilly pink knickers thrust his hips into thin air, his engorged member broken free from the tight lacy underwear.

Digger stared in morbid fascination when the man began ejaculating over his own stomach for what seemed like for ever. 'Christ!' he muttered in disgust.

Eliza slapped Digger sharply on the arm. 'Are you even listening to me or are you too busy getting off watching men come over themselves?' *He might well have turned gay the amount of attention he'd given her recently.*

Digger scowled. 'I heard you Eliza, but I've told you before we need to watch Lacey for the next few days to work out her movements. We need to get this bang on.' *God, the woman was impatient. Did she not realise by now these things took time to do properly?*

Eliza slammed a notebook down sharply on the desk. 'We haven't got fucking time have we! That fat bastard is on the prowl and what if she disappears again? Have you thought of that?' She wasn't prepared to sit around and let that little bitch slip through her fingers for the *second* time.

Neither did she want Lomond steaming in and taking the girl in plain daylight. Exposing them all in his desperation to all and sundry. *She needed to be in control of this.*

'Chill out Eliza!' Digger snapped. 'I've got Lomond under control. Trust me, it's all sorted. Lacey will be back. I just need a couple of days to spec everything out to make sure there are no fuck ups and it can get done in one go.'

Eliza huffed petulantly and stared at her long nail extensions. *He'd better come up with the goods. Men were so bloody laid back half the time and it made her sick.*

'I'm watching her tonight myself and then either I, or Aiden will repeat that tomorrow,' Digger said. 'If everything adds up, we'll take her the day after.'

Eliza nodded. 'Fine. Aiden's with that snotty bitch Anna tonight. He'll be doing some digging at the Wrights whilst they're absent, but I'll make him available tomorrow – that's unless the Wrights get back and in that case, he'll be on another job.'

She'd been surprised to hear Aiden's rather random idea of taking Tina and Anna's mother out, but guessed it made sense. The way he'd planned it meant that Anna would become even more reliant on him, plus there was an extra bonus. Tina had agreed to give him half the life insurance money of which he was willing to split with her and Digger. *Money for old rope.*

Digger nodded. He wasn't quite sure why Aiden had volunteered to dispatch an old woman, but it made no bones to him. It was quite obvious Aiden was trying to prove himself. The bloke wasn't stupid. He knew full well that pulling off a stunt such as this for a few quid proved he was up for anything they could possibly ask of him and it was no secret he wanted more responsibility at Elipse, as well as more money to boot.

Digger shrugged. He couldn't blame the guy. He'd have done the same himself. Aiden was bright enough as well as useful, so they could do a lot worse than having him on side.

Suddenly he noticed the little girl sitting motionless in the corner of the office. *Jesus Christ!* 'What the hell's she doing here again?' he hissed.

Eliza glanced at Emily uninterestedly. 'Oh her? Don't worry about that. I've finally got it into her thick skull that she's to just sit here and say or do nothing if she knows what's good for her.' She glared at the child. 'That bitch of a social worker dumped her on me last minute this morning. It won't be long now before we're signed off and then we can just leave her at the house with a nanny and rarely have to set eyes on her.'

Digger sighed and eyed the child suspiciously. 'The kid best keep her mouth shut.' *Eliza shouldn't be discussing anything with her around.*

• • • •

ANNA MISJUDGED THE height of the table as she placed her glass down unsteadily, but luckily Aiden managed to stop the expensive champagne flute from crashing to the floor.

Despite the near miss, Anna giggled uncontrollably. The champagne had gone right to her head, but it was the second bottle, so it wasn't altogether surprising.

She'd been on edge when Aiden had first arrived, knowing she wasn't allowed anyone in the house, but with the Wrights away and the need to spend some time with the man in front of her, she'd thrown caution to the wind. She was starting to come out of herself and beginning to enjoy life a little. And she liked it.

Anna attempted to focus her glazed eyes on Aiden who got up from his chair and walked around the other side of the table towards her. Standing behind, he pushed her hair out of the way and began trailing his lips down the nape of her neck.

A strange combination of desire coupled with shyness

flooded Anna at the feel of his mouth on her skin and she remained frozen, staring at the table. She hadn't had sex with him since that first time several weeks ago and she was nervous. Nervous in case it hurt like it had before and because she still didn't have a clue what to do in situations.

'Come here Anna,' Aiden murmured, pulling her to her feet. Seeing her stagger slightly, he smirked. *The stupid cow was trolleyed from a couple of glasses of champagne.*

He would have to ensure he made her feel like a princess. He'd got the frigid cow to enjoy herself if he wanted to keep up the act, being as she had doubts over his sincerity. He had no idea how he would pull it off, but he'd give it a damn fine try.

Unbuttoning Anna's blouse, Aiden softly stroked her skin and slipped her bra straps over her shoulders, felt her stiffen. He suppressed his sigh of frustration. 'What's the matter?' he whispered, trailing his lips along her shoulder blade.

'I-I need to listen out for Toby….'

Aiden's fingers inched along the inside of Anna's thigh. 'Don't worry about him. He's fast asleep. We'll hear him if he wakes.' *If I manage to get you going you won't notice if he falls headfirst out of the fucking window!* 'Just relax Anna,' he murmured, his lips next to her ear as he slipped his fingers inside her knickers and gently pressed down on her clitoris.

'Ohhhh!' Anna gasped, a strange sensation flooding her.

Turning Anna around Aiden bent her forward against the table, his fingers continuing to work inside her.

'Aiden? Ohhhh…!' Anna cried, heady currents of sensation flooding from within her.

Aiden smirked, hoping he'd bring her to where she needed to be tonight. 'We'll hear anything that we need to.' *Including if anyone unexpectedly returns.* He upped the speed and pressure of his fingers. 'Just relax and let me make you feel good ok?'

Thirty One

SETH LOVINGLY WIPED THE soft soapy sponge over Jane's breasts as she lay back between his legs in the oversized bathtub.

Jane allowed the hot scented water to lap around her body and tried to let the feel of Seth's fingers on her skin relax her. *What a disaster. They had failed to locate their daughter.*

Seth reluctantly accepted Jane was right. He hadn't had any spark of instinct, which made him feel the little girl wasn't anything to do with him either. Initially he'd made excuses - after all, was it that surprising to have no connection with a child he'd never seen?

But whether he liked it or not, he had to agree. The child bore no resemblance to either of them and certainly gave no impression of being unhappy, of which Jane was convinced would be the case. Her sixth sense was usually bang on, so finding no reason to spend any longer staying in the hotel, they'd packed up and got on the road.

Seth's eyes narrowed. He would wring Mulligan's neck for this. That fat fucker wasn't any better than all of the other pointless leads they'd previously had. He was angry with himself for allowing that burning glimmer of hope into his soul and in turn, giving that to Jane. He knew she was devastated.

He'd be calling that pointless bastard first thing in the morning to question why they'd been sent on a wild goose chase. Mulligan couldn't have got it more wrong and he wanted a bloody good explanation. *That and his money back.*

Seth clenched his teeth. It wouldn't surprise him if Miller had given him the name of a shite PI just to piss him off. He'd be having words with him too.

He desperately tried to contain his rage. He knew he couldn't achieve or change a thing at this precise moment, but by hell – the shit would definitely be hitting the fan very, very soon. *In the meantime, they were back to square fucking one.*

A boiling hot core of red anger remained burning brightly at Seth's heart. They shouldn't even be in this position and there was only one person to blame for that. Both he and Jane knew who that was and he should have taken her advice and finished Digger when he'd had the chance.

Gritting his teeth and feeling the familiar pounding getting stronger in his veins, Seth's thoughts were halted by Jane shifting positions in the huge round bath, raising herself so that she faced him. Leaning back slightly he groaned as she slowly sank down onto him.

Seth placed his hand on Jane's face as she began to move on him, her eyes closed. 'Jane…. I…'

'Shh…' she whispered. She didn't want to talk about Grace or the situation. She was angry. More than angry, but resigned to what had happened and the only way she knew how to deal with that was to take control.

She needed release. She needed to remove some of the frustration which had built up within her. It wouldn't change the outcome of what had happened, but it would take her mind off the heartbreak she was experiencing for a few minutes. And she needed that more than anything.

• • • •

AIDEN SLUGGED DOWN a tot of whisky and stared at Eliza as she perched seductively on her office chair. He knew she was waiting for her, but he was knackered and the day wasn't anywhere near over yet. *Not by a long shot.*

'So,' Eliza purred. 'Are you ready for tonight?'

Aiden nodded. 'Yep. Seth's definitely back?'

Eliza's eyes narrowed. 'Of course he is! Do you think I don't know what I'm doing?' She eyed him maliciously from under her false lashes. He might be decent eye candy and she appreciated what he'd been doing lately – *all of it,* but regardless of any of that, she wouldn't put up with sly comments from the shit head. She glanced at Aiden's crotch feeling a twinge between her legs in readiness of what she expected from him after this briefing.

Aiden wiped the back of his hand across his forehead. 'I didn't mean it like that. Just double checking – it's a habit…' He grinned and attempted one of his cheeky winks he knew went down well with the ladies. Whether he was knackered or not he still had to keep this particular bird on side otherwise things would get difficult.

Placated somewhat and feeling she'd got her point across well enough, Eliza flashed her dentist-whitened smile. 'Glad to hear it. Good job with Anna last night too,' she smirked.

Aiden grinned despite himself. *Yeah, he'd certainly made Anna's legs shake.* Now she'd been baptised in the art of sexual pleasure he knew she wouldn't be able to get enough of him. This was unfortunate from his side as he had no desire to have any more of her, but at least it was useful to the cause. *That was what they paid him for after all.*

Eliza blatantly crossed her legs in front of Aiden's line of sight, giving him an eyeful. 'When will you be introduced to her dear mother? I need that working capital you've promised.'

Aiden smiled. 'It's all in hand.' He didn't intend on giving Eliza anywhere *near* the amount she was expecting. When Tina gave him his half of the insurance pay-out, he'd give this plastic slut enough to let him get out of here. She wouldn't get a penny more unless she wanted Digger to know how she'd been working him. *Two could play at blackmail, couldn't they?*

No, he wouldn't be spending any more time doing her underhand errands. He'd set up on his own perhaps? That was unless Digger and Eliza made him a fully-fledged partner. And while they were at it, he'd insist that greasy fat pervert Lomond was binned off too.

When Aiden had taken Anna breakfast in bed this morning, along with two paracetamol to ease her hangover, he'd casually slipped questions into the conversation about her family to pretend he was interested.

It hadn't taken her long to confide she hadn't seen her mother for a while. He'd pushed on in a concerned way - after all she was supposed to be the light of his life. *She was his Princess and he needed to keep acting the part of the Prince.*

'You should go and see her Anna. My father got killed in a motorway accident and I always wished I'd spent more time with him,' Aiden had choked.

His father wasn't dead at all. He was still very much running his scrap metal business down on the coast, happily shacked up with a twenty-five year old slapper last time he heard, but Anna didn't need to know that.

'Why don't I come along?' Aiden had taken Anna's hand. 'I'm not trying to muscle in on your family, but being as we're serious about each other I think it would be good.'

He saw Anna frown as she tried to weigh up the situation, so felt he'd needed to add a tiny bit more incentive to the equation.

'Unless for some reason you don't want me involved in your life to such an extent. Maybe you don't feel as strongly about me as I do about you…?' Aiden whined.

This had been the winner. The reference to the importance of their joke of a relationship has been what tipped the balance in his favour. Anna had quickly and readily agreed that he was right.

Now he'd just got to make sure it was all plain sailing, otherwise he'd be stuck with not only Anna again tomorrow night, but also – God forbid – her fucking mother as well. Still – everything was in place, so there was little chance of that being an option. *He knew what he was doing after all.*

Eliza rubbed her hands together and watched Aiden stare blankly at the desk in front of him. She aimlessly wondered how long it would take him to notice if she started playing with herself.

Still smiling sweetly, Eliza placed one of her legs up on the desk and slipped her fingers into her knickers. 'Don't forget I'll need you for this business with Lacey the day after,' she said casually, knowing it was only a matter of seconds before he noticed what she was doing.

'God Eliza, I'll have no time to sleep with all the work you've got me involved in!' Aiden quipped, glancing over and nearly choking when he saw where Eliza's hands were.

'Mmm, but sleep is *very* overrated!' Eliza murmured, staring straight at Aiden. *Beckoning him to fuck her. To take her right now.*

Unable to help himself and regardless of his bone-weary exhaustion, Aiden felt the familiar tightening in his groin. *Fuck*, he thought, seeing Eliza's eyes linger on the steadily growing bulge in his jeans. *He'd got no choice in the matter now.*

'Meant to say, I want you to drop another note through the Wright's door later before you visit the 'in-laws',' Eliza smirked, studying Aiden's obvious arousal. *Yeah, when they read this one it would up the ante without a doubt. It was more than time...* She opened her legs impatiently. 'Come on then! What are you waiting for?'

Wearily Aiden rose from his chair and began undoing his jeans.

• • • •

DIGGER GRINNED WIDELY as he accepted the drink Steve Lomond placed on the table. *He* was usually the one buying the drinks. Lacey's movements and whereabouts had now been confirmed for two days and nights in a row, so it was fair to say they were pretty much home and dry.

The route had been worked out and Eliza had settled on a

snatch point where there was no chance of anyone spotting the actual take. *It was all good.*

Digger frowned. It was a good job they'd wrapped up the planning when Lomond had burst into the office earlier. If he'd realised they knew where Lacey was, his desperation for the little bitch would have overtaken any necessity to sensibly execute her return.

He fished his cigarettes from his pocket. 'Fancy one of these Steve?'

Lomond swivelled his owl like head around and his beady eyes stared at Digger. 'No thanks. We need to get going.'

Digger looked confused. 'Get going? I thought we were out for the night? Having a few beers and all that?' *Lomond's generosity had obviously been overstretched by the three pints he'd funded.*

Steve Lomond smiled. It was more of a sneer than a smile, but due to the general state of the man's face it was relatively difficult to differentiate as to what half his expressions signified at the best of times. *He really was a pig-ugly fucker.*

'I was just beginning to chill out,' Digger griped.

'Who said we're not out for the night?' Lomond grinned, unusually jovial. 'At least for a bit longer anyway.'

When Steve Lomond pushed his great bulk up and out of the wooden chair, Digger felt he should probably do likewise. He quickly tipped what remained of his lager into his mouth and got up. 'Where's the next stop then?'

Lomond grinned. 'It's a surprise....'

Thirty Two

LACEY DESPONDENTLY PUT her things into her handbag and prepared to set off for Pegasus Place. She glanced at the clock. *Almost 9…*

She sighed. She may as well live at the bookshop and probably would do so if it were possible. The atmosphere at the hostel was at the point of being unbearable. She'd tried to speak to Jennie several times since her outburst, but her former friend had made it very clear she'd said all there was to be said and wasn't prepared to discuss it further. *Apparently she knew what she'd done…*

The problem was, she didn't. Lacey still hadn't the faintest clue and sadly came to the conclusion she was left with very little choice apart from moving on somewhere else. Although she'd paid her contribution for her upkeep to the hostel, she'd still managed to put a bit aside. Another couple of weeks working and she should just about have enough to rent a small bedsit.

Rising from her desk, Lacey picked up her bag and after a quick glance around the shop, flicked the lights off and opened the front door.

••••

DIGGER WISHED HE KNEW why Lomond wasn't happy to go to one of the pubs around the corner from where they'd been, but instead he'd insisted on getting in the bloody car.

He didn't much like going too far out of his neck of the woods at night for a jolly for obvious reasons. Not that he'd class drinking with Steve Lomond 'jolly'.

Digger forced himself to concentrate. He was looking forward to hitting the sack to be honest because he was shattered. Putting a cigarette in his mouth, he flicked his lighter into life and reached towards the window to open it, when it suddenly dawned on him where they were.

As the car came to a halt and Lomond carefully reversed into the mouth of an alley, Digger felt his heart pick up an unexpected thunderous pace. The cigarette dropped from his mouth as Lomond, without uttering a single word or even looking at him, hastily got out of the car.

Digger scrabbled with his seat belt. *He was kidding right? The silly stupid fucking ponce!*

Throwing himself from the car, Digger lurched after Lomond. 'Steve,' he hissed. 'You can't do this. Seriously!' *If Lomond attempted to snatch Lacey they'd be fucked.*

Steve swung around and yanked Digger's hand off him. 'Oh yes I can and I *will…*' he growled.

'But…'

Lomond's eyes were wild. 'But nothing. If I hadn't heard you and Eliza discussing this earlier, I'd have still been in the fucking dark!'

Digger paled. *So, he'd heard? He'd heard their conversation? Bollocks!* 'But the jump's sorted for tomorrow night,' he explained, hoping the idiot would see sense. *If he tried to pull it off this way, they'd all be going down.*

Lomond stopped in his tracks and turned to face Digger square on, his expression adopting that of a rabid animal. 'Listen, you cunt, I'm having that girl. *Now*! I'd be waiting until the sea froze over if it was for you lot.'

Digger paled further. *He was serious alright.* 'You'll fuck it up. This isn't the best place to do it from. We've scouted the route out and you need to d...'

Lomond's meaty hand quickly gripped Digger around the throat. Despite the massive size of his neck, the man's hand easily spanned it enough to crush his windpipe and he was abruptly cut off in his reasoning.

'I won't tell you again,' Lomond growled. 'It's happening and it's happening *now*. You'd best fucking help me Digger, or I swear to God I'll chop all your remaining appendages off.'

Looking at Lomond's manic expression, Digger realised he had little choice in the matter and knew without doubt the man would carry out his threat. Thanks to Seth-fucking-Wright he wasn't as well able to defend himself as he'd once been.

Sensing Digger's silent agreement, Lomond smiled nastily. 'Now hurry the fuck up!' He strode a few more paces away from the mouth of the alley where the car had been parked before stopping. 'Here will do nicely.'

• • • •

MAGGIE KNEW IT WASN'T a great idea to go to the shop to buy another bottle of wine. Being as she'd already had a whole one to herself, she knew she probably shouldn't have got into the car to drive halfway over town either.

The trouble was she didn't want to return to the same off licence by where they lived and from where she'd bought the first bottle. She knew what this place was like. It wouldn't have taken much time for word to get back to Dan and she'd promised him she wouldn't hit the wine again.

Maggie readily accepted wine only made her more depressed but she couldn't help herself right now. Dan had promised her it wouldn't be like this. *Promised* things weren't like she thought – whatever had happened in the past, it wasn't like that now. Seth wasn't like that anymore and Dan was keeping him under control. He'd *tell* her if things began to go wrong and if there was any reason for her to worry…

Except there was plenty for her to worry about and Dan

hadn't said a word...

Feeling the tears prick the back of her eyes, Maggie shook her head to try and push the racing thoughts away. Dan was keeping *everything* from her and there was a *lot more* going on than he was letting on. She was sick of it.

She'd brought up what was on her mind *yet again* and Dan hadn't been able to get out of there fast enough. He'd had to go to the Glint to make sure everything was alright for Seth. *That's right. Go running off for Seth like a good boy!*

It was all more important that her. *Everything and everybody was more important than her.*

Maggie screeched to a halt outside a corner shop. *Fuck it. This would do.* She couldn't be arsed to drive too far. This shop was far enough away not to come to Dan's attention. Besides, why she was so bothered about what he thought anyway?

Getting out of the car she stomped angrily towards the shop, tutting with annoyance as someone opened the door from the inside and pushed past her on to the pavement.

She glared at the man who glanced uninterestedly at her from under his skanky cheap hooded top and quickly loped up the road clutching a four-pack of lager.

Scrubber, Maggie thought, irritably walking into the shop. As she made her way towards the chiller fridge, she stopped dead in her tracks. *That was the bloke from the hospital! That Aiden - Lacey's supposed boyfriend!*

Turning on her heels, Maggie raced from the shop and stood on the pavement, blindly looking up and down the road. It was no good. There was no sign of him.

• • • •

LACEY TURNED THE CORNER, putting her hand in her pocket to search for some change. She might pop into the shop down the road to see if they'd got any pasties left. Continuing down the road, she was so lost in her thoughts she didn't notice the two men step out of the doorway until it was too late.

Fear lurched through her when her path was blocked and

shock spread across her face when she recognised who exactly these people were. *Oh Christ!*

Lacey opened her mouth to scream in terror, but a large hand covered it. Before she could formulate another thought, she was dragged roughly into the doorway.

'Missed me have you sweetheart?' Lomond growled, an inch from Lacey's face as he pressed his fleshy body into hers, squashing her against the wall.

Lacey felt herself begin to involuntarily gag from the all-consuming stench of stale cigarettes coming from the hand clamped tightly over her mouth and the confirmation that the person crushing himself against her was none other than *that man*.

That monster what had put a baby inside her and the one who enjoyed hurting and humiliating her.

Lacey's eyes burnt with tears and her gaze darted manically around. The large figures in the doorway blocked anything else from her view and even though she could see very little, she knew they were all but invisible within this darkened recess.

As Lacey felt Steve Lomond's erection pushing against her she tried to focus on the second man in the hope he may possess marginally better morals than this perverted freak.

As her panicked eyes locked on Digger's recognisable bull-headed outline in the shadows, Lacey's heart sunk to the pits of despair. *Digger as well? This was worse than hell...*

'Don't struggle baby,' Lomond growled in Lacey's ear. 'It will make things more palatable if you play along.' He stuck his hand roughly between Lacey's legs, pushing his fingers against the denim crotch of her jeans. 'I'm sure as hell looking forward to getting these off you. I've missed you sweetie. More than you know...'

Feeling the man's tongue push into her ear, Lacey felt her stomach heave. Realisation dawned she would be returned to the Elipse to be this bastard's plaything and she began thrashing around and kicking out.

She couldn't go back there. Couldn't and wouldn't. No, no,

NO!

Seeing the girl flailing around like a banshee, Digger stepped forward and painfully twisted her arms behind her back. 'Don't make this more difficult for yourself you little cunt. You seem unaware just how much trouble you've caused, so do what you need to do without the fucking hysterics yeah?'

Lacey was deaf to Digger's words and continued thrashing about in pure panic.

'You know you want me you little slut. *Tell me.* I want to hear you say it!' Lomond shouted, his hands pulling at Lacey's top, his fingers running over her breasts. His breathing was laboured, feeling her skin under his touch once more. *He'd have to take her now. He'd waited too long...*

Lacey hastily slammed her knee into Lomond's groin sending him staggering back howling in pain.

Digger scowled. *He needed to do something. She was going to scream!* Raising his good hand, he slammed it into Lacey's jaw and she crumpled to the floor.

Digger stared at her inert body. *Shit! This had all gone tits up!* He knew it would with Lomond pulling a bloody stunt like this. Why couldn't he have just waited and done it *his* way? *For fuck's sake. Eliza was going to go loco!* 'Help me get her in the car then for Christ's sake!'

Lomond leant against the wall, trying to regain his breath from the crushing pain. He stared at Digger, momentarily losing the ability to think of anything other than the uncontrollable need to stick his cock in the girl. *Couldn't he just have her first and then they'd shift her?* Feverishly he pulled at the zip of his trousers.

Digger stared at Lomond incredulously. 'What the fuck are you doing? You haven't got time for that! We need to get away from here before someone sees us. What's the matter with you man?' he snapped, roughly pushing the man out of the way. *The fucking idiot! The fucking nonce!*

Digger didn't care if he'd offended Lomond or even if he refused to help them anymore. If they were discovered right now there would be no turning back. *He wasn't going down for this prick.*

He eyed the girl lying in an awkward position and could see her jaw was broken. At least she was still out cold. He sighed. Eliza wouldn't be happy about the state of her face and he was bound to get it in the neck for that, but what was he supposed to have done? Let her scream and get them all nicked?

Quickly scooping Lacey up in his big arms, Digger elbowed Lomond heavily in the ribs. 'See if anyone's around,' he hissed. 'And hurry the fuck up.'

Coming to his senses, Steve Lomond forcing his engorged cock back into his trousers, pulled his zip up and stuck his large head out of the doorway. 'We're ok,' he whispered, stepping out onto the pavement.

Lomond walked briskly back to the car, pulling the keys from his pocket. Despite the pain in his groin, he smiled knowing Digger was following with the girl in his arms. *He'd got Lacey back and this time he wasn't going to let her go.*

THIRTY THREE

SETH CUPPED JANE'S FACE in his hands and lowered his mouth onto hers. Feeling her soft lips yield under his, he desperately wanted to take her back to bed. 'Do I *really* have to go into the club yet? Can't I just stay here with you a bit longer?'

Jane would have loved nothing more than to let Seth take her back upstairs, but she knew they'd been absent three days already. He should have checked in at the Glint yesterday once they'd got back, but they'd agreed another day together was warranted.

Reluctantly Jane pushed Seth back to arm's length and cheekily ran her hand across his crotch. 'I'll still be here when you get back,' she smiled.

'You're a wicked woman!' Seth replied huskily, not at all convinced he was up for leaving.

'It's already 11 o'clock and you've got to give Dan a break. Besides, you need to catch up with what's been going on. See if there's been any developments in our absence *and* you need to be speaking with Mulligan.'

Seth nodded. Jane was right. He did need to find out what was going on. He hoped there wouldn't be any unpalatable news awaiting him. Bashfully rearranging himself in his trousers, he smiled. 'Don't you worry about that. It will all be taken care of, but I want to pick this up where we left off later right?'

Seeing Jane grin, he kissed her once more. 'Are you coming in today?'

Jane pulled her satin robe around herself. 'I was going to see Maggie, unless you need me at the Glint of course?'

Seth grinned. 'I *always* need you, but go. In fact, you should take a leaf out of Maggie's book – be a lady of leisure…'

He laughed seeing Jane's horrified expression. She'd hate having nothing to do. The concept of being content lounging about all day was not something she'd ever entertain. Still, he did want her to start taking it a bit easier. 'I was only joking,' he laughed. 'But not about taking it a bit easier.'

Seth gave Jane one more kiss. 'I'll see you later ok.'

Jane watched Seth walk up the hall and shrug his jacket on. He bent down to pick up the post from the mat so he could open the door.

'There's a couple for you here,' Seth called as he ripped open an envelope.

Jane was about to go upstairs to get herself a shower until she saw the expression on Seth's face as his eyes ran over the contents of the letter. 'What is it?'

Getting no response, Jane moved up the hallway. She leant against him, putting her head on his upper arm, loving the big muscles she could feel underneath the material. 'What is it?'

Seth's eyes were ablaze. 'I don't know what the fuck this is or who it's from but I'm going to goddamn kill them!'

Snatching the letter from Seth's grip, Jane's eyes rapidly scanned the contents and paled.

Do you know what it's like to have your life ruined?
If you don't, then you will do shortly.

You've already mislaid one kid, so make sure you look after the other. It's always upsetting when things go missing.

Jane leant against the wall, her breathing coming in short rasps. 'Who the hell sent this?' she whispered.

'How the fuck do I know?' Seth raged. He'd kill the fucker, whoever it was. Threatening to take his son? *Over his dead body.*

Jane's eyes narrowed, not forgetting Seth's previous comments. 'And *this* is down to paranoia too is it?'

Seth scowled. 'No time for sarcasm Jane,' he seethed, snatching up the phone. 'I'm not going *anywhere* until I've got backup. This time there'll be someone with you and Toby at *all* times - Anna included when she's got our son with her.'

• • • •

'I'M SORRY MR WRIGHT,' Tom said awkwardly. 'I've been told by Mr Miller that you aren't welcome here.' He shifted uncomfortably from foot to foot, wishing he hadn't been the one on the door at the Limelight when Seth Wright had arrived.

He'd always had great respect for the man and was shocked to receive orders not to allow him admittance under any circumstances. He can't say however that he was surprised.

It was no secret Seth's latest exploits had caused a ruckus within the Limelight ranks. A lot of the staff had expressed their disappointment because the general consensus had previously been, aside from Seth's formidable and well-deserved reputation, he was a fair man – providing he was not crossed, but *not* the sort to turn on a woman.

Even though very few had been swayed by the initial rumours, the last newspaper story had made it less easy to ignore. Of course, Jason Miller's reaction had left little room for personal opinions because they had little choice but to obey his wishes. Miller paid their wages at the end of the day.

Seth's eyes narrowed into slits, his anger bubbling dangerously close to the surface. He was in a bad enough mood as it was since getting that note. It had then got worse after he'd called Mulligan, where he'd discovered that he'd somehow cancelled their contract. *Apparently…*

In the past it was feasible he could have done something like that during one of his frequent blackouts, but not these days. Hence he'd insisted Mulligan better get his arse into gear and come and see him so he could find out what the fuck the man was going on about. *And now this shit with being stopped on the door of the Limelight?*

'I always thought you had a bit more about you than this Tom,' Seth sneered. 'It appears a lot of people aren't what they seem...' He'd expected a lot more from Jason Miller and his crew after their joint involvement over the past couple of years, however it looked like loyalty counted for jack shit.

'I'm sorry Sir, it's orders,' Tom said. Even though he didn't agree with how the Limelight was treating this man, he was determined to hold his head up straight and look Seth Wright straight in his steely green eyes.

'I appreciate you have orders Tom - I know how it works remember, but on this occasion, you'll have to bypass them. This is important.'

Tom's stomach sank. He really didn't want to have to argue with this guy. 'I'm sorry but I c…'

'Fair enough,' Seth snapped, forcibly pushing past the huge man. 'I'll just see myself in.'

Momentarily astounded, Tom hastily regained his composure. Placing his massive hands on Seth's shoulders, he pulled him backwards. 'Like I said, it's been requested th…'

Tom may have been a massive bloke, but very little could equal Seth's panther-like aggression. Twisting out of the man's grip, he delivered a head butt to the bridge of Tom's nose, immediately smashing it into his face.

Unwilling to have to pummel the doorman he'd known and respected for so long, Seth was glad the big man had been quickly reduced to dropping to his knees, clutching his crushed nose.

'Don't want to damage you Tom, but I will if I have to,' Seth warned watching Tom's eyes watering with pain, temporarily rendering him useless. 'Now I'm going in.' He pulled a handkerchief from his pocket and dropped it into the man's lap. 'There you go mate. Sorry about your nose.'

• • • •

ANNA CLUTCHED AIDEN'S hand gratefully as they walked from where he'd parked towards her mother's house. Her heart pounded almost painfully in her chest. She knew she'd be faced with a host of awkward questions about why she hadn't been in touch for so long and she wasn't quite sure how to answer them.

She was glad Aiden was with her. Not only did it take some of the pressure off, but it also meant he was serious about her. She squeezed his hand tighter, hardly able to believe her luck. It was finally beginning to sink in that how he felt about her was real. And it felt *amazing*.

Almost as amazing as how she'd felt when they'd last made love. Anna smiled shyly to herself. The difference between the first and second time had been astronomical. She now understood the noises she'd heard coming from the Wright's bedroom.

She glanced up at Aiden and smiled. 'You seem to know where you're going,' Anna joked as he turned towards the group of houses containing her mother's.

Aiden forced a laugh. 'Lucky guess!' *Damn! He really must pull his socks up*. His mind was on overdrive and he was on edge. *A fucking massive edge*. If they rounded this corner and the place was cordoned off with police tape then everything would be ruined. They'd taken a risk by making the decision to let Anna discover her mother's body, but Eliza said it would have more impact. *Still, it didn't mean he had to get slack on what he was doing.*

'You realise she'll bombard you with questions, don't you?' Anna said, hoping her mother's overbearing attitude wouldn't put off the man she'd heavily fallen in love with.

Aiden stopped and gently tilted Anna's face up toward his. *The old bat had bombarded him with fucking questions last night, but she wouldn't be asking any more...* 'Nothing could make me not want you,' he lied, gently pressing his lips down on hers.

He tried to concentrate how his reaction should unfold when Anna opened the front door to find her mother in a heap in the back lounge. *He needed to act as surprised and horrified as she was, right? Remember, remember, REMEMBER*, he chanted silently.

Aiden silently wondered how long he'd have to listen to her anguished wailing. *Probably all fucking night knowing her. For God's sake. This was all such a ball-ache.*

He'd been hoping to see that juicy barmaid for another session tonight, but again that had to be postponed. It would have been so much easier if Anna was more like her sister: dead from the neck up.

When he'd got back last night to report to Eliza the job had been done, Tina had been so happy she'd even offered him a blow-job for his services. He'd rather have had oral sex with a fucking alligator than allow that skank anywhere near his cock, but saying that – even that might have been preferable than having to put up with Anna crying in his arms all night.

He grabbed Anna's hand. 'Come on, we want to see your Mum, don't we?'

'You're so thoughtful,' Anna gushed as she walked besides him. *How could she have got this lucky?*

• • • •

'WHAT THE FU….' Jason Miller nearly dropped a tumbler of whisky down himself in shock when Seth burst into his office.

'Jason!' Seth smiled far too brightly. 'Good to see you. Got a minute?'

Jason glanced around, completely off guard. He'd given the staff strict instructions not to let Seth Wright in. Not that he was overly bothered by the man, but on the same vein he didn't want a face-off with him either.

It didn't change the fact he didn't want any involvement - publicly or otherwise with Seth Wright. Even though the 'we have a good marriage' damage limitation story had made some amends to public opinion of Seth's reputation, there was still general suspicion – especially within the Limelight.

'What do you want Seth? I made it clear I wanted you to keep your distance until all the shit died down. You sh…'

Seth stepped forward so his face was an inch from Jason's. 'Except you didn't have the decency to say anything to *me,* did you?' he snorted. 'You thought you'd send the message via one of my men.' *How he'd love to pour petrol all over Miller's orange fucking hair and then light it.*

Jason stepped back a pace, not liking anyone in his personal space. 'Is this what it's been reduced to? You coming in here playing the big man? I'm not frightened of you,' he growled, matching Seth's harsh stare.

Seth felt his temper may erupt beyond control at any second. 'I don't expect you to be frightened of me Jason,' he snarled. 'Exactly what would be the point of that? What I *do* expect though is more respect than you've fucking delivered of late. The last thing I thought you were was a coward.'

Jason Miller clenched his teeth. *He refused to rise to the bait.* It was true he should have spoken to Seth personally about stepping away, but he'd been busy and - well, Seth hadn't been available. 'You were the one who was locked up if I remember rightly?'

Ignoring the fuelled jibe, Seth continued. 'We've worked well together for some time, but the first sign of shit on the horizon which could raise questions and you fuck off in the other direction. That doesn't say a lot to me!' He ran his hand across his beard thoughtfully. 'I doubt your old man would be impressed if he knew your spine's gone bendy,' he spat, knowing his words would simmer in Miller's brain because they were true. *All of them.*

At the insinuation of disappointing his father, Jason's eyes flashed with rage. Lunging forward, he grabbed Seth's lapels. 'You cunt! You know jack shit about my father!'

Seth grinned, happy he'd achieved the desired reaction. 'Oh, but I do. You've fucked up by turning your back on me, Miller and you know it!' Putting his hands over Jason's, he yanked them away. 'I've been doing the work around here trying to find out who's been upsetting things for far too long. *I'm* the one putting *my* neck on the line to make sure *both* of our clubs remain undamaged and profitable, but you and your crew have done *nothing*! You've happily sat back leaving everything down to me. Bit strange don't you think?'

Jason scowled. 'What's *that* supposed to mean?'

Seth laughed. 'You think I don't know what you're trying to do Miller? Setting me up won't work.'

Jason seethed with Seth's words. 'Setting you up? You're being ridiculous!'

Seth helped himself to a glass of Jason's whisky and perched on the edge of the mahogany desk surface. He casually inspected his fingernails before moving his stare directly back to Jason. 'I might add *all* this started from your vindictive fucking dried-up trout of a wife's big bitchy gob, but you've gone too far this time!'

Jason clenched his fists. 'Leave Linda out of it!'

Seth laughed loudly. 'Why? Pretending that's not true either? That she doesn't bitch-slap you into whatever she wants? That she loved the opportunity to have a dig at me because I refused her?'

Seth pulled himself away from the table and moved back into Jason's face. 'Yeah, that's right. She tried it on with me *ages* ago. Obviously I turned her down. I mean, why the fuck would I go there when I've got *Jane*? You know – my *wife* – the one your dick keeps pointing towards?'

Seth's hand shot forwards, gripping Jason tightly around the throat. 'Don't try to deny that either! You think I've been blind the past few years, do you? The difference is *I* have the fucking decency to see past that. *You* on the other hand…' He forced control back into his raging mind. 'Think you can set me up!'

Seth pushed Jason backwards and away from him, knowing if he didn't get the two-faced bastard away from him then he'd surely clump him. *And he wouldn't be able to stop once he'd got started.*

Staggering back, Jason raised his hand to his throat and steadied himself against the table. *Linda had tried it on with Seth Wright? The fucking bitch. He might have known... And what was all this about setting him up? More like the other bloody way around...*

Jason kept his expression level, not wanting Seth to see that his scathing comment had cut deep. 'At least my wife doesn't fight my battles!'

Seth laughed. 'My wife *believes* in me and has short shrift with bitches and yellow-bellies? That wrong is it?'

He folded his arms across his chest and raised his eyebrows. 'Sinking in yet is it Miller?' Seth snarled, enjoying that Jason's attempt to conceal what was going through his mind had failed miserably. 'Sorry to have to force you to swallow some home truths, but life's hard sometimes.'

Jason pulled himself up to his full height. *He needed to claw back some standing.* 'I think you should leave now.'

Seth smiled. 'Do you now? Well, I think you should tell me why you purposefully gave me a fucking shite PI for a start! Another dig was it? I'd never stoop so low to aim for your kids Miller. Not that you have any, so you wouldn't understand how important they are.'

Jason sneered. 'Oh, for God's sake! Mulligan not up to your standards now is that it?'

'No, he goddamn isn't! The guy looks like a mashed-up retarded fucking thug! He sent us on some bloody pointless trip around the country for a load of bollocks. I don't care if you hate me Miller, but you hurt Jane with that cheap stunt,' Seth raged.

Jason momentarily forgot the argument. 'What are you talking about? A *thug*? Mulligan doesn't look like a thug! He's an old man! He looks like someone's Grandad!' *It was true. Carl Mulligan may well look like someone's Grandad with his brown tweed jackets, but he was one of the BEST private investigators around.*

Seth sneered. 'Fucking funny Grandad you've got if he looks like that! Another wind up is it? Well screw you Miller! I suggest you open your eyes and take a look around at what's going on here. You never bothered to find out who cut up that poor girl of yours did you?'

He watched Jason shift uncomfortably. 'It had to be one of your staff and you're ok with that are you?' Seth's voice raged. 'Cos I'm not! You need to get a fucking grip, Miller!'

Seth pulled a piece of paper from his pocket and thrust it into Jason's face. 'Look at this! Go on, *look* at it!' He pushed it further forward. 'Some cunt is now threatening my *child*!' he roared. 'Know anything about this do you? Or is that supposed be to my doing as well?'

Jason stared at the typed words on the paper. 'That's nothing to do with me! Who's it from?'

Seth snatched the paper back. 'Do you think if I knew that I'd be wasting my time talking to *you*? If it isn't you, then I don't know who sent it, but I'll be finding out. *Everyone* right now is a suspect. *Especially* wankers who play fucking games!'

Jason's eyes narrowed and he stepped forward incensed. 'I hope you're not suggesting I had anything to do with that! I'd never do som…'

'Shut it Miller!' Seth screamed. 'I wouldn't put *anything* past you if you thought it would save your fucking skin or enable you to stick your cock in my wife!'

'Now wait a minute! You…'

'No, *YOU* wait a minute. You've shown your true colours and I won't forget that. You've made a fucking *huge* mistake.'

Jason sneered. 'Are you threatening me?'

Seth laughed. 'I'm not threatening you Miller, I'm *promising* you!' He slapped Jason Miller in a mock-friendly gesture on the shoulder which meant anything but and then casually strode out of the office, leaving the man standing alone.

THIRTY FOUR

'WHY HASN'T SHE ANSWERED the door?' Anna cried, panic evident in her voice. Her mother never went out in the evening. *Something was wrong. It HAD to be.*

'Calm down,' Aiden said gently, pleased things were progressing nicely. He forced a worried look on to his face and pulled Anna towards him. 'There must be a rational explanation. She'll be fine.' *She wasn't though, was she? She was far from ok.*

He knew first-hand what Anna would see when he played the Knight in shining armour and got her inside the house.

Anna's eyes were frantic. 'But you don't understand!' *It was no use. She'd have to tell him. Otherwise he couldn't take on board just how serious this may be.*

She clutched onto Aiden's arm and her heart pounded so hard she was sure it was going to fly out from her chest. 'My sister Tina, she works for this place…'

'Didn't know you had a sister? What place?' Aiden interrupted. *How much did Anna know?*

'I-I don't know. We don't get on. She's, erm, it doesn't matter – but the place she works for – it won't be 'nice' if you get my drift?'

Aiden shook his head, trying to play dumb. 'Not really, but carry on.' *So, she didn't know anything about the Elipse? That was good. Well done Tina!*

'Tina's been blackmailing me. She's run up a debt she needs to pay off and she needed some info from me that would do this. If she didn't get the info or the money, then she'd get hurt or perhaps even our Mum would instead.'

Aiden acted surprised. 'Information? What sort of information?'

'The people Tina owes money to have some kind of issue with the Wrights,' Anna garbled.

Aiden frowned, pretending to try and work out what Anna was saying. 'Are you telling me you've been getting dirt on the Wrights and passing it to your sister?' he asked incredulously.

Anna stared at the floor in shame. *What would Aiden think of her now?* He'd be horrified being involved with someone who would behave in such an underhand manner. 'I-I know it was wrong and I didn't want to do it. Oh, *please* don't hate me Aiden,' she begged, clutching at his arm. 'I-I love you. I really love you and I know I shouldn't have done it, but…'

'Hey, *hey*!' he cried, pulling Anna towards him. 'I don't hate you. The opposite. I understand, *really* I do. What choice did you have? I'd have done the same.'

Anna sagged with relief. 'I've never done anything like this before. I didn't even really get anything of any use. I…'

'Shhh, it's ok.'

'But it's not. I'm worried th…'

'Listen, I'm sure nothing's happened to your mum. I doubt whether your sister's bosses – whoever they are – would *really* go through with doing something like that to an old lady anyway,' he reasoned. 'Besides, it's probably a good job you weren't able to dish any dirt. The people to worry about wouldn't be your sister and her lot, it would be the Wrights!' Aiden smiled reassuringly.

Anna felt less panicky for one moment, until with a jolt she realised she *had* got the Wrights into grief – inadvertently of course.

She raised her hand to her mouth. 'But I have haven't I!' Anna wailed. 'You called the police after I phoned you and I'm sure they know it was me. Then there was that thing about what I said to the press and then you walked me home an...'

'But you didn't give my name,' Aiden said a little too urgently.

Anna shook her head. 'No, I didn't, but I don't think they trust me.'

'You're jumping to conclusions. We don't even know what's going on yet.'

'What shall I do?' Anna cried, her panic resuming four-fold. 'I need to make sure Mum's ok.'

Aiden perfected the sincere expression plastered across his face. 'Then let's get you into the house so you can put your mind at rest ok?'

• • • •

DIGGER HAD BEEN OUT most of the evening and Eliza had been waiting *hours* to tell him that it was all almost cut and dried that they'd won legal guardian status of Grace Wright, or Emily Someone-Or-Other as she was now known.

Social Services had called her last thing this afternoon with the 'good news'. They'd passed the child visit assessments and the court papers were now being prepared for the date of the adoption. Once they'd received the paperwork, all they had to do was turn up at court on the allotted date, sign a few things and then they'd be taking Jane and Seth Wright's daughter home with them as their own child. *Legally*.

Eliza just needed to get these last loose ends tied up and all in all she was in a splendid mood. That was until she clapped eyes on Lomond directly behind Digger on the CCTV monitor, dragging Lacey with him.

'What the fu...' Eliza cried as they barged into the office. *What the hell was going on? Why had they jumped Lacey? That was Aiden's job and was set for tomorrow!*

'Don't ask…' Digger muttered. 'Where shall we put her?'

Eliza was gobsmacked at this turn of events and unable to answer. She stared at Lacey's broken jaw hanging loosely with a trail of bloody saliva dripping from her chin. Her smashed face lolled against the ripped top of her chest as, semi-conscious, she was forcibly held upright by Lomond.

'*Eliza*!' Digger hissed. 'Where shall we put her?'

'What the fuck have you done?' Eliza screeched, reality overruling her confusion. 'You've mashed her fucking face up!'

'Just tell me where to put her!' Digger pressed. *He'd deal with Eliza later. Right now he needed to get Lacey out of sight.*

'Room Twelve,' Eliza replied, her eyes darting frantically to the row of security monitors to check whether anyone was milling about. 'You'd better hurry up!'

Steve Lomond dragged the girl through the door to Room Twelve and went to push the door shut behind him. 'What is it?' he snapped irritably, realising Digger was still behind him.

'Leave her for tonight,' Digger said. 'See her tomorrow.'

Lomond's eyes narrowed. 'You've got to be joking! I've waited far too long as it is and I won't wait a minute longer. Now fuck off and give me some peace.'

Slamming the door, Lomond put Lacey on the bed and impatiently tugged at his flies. He'd had the most uncomfortable hard-on since the alleyway and if he couldn't offload it into her soon, he'd explode.

He gasped with relief as he freed himself and wrapped his fist around his cock, grateful for the pressure his hand temporarily offered. 'You've been a very bad girl haven't you Lacey? A *very* bad girl, do you hear me?'

Lacey moaned incoherently, still semi-conscious.

Lomond stared at the mess of her face as he hastily yanked her jeans down. *He couldn't look at her in this state. She looked a right ugly cunt.*

Quickly turning her over onto her front, he slapped her naked buttocks hard. 'Wake up bitch!' he screamed. 'You've got some fucking apologising to do.'

'Uuurgh,' groaned Lacey, partly aware something was going to happen that wouldn't be good, but the agonising fire of the pain was rendering consideration of anything else impossible.

'Get on your hands and knees, slut!' Lomond panted, forcing his fingers into Lacey, his cock twitching in his other hand.

Struggling, Lacey got on all fours. *She'd kill this bastard when she got her head together.*

Unable to close her mouth because her lower jaw was hanging loosely, she couldn't stop the constant trail of bloody saliva from dripping out from her mouth and she knew she was making loud animalistic howling noises, but couldn't help it. It was surreal – like she was watching herself in a sick film.

'Shut up your moaning!' Lomond screamed, wrapping a meaty hand around Lacey's waist whilst he forced his cock into her. 'You're going to suffer for running away. Say sorry,' he panted. The feel of the girl around him again almost made him come on the spot.

Aware she hadn't answered his last question, Lomond grabbed Lacey's shoulders from behind and he shook her roughly. 'I didn't hear you! Answer me, bitch!'

Lacey felt vomit rising from deep within her throat and was unable to hold her own weight up on her arms. Groaning in agony she slumped forward from sheer pain and exhaustion, but hands pulled her back up by the throat from behind.

'Don't lie down on me, you slut! I need your full attention!' Lomond barked, his hands tight around Lacey's throat. *This would keep her upright*. He thrust harder and faster. *Oh, this was good. This was TOO good. Oh God....*

He tightened his grip, feeling a long overdue orgasm moving upwards.

• • • •

'DIGGER, WHAT THE FUCK is he doing?' Eliza screeched as she stared at the monitor. 'He's strangling her!'

'Nah, he just wants a fuck. Desperate so he was. Where's the harm? She's too far gone to notice anyway,' Digger mumbled.

He was just glad to be away from Lomond for a while, but not glad he'd now got Eliza harping on instead.

'No seriously! Look!' Eliza yelled.

Begrudgingly, Digger pulled himself up from the chair. Personally, the last thing he wanted to look at was Lomond at it. He thought the man should have left the girl alone for the night to be honest, but it was easier to let him just have his own way. *The prick was like a spoilt child.*

He glanced uninterestedly at the monitor Eliza was flapping over and paled. Lomond had his hands around the girl's throat and was pulling her backwards while he thrust into her. He was staring blindly at the ceiling, his face locked in a grimace. *He'd got her too tight.* 'Oh SHIT!'

Digger raced from the office and up the stairs to Room Twelve with Eliza hot on his heels.

• • • •

ANNA COULDN'T HELP but be impressed with the way Aiden had selflessly come to her rescue. She didn't know what she would have done if he hadn't have been here. She watched him brace himself against the wooden front door.

Aiden slammed his shoulder into the door just above the lock and winced as the door stayed firm. *Bloody thing.* He'd had to lock it last night so it wasn't obvious someone had been let in. He'd left the back door open, which Anna would soon discover, but he could hardly suggest going in that way.

He glanced at Anna watching wide-eyed. Even in this situation he could see the clear infatuation for him visible in her eyes. *The daft bitch.*

Refusing to rub his shoulder which was hurting like hell after that botched attempt on the door, he puffed his chest out. 'It's definitely locked. I'll kick it in instead. Failing that, we'll smash a window.'

Anna glanced up at him admiringly. *It was hopeful if it was locked as that meant no one could have broken in.*

'Don't worry,' Aiden smiled. 'I'll pay for the door and

window, so don't stress about that ok?'

Anna smiled gratefully. *She was so lucky to have him.*

Raising his foot, Aiden gave the door a hefty kick and was heartened to see the door begin to give. 'One more should do it I think,' he muttered. He didn't want to put the window through because he'd probably severe an artery the way things were going today.

Still, on the bright side he'd get a *big* pay out for pulling this job off, so it was worth it. He'd also be putting in for some overtime for those extra hours he'd be stuck with Anna too. Eliza could afford it and by Christ, they sure as hell needed his services at the moment.

Giving the door another hefty boot, it gave on his hinges, the cracking sound loud as the wood splintered.

With the door now wide open, Anna immediately pushed through. 'Mum?' she called.

Aiden grabbed Anna's arm before she could go any further. 'Let me go in first,' he said. *He needed to at least pretend her safety was a concern.*

Anna smiled weakly. 'No. Mum will have a coronary seeing a strange man in the house. She'll presume you've come to rob her, or worse.'

Aiden smiled. *Yep and she'd have been right.* 'Ok, but I'm right behind you.' He followed Anna as she walked into the small square hallway.

'Mum?' she called again. Receiving no answer, she stuck her head into the tiny kitchen finding it empty. 'Maybe she's upstairs?' Anna mumbled. '*Mum!*'

Continuing into the lounge situated at the back of the house, Anna glanced in. 'Mum? M… OH MY GOD!'

'What is it?' Aiden cried, racing to her side already knowing what the problem was.

Anna froze in the doorway as her eyes came to rest upon the body of her mother crumpled in a heap upon the sheepskin rug. 'M-Mum?' she whispered almost inaudibly, a tremoring shaking vibrating up through her toes, up her legs, along her arms and up to the ends of her fingertips.

Her breath came in short, rasping gasps as her eyes moved over the once beige rug, seeing a dark red patch spread out in a large circle from under her mother's head.

'Don't,' Aiden whispered, grabbing Anna's arm as she made to move forward.

Anna shook his hand away and forced her shaking legs to propel herself across the carpet towards the figure on the floor. *She needed to get to her mother. Needed to help her.* 'Mum,' she choked. 'It's me, Anna. I'm here.'

Moving closer, Anna could clearly see there was nothing that she could do to help her mother.

Vomit rose into her throat when her eyes moved to the caved-in hole at the back of her mother's head. Her skull looked like it had sunken from the inside out. Part of the skull was missing and the brains had spilled out from her mother's head, causing a gelatinous mess to mix with the sheepskin rug fibres.

It was more than she could bear and a projectile wave of vomit spewed from Anna's mouth and nose as she sunk to her knees on the carpet.

Aiden sighed as Anna began screaming hysterically. *It was going to be a long night.*

THIRTY FIVE

SETH WAS STILL NOT in anywhere near a good mood. In fact, it was a gross understatement to suggest he was experiencing anything other than a combination of rage, disbelief, confusion and downright terror. Although he'd given Jane a quick low down over the phone of the latest news, he knew there would still be an awful lot she'd need answers to. *The problem was he didn't have them.*

On returning to the Glint after his fruitless run-in with Miller, the second Seth had stepped into his thickly carpeted lobby he'd been informed there was someone waiting to see him. He'd been irritated. He didn't appreciate off the cuff callers. The rule was 'Appointment Only' and he had little time for *anyone* who felt they could bypass this.

Raking his fingers through his hair, Seth had been all set to tell the receptionist to inform the caller to come back once they had an appointment. That was until he'd learnt the person waiting was none other than Carl Mulligan. Being as he was very much in the frame of mind to tell the useless bastard what he thought of him, he'd figured now was a good a time as any, so he'd stomped up to his office.

Yanking the door open, Seth had barged into the room ready

to let rip, until his eyes focused on the short, kindly-looking old man sitting patiently in a chair.

'Mr Wright?' the old man said, stiffly rising from the seat. 'Good to meet you at last. Have you changed your mind and want to continue in the search for your daughter after all?'

Seth had been taken off guard and stood dumbly staring at the man dressed in a brown three-piece suit, with wisps of greying hair combed delicately over his balding crown.

The man stepped forward, his hand outstretched. 'Sorry, I should introduce myself. I'm Carl Mulligan. We spoke some time ago about your missing daughter? You called again this morning? Some confusion over cancelling contracts? I have to say I was surprised when you previously cancelled my services because you seemed so eager to lo…'

'*You're* Carl Mulligan?' Seth had exclaimed. He needed to sit down. If *this* was Carl Mulligan, whom he might add, fitted Miller's description down to a tee, then who the hell had he seen before? The one who'd given him the location of his daughter?

Flopping onto the sofa, Seth forced himself to smile at Jane as she topped up her vodka. He was exhausted - mentally and physically.

'What going on Seth?' Jane asked, her eyebrows knitting closely together. She needed to know the ins and outs of what had happened. She'd rapidly realised after his phone call that things were even more worryingly complex than they had both suspected.

Seth glanced around the room. 'Where's Anna?' he asked quietly.

'She's giving Toby a bath and then putting him to bed. Can you just please tell me what's happening?'

Seth cracked his knuckles. 'That's the thing,' he muttered. 'I don't bloody know.'

Something untoward was going on alright - that much was obvious. After seeing Carl Mulligan for himself it hadn't been difficult to work out someone was impersonating the man, but the question still remained as to *why*? It also hadn't been rocket science to deduce that the same person, or someone *linked* to that person had also impersonated *him* to cancel the *real* Carl Mulligan's contract.

Seth slugged greedily at his whisky. *All this shit was making his head hurt. It was too crazy.* 'I told Carl the girl we'd been falsely led to was in no way our daughter and he's promised to get back on the case straight away. He'd already done some prep work before he'd been 'cancelled', so reckons he should have something concrete to give us - hopefully by the end of the week.'

Jane nodded, getting the distinct feeling there was more.

Seth sighed. 'I also touched briefly on the other events which have been going on, including the latest threat to Tobes. Mulligan's warned me all the signs definitely point towards somebody is intent on kidnap as well as trying to impede everything we're doing. Or *both*…'

Jane's hand flew to her mouth. '*Kidnap*? Oh fuck, Seth, NO!'

Seth grabbed Jane's hand and pulled her close. 'Listen, don't worry. We have to be extra vigilant and in the meantime, do everything we can to discover who's behind this crap. I won't let anything happen to you or our son, Jane. Over my dead body ok? Trust me, it won't be *me* who's dying at the end of this. Neither will it be you or Tobes,' Seth snarled.

Jane shakily reached for her drink. 'So, what the hell do we do?'

Seth ran his fingers though his beard. 'I don't know yet. I thought all of this was to do with Miller, but now I'm beginning to wonder…'

'Jason Miller?' Jane cried. 'Regardless of anything else, he wouldn't threaten *kids*!'

'Well that's what I thought, but you never know. Still… leave it with me. I *promise* I'll get to the bottom of this somehow. Now on to another subject, have you had any more letters regarding Toby?' Seth asked.

Jane shook her head. 'Thankfully not, though I'm half

expecting more,' she scowled. 'I won't leave anything to chance where Toby's concerned.'

Seth pushed himself forward to the edge of the sofa and spoke quietly. 'Martin wanted a word the other day, but my priority was to get him to tail you when you went to Maggie's. I won't take any chances either and that includes *your* safety too Jane.'

He reached forward, grabbing his glass of whisky from the coffee table and gulped at it greedily. 'Yeah, like I was saying, Martin finally grabbed hold of me this afternoon and it turns out whilst we were in St Ives, Anna was with a bloke.'

Jane sat up. 'What? Again?' She knew Seth had his misgivings about Anna and also knew he'd previously questioned her over the police incident. He was convinced she wasn't being honest and she'd begun to suspect he might be right. 'Well who is it then? A boyfriend she hasn't told us about?' One of the reasons she'd hired Anna because she allegedly had no interest in relationships.

Seth shrugged. 'That's the point. I don't know. I wish I'd made the time to listen to Martin before now, otherwise I might have already got to the bottom of it.'

'Has this bloke been in our house?' Jane asked, anger simmering. *If Anna had been lying all of this time....*

'Again, I don't know. Martin said he'd seen her in the park with this guy. She'd got Toby with her...'

'She took my son to meet up with a bloke no one knows from Adam?' Jane yelled.

Seth pulled Jane back down trying to calm her. Even though he was also steaming about it, he didn't want her to pick up on that. 'When I spoke to her about it, she said the guy was just a friend. Martin doesn't know whether he was at the house this time around.'

'And why the fuck not?' Jane barked.

'Because I pulled everyone off watching the house after we realised there was no need,' Seth mumbled.

Jane seethed, knowing Seth was referring to his belief that

her thinking people were casing their property was down to her paranoid delusions. 'Well maybe they *were* watching the house! Especially after this!'

'Here's what's going to happen,' Seth said. 'Martin can't be sure because he hasn't seen the man close up, but he did say the guy reminds him of someone. He's not saying it's *definitely* this person, but there are lots of similarities.'

'So, who the hell is it?' Jane asked, getting more and more impatient.

'It's a guy who works for Miller... A bit of a nobody. I want him brought to me at the Glint for questioning,' Seth stated. 'I'll get Dan to bring him in asap.'

When Martin had said it could be one of Miller's guys it was hardly a surprise. That was the *second* person who'd linked Miller to all of this shit. Seth's teeth grated together. Regardless of what Jane said, if he found out the treacherous cunt was behind this like he'd suspected all along, then he'd be personally disposing of him.

Jane stared at Seth. 'Was it *you* who did those two reporters?'

Seth looked at Jane quizzically. 'What makes you think that?'

Jane raised an eyebrow. 'Just seems a bit coincidental both reporters who ran a non-favourable story on you met untimely ends... Stop playing games with me Seth.'

'It had to be done,' Seth shrugged. Although he'd planned on taking the second reporter out anyway, he'd had an unexpected opportunity where that bloke was concerned. A chance encounter one night whilst driving home had given him the opportunity to pull off a convenient hit and run. He'd had to make no effort whatsoever. It couldn't have been more handy. *Right place, right time – at least for him...*

Jane huffed angrily. *She knew it.* 'And like doing that will help us get our daughter back? Do you really think I need anything else to worry about?'

Seth sighed and pulled Jane into his arms. 'That's why I

didn't tell you. I knew you'd get stressed.'

'I've every right to!' she raged. 'You'll fuck the court case up.'

'And so would lots of damaging press articles. Two were bad enough and I couldn't have any more!' Seth snapped. 'Hence me trying to sort all this stuff out.'

'But I could do without you not levelling with me. There's enough people doing that without you!'

'Listen, we won't have a court case to go to if I can't resolve this shit, so let me get on with it,' Seth said gently. Although Jane had always dealt with everything well and taken it on the chin, he knew she'd been so very disappointed with the let-down where Grace was concerned and he'd been reticent to add to her worries. 'I'll tell you all the gory details from now on then, but you may not like or agree with them.'

Jane scowled. *That was hardly anything new was it?*

• • • •

ELIZA WATCHED STEVE LOMOND casually refill his glass from her best and most expensive whisky as usual. If she could have got away with smashing the heavy decanter into his rotten stinking teeth, she would have done. *This was a total and utter bloody disaster. In fact, it wasn't just a disaster, it was a catastrophic calamity!*

She irritably wiped the thin film of sweat from her brow, scowling at the streak of brown foundation smeared across her hand. *So much for bloody waterproof makeup. Cheap shit.*

Eliza studied Digger staring out of the window. She didn't know why he was bothering. The view was hardly delectable - a brick wall. He was obviously waiting for *her* to come up with a solution. *Again.*

Snatching the decanter from the table before Lomond could get his greasy mitts back on it, Eliza tipped an overly large measure in a glass and placed the heavy bottle next to her, rather than back where it had sat, knowing Lomond would have to physically get up if he wanted any more. And if he so much as asked her to pass it to him, she'd insert the bloody thing up his goddamn arse.

She let out a deep sigh and opened her cigarette packet for the tenth time in as many minutes. *As if she hadn't got enough to deal with.* She was trying to keep tabs on Aiden too and she needed to touch base with him and hadn't been able to as yet because thanks to Lomond, she'd had to deal with *this.*

For God's sake. Lomond couldn't help himself could he the stupid, STUPID bastard.

Eliza felt her blood pressure surging at an alarming rate. 'Are you going to explain what the fuck you were thinking of or what?' she screamed, making everyone else jump out of their skins in the previous silence of the room.

Steve Lomond glared at Eliza. 'Just one of those things,' he muttered dismissively. 'It'll resolve itself.' Not that he would admit it, but he was gutted. He'd been looking forward to having that tasty bit of skirt to himself for the foreseeable future.

'One of those things?' Eliza screeched. 'You fucking kill a girl because you can't control yourself, you moronic bastard and it's *one of those things*?'

Lomond hefted himself up from the chair angrily. 'Now wait a minute, you plastic bitch, you…'

'FOR GOD'S SAKE!' Digger roared. 'I've had enough of this! Are you going to bitch and moan all fucking night? It's irrelevant how, why or who. We have a problem. A *big* one and we need to work out what the hell we're going to do about it.'

He ground his cigarette out in the ashtray. 'I don't know about you two, but I don't fancy going down for a long stretch over this!'

Eliza, shocked into silence, stared at Digger. *He was right. She still wanted to rip Lomond's dick off for putting her in this position, but it would have to wait.*

She glanced at him evilly for several seconds before turning away. Leaning back in her chair, she folded her arms across her chest to make out she felt in control of the situation. Realistically it would have been better described that she felt up to her neck in quicksand. *Quicksand that was gradually sucking her under...*

'Ok - the situation as you know is dire. We have the body of a young girl concealed in our cellar, which will be discovered sooner rather than later from the fucking smell alone!' Eliza inspected her fingernails, her voice dripping with sarcasm.

'The other point to note is that it's quite obvious death was from strangulation and...' Eliza didn't even attempt to hide the smile that crept across her face when she turned towards Lomond. '...anything on her body will belong to *you*.' *If anyone was going down for this it would be him.*

Eliza's bravado was fake. She knew if any investigation got near it would only be a matter of time before the past came to light – including the kidnap. She felt sweat creeping along the back of her neck as the finality of their situation sank in. Being tugged for this would totally blow their adoption to the moon and back.

'*I'm* not taking the rap for this!' Lomond boomed. 'If you'd delivered when you should have then I wouldn't have been forced to take matter into my own hands.'

Digger's mouth set into a hard line as a glimmer of an idea began to form in his mind. *Maybe there was a way that none of them would be held accountable which would be the icing on the cake.*

'I suggest you determine the location of one of Wright's lock-ups Lomond. He's bound to still have some,' Digger grinned. 'We'll dump the fucking tart's body at one of those and then none of us need to worry.'

Thirty Six

SETH HAD RECEIVED A call from Dan twenty minutes ago to say he'd got hold of Alan Barber and they'd be at the Glint shortly.

Leaning back in his chair, he cracked his knuckles and frowned. He'd been hoping to get to this Alan bloke long before now, but two long days had passed before the opportunity had arisen. After all it wasn't like he could expect any help from Jason Miller.

He wanted to be at home. He always wanted to be with Jane and Toby, but the need to be close to them today was all consuming. He hadn't mentioned it to anyone, but this morning he'd received another letter.

Seth pulled the crumpled piece of paper from his trouser pocket and hesitated slightly before opening it. The contents had made him feel ill enough the first time around.

> *We realise your concentration is slipping because you're on edge, but it will be some comfort to know your daughter will be very happy with us.*
>
> *Also, being as your au pair is clearly too upset about her*

Mother to properly look after your son, it leaves the way nicely open doesn't it?

Your entire family will soon be ours and you are done.

Fighting the urge to shred the letter into tiny pieces, Seth shoved it back in his pocket. There was no arguing with that. This was the first mention of his daughter and he had no clue whether whoever this was, had her or whether these words were purely to instil utter fear, but it had certainly achieved that.

Whoever was sending these letters knew things that weren't public knowledge. Very few people knew about their daughter and no one, as far as he was aware - apart from the police, knew what had befallen Anna's mother.

So was the writer connected to the perpetrator, or was it the killer?

Seth racked his brain for who knew about Grace. There was close friends, Mulligan and *Miller* – and of course whoever was impersonating Mulligan…

His body thrummed with dread. There was no mistaking the warning. This was no veiled threat. It was *blatant*. They were coming for his son and when he found out who was behind this, he would rip them to shreds – very slowly and *very* painfully.

• • • •

ALAN BARBER COULDN'T help but feel unnerved. He risked a sideways glance at the man driving the car.

The minute someone had stepped from the shadows when Alan had got out of his car for the second shift of the day, he'd known something was afoot.

The man who'd introduced himself as Dan, had been polite, although firm in his request and Alan had immediately realised there was little point attempting to resist a request to meet with Seth Wright. To do so would have invariably brought him trouble. *Well – more than what he found himself in at this present moment in time.*

He shifted slightly in the car seat, not having the faintest clue what they could want with him. He wasn't privy to *anything* which could be of interest to the likes of Seth Wright.

He was aware things went on at the clubs. Name a club where it didn't? But he wasn't party to inside information and neither did he want to be. He kept his nose out of that side of things and that was the way he liked it.

However, he *was* tuned in to the atmosphere at the club that had changed considerably over the last couple of months. Only being blind and deaf would have escaped that.

There had been high levels of suspicion even between his colleagues ever since Billie-Jo's attack. No one liked to think it was one of their own who could have done it, but it *had* to have been one of them. Either that or a psycho stranger had been wandering around invisibly amongst them all. *He wasn't sure which was worse.*

This knowledge had upset the general equilibrium. Gone were the good-natured chats, jokes and associating out of hours. Instead everyone eyed each other with ill-concealed distrust and it was horrible. It had become so uncomfortable Alan had even begun to think of leaving.

When Miller had publicly pulled the club's association with Seth Wright and the Glint, it had opened up even more speculation. Rumours had been circulating for a while about the Wrights, but since all that business in the paper and then Miller taking a step back, it had only put more fuel on the fire. There *must* have been substance to the hearsay and rumours.

Alan stuck his finger into the neck of his collar, hoping to loosen it. It was feeling exceptionally tight. If word got out, he'd been seen at the Glint, then he too would become a target for finger pointing.

'Here we are!' Dan said, as the car came to a sudden and abrupt halt outside the side entrance of the Glint.

Alan swallowed nervously. He hadn't noticed how quickly they'd crossed town. Taking a deep breath, he reluctantly got out of the car.

• • • •

JENNIE WEARILY TRUDGED down the road and glanced at her watch. She'd still got half a mile to go before she reached Hadley's for her evening shift and would be late if she wasn't careful.

As much as she didn't like to admit it, she'd really missed Lacey's company since they'd fallen out. It had been strange not having the easy camaraderie that she'd experienced with the girl from day one.

Jennie had been thinking about making things up with her and thought perhaps she'd been too hasty jumping to conclusions, or at least not giving the girl a chance to explain. That was until Lacey had done a runner.

Two days ago she'd gone to work and hadn't come back. Sylvia had opened her room, but none of her belongings were missing. Not even a toothbrush or a change of clothes. Alarm bells had begun to ring.

Sylvia had been less concerned. 'Jennie, don't worry. You say you two had a falling out? I'm not going to ask what it was about and it doesn't really matter, but I will say I had noticed that as well as from you, Lacey was getting blanked by all the other girls too…'

Jennie had hung her head guiltily. It was true she'd made sure the other girls had been informed of Lacey's lies. *Was this all her fault?*

Sylvia had put her hand on Jennie's shoulder. 'Listen, it's extremely unlikely anything dreadful has happened. I've been doing this a long time and lots of girls who haven't had the best start in life find when something – even something relatively small – causes problems, they go off the deep end.' She smiled kindly. 'They return after a day or so after a bit of time out.'

Jennie hadn't been convinced and it must have showed on her face.

'*When* she returns, I suggest you make up your differences. You obviously care a lot about her and so therefore whatever caused you to fall out can't be *that* important can it?'

Jennie had slowly nodded her head, acknowledging that Sylvia had been right.

'Good!' Sylvia had exclaimed. '*If* Lacey hasn't returned by tomorrow night, *then* I'll think about phoning the police to report her missing, but I can only repeat I've never known a girl not to return.'

What Sylvia had said had put Jennie's mind at ease to a certain extent, but not completely. There was still something which hadn't seemed right.

She continued miserably down the road, scornfully watching a large car pull up at the side of the road outside *THAT* alley. Word had it there was a place down there with a dodgy quack who dealt with prostitutes – sorting out their contraception, STI checks and abortions. Rumour said his fee was freebies from the girls. Her nose wrinkled up in distaste. *Bloody men. All out for one thing...*

A man got out of the car who resembled a monster. From this distance he resembled the epitome of a psycho in the films. She watched six girls pile out the back of the large saloon who were then shepherded down the alley. Her blood ran cold when her eyes fell onto the final girl in the group. *It was THAT girl - the one from the café.*

Remaining motionless, Jennie squinted against the late-afternoon sun as the girls disappeared from view. A horrible sinking feeling enveloped her. *Lacey hadn't been lying about a thing. She hadn't done a runner. Something bad had happened. She was sure of it.*

Deciding going to work was nowhere near as important as updating Sylvia with what she'd discovered, Jennie turned on her heels and ran as fast as she could back to Pegasus Place.

Thirty Seven

JANE SIGHED AS, with some effort she pushed herself up from the armchair and irritably put her notebook down on the coffee table. She'd only just got Toby off to sleep and had used this rare spare time to jot down some ideas she'd had about the Glint.

She was losing her patience with Anna. There was something niggling at the back of her mind about the girl. Despite a great start, things were going off track. She couldn't afford to have someone around that was showing signs of being untrustworthy.

Jane moved towards the door. *For a start, why the hell was she paying Anna all this money if she wasn't around when she needed her. Like to answer the door or look after Toby?*

Jane glanced at the front door, an unfamiliar pang of nervousness washing over her. *It was late, so who would be knocking at this time?* Unwilling to admit that the threats and weird business had unnerved her more than she cared to acknowledge, Jane reprimanded herself. Martin or Barry were watching the house again, so anything untoward would have been taken care of.

Jane yanked open the door, finding Martin standing on the doorstep, his hand firmly on the shoulder of an unkempt woman.

'Sorry to disturb you Mrs Wright,' Martin said. 'This 'lady' has asked to speak with Anna.'

'*Anna*?' Jane couldn't hide the incredulity from her voice as her eyes ran over the woman's lank greasy hair and sunken eyes. She always prided herself on not being judgemental, but she'd failed miserably in this instance. *What on earth did this woman want with Anna?*

'I'm really sorry to bother you. I didn't know what else to do. I've got no other means of contacting Anna,' Tina said, trying her best to put on a voice which hid the traces of the heroin she'd smoked earlier.

Jane raised an eyebrow. 'Could I ask what you want to speak to Anna about? She's working.'

Tina watched Jane as she spoke. *The stuck up bitch, standing here all snotty-like, the jumped up cow.* Quickly remembering herself, Tina applied the look of a desperately sad person to her drug-ravaged face. 'Anna's my sister, Mrs Wright,' she said, enjoying the look of shock briefly washing over Jane Wright's face. *How she'd love to smash her fist into that perfectly pretty mug.*

Quickly dragging her composure together, Jane opened the door wide. 'Please, come in.' She glanced at Martin frowning questioningly from behind and nodded her approval. She could hardly turn the woman away.

'Sit, down, erm… I didn't catch your name?' Jane said, whilst Martin followed them into the house.

'Tina. I'm Tina,' the woman said, sitting down in her grubby tracksuit.

'Ok Tina, I'll go and get Anna,' Jane said, walking from the room. *Tina? Didn't Lacey tell Seth the woman who'd groomed her was called Tina?* Her hackles began to rise and suspicion welled.

• • • •

ALAN HADN'T KNOWN what to expect when he'd followed Dan to Seth Wright's office on the top floor of the Glint. He still didn't understand why his presence was required.

All that had happened since taking a seat was to be intensely scrutinised in silence by Seth's infamous green stare. *And it was utterly unnerving.*

Although Alan had seen the man on countless occasions, he'd never seen him close up before and Seth Wright had never *ever* uttered a word to him, or even glanced in his direction before, so why would he bother to acknowledge him now? There was no reason – he was a mere grunt.

Even Jason Miller barely knew his name and he'd worked for him for *years*. Now for some reason he'd fallen onto the radar of Seth Wright and that was *definitely* not on his 'to do' list.

Without making it obvious, Alan had stolen a few surreptitious glances at Seth. The man emitted an intense persona without even speaking. His physical strength was clear due to his build and his heavily-muscled forearms - on show courtesy of his rolled-up sleeves, but the *mental* force was suffocating. The vibe and magnetism radiating from him was something Alan didn't think he'd ever experienced.

Seth frowned and his dark eyebrows knitted together in concentration. *He half-recognised this guy...* 'Have we spoken before Alan?' he asked, resting his forearms lightly on the paperwork littering the top of his desk.

'N-No Sir,' Alan stuttered, momentarily flummoxed when the silence was unexpectedly broken. 'I don't think so. I-I mean, I've seen you on many occasions, but never had the pleasure of speaking with you.' *Christ, he was grovelling and simpering like a twat.*

Seth nodded dismissively, recognition still jangling somewhere in the recesses of his mind. 'A social occasion perhaps?'

Alan frowned, doubting very much that he would have ever been invited to a gathering hosted by Seth and Jane Wright *or* any of the people who would have them on their esteemed guest list. *Unless...*

'Actually, there may have been *one* event – Linda Miller's birthday? Mr Miller invited all of his long-serving staff,' Alan gibbered, trying to justify why the likes of him had been invited.

Seth rubbed his fingers lightly over his beard without moving his gaze from Alan. *That may have been it, therefore this guy could be a feasibility.* 'So, I take it you know my son's au pair?'

'Your son's *au pair*?' Alan spluttered. 'N-No. I don't th…'

'You met at Miller's party? Is that how you know her?' Seth interrupted once more.

Alan was unsure how to answer. It hadn't escaped his notice Seth's tone of voice had taken on a definitive snarl. 'I-I've never met her Sir. I-I mean I've seen photographs in the paper, but I've never had the pleasure of meeting her personally.' *Was that the right thing to say?*

'Are you *sure* about that Alan?' Seth hissed, leaning forward and watching the man visibly shrink before his very eyes.

Alan swallowed nervously. 'I-I'm sure. I've never spoken with or met your au pair.' *He had no idea what this woman had got to do with anything, but was damned if he was going to ask.*

Seth scrutinised Alan's nervous body language. From instinct he felt the guy was telling the truth, but he fitted the description of who Anna had been seen with. And of course, Martin had put forward his name as a possibility….

'Ok, let's try this…' Seth smiled. A smile that didn't reach his eyes. 'Do you know *who* has met my au pair if you haven't? Either that night or since.'

Alan didn't know where to look. He didn't want to look into Seth's eyes in case he got turned into stone, but neither did he want to *not* look at him because that came over like he'd got something to hide. *Oh God. This was awful. He didn't have a clue who Seth Wright's au pair had met! Why would he?*

Seth rose from his chair and casually pulled open the middle drawer in his filing cabinet, ensuring Alan Barber got a good view of the handguns he kept there for occasions such as these, as well as the camera, which he pulled out flamboyantly.

Noticing Alan flinch, Seth hid a smile. 'You don't mind if I take a quick snap, do you? Identification purposes.'

Alan shook his head and swallowed down the large brick stuck somewhere down his gullet. *Identification purposes? What for? His body?*

Mentally kicking himself for allowing his mind to run away with itself, inflaming his already fragile state of mind, he pulled his brain back to reality. *He was being silly. He was being asked a perfectly acceptable question for God's sake! Wasn't he...?*

Never being a very good liar, Alan tried to look normal and not like a recently released lunatic who hadn't been taking his tablets and stared down the lens of the camera.

'Thanks Alan,' Seth smiled, placing the camera back in the drawer.

'N-No problem,' Alan murmured, hoping he wouldn't let himself down by toppling off the chair in fear. If he got out of here – no, *when* he got out of here – *think positive Alan, stop being so melo-bloody-dramatic* – then he was going for a drink. He was already late for his shift at the Limelight, so a bit more time wouldn't matter.

Maybe Aiden was about? They said they'd catch up for a drink, but that was *weeks* ago and… *Hang on... Aiden came to that party. It couldn't have been him could it?* People said they looked similar…

Aiden *had* been present at that party, but the only person he'd seen him talking to was that hideous cougar who'd jumped on the pair of them when they'd arrived. Admittedly he hadn't taken that much notice of what his brother had been doing the rest of the night, but surely he'd have mentioned it if something important had happened?

They told each other *everything*. It had been the same since they were little. Having only eighteen months between them ensured they'd always been close. It was only since leaving school they'd inevitably drifted apart as they'd both got on with their lives and they didn't see each other as much as they'd have liked.

Seth was studying the expressions running across Alan's face. 'Has something come back to you?' he barked.

Alan jumped in his seat. He'd allowed himself to get sidetracked. *Shit. He'd never been much good at hiding things.* 'No, sorry. I was worrying about being late for work that's all.' *Oh God. Now he'd lied. He'd lied to Seth Wright...*

There was no way he'd bring Aiden into this by mentioning his name. What was the point? There was no chance Aiden would have done anything untoward. Besides, he was his younger brother and he'd *always* looked out for him and that hadn't changed.

Seth leant casually against the front of his desk close to Alan. 'Just one last question... Has Miller found out who disfigured that poor girl yet?'

Alan was taken aback by the question. He hadn't expected it. He couldn't say anything against Miller, even if he had thought along the same lines himself. *For all he knew this could be a set up.*

'My understanding is that he's still looking into it, Sir,' Alan replied steadily. *Well, it was probably true.*

'Ok,' Seth said breezily, pushing himself up to his full height. 'Thanks for your time Alan. Remember to get in touch *straight away* if anything comes back to you.'

Alan stood up, praying his jelly-like legs wouldn't let him down. He forced himself to meet Seth's eyes which were drilling into his.

'Or of course if you hear of anything which rings alarm bells that might also be of interest to me.' Seth smiled coldly. 'Dan, take Alan wherever he needs to go.'

Dan quickly ushered Alan out of Seth's office and down the stairs. As they walked to the car in silence, Alan recalled Aiden had been in the Limelight the night Billie-Jo was attacked.

He shook his head to remove the ridiculous suspicion which had begun to form.

• • • •

ANNA RAISED HER HAND to her face when Tina delivered another stinging slap to her cheek.

'It's all your fault, you stuck up bitch!' Tina screamed, spittle spraying into Anna's hair. 'If you hadn't broadcast your involvement with the Wrights, then *none* of this would have happened.'

Oh, she was loving this. Loving EVERY minute. She'd have descended on Anna before now, but knew she'd needed at least a couple of days to tone down the joy and relief that their mother was no longer around. *She could hardly deliver a genuine-looking angry bashing with a big smile on her face, could she?*

Tina had literally danced with glee when Aiden had returned, telling her the job had been successfully carried out. It was like a grand piano had been lifted off her shoulders – one that had sat there crushing her from the outside all her bloody life and now it was gone.

Never again would she have to listen to bitchy comments about what a dreadful daughter she was or what an embarrassment she'd been all her life. No more would she have to pretend her mother's words didn't bother her, when really they cut her to the bone and neither would she have to hear ever again how much of a failure she was in comparison to her sister. *The perfect Anna...*

'If only you'd bothered to get me more information,' Tina raged, lurching towards her sister who had now dropped to her knees. 'You had the perfect opportunity to get all the dirt in the world on the most dangerous couples in town, but you didn't. I could have paid my debt off, but you didn't want that did you? Oh no, you'd rather make it a dead fucking cert someone would cop it and you were hoping it would be me, but it wasn't. It was *Mum*. YOU'VE done all of this Anna. *YOU!*'

Tina hid her smile. All that mattered was if Anna believed *she* was to blame for their mother's death, that would be her downfall. It couldn't have turned out more perfect. *God, it was almost orgasmic.*

Anna could barely formulate any words her sobbing was so

intense. She'd been surprised to learn her sister was in the living room and she'd dreaded going downstairs as she knew what was going to happen, so she'd quickly ushered Tina out of the house and down the road to the small park and there she'd let rip. But everything she'd said was true. *Everything!*

Anna looked up at Tina with her tear-stained face. 'I'm *so* sorry Tina. I tried my best but what can I do?'

Tina scowled. 'What *can* you do? That's the problem. You didn't do *enough* and certainly didn't do your best!'

Anna grasped at her sister's grubby tracksuit. '*Please*. You've got to listen to me. What if they come for you next?'

Tina raised her eyebrows in mock thoughtfulness. 'Has it ever crossed your mind that this may have had *nothing* to do with my debt, but *everything* to do with your beloved Mr Wright? Do you think he was happy discovering the source leaking his dirty washing to the press was none other than *you*?'

Anna's sobs quietened to soft hiccups. 'That's not possible…' *Could that have been it? She'd certainly seen a different side to Seth lately…*

Tina smiled watching the cogs whirring in Anna's head. 'Yep, it's sinking in isn't it? The people I owe money to wouldn't have got much by knocking off an old woman, would they? What would they do? Pawn her shitty furniture?' she laughed loudly.

Dropping down onto her haunches, Tina squatted in front of Anna. 'They were still getting info from me via you which they could use, so although your efforts have been feeble, it was still *something*. No Anna, I think you need to look closer to home for the culprit.' *Oh and how true was that!*

Anna felt thoroughly sick. *It was feasible.*

'Furthermore,' Tina drawled, loving seeing Anna squirm like the worm she was. 'I heard the story you enabled the papers to print has fundamentally damaged the chance of the Wrights ever getting their daughter back. Know that did you? Not that they stood a chance of finding her, but that's not the point.'

Anna looked at Tina. 'How do you know about their

daughter?' As far as she knew no one knew about that. She only knew because she'd overheard yet another of their arguments. She paled further. If that was true then there was definitely a motive for hurting her through her mother.

'Although it could equally be my debtors,' Tina continued glibly. 'I guess we'll never know. It's not like I'm going to fucking ask them if they killed my mother is it?' she sneered. 'And if it's them, then yes – they'll be coming for me next.' *Oh, she'd got her. Look at her face. She'd got her well and truly.* 'Either way Anna, it's on you isn't it!'

Anna looked up. 'Tina *please*. I'm still in a position where I can do what you need. Just tell me what you want me to do.'

Tina scowled. *She didn't want to look too eager.* 'How can I trust you now?'

'Tina! You need to let me put this right. I need to do this,' Anna begged, grabbing her sister's arm.

'You need? *You* need? It's always about you isn't it?' Tina snapped, shaking Anna's grip from her sleeve.

'I'll do whatever you want,' Anna insisted.

Tina pulled some paper out of her pocket and shoved it in Anna's hands. 'In that case, the first thing you can do is put this on Jane's desk in her office. Secondly, get me Seth's hairbrush and thirdly – I want the kid.'

She didn't know why she hadn't thought of this before. Eliza would *love* it if she could get her hands on that baby – she knew how much her boss wanted revenge on the Wrights and if she could surprise her with *that* on top of everything else, then she was sure she'd be handsomely rewarded.

Thirty Eight

JANE TRIED NOT TO fidget whilst she waited for Carl Mulligan to get to the point. She knew it must be important for the man to have called so late last night asking for an urgent meeting as soon as possible, especially as he had been reluctant to discuss details over the phone.

Even though Seth had tried to get her to remain at home, Jane had insisted on being present at the meeting. If this man knew something about Grace, then she wanted to be there to hear it.

Carl Mulligan shuffled some paperwork in his hands and looked between Seth and Jane in turn. 'As I said, I'm sorry to have asked you to drop everything at such short notice but I felt th…'

'It's fine Carl,' Seth interrupted. 'There isn't anything that's more important than news of our daughter, so with all due respect, cut the waffle and just tell us the score.'

Jane glanced at Seth, watching the nerve twitch in his neck. He was clearly as pent up as she was about this and personally thought that if this man felt the need to procrastinate, then it looked like whatever he had found they weren't going to like.

'Very well…' Mulligan took a deep breath. 'I've located

your daughter an…'

Seth stood up, knocking a jar of paperclips over in his haste. 'Great! Where is she? Can we have the details? I wa…'

Mulligan raised his hand. 'It's not quite as simple as that I'm afraid.'

Seth's eyes narrowed. 'What do you mean it's not simple? You've either found her or you haven't! Which fucking one is it?'

'*Seth*!' Jane hissed. *Having a go at this bloke wasn't going to get them their information.*

'Well,' Mulligan continued, 'I've located your daughter's records. She's been renamed twice and the birthdate was entered incorrectly on one set of official paperwork, which is what has most likely flummoxed previous investigators.' He laid a sheet of paper on the desk, swivelling it around so it faced Seth and Jane.

'What's this?' Jane asked, scanning the list.

'These are the temporary foster placements and children's homes your daughter has been placed in over the last few years.'

Jane looked down the list of names. There were at least thirty all over the country that she could see at first glance. Hot tears burnt at the back of her eyes. 'Are you telling me our daughter has been constantly moved from one place to another all this time?' she snapped angrily.

Mulligan nodded sadly. 'I'm afraid so.'

'Look Seth,' Jane stabbed at the paper. 'In that month alone, she was moved *three* times!'

Seth's teeth clenched as a myriad of emotions ran through his mind. It looked like Jane's sixth sense had been right after all.

'Who's that?' Jane asked, pointing to a name at the top of the list.

Mulligan peered at the sheet. 'That's what your daughter is called now. Emily. Emily Benson.'

'*Emily Benson*?' Seth muttered almost to himself. 'So how do we move forward? What's the next stage? As you know there's quite a few things going on here and so we need to get this wrapped up sooner rather than later.'

Jane watched Carl Mulligan absentmindedly scratch his chin and she felt a rush of foreboding creep up on her. *He was stalling. They weren't going to like his answer, were they?*

Mulligan cleared his throat. 'That's where there's a slight issue…'

'Well spit it out then man!' Seth growled. 'You don't need to sugar-coat it. We need to know the crack.'

'I heard back from the authorities last night. They've confirmed there's an adoption in process.'

Jane felt like she might pass out. 'My daughter's being *adopted*?'

'It hasn't been finalised yet,' Mulligan said hastily. 'It's about to be though. Everything else has been completed and they're at the last stage - the formality of the court's signing of the papers. Although I can't get the date for this.'

'You've got to stop it!' Seth raged. He snatched up the telephone. 'I'll call the solicitor now.'

'The notice for adoption was listed some time ago. No one came forward with any objections…' Mulligan said quietly.

'It has to be stopped!' Jane cried. 'She's *our* daughter! Tell us where she is.'

'Well that's just it. I can't. They won't release that information at this stage unless we have a legal warrant, so we need to apply for it.'

'How long will that take?' Seth snapped. He was fast losing his temper. If anyone thought he would stand by and let his flesh and blood be adopted from under his nose they'd got rocks in their head.

'It depends. It could be months.'

'When's this adoption set to go through?' Jane asked, her voice barely audible. She felt like she was sinking and could hardly bear to ask the question.

'The final granting usually goes through a month or two after everything else has been completed,' Mulligan answered, seeing deep emotion flood the faces of the couple in front of him. 'And it was filed over a month ago…'

Seth's eyes narrowed. 'So, you're saying it could be any time now?'

'What can we do?' Jane cried in desperation.

Mulligan sighed. 'We need to get on top of this as soon as possible. At this stage, there's not a lot anyone can do once it's happened.'

Seth's mouth set in a hard line. Tomorrow he'd be back on the case finding out who was sending those threatening letters. Thankfully none had arrived today, but he suspected it was only a matter of time before the next one arrived. He would get to the bottom of this and finish it before the threats moved past mere letters and he was fairly certain that whoever was sending those letters had something to do with this adoption. *What did they say again? 'We've got your daughter...'*

Standing up suddenly, he swiped the entire contents of his desk to the floor and stormed from the room, leaving Jane staring at Carl Mulligan in abject shellshock.

• • • •

ALAN RUSHED DOWN THE road towards the car lot. He glanced at his watch and didn't dare run the risk of being late back. He'd only got a two hour slot between shifts today and it had taken him the best part of three-quarters of an hour to get over the other side of the city.

He'd got grief for being late the other night after his run in with Seth Wright, but had instinctively felt it wouldn't have been a wise decision to explain *why* he'd been so late. He was uncomfortable enough about all of this as it was and certainly didn't want anyone else – like Jason Miller – on his back as well.

He'd been hoping to catch up with Aiden before now, but there had been no gaps in his schedule which corresponded with when he knew Aiden would be at work. Being as he didn't even have an address for his brother these days, he had no choice but to do it this way.

Thankful to see the bright red signage of the car sales forecourt ahead of him, Alan crossed the tarmac, impatiently waving away an approaching salesman who had hastily moved in his direction clearly about to embark on a sales pitch. *He wasn't here to buy a fucking car!*

Alan pulled open the heavy door to the plush interior of the sales office, the strong air conditioning blasting him fully in the face.

He glanced around the desks positioned at widely spaced intervals around the large expanse of the room. *Where was Aiden? Maybe he'd finally been promoted and moved up to one of the sales offices upstairs?*

Alan looked up at the high galleried level of fishbowl glass-fronted offices and realised there was no way of knowing who was in any of them without being up there. He sighed, hoping after all of this Aiden wasn't out to lunch.

'Good afternoon Sir,' a suited man approached from behind, his hand already poised to shove a sheaf of shiny brochures in his hand. 'Any particular model you're interested in? Diesel? Petrol? An automatic perhaps?'

Alan glared at the man in irritation. 'I'm actually looking for someone. My brother – Aiden Barber. He works here. Do you know where I can find him?'

The salesman frowned. 'I'm afraid I don't know anyone of that name, but I've only recently joined the company. Let me go and ask my colleague.'

Alan impatiently watched the man lope over to the nearest desk and converse with another man. He saw the seated man glance up and look in his direction before getting up and making his way over.

Alan forced a smile. *Finally. Perhaps now he could get on with it? He hadn't got much time.*

'Hello Sir. I understand you're looking for Aiden?' the man said, extending his hand.

Alan nodded and shook the proffered hand. 'That's right. I need to speak to him. It's quite urgent.' *Get the hint. And I don't want to buy a car!*

The man looked slightly embarrassed. 'I'm afraid Aiden doesn't work here anymore Sir.'

Alan couldn't hide the shock from registering on his face. *Oh no! Had Aiden got sacked? Bloody hell!* 'W-What?'

The salesman cleared his throat. 'I'm guessing you haven't spoken to him for some time. Aiden left us over a year ago.'

Alan's mouth dropped open. 'A *year* ago? Oh, erm…' *What the hell?* 'Where did he go?'

The salesman shook his head. 'I can't help you with that either Sir. I don't know. He didn't work his notice out and no reference requests ever came in for him. He just arrived for work one day, said he was leaving and that was that.'

'Ok, thank you,' Alan muttered, hastily leaving the salesroom. He walked quickly down the road. *So now what?* He and Aiden had *always* been honest with each other, so why hadn't he been straight about leaving his job? And where was he now? Furthermore, *why* didn't his brother want him to know?

A glimmer of fear sprung forth and began to gain momentum in Alan's mind.

• • • •

'YOU'RE SUPPOSED TO fucking knock, you slag!' Eliza screeched when Selena unexpectedly walked into her office, straight into an eyeful of Aiden taking her over the desk.

'Sorry, sorry!' Selena squeaked, hastily backtracking out of the room and slamming the door firmly behind her. She leant up against the wall in the corridor and tried to steady her breathing already threatening to turn into hyperventilation. *Shit the bed! Eliza was doing that Aiden? Not something Digger would be pleased about.*

Selena shrugged. Not her business. *Nothing* was her business and she wouldn't be mentioning it to anyone. *She didn't want to end up like Lacey.*

She wiped the cold sweat off her forehead and made her way back down the steep staircase. She'd promised herself she wouldn't think about what had happened to Lacey, but it kept creeping back into her mind regardless and she wished it would go away.

Admittedly she'd spent the last week waiting for it to be discovered that she'd witnessed what they'd done. If they'd watched the CCTV footage back from that night, they'd have spotted her at the end of the corridor, clearly watching Aiden and Digger drag a large object wrapped in a bedsheet out from Room Twelve.

She'd only got up to get a drink. No amount of drinks, toothpaste or Polo mints had been effective in removing the foul taste of her last punter from her mouth and she hadn't been able to sleep. Selena closed her eyes in despair, unable to formulate just how much she wished she'd put up with the revolting taste lingering in her mouth, rather than getting up in the middle of the night only to end up being dragged into a nightmare.

Selena hurried into the communal lounge, glad to find it empty. The minute the door was safely closed away from prying eyes, she burst into tears. She'd known instinctively as she'd stood frozen in the shadows that the object wrapped in the bedsheets was a body. *And that the body was Lacey's.*

Any doubt she may have managed to convince herself of was quashed when she'd clearly heard Eliza ranting at Steve Lomond who'd also been in Room Twelve. That dirty foul sicko had killed his favourite girl. Whether intentionally or not she couldn't make out, but kill her he most definitely had.

Selena swiped the angry tears away from her face. She didn't care if she looked a state for her next punter due soon - he'd have to put up with it.

This was her fault. If she hadn't told them where to find Lacey, then she wouldn't be dead.

Selena had struggled through the last few days on auto-pilot. She'd gone through all the expected motions whilst successfully avoiding thinking, feeling or remembering *anything* about what she'd seen and what she knew to be true. Now it was starting to catch up with her and weigh heavily on her mind.

Sighing, she slumped down onto the saggy sofa and turned on the television. Seeing the news, she was about to turn it off when something made her pause.

Her finger hovered over the power button on the remote control as a photograph of Lacey flashed up onto the screen. Her ears began ringing as the presenter's muffled voice droned on about concerns for a local girl's safety since she'd gone missing a week ago from a hostel. It then switched to Jane Wright delivering a press appeal.

Selena studied the exceptionally beautiful and infamous Jane Wright. From the woman's eyes alone, it was clear to see this was a woman not to be messed with. The hardness behind those long lashes was evident for all to see and contradicted with the emotion evident in her voice.

So, it was true then? Lacey *had* been involved with Seth and Jane Wright? Oh, she'd heard rumours on the grapevine but hadn't believed any of them at the time.

The camera panned back to a close-up of Jane's face and Selena's jaw almost hit the floor hearing fifty thousand pounds reward money being offered to anyone with information leading to Lacey's whereabouts.

She knew where Lacey was… It wasn't about the money – not that fifty grand would go amiss, but it was because it was the *right* thing to do.

Selena's face fell. *What was she thinking?* She couldn't do or say a thing. If she opened her mouth, she'd invariably end up joining Lacey… On top of that, if she spoke of what she knew, then everyone would know *she'd* been the one who had set Lacey up. *She was the one responsible for Lacey's death.*

She may not have been the one who *physically* did it but was as near as damn it.

Thirty Nine

'DO YOU THINK IT was a good idea doing a press appeal?' Maggie asked.

Jane glanced up. 'Yes, of course I do. I wouldn't have done it otherwise. Why?'

Maggie shrugged. 'No particular reason. I just worry about you, what with all this stuff that's going on with Toby and this latest thing regarding Grace.'

Jane sighed. Didn't Maggie think the main reason she'd done the press appeal was because she believed the people involved with Lacey's disappearance may well be the same people behind everything else?

She looked out of the large window of the coffee shop overlooking the main road, well aware Barry had her clearly in his sights from his position on the pavement opposite.

She was getting fed up with being constantly followed. It made her feel like a wanted suspect. She'd had *more* than her fill of that over the years, but also sadly acknowledged at this precise moment in time it was an unfortunate necessity.

Maggie faltered. She realised she needed to come clean about something which had been bothering her. 'I should have mentioned this before,' she said. 'I hope it won't make a difference to anything?'

Jane frowned. 'What are you talking about?'

'That bloke. The one who was at the hospital the day we met Lacey…'

Jane sat up, her senses alert. 'What about him?'

Maggie stared at her fingernails and started picking at bits of imaginary dirt underneath them. *She knew this wasn't going to go down well.* 'I saw him…'

'*What*?' Jane screeched. 'When? Where?' If Maggie could ID the bloke connected to Lacey and it was the same one as the guy on Seth's photograph, then they'd got their man. It would prove her theory that this person knew something about Lacey's disappearance, but furthermore, she also thought these people were somehow linked to this weird vendetta, including the threats to Toby and the ones who had, or were trying to get their daughter.

'I saw him in a corner shop halfway across town,' Maggie admitted.

Jane's face flushed with anger. 'Why the hell didn't you say something sooner?'

Maggie couldn't quite meet Jane's eyes. 'I should have done.' She lowered her voice from embarrassment. 'I didn't want Dan to find out I'd been sneaking to the off-licence.'

Seeing the disbelief on Jane's face, Maggie attempted to justify her reasoning. 'I said I wouldn't go over the top with the drinking. You know how I get when I'm on it. I needed someth…'

'Oh, for God's sake!' Jane snapped angrily. 'You should have just told us straight away! It's more important than whether you get caught getting pissed!'

Maggie hung her head shamefully. 'I know and I'm sorry. I just hope it doesn't affect what they're doing.'

Jane stopped in her tracks. 'What do you mean?'

Maggie paled slightly, realising that she'd managed to put her foot in it. She'd presumed Jane knew of Seth's plans.

'Maggie, just tell me! Don't hide anything else for Christ's sake!'

Maggie fiddled with her fingers. 'Well, I er, don't really know much about it. Dan's been asked to go with Seth on a house call to see a bloke Seth thinks can shed more light on what's going on.'

Jane clenched her teeth. 'Typical!' she muttered, getting to her feet.

'Oh Jane, don't go! I wish I hadn't said anything,' Maggie pleaded.

'I'm glad you did Mags,' Jane said. '*Very* glad you did…'

• • • •

SETH BANGED HIS FIST on the front door and waited impatiently for it to open. He was convinced Alan Barber was the person behind it all, even though he'd admitted he'd thought the man was telling the truth the other night.

Seth knew Dan thought he was going out on a limb by revisiting Neil Batchelor, but Dan seemed to have forgotten a glaringly obvious point that very much pointed the finger at Alan Barber.

It was only after Alan had left the other night had it come back to Seth that the last time they'd paid Batchelor a visit, the man had said the runner who had asked him to make inroads at the club's name had begun with the letter 'A'.

Alan. Alan-Fucking-Barber. It all made sense. Martin said it looked like Barber. *Not difficult was it?*

Dan stood behind him. He knew Seth was hell bent on getting to the bottom of everything and he couldn't blame him for that because he'd have felt the same. He still couldn't help but feel he was barking up the wrong tree, but wisely decided to keep his opinion to himself.

'The fucking prick best hurry up,' Seth muttered, banging on the door again. 'Otherwise I'm just going to put the bastard thing through.'

'Yeah?' Neil Batchelor said yanking open the door, his red-rimmed eyes struggling to focus and his voice thick with cannabis.

'Neil!' Seth grabbed the man around the throat and frogmarched him backwards into his own hallway. 'Hope I'm not interrupting anything?'

The impact of having his windpipe crushed sank into Neil's stoned mind and his eyes widened in shock, realising it may have been more sensible to remain face down on the sofa and bin off the Chinese delivery he'd thought had arrived.

'I won't keep you long,' Seth growled, pushing Neil into the lounge. 'I just want you to ID someone.'

'ID someone?' Neil stammered.

'Yeah mate. It means I want you to look at a picture and tell me who it is,' Seth spoke slowly as if he was speaking to someone with reduced mental capacity.

Dan snorted back an inopportune giggle brewing at the back of his throat. It wouldn't have been a good plan to laugh.

Seth fished out the photograph of Barber from his inside pocket and shoved it in Batchelor's face. 'Recognise *him*?' He rolled his eyes watching the man struggling to focus. 'For fuck's sake!' he snarled. 'Look at the bastard picture you thick cunt! Is *this* the guy who asked you to make enquiries or what?'

'Erm…' Neil desperately tried to focus. *He shouldn't have smoked all that dope. Fuck!*

'Turn that shit down!' Seth yelled to Dan and nodded towards the television. *He didn't want to be watching the fucking news whilst dealing with this dickhead.*

'WAIT!' Seth barked as Dan reached for the power button when Jane flashed up on the screen. *What the hell?* His jaw clenched in fury listening to his wife rattling on about Lacey Garner's whereabouts. *Fifty grand reward? Was she mad? She needed to concentrate on her own daughter!*

Dan anxiously watched Seth's reaction to Jane's pleas. He could tell from the nerve twitching madly in Seth's neck that he was far from happy. He moved his focus to Neil Batchelor, who hadn't seemed to notice Seth's concentration was elsewhere and was painfully scrutinising the photograph rammed almost in his face.

'Turn it off!' Seth yelled once more. *The stupid fucking bitch! Was she crazy?* This would only serve to make her and Toby and every fucker that mattered more of a target! He ran his hand aggressively through his hair. *And she wondered why they were receiving threatening letters?*

Seth's adrenaline levels were nearing boiling point and he glared down at the stoner still vacantly staring at the picture of Alan Barber. *He wanted to pull his head off.* 'Well?' he snarled. 'Is it the same guy?'

'He looks similar…' Batchelor slurred.

'*Similar*? For fuck's sake – it's either him or it isn't surely?' Seth muttered. Bored, he delivered an upper cut to Batchelor's jaw, which sent him sprawling on to the grubby carpet.

Seth dropped to his haunches over the man who lay holding his jaw, looking dazed, confused and plain scared. 'Do you want to try again? Is *this* the guy?'

Neil swallowed. *What was he supposed to say again?* 'It does look a bit like the guy who I spoke to, but he…'

'What's his name?' Seth interrupted, getting even more frustrated. He was sick of people like this. *Totally fucking sick to the back teeth of them. They were so screwed up they didn't know what day it was half the time.*

He yanked his pistol out from his back pocket and rammed it into Neil Batchelor's mouth, forcing it wide.

'AAARGH!' Batchelor screamed, the acrid taste of the metal sticking to his tongue.

Dan shifted uncomfortably on his feet. '*Seth!*' he hissed. *He didn't need to go this far.*

Seth glared at Dan. 'What? I'm getting the information out of this wanker one way or the other. I've had enough!' He turned back to the man on the floor. 'His name?'

Neil Batchelor attempted to flail around on the floor, but it was pointless as Seth's other hand had him pinned firmly to the ground.

'His *name*?' Seth growled. 'Tell me his fucking NAME!'

Neil Batchelor blinked, the metal of the gun scraping uncomfortably against his teeth. He knew who this was but couldn't be sure it was the same bloke who'd spoken to him about the clubs. *He was too stoned.*

'*NAME?*' Seth screamed, cocking the trigger.

'Yyllan Rwarbr' Batchelor garbled.

'*What?*' Seth yelled impatiently. 'Speak fucking properly!' He yanked the barrel of the gun out of the man's mouth.

'T-That's Alan Barber,' Neil babbled, sweating profusely. 'But I don't th…'

'Thanks,' Seth said quickly, shoving the barrel of the pistol back in Batchelor's mouth. 'That's all I wanted to know.'

Seth pulled the trigger and Dan cringed when the man's skull shattered and bits of brain splattered up the wall. *Great. Just fucking great…*

Seth pushed himself to his feet, put the pistol back in his pocket and casually wiped his hands down his trousers. 'Come on,' he said dismissively.

Dan glanced around the room eyeing the gore. 'But…'

Seth glared at Dan as he walked towards the front door. 'But nothing! I'll send someone to clear this up. I need to get home. I want to find out what the fuck Jane was thinking.'

FORTY

SETH WHEEL SPAN ONTO his drive leaving deep furrows in the grey gravel. He got out of the car not bothering to acknowledge Martin watching the house from the end of the driveway.

All he could think of was getting it out of Jane what on earth she'd been doing. He'd been seething the entire way back and in all fairness, could do with a few stiff drinks to calm himself down before he caught up with her, but it was too late for that now.

It was almost guaranteed he would fly off the handle because he couldn't think of *one* reason why she'd put herself in that position. Or Toby. Or *him*. Didn't they have enough bloody things going on without Jane causing more problems?

Seth raked his hand through his hair as he strode up the path and then glanced at his hand. He'd tried to clean himself up on the way back, but there were still remnants of that twat's blood on him and his clothes. *More stuff he'd have to burn.*

Dan had nearly got a whack in the eye too. Going on at him about unnecessarily shooting that bloke. Seth scowled. *What the hell had he expected him to do?* The guy had been getting on his tits from the off, mumbling on incoherently. As far as he was concerned he'd done everyone a bloody favour. Besides, he'd got the info he needed in the end and that was all that mattered.

His teeth clenched together. He'd known it was that Alan. He'd just *known*. He felt angry for allowing the dickhead to make him believe his lies about not knowing anything, but he would be rectifying that as soon as possible.

Before dropping Dan home he'd given him *clear* instructions that Alan bloody Barber was to be brought back in as soon as possible. *No excuses and no stalling*. He didn't care whether Dan agreed with his reasoning or not – either about Alan Barber or that pointless bastard, Neil Batchelor, or whatever his name was. He had a job to do and he was damn well doing it. It was *his* fucking family at stake here – not Dan's – not *anyone's. HIS. He'd do it all on his own if needs must.*

Seth fumbled for his keys in his inside pocket, cursing loudly as they dropped to the ground. Retrieving them he rammed them into the lock and pushed the door open, slamming it closed with his foot. He walked in the direction of the kitchen. 'Jane!' he roared.

He scowled further spotting Anna lurking in the kitchen. *The last thing he wanted was to have to see HER.* He still didn't understand why she was still here. Anna had broken his rules and so as far as he was concerned, she should have been given her marching orders well before now.

Seth glared at Anna eyeing him nervously over by the work-top. 'Where's Jane?'

Anna attempted to smile. 'I-I'm not sure Mr Wright. She went out earlier, but hasn't come back yet.'

Seth went cold. *It was late. Why wasn't she back?* 'Went out? Where? Where did she go?'

Anna shook her head. 'I don't know…'

'Why don't you know?' Seth roared. 'And where's Toby?'

Anna smiled weakly. 'He's upstairs asleep.'

Seth nodded, slightly placated and sat down at the kitchen table.

'Let me get you a drink,' Anna said, her face hurting from

the smile she was continually forcing over her face. *The last thing she wanted to do was wait on this man who might have killed her mother.* 'Whisky?'

She grated her teeth as she walked to the cabinet to fetch the bottle of whisky. Judging by Seth's mood, he wouldn't care whether his drink came from the bottle instead of the decanter.

Whether she liked it or not, she *had* to remain under this roof. She'd done what Tina had asked and now had to wait for the opportunity to put the rest of what she'd requested into motion. She didn't pretend to understand why she'd been asked to do the things she had, but no longer cared. She needed to do what Tina said without question. *Or guilt.*

'Some mail came for you today,' Anna said quietly as she handed Seth an extra-large measure of his favourite whisky.

Seth's head shot up. 'Where is it?'

'I put it all on Jane's desk in her study. Most of it was for her. Sorry - I should have sorted it.'

'No matter,' Seth muttered, downing the whisky in one.

Rapidly leaving the room he strode up the stairs to Jane's office, seeing a pile of mail sitting on top of a green folder on the desk. Recognising the envelope on top of the pile, Seth snatched it up and quickly put it in his pocket. He didn't need to open it to know *exactly* what it was about. *That was it. Decided.*

Seth nodded almost imperceptibly to himself. He'd made his decision. He wouldn't wait for Dan and neither would he sit up waiting for Jane. He'd go and do what he should have done earlier.

Unlocking his cabinet, Seth pulled out a sawn-off shotgun. *That would be the last threatening letter they'd be receiving.*

• • • •

'ANNA?' AIDEN SAID breathlessly, recognising the voice on the other end of the phone. He'd finally got a night off and he'd hoped he'd spend it in peace without having to deal with *her*. 'What's up?'

'Just wanted to see how you are,' Anna said quietly. She was missing him like crazy. She'd have to wait until her next day off until she saw him again and that was *days* away. Since she'd realised Seth's guys were tailing her each time she left the house with Toby it had scuppered the routine she'd got into for meeting up with Aiden every day when she took Toby for his afternoon walk in the park.

She couldn't risk being caught after the grief she'd got in before, especially with the little boy in tow. That would *definitely* get her in the shit and she couldn't afford to be kicked out now. *Not for anything.*

'I've missed you,' Anna whispered, hoping Aiden would say the same. She had missed him. Missed him *desperately* and wanted to unburden herself over what Tina had asked her to do. Especially regarding Toby. She felt more than uncomfortable about trying to snatch the child. *Surely that had to be so wrong?*

She'd been trying to convince herself Toby would be better off somewhere else. *Look how unstable the Wright's relationship had become and how dangerous things were.* A child should not be subjected to that.

Anna needed to hear that Aiden agreed with her. *Maybe even help her carry things out*? He'd been so good about the nightmare with her mother and had been so understanding.

She sighed despondently. This was different. She couldn't put this on him. It wasn't fair. Although she trusted him, what if he was so horrified that he left her? *It wasn't worth the risk.* No, she'd just have to deal with this on her own.

'Aiden can you hear me?' Anna asked when she received no response.

'Oh yeah, sorry. Of course I can hear you, babe,' Aiden muttered. He was distracted. Distracted by the naked body of the girl writhing on his bed whilst his fingers worked overtime on her. He ran his other hand down his rigid cock in readiness, whilst ensuring the phone didn't slip from where it was wedged in his neck. *Why did Anna have to phone him now of all times?*

He'd waited *weeks* to get back in the sack with this gorgeous barmaid and now Anna was ballsing it up.

'When will I see you again. *Properly*?' Anna asked, her voice pleading.

Aiden pulled a face. *Christ she was so desperate – unlike this beauty.* His eyes ran over the girl's pert breasts, across her flat stomach and down to where his fingers were delving. He watched the girl bite her lip and raise her hips. *God how he wanted to put it in her.*

Smiling he upped the pressure of his thumb circling her clitoris and his fingers continued working hard inside her.

'Ohhhh...' the girl groaned.

'Who's that?' Anna cried. 'Who's with you?'

'What?' Aiden said, winking at the girl below him and raised a finger to his lips. 'What do you mean?'

'I can hear something,' Anna said, panic in her voice. *It sounded like a girl. Was he with another girl?* She felt tears stinging in her eyes.

'No one baby. There's no one here,' Aiden said, pulling his hand back down his length. *There was no way he'd lose his hard on because of this whining cow.* 'Just the TV... I'll turn it down.'

'It's horrible here Aiden,' Anna moaned. 'Seth's in a foul mood.'

Aiden suppressed a gasp as the barmaid took him into her mouth. 'Oh god, that's good.'

'Good?' Anna asked confused. 'What are you talking about?'

Shit! 'Oh, erm nothing. Don't worry about it. Listen, I'll see you soon,' Aiden sighed. *He had to get rid of her.* 'As soon as I can ok?'

Without waiting to give Anna the chance to start rambling, Aiden quickly put the phone down. Realising he'd lost his erection, he lay down on the bed and pulled the pretty barmaid across to lay on his chest.

'Sorry sweetheart. Just give me a few minutes. Things have been getting complicated around here lately.' He stared up at the ceiling thinking what a gross understatement that was. *Complicated? Things were more than complicated.*

He'd been filling his car up with petrol this afternoon when his name was called across the forecourt. Turning, he'd been surprised to see his brother crossing between the petrol pumps, waving frantically.

'Christ, I'm glad I've seen you!' Alan had gasped. 'What the fuck's going on?'

Confused, Aiden had beckoned Alan into his car. He knew he was up shit creek the minute he was asked why he'd been lying about where he was working.

He hadn't meant to come out with another lie – especially not to Alan. He'd never lied to his brother before, but it was for *his* sake not his own. *He'd lied to keep Alan safe.*

It never ceased to amaze him how easily the lies tripped from his tongue these days. 'The guy's lying, Al. I didn't walk out of that job. They gave me the boot and I've been out of work ever since. I was so embarrassed, I pretended I still worked there. I didn't want you to be disappointed in me…'

That was *partly* true. He hadn't wanted to tell Alan the truth about where he was really working. Plus, he hadn't wanted to admit to his brother the type of work he'd found himself involved in. *Especially lately.* Alan was a nice person. A lot nicer than him and he'd have been mortified, not to mention frightened if he knew the truth.

'I got pulled in by Seth Wright…' Alan had said.

Aiden had hoped sitting inside the car had detracted from the pale colour his face had most likely become when he'd heard that. This revelation about Seth Wright had turned out to be even *worse* than he'd first thought.

From what Alan had said, it was clear Seth was putting two and two together. He'd been grilling Alan over Anna and about sending runners into the clubs. Now it appeared Toby had been added to the list. It turned out that he'd been seen on several occasions and it was a clear case of mistaken identity. *Mistaking him for Alan…*

Aiden sighed. He and Alan had always looked alike, but he'd never thought about the possibility of something like this happening.

'You've got to be honest with me bruv,' Alan had said. '*Was* it you? Is it *you* they're after?'

Aiden had felt like shit. Alan had looked terrified. It wasn't supposed to be like this...

'Are you seeing that au pair? What the fuck have you done to make the likes of Seth Wright come for you?' Alan barked.

Aiden had needed to make a split-second decision. His eyebrows knitted together as he aimlessly twirled the barmaid's hair in his fingers. He hoped he'd made the right choice. He'd had two: Lie to his brother, or level with him.

He kept telling himself the choice to lie was the right one because it would protect Alan – no other reason.

'Of *course* it's not me!' he'd chuckled. 'Have you seen the state of her? Hardly my type, is she?'

But then Alan had started grilling him about Billie-Jo.

'Who's Billie-Jo?' Aiden had asked weakly, trying to act none the wiser and hurt about Alan's obvious suspicion. *He knew who she was alright. So, they'd linked him to that too? Holy God.*

'I'm sorry, but I had to ask you Ade,' Alan had explained. 'I just can't work out why anyone thinks it's me.'

'I don't know either, but I *promise* I've got nothing to do with any of this,' Aiden had lied for the hundredth time. 'Maybe someone from the Limelight's got it in for you?'

'Seth Wright has *threatened* me Aiden and I get the distinct impression it's not over. I won't be angry, but you *have* to tell me whether you know anything about this.'

Alan had been giving him a final get-out-of-jail-free card. He knew that, but still couldn't bring himself to tell the truth. *Not even to his brother*. He didn't want Alan to know what he'd become and what he'd done. He didn't want to have to tell him that on top of what he already knew, there were worse things. *A lot worse.*

Aiden knew Alan would be disgusted. He also knew he was putting his brother in a precarious position, so what choice did he have?

If Alan knew the truth he wouldn't serve him up, so knowing the score would give him a heads up. Aiden owed him that at least, didn't he?

Apparently not. Shamefully he'd kept his mouth well and truly shut.

Alan wouldn't end up taking the rap for it all anyway. It was all something and nothing. It was only a matter of time before Seth and his crew worked out things didn't add up and it couldn't be Alan.

Aiden swallowed uncomfortably. This meant conversely that it would take an equal amount of time for it to be discovered that *he* was the one they were really looking for. *He needed to up his game and fast.*

He sat up in bed and smiled at the barmaid. He didn't know what he'd been thinking. He hadn't got the time for a night off during all of this shit. 'Sorry love. I'm going to have to take a rain check on the rest of the night. I've got things I need to do.'

Giving Aiden a withering glare, the barmaid threw herself quickly out of his bed and pulled on her clothes. 'You've got fucking rocks in your head if you think you'll get another chance with me after this!' she snapped, huffily stalking from the room.

Aiden exhaled raggedly. *For fuck's sake.*

Forty One

SETH PULLED HIS CAR into the alley behind the garage. Fishing the keys out of his pocket, he yanked the metal door up. Getting into the van, he reversed it smoothly out of the garage and pulled the handbrake on. Leaving the engine to run, he jumped back out and pulled the metal door down.

Safely back in the van, he sped along the road in the direction of the Limelight. *Fucking Jason Miller and his bastard cronies*. The true reason why he'd pulled out of their association was coming to light. *All of this shit was a set up.*

Seth frowned. It was below the belt orchestrating threats on his child to get to him. And to think he'd trusted the guy. If he'd wanted full rein of the business, he should have just had the bollocks to say so, not pull all of these extravagant mind-fuck stunts.

His anger was palpable and he willed his brain to slow down to the point where he could function. He'd be no good to *anyone* with his mind speeding and considering he was on his own, then he'd best pull himself together.

Seth crunched the van into fourth gear, cringing as the grinding metal noise vibrated through his teeth. He might not be quite as hands-on in the business as he used to be, but he was still very capable. He still owned and controlled access to all the lock ups and equipment his crew utilised on a regular basis and he knew *exactly* when these were being used. One was vacant tonight, which was a good job – because he needed it. *He was doing this job. It was personal.*

He'd kept abreast of the notes Dan had collated on Alan Barber's movements so he knew when the man's shifts were, where he parked and at what time. He also knew where the guy would be heading *right now*. He'd pick up the tail as he made his way towards the car park and take him from there.

He scowled. *Jason Miller was next on his list, but he needed to remove the monkey first.*

Waiting at the underpass with the van's engine on tick over, Seth's eyes scanned both carriageways of the road ahead. He pulled out his wallet and looked at the well-thumbed photograph he kept in the see-through window and touched the image of Toby's curly little head as he sat in Jane's arms. *How dare this cunt threaten his baby boy!*

Spotting Alan Barber's car approaching, Seth slipped his wallet back in his pocket and shoved the van into gear.

• • • •

ELIZA COULD HAVE DONE without Aiden's bleating. She was up to her neck as it was. Jane bloody Wright doing that appeal on the news hadn't helped. The more clout behind Lacey's disappearance, the more the police would dig and at this precise moment all leads led back to the *Elipse*.

Aiden fidgeted on his seat whilst Digger glared at him out of the corner of his eye. He knew no one was paying much attention to what he was saying, but it was important. *Very bloody important*.

'Listen, I've already gone above and beyond for you and this business,' Aiden stated clearly before he lost his nerve. 'My brother's in serious danger. Seth Wright is suspicious and thinks *Alan's* been the one seeing Anna, sending letters and sending runners into the clubs.'

Eliza stared at him in amazement. *Was he saying he expected special treatment for doing his job? Seriously?* 'For fuck's sake Aiden, you should be glad. Whilst they're convinced Alan's the culprit, *you're* in the clear. Think yourself lucky!'

Digger guffawed loudly in the corner at Eliza's comment.

Aiden glared at him, red-faced with rage. 'He's my fucking brother! He wasn't supposed to be involved! I said from the off I didn't want him dragged into anything! You sa...'

Digger launched himself from the chair and wrapped his hand around Aiden's throat, squashing him painfully against the back of his seat. 'Less of the fucking lip! You work for *us* and therefore do what we say. That's part and parcel of having a bloody job dickhead. *We* never involved your brother - you two shouldn't look so alike! If you're that similar then get plastic surgery or buy Seth Wright some fucking glasses!'

Eliza smiled. *That was quite amusing for Digger.* She stared at Aiden. She understood to a point what he was saying, but it didn't mean anything. It wasn't *their* problem. 'Nothing's going to happen to your brother. It's all hot air. You said they've already spoken to him didn't you, so what are you worrying about?' She laced her fingers together. 'I'm more concerned about things leading back to us...'

Aiden tried to take solace from Eliza's words, but failed. He was sure it wasn't over. He was sick to death of this stupid vendetta Eliza and Digger had against Seth and Jane Wright and felt tempted to bin off the whole thing - including his job.

Yes, he'd been part of it, but only for *their* sakes. He'd never had any run-ins with the Wrights. Was his job *so* important he'd risk his brother's neck? He needed to think fast on this before things progressed further.

'*My* main concern right now is stopping Jane Wright from bringing even more attention to Lacey Garner's disappearance.' Eliza said spikily.

Digger lit a cigarette and blew the smoke out slowly. 'The cops won't dig too deep over a scatter-brained hooker. You worry too much. The body's gone now so there's no reason to link it to us. No one even knew Lacey worked here and let's face it, none of the tarts here will open their gobs.'

'You've dumped the body?' Eliza cried. *He could have said. She'd been bloody worrying about that for DAYS.* 'Did you use the hair I gave you?'

'Yes I did. It's all done and sorted.' Digger had made sure that a liberal amount of hair from Seth Wright's brush Tina had managed to produce was wrapped between Lacey's fingers. *It was a done deal.*

Eliza scowled. Ok, so that was good, but the baseline was a sixteen-year-old had gone missing and that sort of thing *always* gained public support, which put pressure on the authorities to make a double effort to get to the bottom of it. 'Anything else we can do to point them further towards Seth?'

Digger shrugged. Eliza was so melodramatic and caused extra work for them all for no reason, but if it shut her up? 'Aiden any ideas?'

Aiden stared at the floor. He was reluctant to do anything else to help them in their twisted quest. What was *he* going to get out of it anyway? It was him who was constantly putting his neck on the line. Although if their plan meant Seth Wright wouldn't be on the scene anymore, then maybe both Alan *and* him would be ok. *And where was this life insurance pay-out Tina had promised him?*

Eliza felt more than frustrated. 'How's Anna by the way?'

Aiden scowled. 'She thinks Seth's a suspect in her mother's death and hates him almost as much as you do, I reckon.'

Eliza grinned. *Unlikely. No one hated Seth and Jane Wright as much as she did.*

• • • •

ALAN BARBER STRUGGLED pointlessly as he was pulled from the back of the van.

He'd parked up in the car park ready for his shift at the Limelight and hadn't even had time to react when a van had screeched to a halt in front of him. He'd been yanked from behind the wheel of his car, a hand had clamped over his mouth and he'd quickly lost his footing when he'd been bodily dragged backwards.

The last thing he remembered was hitting his head on the metal wheel arch as he'd been thrown into the back of the cavernous hulk. Sometime between then and arriving wherever he was now he'd been bound and gagged with duct tape.

He was roughly thrown to the floor in what looked like a small warehouse and his frightened eyes stared up at Seth Wright standing over him

'Hello again Alan,' Seth smiled, his white teeth glinting in the light cast by the single florescent strip light hanging from the ceiling. 'I'm afraid your lies have caught up with you.'

Alan frantically shook his head from side to side, unable to utter a word. *How had it come to this? How could he be held responsible for something he had no knowledge of?*

Seth moved forwards and painfully ripped the duct tape from Alan's mouth.

Feeling sick as the first couple of layers of skin was removed from his lips, Alan stared up into Seth's manic eyes.

'Anything to say?' Seth snarled.

'It wasn't me. None of what you asked me about the other day was *anything* to do with me. I can assure you th…'

'*Assure me,* can you?' Seth sneered, his face contorting into a savage snarl. 'You fucking LIAR!' He brought his boot down hard on Alan's ribcage and smiled hearing bones snap. Ignoring Alan's howls, he dropped to his haunches. 'I presume Jason Miller put you up to this did he?'

Alan didn't reply. He knew whatever he said wouldn't make a difference. *The guy was deranged like everybody said.*

Seth calmly lit a cigarette. 'I take it by your silence I'm right!'

'No!' Alan said, finding the resolve to defend himself once more, the pain in his ribs making it increasingly difficult to him to speak.

'Playing games?' Seth laughed. 'Good luck! Oh and by the

way, that mug shot of you I took… Remember that?'

Seth watched Alan Barber nod, thoroughly enjoying the fear visible in the man's eyes. 'You were ID'd as the one to send runners into the clubs.'

Alan frowned. *ID'd? Who could have ID'd him? He hadn't even known about any questions.* He shook his head vehemently.

'That also means *you're* the one responsible for sending letters too yes?' Seth growled, pulling his wallet out. Opening it he shoved the photo of Jane and Toby in Alan's face. 'You see this? This is my wife and my kid. *This* is the kid you've been threatening and you think that's ok, do you?'

Shoving his wallet back in his pocket, Seth grabbed Alan around the throat and applied pressure. 'I also want you to tell me what you know about my daughter!'

Alan began choking as his windpipe was crushed. He couldn't move his arms because they were bound tightly behind his back. *What daughter? Did Seth Wright have a daughter? He was going to die. Going to die for something he had had no part of.* 'It wasn't me…' he gasped.

Seth laughed. He pulled the man's head up by his hair, then slammed it hard against the concrete floor. It was tempting to kill him, but he was determined to drag it out a bit longer. *After what this cunt had done. After he'd threatened a child? His child? There was no way he'd be walking away from this.*

'You would say that wouldn't you? It's not you – just happens to *look* like you, yeah? Convenient that…'

Alan's head pounded with pain, the sickening crack he'd heard when his skull connected with the concrete had not sounded good and was still very much resounding in his brain in more ways than one.

Seth got up and pulled out his sawn-off from the inside of his coat, watching as Alan stared at it with terrified eyes. He paced up and down in front of the shaking man. 'You know, I wouldn't have thought you were the type to resort to threatening kids. You don't look the sort…. Thought you were more into *older* women?'

He laughed watching Alan's confusion. 'I remember quite clearly now seeing you at Miller's party being chatted up by that woman old enough to be your bloody mother.'

Alan frowned. *Who? Oh fuck. That was Aiden. Seth Wright thought he was AIDEN.* He felt desolation sweep over him. *All of this was about Aiden... His brother had lied and now he was paying the price.*

Seth sighed. He could tell the bloke was hiding something. He'd been in this game far too long not to see the signs.

Grabbing Alan by the lapels, Seth yanked him to his feet, holding him upright when his legs buckled. He dragged him to the other side of the lock up, knowing the man's eyes were glued to the sawn-off he was still holding. Not that it appeared to be tempting him into giving over any further information. *Let's see if this would help...*

'I need you to tell me who's behind this,' Seth growled. 'Is it Miller?' He waited for a response, but got none. 'I *will* get this info out of you Barber. Either that or you'll die.'

Alan stared at the sawn-off Seth Wright was still clutching. *What could he say? He couldn't serve Aiden up to this man. Aiden was his BROTHER.*

Seth shrugged, placed the sawn-off on a table and flipped off the top of a large metal barrel. 'Suit yourself...' Turning Alan around so he was facing him, he lifted him up onto a step and roughly pulled his arms away from his back.

Alan whimpered, both from pain and fear as a horrible acrid chemical smell assaulted his nostrils.

'I. Need. A. NAME...' Seth roared, pushing Alan Barber's hands into the liquid the barrel contained.

Alan howled, vomit rising as acid burnt into his skin, first on his fingertips and then the rest of his hands. He tried to struggle, but he was being held fast, his body crushed up against the barrel. *There was nowhere to go. Nowhere to move...*

Seth's nose wrinkled up from the caustic smell of the acid combined with burning, disintegrating flesh. 'Still nothing?'

Alan gasped in a big lungful of air as he desperately fought to override the crushing pain overtaking his body like wildfire, his mind seeing flashes of light. He hoped he'd pass out very soon.

Seth watched the man's face, accepting he wouldn't give up anything now. He had to take his hat off to him. To not fold under this took some doing. He couldn't let him go now even if he wanted to though. *Which he didn't.*

Everyone had a fucking choice and he'd made his choice when he'd agreed to send those letters.

And he'd been in his house. Further rage and indignation bubbled in Seth's veins. This twat was the one knobbing that stupid bitch Anna. *Not any more he wouldn't be.*

Seth backhanded Alan Barber around the face. 'Stay with me Barber, stay with me. It's not quite over yet…'

Alan felt vomit rising and began to heave. *Why did you do this to me Aiden? Why?*

Asking himself these questions now was pointless. There could be no answer.

It was a blessed relief when Seth whipped out a hunting knife. Alan felt no pain as the blade sliced cleanly through his throat. When he crumpled to the floor, his last thoughts were only of his brother.

Forty Two

SETH WOKE WITH A start and glanced at Jane fast asleep next to him. She'd been out for the count by the time he'd got in last night, which was a good job because he'd been covered in blood and wired to fuck.

He'd also been poised ready to lay into her about both where she'd been that evening and furthermore, what the hell she'd been thinking by putting out an appeal to the bloody nation. However, once he'd finally got through to Barry, informing him there was an urgent clean up and disposal job that required his attention and then had a long hot shower, he'd calmed down.

Whatever Jane had done didn't dampen his contentment when he'd pulled the duvet back to see her lying resplendently naked. He'd got into the super-king bed and lay behind her, ignoring the erection he'd acquired the minute he'd laid eyes on her.

He'd happily drifted off to sleep secure in the knowledge that one piece of the problem had been removed tonight. However, it was now morning and he still needed to say his piece. He needed to make Jane understand that under no circumstances was she to engineer a repeat performance of going to the press in someone else's defence.

'Jane,' he whispered in her ear, his hand running up her thigh. 'Wake up.'

Jane moaned softly and turned onto her back. She opened her eyes to find Seth propped up on his elbow over her.

'Morning gorgeous,' he smiled, kissing her gently on the lips as she pushed herself up on the pillows.

'You shouldn't have done that yesterday - it was stupid.' Seth said, his voice stern.

'What now?' Jane sighed.

'That stunt with the press. It was dangerous. Drawing attention to yourself,' Seth continued. 'I don't want you becoming more of a target.'

The memory of her conversation with Maggie immediately shot back into her mind. 'It had to be done Seth. I know the people who prostituted Lacey are the ones who have something to do with her disappearance. They'll be working her again or they'd have killed her for escaping. We need to find them.'

Seth's eyes narrowed. 'You just don't get it do you?'

'Seth, I think they're the ones threatening us. Threatening *Toby* and who have something to do with Grace.'

'So why the fuck are you giving them extra ammo?' Seth snapped, his voice rising.

'Extra ammo? I'm not!' Jane cried. 'I want it all to stop Seth. I want my daughter!'

'For fuck's sake, Jane!' Seth shouted. 'Can't you see this is *Miller's* work? The letters will stop now so that's one thing.'

Jane's face grew hard. 'Oh yes, you had a lead, didn't you? One you didn't bother informing me about. One you were going to follow up on apparently. Maggie let it slip.'

'Relax babe. I'm not trying to hide anything. I just needed to get on with it,' Seth said dismissively, refusing to get riled. 'It's sorted.'

Jane raised an eyebrow. 'What have you done…?'

Seth grinned. 'What I needed to do. I won't have my child threatened or my wife worried anymore.' He drew circles on Jane's thigh with his fingers, gradually moving higher. 'Just let me to get on with my stuff Jane.'

'But Maggie saw the man with Lacey at the hospital. She can ID him!'

'Will you stop going on about that fucking girl!' Seth barked. *He was sick of hearing about her. Toby and Jane were his priority, not Lacey.* 'All I'm bothered about is that this was the guy sending the letters. If he's connected to Lacey, then that's two birds with one stone.'

'But what if it's not the right person?' Jane asked, squirming as Seth's fingers slipped between her legs.

'It *is* the right person, trust me. He was obviously working for someone and they'll be next in line.'

'But…'

'But *nothing* Jane,' Seth said. 'It's like you want it to be more complicated than it is. You need to stop this. You'll soon see. Take a look at Anna's face when she finds out her boyfriend is no more.'

Jane's face paled. 'Anna? Are you sure she was involved with this person? What about Miller?'

Seth nodded. 'I'm sure, ok. It all adds up. Jane, you need to get rid of her and Miller's next believe me! Now, back to us…'

Swiftly flipping himself over Jane, parting her thighs under his hips, Seth kept his body raised above hers, the tip of his cock resting tantalisingly against her entrance.

Jane raised her hips, desperate for him to enter her. She reached and gripped the velvet skin of his length. 'You'd best take my mind off all the shit going on hadn't you!' she winked.

Grabbing Jane's wrists, Seth pulled her arms over her head, holding her firmly to the bed and pushed himself into her, up to the hilt. 'That I can promise to deliver *right now*,' he growled, thrusting hard.

• • • •

JENNIE HAD GOT HALF a mile from the address she'd found for Jane Wright. It hadn't been difficult to find but now she'd got cold feet.

What could she possibly say? She didn't know what had happened to Lacey, but she *did* know that whatever it was wasn't good.

Everyone had seen Jane Wright on the television yesterday and the hostel had been a hive of activity from the minute the appeal had aired. Press reporters, clamouring for information about Lacey's relationship with Jane and how it had come about - down to the other girls in the hostel speculating over their take on it. Some even pretended they'd had a close relationship with Lacey and that she'd told them *all* the details. *They'd sell their story for the right price...*

No one knew anything. None of them. The only person who knew *anything* was her.

Lacey had divulged snippets to her, almost accidentally one night as to what had really happened with where she'd come from and what Jane Wright had done for her. Jennie had not believed it to be true – that was until Jane Wright had appeared on the television offering a reward.

But she didn't know anything other than that. No names had been given. The only reference Lacey had ever made about the horrible place she'd been forced to work was something to do with 'digging' and Jennie had no idea what she'd been talking about. Whatever it was, wasn't particularly important or useful. *Especially now.*

If she turned up at Jane Wright's house off the cuff and if, on the remote chance she was given any time with the woman herself, then what could she offer to the equation? Not a fat lot.

There was no point. *It was a stupid idea.* Turning around, Jennie began the long walk back to Pegasus Place.

• • • •

JASON MILLER WAS NOT impressed by the 5am call telling him he was needed immediately at the Limelight. He'd been even less happy when he'd arrived to discover the body of Alan Barber had been dumped on his steps.

The night watchman had been on patrol and thankfully

spotted it minutes after it had been dumped, quickly moving it. Unfortunately, he hadn't witnessed who had delivered it. The CCTV footage only showed a white van slowing down, the side door opening and the body, wrapped in sacking, being launched from the van onto the steps. But it was obvious who was behind this. *Seth Wright.*

At least he had conscientious staff who'd know better than to involve the police. At this precise moment in time Alan Barber's body was being kept in the cellar until he decided the best thing to do with it.

Jason cracked his knuckles and stared at his address book. He needed to contact the man's family, but didn't know a bean about him, apart from some of the staff said he had a brother living locally.

Jason vaguely remembered Alan Barber bringing his brother to Linda's birthday bash – it stuck in his mind because he'd done a double take, thinking he'd just seen two copies of the same man wearing different suits. The two of them were very much alike.

As the boss of the club, it was only right he should be the one to break the news to Alan Barber's family, so he'd get one of the staff to find an address or number for this brother as soon as they came in.

In the meantime, he'd work out *exactly* how he would deal with Seth Wright.

FORTY THREE

'I DON'T BELIEVE YOU'VE done this!' Seth raged, staring at Jane in disbelief, his face like thunder and his green eyes flashing with fury.

Jane stared at Seth in shock. He'd been fine a moment ago, but now he was screaming blue murder. 'What the hell are you talking about?' she yelled. She knew Anna and Toby were in the sitting room and could hear every single word Seth was shouting and she didn't appreciate it.

'You've put everyone through hell for what? For fuck all!' he screamed. 'Are you really that desperate for attention? I was right about you a while back, wasn't I? You're losing your fucking mind, you stupid bitch!'

Jane's face flashed with anger. 'Keep your voice down?' she hissed through gritted teeth. 'Do you want to tell me exactly what I'm supposed to have done before you continue trapping off?' She wasn't having this. It was *him* who was losing the plot, not her.

Striding over, Seth thrust a green folder into Jane's hands. 'Yours I presume?'

Jane took the folder and stared at it. 'What's this?'

Seth paced over to the kitchen table and slammed his fist on the surface making her jump. 'Don't give me that! Don't you *dare* pretend you know nothing!'

He slumped in a chair and ran both his hands through his hair so frantically it looked like it might rip from his scalp. 'How could you do this Jane?'

Jane glanced at Seth and then at the folder, completely clueless as to what he was talking about. His problem, whatever it was, was fast getting on her tits. Angrily she lifted the flap of the cardboard folder and pulled out several pieces of paper.

'Don't you dare insult me by saying you don't know about this, you crazy bitch,' Seth muttered, unable to look at her. *How could she? She knew he'd been losing his mind over this. How could she have done such a thing?*

Remembering he'd still got some unopened mail that Anna had put on Jane's desk last night, he'd thought he'd grab it in case there was anything important there. He didn't like getting behind with bills, but how he wished he hadn't found the folder. It would have so much less hurtful.

Walking into Jane's study, he'd grabbed the small pile of letters still on her desk and glanced absentmindedly at the green folder underneath. Thinking it may contain mail too he'd looked just to check and part of a sentence had caught his eye.

Recognising the wording, Seth's heart had lurched. He'd pulled the paperwork from the folder and his hands shook with pure fury seeing it contained none other but copies of the threatening letters he'd received.

Not only were there copies of what he'd got, but also other versions of the same thing, which were first drafts – amended until they'd become the ones which had been sent. And as if that wasn't bad enough, it also contained notes for the *fake* Carl Mulligan.

It had taken a few minutes of utter confusion before the penny had dropped – probably because he hadn't wanted to accept what had been staring him in the face.

Jane had sent those letters. Jane had been faking threats to her own son and was behind the scam with her daughter!

Jane had planned the whole thing. She'd led them on this wild goose chase to find a daughter she'd *known* wasn't theirs. She'd got that bloke - whoever he was, to pose as Mulligan and she'd probably had something to do with Lacey disappearing too... *Oh fuck. She was a bloody good actress! What the hell...?*

Seth glared at Jane, watching her flick through the paperwork with a puzzled expression. *Nice try Jane,* he thought. *You won't get out of this one...*

'You need help,' Seth muttered. 'You need to see someone.'

'Wait!' Jane cried, suddenly realising what she was being accused of. 'You actually think *I* did this?'

Seth laughed sarcastically. 'Funnily enough, yes.'

'I don't believe this!' Jane yelled, throwing the folder on the kitchen table and moved to leave the room.

Leaping up from the table like a panther, Seth caught hold of Jane's arm, quickly swinging her around to face him. 'I don't think so,' he snorted. 'I fucking *killed* a man for this last night and all along it was *YOU!* Pretending this was all to do with some crazy conspiracy theory about people using young girls in brothels and all that bullshit!'

He gripped Jane's face. 'You're actually that deranged to set out all this bollocks about Grace too?' he raged. 'Who the fuck was it? Who the fuck was the bloke you paid to impersonate Mulligan?'

Jane couldn't comprehend any of this. '*What*?'

'The pretend Mulligan? Who the fuck was it? I'll kill him. That is, after I've killed *you*!' Seth spat. Suddenly another realisation seeped into his brain. 'Oh my God! The adoption! Who's *really* adopting Grace? You clearly know and have set this up from the off haven't you? You've done all this so we can't get her back! Feel guilty, do you?'

'If you couldn't cope with getting your daughter back after you let her go in the first place, then you should have said, you crazy pathetic attention-seeking *bitch*!' He raked his hand through his hair once more. 'Oh my God! I still can't believe you've done this!'

Tears welled up in Jane's eyes. 'Seth, I haven't! It's not me! You've got to believe that!'

'What sparked this off? Have you been lashing out at everyone around you because you *can*?' Seth raged, his face inches from hers. 'What the hell's wrong with you?'

'NO!'

'Ah, so you're admitting it was to do with something then? Well what the fuck is it? I knew you were crazy. Just *knew* it! Getting back with me was to set me up once and for all - for what happened in the past, yes? It all makes sense now.'

He walked over and grasped Jane by her shoulders. 'You've been too quiet and nice all along – it's just not like you. You've never been emotional and then suddenly you're telling me you love me, we get married, have Toby… Oh fuck, I expect *that* was an accident as well yeah?'

'How *dare* you!' Jane screamed. 'You're the crazy one if you think *any* of this is true!'

Seth laughed hollowly. 'Oh God, I've been so stupid. So fucking stupid… Then there was all that paranoid shit. The shit about me and Lacey? The phone calls? None of it happened did it? Just admit it!'

'How can I admit it?' Jane screamed. 'It's not fucking true! I can't believe you'd actually think this is down to me.' *How could he? How could he think she'd do this?*

'Do you know what?' Seth stared into Jane's eyes, his gaze cold as ice. 'You could do with a hard slap!'

Jane bit back the tears burning in the back of her eyes. 'Seth, how could you th…'

'It's probably a good job Grace is being adopted – although I wouldn't trust who you've set up to do that. And I'll be stopping it!' Seth placed his large hands either side of Jane's face. 'You don't deserve Grace and neither do you deserve Toby. You deserve *fuck all*! I want to wring your goddamn neck!'

'You bastard!' Jane screeched, punching Seth squarely on his jaw. 'You're not listening to me!'

Seth wiped the blood from his cut lip irritably. 'Christ Jane, you need to see someone and I'm going to make sure that happens.'

'You're the one that's crazy Seth. For thinking any of this in the first place!'

'You need a fucking doctor Jane!' Seth roared.

Jane lurched forward, her fists beating against Seth's chest. 'Don't you dare! I'm not mad! I don't need a fucking doctor!'

Seth sneered at his wife. *He couldn't deal with this.* 'Oh yes you do. By God Jane, you sure as fucking hell do. And you'd best not stop me getting you sectioned because otherwise I'll kill you with my bare hands.'

• • • •

EVEN THOUGH HE'D apologized several times, Aiden had been getting daggers from the barmaid who he'd had to bin off the other night and she was showing no signs of budging. She had a face like a fucking slapped arse every time she looked at him.

After a couple of hours, it was obvious he wasn't going to get anywhere with her and unlike most women, she'd actually meant it when she'd said he wouldn't get another chance. *Her loss at the end of the day...*

All was not lost. There was a tasty little brunette with big tits who'd been giving him the eye half the night and she'd happily accepted a drink off him. Now seated with her at a table, Aiden had been putting pints down his neck and his usual charm and bravado was on top form.

He winked at the brunette and casually squeezed her thigh under the table. As long as Anna didn't suddenly show up in some kind of horrible twist of fate, then he was on to a winner.

Deciding he'd happily forget about the barmaid now he had this nice little stunner's interest, he sauntered back to the bar to get his new acquaintance another drink.

• • • •

JASON MILLER DIDN'T LIKE showing his face around the backwoods of town – it gave the wrong impression, but he hadn't a lot of choice.

Five crummy dumps he'd been round looking for Aiden Barber and it was like looking for a needle in a haystack. He'd begun to wonder whether his staff were taking the piss judging by the list of pubs they'd compiled where they thought Alan's brother could be found.

Jason had garnered a hefty collection of strange looks as he and Tom had got out of the back of his saloon with the blacked-out windows when it had pulled up outside the front of these dives.

He'd also noticed the uncomfortable silence which had descended when he'd walked in with the larger man trailing two paces behind him. The rollup-smoking collection of drongos had all but virtually chucked their pints of Stella down their football tops in shock.

He *hated* these types of places and the deadbeats within them. Jason sneered. This was why he ran a *classy* joint, rather than a dump and probably why Seth Wright felt at home in these sorts of joints. The man might have the posh club and expensive house now, but it was no secret where he'd come from.

Whichever way he looked at it, he was right to pull his association with the Wrights. Especially now they psycho had wiped out one of his staff, if not two. The more he thought about it, the more likely it was that Wright was behind that despicable attack on Billie-Jo.

Jason glanced up at the forlorn façade of the pub they'd pulled up outside of, thankful this one was the last on the list. If Barber's brother wasn't in here, then that was it. He wasn't prepared to do anything further. His conscience was clear in as much that he'd tried his best to find the man.

Stepping from the car, Jason straightened his suit and stepped into the pub.

• • • •

MAGGIE HADN'T FULLY understood why Jane needed her to come over so urgently until she'd arrived at the house. Anna had looked extremely nervous when she'd let her in and as she was shown through to the kitchen, she'd realised why.

Seth had blood down his shirt from his bust lip and Jane's tear-stained face was smeared with black from her smudged makeup. The atmosphere was like ice, not to mention the large amount of smashed glass and crockery littering the tiled floor.

Maggie looked at Seth and Jane facing each other off from opposite ends of the room, eyeing each other with distrust and her heart sank. They'd obviously had a blazing argument and the *last* thing she wanted was to be dragged into it. 'W-What's going on?' she stammered nervously, wishing she'd insisted Dan come with her.

'Ask *Jane*!' Seth seethed, his green eyes spitting fire.

'Seth thinks *I'm* the one behind all these fucking letters threatening Toby, behind the fake detective and behind *everything*!' Jane spat. 'Tell him, will you?'

'Tell him what?' Maggie cried. *What was she supposed to say?*

'Tell him it wasn't me of course!' Jane shouted exasperatedly. *Was Maggie EVER going to get less dense?*

Maggie didn't want to look at Seth, let alone argue with him. He'd *always* scared her. Especially when he was like *this*. She sneaked a glance as he paced up and down by the work surface cracking his knuckles, his eyes manic. *She didn't want to get involved.*

Jane frowned at Maggie's lack of response. 'Aren't you going to say anything?' she hissed.

Maggie forced herself to look Seth in the face. 'Jane wouldn't have done this.' *Surely she wouldn't have?* She might have been acting off lately, but to do *that?* No. She couldn't have.

'But you don't know that for a *fact* do you?' Seth raged, facing Maggie head on. 'What else explains *this*?'

Maggie took a step back, unsure where to place her eyes being as Jane was also staring daggers at her. 'Well no… I can't know anything for sure, but th…'

'She needs to see a fucking shrink!' Seth barked, pouring whisky into a tumbler, his hands shaking so violently with pent up rage it splashed all over the worktop.

'Maggie!' Jane hissed. 'You're not being much help. Tell him it couldn't have been me!'

Maggie's eyes flicked from Jane to Seth and back again. 'I-I've already said I didn't think it co…'

'*You're* the one who said Jane wasn't herself, Maggie,' Seth barked.

Jane's eyebrows knitted together fiercely. 'I see you've both been discussing me then?' she yelled. 'Going crazy, am I? How dare you! You have the cheek to do that with the state of *your* fucking head?'

Maggie felt tears bite. She hadn't come here to get a round of abuse. 'I never said anything of the sort!'

'*LIAR!*' Seth raged.

'I never said Jane was crazy, Seth!'

'Didn't sound that way to me!' Seth added.

'I was worried when you kicked off at the spa, Jane. You were acting strange.' Maggie explained, even though she knew it wouldn't make a blind bit of difference.

'Maybe *you'd* act weird if the fucking papers were going round accusing *you* of having abortions and getting phone calls about your husband shagging a school girl!' Jane slammed her fist down on the green folder sitting on the kitchen table. 'I'm *sick* of people trying to set us up. This is another example! You both think I'd do this sort of shit to my own family?'

Jane's eyes narrowed. 'Good job I wasn't so narrow-minded and easily taken in to not believe you when it was *you* in the firing line, wasn't it, Seth?'

Seth smirked nastily. 'You probably set that up too!'

'I don't believe this!' Jane screamed and turned to Maggie. 'Well get this Maggie, he's only gone and topped the bloke he reckons was sending the letters and who I reckon was involved with Lacey and now he feels guilty because apparently it's not him, it's *ME*!'

'You've killed someone again?' Maggie wailed.

'Oh, shut up!' Seth hissed, aware Anna was still in the next room. 'And for the record, I feel guilty over *nothing!*'

'Yeah, he killed him and a few more besides I don't doubt, but Seth being Seth went ahead without bothering to tell me. It appears he tells me *fuck all* these days. If he had then I'd have made him show the picture of the bloke to you first to ID him.'

Glancing between them both, Maggie wished more than ever that she hadn't answered the phone when Jane had called.

'Go on then Maggie,' Seth raged. 'You fount of all knowledge, you. This guy you saw – you know the one with the girl who I was apparently fucking and the one that was sending the letters. This is the guy, right?' He fished the crumpled photo from his wallet and shoved it in Maggie's hand.

Flinching, Maggie took the photograph and stared at it.

'Well?' Seth barked, throwing a sarcastic smile in Jane's direction whilst he waited for Maggie's answer, proving he'd been right all along.

Maggie glanced up. 'He looks *similar*... When was this taken?'

'The other week,' Jane said, looking at Seth. 'Why?'

Maggie shook his head. 'Then it's not him…'

'*What*?' Seth cried.

Maggie looked directly into Seth's emerald eyes. 'It's *definitely* not the same man. The guy I saw on both occasions had a tattoo of a swallow on his neck.'

Jane squared up to Seth. 'This is NOT down to *ME*!'

Seth stared at Jane and slugged the whisky down in one. *Fuck! Fuck! FUCK!*

• • • •

AIDEN HADN'T NOTICED the hush descend in the bar because he was already fairly drunk and was also too busy concentrating on looking down the brunette's top to let much else distract him. That was until he heard his name mentioned.

'Is there an Aiden Barber here?' Jason asked the barmaid.

The barmaid eyed the man's expensive tailored suit appraisingly and smiled. 'Yeah, he's here, but personally I wouldn't bother. He isn't much cop in *any* way,' she said scathingly. 'What you drinking?'

Jason smiled coldly. 'I'm not interested in your personal opinions love and I don't want a drink either. I just want to know who he is.'

The smile fell from the barmaid's face and she nodded behind him curtly. 'He's over there. Blond hair. Sitting at the table with that brown haired tart.'

Aiden glanced over his shoulder just as Jason Miller turned around to follow the barmaid's gaze and his stomach dropped into his shoes. *Jason Miller? What the fuck was he doing here?*

'Aiden Barber?' Jason said, stepping over to where Aiden sat.

'Yes,' Aiden acknowledged. *How should he play this? This could be either good or bad. Maybe he was going to offer him work?* 'How can I help you?' He extended his hand.

Jason Miller ignored Aiden's outstretched hand and jerked his head. 'A word?'

Aiden got up unsteadily, shooting the brunette at his table a nervous smile. He eyed the big bloke flanking Miller and hoped they hadn't got wind of his dealings. Warily he followed Miller and the big man out to the corridor by the toilets where it was quiet.

'I'm Jason Miller,' Miller stated. 'Your brother worked for me.'

Aiden nodded. 'That's right. What can I do for you Mr Miller?'

Jason Miller cleared his throat. 'I'm afraid I have some bad news…'

A knot of fear pulsed through Aiden's body at Miller's words. Not knowing what else to do or say, he decided to remain silent and that waiting for Miller to continue was the most sensible option.

'I'm afraid your brother Alan has been killed….' Jason said

abruptly.

'W-What…?' Aiden spluttered, unsure whether he'd heard correctly.

'He's been murdered. I'm so very sorry…'

'M-Murdered?' Aiden garbled. The world swam before his eyes and he put his arm against the wall to steady himself as waves of nausea rushed over him. 'H-How?'

Jason Miller pursed his lips. 'I'm not sure. Nor are we sure as to why, but I can assure you we'll be looking into it.'

Aiden blinked rapidly, still unable to digest the information. 'B-But, but…'

'I know this is a shock, but there isn't a lot else I tell you at this moment in time.' Miller fished a business card from his inside pocket and handed it to Aiden. 'Call me in a few days and I'll let you know if we have any further information.'

Without waiting for an answer or further questions, Jason Miller nodded at Aiden and walked back out of the pub.

Aiden staggered against the wall and put his head in his hands before slowly sliding to the ground. As a low guttural howl escaped from his mouth, he rapidly realised he knew exactly why his brother had been killed and who was responsible for it.

He'd got his brother killed because Seth Wright thought Alan was HIM.

FORTY FOUR

SELENA WAITED UNTIL ELIZA had bundled the terrified little girl roughly into her car before she dared to make her move. She glanced at the collection of zoned out girls slumped on the saggy sofas spaced around the perimeter of the shared lounge. She was confident their daily late-afternoon dose of brown had rendered them incapable of taking a blind bit of notice as to anything she may be doing. *It was now or never.*

Digger was out with Steve Lomond and there wasn't much of a window before they got back. It had been bad enough watching that poor child sitting miserably in the corner all day looking like the weight of the world was on her shoulders, but she'd been powerless to help or even speak to the kid.

Eliza went berserk if anyone so much as *smiled* at the terrified girl, so how those two had ever been deemed acceptable to adopt was well beyond rationality. Selena knew they were formally adopting the kid any time soon because Eliza had been boasting about it. As to why, she had no idea.

Eliza and Digger had no time for children and appeared to despise this particular kid more than most, which only made it even more unfathomable.

How she'd love to go to the police and tell them that those

two were allowing a little girl to sit in the corner of a brothel all day. In fact, how she'd love to tell the police *everything* she knew about that pair…

Maybe she would. But she had to get what she needed over and done with first and foremost. If she got away with that without being murdered then she had her insurance sorted as well as the proof she needed to get out of this shit hole for ever.

It was bad enough Aiden was behaving like the local lunatic now. According to rumours his brother had been murdered. She didn't know why, or if it was true, but there was some shit going on around here and she didn't want to be part of it. She needed to get away as soon as possible. *That was a definite.*

She didn't know how she would achieve that but achieve it she would. The leverage one specific CCTV tape could give her meant she stood a very good bloody chance.

Selena glanced back around the room just to check everyone was still in a state of blissed-out blankness and got up from her seat just as the television flashed up the latest breaking news.

Absentmindedly watching as she edged towards the door, her heart suddenly accelerated when a photograph of Lacey flashed up on the screen.

The newsreaders mouth moved up and down and Selena froze hearing a body strongly suspected of being Lacey Garner's had found earlier today, dumped in a trade bin at an undisclosed location not far from here.

Selena felt nausea rush over her. *That was it.* She'd have to speak to Jane Wright. She had to tell her who was behind this and that she hadn't meant to be part of it. Maybe the woman would believe her and do something to help? *But first she had to get that tape.*

• • • •

SETH SAT IN HIS office at the Glint and put his head in his hands for what felt the ten-thousandth time. He couldn't apologise to Jane any more than he had done already. Neither could he blame her for not forgiving him.

He wasn't sure whether he'd *ever* forgive her if she'd accused him of the things he'd thrown at her last night. Contrite was an understatement of how he felt. The whole thing was such a bloody mess and he had little idea how to even start rectifying it. But he would. *Somehow.*

Seth knew he'd grossly fucked up, but he had to put things into perspective. Whatever he'd done, he needed to find the man who he *should* have finished rather than the one he had.

He'd killed the wrong man, he knew that and there was fuck all he could do about it. It also proved that he'd been incorrect about Miller. *Jesus Christ! How could he have got everything so wrong*?

Seth reached for the decanter and poured himself an extra-large whisky. He knew it was early, but he didn't care. He glanced at Dan, who understandably hadn't been pleased to discover Maggie had been put in such a horrible position last night. Again, he could only apologise so much and so many times to everyone – it changed *nothing*. Neither did it change that this clown with the swallow tattoo knew the answers.

Seth clenched his jaw. Because of his own screw-up, the bastard was still walking around somewhere.

This guy knew the reasons behind this elaborate set up and Seth was struggling to imagine why someone he didn't know from Adam would be so hell bent on destroying his life. He had to find out. *Quickly*.

Regardless of what state his and Jane's marriage was in presently because of his wild accusations, they'd agreed all they would concentrate on right now was to find out who was doing this. The most important part of that being to stop this joke of an adoption.

Seth snatched the telephone from its cradle as its shrill ringing pierced his eardrums. 'Yes?' he barked into the mouthpiece.

'Mr Wright? Carl Mulligan here,' the voice said.

Seth exhaled nervously. 'Carl. Any news?' *He needed some news. Some GOOD news.*

‘Well, yes and no…’ Mulligan said. ‘I’ve got a date to hear your request for a warrant to lift the anonymity of the potential adoptive parents.’

‘Good!’ Seth said eagerly. ‘When is it?’

Carl paused. ‘A week today.’

‘A *week*?’ Seth roared. ‘That might be too late!’

‘I know,’ Carl agreed. ‘I explained the urgency, but this is the soonest they can do it. They originally set you a date for three weeks’ time, so what we’ve now got is certainly an improvement.’

‘Yeah, that’s great that is,’ Seth spat. ‘Bloody super! What if it’s gone through by then?’ He could almost hear Mulligan shrug on the other end of the line.

‘I appreciate it’s frustrating Mr Wright, but there really isn’t any other way we can do it I’m afraid. I can’t make it any quicker, even with my contacts.’

Seth nodded to himself resolutely. *Fuck*! ‘Right, ok thanks,’ he muttered. ‘Keep me updated.’ Putting the phone down, he stared at Dan for a few seconds before placing his head in his hands again.

‘Got anything to say?’ Seth snapped, aware that Dan had still not uttered a word.

‘Not really. What is there to say?’ Dan mumbled. Things didn’t get much worse than this. Everything was unravelling quicker than the speed of light. If Seth hadn’t jumped off the deep end without checking his facts, or thought things through a little more, then perhaps things wouldn’t be quite so untenable.

‘This had all gone tits up hasn’t it?’ Seth said, realising as he spoke it was a classic ‘state-the-obvious’ remark.

‘You could say th…’

‘Sorry for interrupting,’ Martin burst into the office.

Seth glared. *Would he get no time to fucking think straight today or what?* ‘What is it Martin? I’m snowed under here.’

‘I thought you should know that a body’s been found. They think it’s Lacey Garner’s. Thought I’d tell you because of Mrs Wright’s appeal bu…’

Seth groaned. He knew Jane would start blaming him again for making the girl leave and now it looked like she was dead. 'Oh well, I guess that's that then.'

Martin looked uncomfortable as he glanced at Dan and then back at Seth.

'Anything else?' Seth barked. He knew he was being snappy but didn't have the time, nor energy for extra grief on top of everything else.

'Yes there is actually. The body was found in a trade waste bin. They showed it on the news – it's all cordoned off, but from what I could see, I'm certain it's the bin outside that lock up of yours on East Yard.'

Seth sat bolt upright. '*What*? My lock up?' He looked at Dan who was staring straight at him. *Oh shit! Shit, SHIT!* 'Thanks Martin. If anyone comes sniffing around, contain it as best as you can.'

Nodding, Martin left the room and once the door had closed, Seth turned to Dan. 'Before you fucking ask, it wasn't me!'

'I never said it was, but Jesus, someone's managed a top job on you, haven't they?' Dan said. He could hardly believe this consistent chain of events had been so meticulously engineered and was astounded as to the detail and ingenuity behind it all.

'Haven't they just,' Seth muttered, topping up his whisky. 'The problem is the remains of Alan Barbers' body is still busy disintegrating in a barrel of acid in my lock up in the other yard. The yard *opposite* where someone's dumped Lacey's body.'

Dan stared at Seth vacantly, unsure he was hearing correctly, but judging by Seth's expression, presumed he was. 'Jesus fucking Christ!' he said quietly.

Seth felt like giggling with hysteria. He sparked up a cigarette. 'What else is going to go wrong?' he snarled.

'*This* perhaps?' Jason Miller roared as he kicked the office door open and pointed his gun at Seth's head.

• • • •

JANE WAS STILL SEETHING after Seth's accusations. And

hurt. However, all that mattered at this point in time was putting an end to all of this shit. Only then would she decide what she was going to do about him. *For now she'd take some of her anger out on that two-faced bitch of an au pair.*

Aware Anna had put Toby down for his mid-morning nap, Jane knew now was the time to act. She'd only managed to keep her temper contained last night and so far this morning purely because she refused to do anything in front of her son which could upset him.

Now Anna was on her own, she'd deal with her and once she had, the bitch had better make a very sharp exit before she completely lost her self-control and killed the lying whore.

Jane would love nothing more than to kill Anna, but couldn't. Not whilst there was a smidgen of a chance they'd still be able to get Grace back.

If she got Grace back *then* she'd hunt Anna down and finish her, but that would have to wait. For now, at least. *This part however, couldn't.*

Walking into the kitchen knowing Anna was sipping her tea at *her* kitchen table and still believing she hadn't been sprung in all the shit she'd pulled, Jane stomped over, grabbing her around the throat.

Pulling her out of the seat, she slammed a terrified and shocked Anna hard into the fridge-freezer. 'Right you fucking lying bitch!' she snarled, squashing her face painfully against the door of the fridge. 'Tell me what your part in all of this has been.'

Anna tried to control the escalating terror fast threatening to overcome her and render her useless. 'W-What do you mean?'

'What do I mean?' Jane raged, grabbing Anna by the shoulders and twisted her around to slam her back against the unit. 'What I mean is, tell me what *you've* done to help this intricate set up work?'

'I-I…' Anna faltered. *What could she say*? Although she hadn't agreed with anything which had been asked of her by Tina, she could still do well to remember these people may have killed her mother. For that alone she wouldn't breathe a word.

She'd already caused enough problems for her sister. *No, she'd find the resolve to stand her ground.*

Jane's eyes narrowed menacingly. 'Listen you little bitch, you've been lying all along. Sitting there all nervous, like butter wouldn't melt. Who's your boyfriend?'

'B-Boyfriend?' Anna tried to squirm out of Jane's grip. What had Aiden got to do with it? Ok, so she wasn't supposed to have anyone in the house, but it wasn't *him* who'd caused their problems.

'Don't insult me by pretending you haven't been seeing a man. Who is he?' Jane snarled. Anna's lack of response flicked a switch in her head and she delivered a crushing head-butt to the bridge of Anna's nose.

With Anna wailing in shock and pain, Jane gave her an additional backhander to silence her. 'Be quiet, you silly girl – you'll wake Toby. Your boyfriend, whoever he is, will soon be fucking dead. *He's* the one setting us up, isn't he? And *you're* helping him!' She prodded Anna hard in the chest.

Eyes watering from the stinging pain in her nose, Anna stared at Jane. 'I haven't done anything! I don't know what you're talking about. He's got nothing to do with it!' *Their true colours were seeping through now, weren't they? Aiden was right. They must have killed her mum. She had to get out of here.*

'Now you've admitted you have a boyfriend, tell me his fucking name,' Jane spat, her grip back tight around Anna's throat.

'You're hurting me!' Anna wailed. She needed to distract the woman. *Come on Anna. Think. THINK! These people are psychotic*. 'He's a friend that's all. He hasn't had anything to do with any of your problems.'

'How come things in the house keep 'appearing' seemingly from nowhere? Explain *that*!' Jane snarled. She was getting impatient. The best plan was to put the little cow in the cellar.

Yes, she'd do that. She'd tie her up and keep her in the cellar until she decided to be honest. Whether she liked it or not,

Anna's boyfriend – whoever he was, was connected to this and she would get the information out of her. It was clear Seth had failed with bells on, so this was their only option right now.

'Your boyfriend has been linked to lots of incidents Anna, including a violent attack on a woman, plus involvement in prostitution rings with young girls. Know that did you?' Jane seethed, venom pouring from her voice.

How she wanted to slice this dumb girl up piece by piece for giving a monster like that an inroad to her house and her child. 'And that's just the *tip* of the iceberg!'

'Y-You're lying!' Anna garbled. *It couldn't be true.* Jane Wright was feeding her this to assuage her own guilt. Well it wouldn't work. Aiden loved her and he was a gorgeous, kind and thoughtful man. How could this woman even suggest such a ridiculous thing? 'It won't work Jane. You can't make me believe your lies. From what I've heard you've gone crazy. Even your own husband doesn't believe you!'

Jane began raining punches down in Anna's face one after the other. 'You stupid bitch!' she screamed. 'You can't see the wood for the trees, can you?'

Anna's eyes rolled back in her head as she slumped to the ground. She lay panting breathlessly on the floor in a pool of her own blood and tried to formulate rational thoughts in her spinning mind.

Deciding playing dead for a minute or two might give her the breathing space she needed, Anna overrode the urge to sob and scream out of pain and remained lying motionless on the quarry tiles.

Glancing at Anna as she lay prone, Jane busied herself with collecting the things she needed from the drawer in the pantry. There was a roll of heavy-duty duct tape in there which would do nicely to bind Anna to a chair in the cellar until she decided to talk.

Jane didn't even see it coming when she was whacked in the temple with a copper saucepan.

Forty Five

AS SOON AS SHE heard the car pull up, Anna peeked out from behind the bushes. Confirming it was Aiden's car, she ran out from her hiding place and jumped in the back seat, clutching Toby tightly against her chest.

Without uttering a word, Aiden screeched off and Anna was finally able to take a deep breath of relief. She'd wiped the worst of the blood off her face with the back of her sleeve before she'd left the house. Knowing she had no time to waste, she hadn't bothered washing herself up further or changing her bloodied clothes before she'd quickly lifted Toby from his cot and rushed down the stairs.

She knew she looked a frightful state, but Aiden hadn't even commented, even though she could see his eyes in the rear view mirror as they sped along the road. 'Thanks for coming to get me. It was awful,' she said.

'Yeah, everything's awful for you, isn't it? Shut up for once, will you?' Aiden snapped.

Anna swallowed, feeling the overwhelming need to burst into tears. She'd been expecting him to be angry about what had happened to her, but he hadn't even remarked on her dishevelled and obviously injured appearance. Neither had he said anything about why she was clearly distressed and had called him from a phone box in a state of panic asking him to come and pick her up.

'Aiden?' Anna said nervously. 'What's wrong?'

'*What's wrong*?' Aiden roared, his eyes glaring menacingly in the rear view mirror's reflection. 'I'll tell you what's wrong – Seth-Fucking-Wright is what's wrong. He's murdered my brother!'

Aiden drew in ragged breaths through his all-encompassing rage. He'd lost it big time since Alan had been taken out and didn't give a flying fuck what he did, or how he did it anymore.

'Killed your brother?' Anna whispered, shocked. 'Oh my God, that's terrible! Why would Seth have done that? What on earth was your brother involved in?' *So, it was true. The Wrights went around killing people left, right and centre.*

She glanced down at the little boy in her arms, still sleeping peacefully. Seth and Jane didn't deserve children. She'd done the right thing by taking Toby with her. Regardless of anything else she couldn't leave him with that crazy woman and her serial killer husband.

'What do you mean what was he involved in?' Aiden screamed. 'Why did he have to be involved in *anything*?'

'I-I didn't mean... I just meant…'

'That's the fucking point, Anna. My brother wasn't involved in *anything*. He was a good man. A *nice* man,' Aiden shouted, the anger he felt about selling out his own brother to save his own skin bubbling to the surface again like a volcano.

'I-I'm sure he was,' Anna said gently, hoping to calm Aiden down. *He was obviously upset.* She leant forward from the back of the car and placed her hand on his shoulder.

'Get the fuck off me!' Aiden screamed, the car swerving violently.

Anna cried out as she slammed against the side of the door. 'Aiden?' she whimpered. 'What are you doing?'

Aiden glared at Anna in the mirror. He wanted to kill her. He wanted to punch her stupid fucking face full of holes. The stupid,

stupid bitch. He'd had enough. Enough was more than well and truly enough. He was done with it. After all this with Alan he was finished. He wasn't putting up with this bullshit any longer. Anna could go and fuck herself.

'Alan was murdered because Seth Wright thought he was *me*!' Aiden said, his voice a lot calmer than he felt.

Anna tried to smile. 'Oh don't blame yourself.' *Poor Aiden. He was taking this really hard. She had to make him see none of it was his fault.* 'When Jane was threatening me just now, she said all this rubbish about you being responsible for awful things. Don't worry, I told her quite clearly that sh…'

'Shut up!' Aiden snapped. 'What the hell do you know? I'm done with listening to your pathetic bleating. Just piss off!'

'What?' Anna cried as the car abruptly screeched to a halt at the side of the country lane.

'Get out of my car,' Aiden growled.

Placing Toby on the back seat next to her, Anna sat forward and put her hands on Aiden's shoulders. 'You've had a dreadful shock with your brother, don't be si…'

'I said get the fuck out…' Aiden snarled, twisting around in his seat to face Anna. He ripped her hands away from him. 'I could *never* be paid enough to put up with you. The longest fucking time of my life this has been and I'm not doing it anymore.'

Anna stared uncomprehendingly at the man she loved. 'P-Paid?'

Aiden laughed. 'Yes, *paid.* Your sister's idea actually. It helped pay off her debt, but I'm done with it.' He looked her up and down slowly. 'I mean for fuck's sake – look at you! You really think I'd have done you without some big reason?'

A single tear rolled down Anna's cheek. *Was he being serious?*

'Oh and you're wrong about Seth,' he smiled. '*I* despatched your mother, not him. Easy fucking money that was. Again, your sister's idea. Now get the fuck out of my car and my life. I won't tell you again.' Leaning over, Aiden opened Anna's door and effortlessly slung her out onto the grass verge.

Slamming his foot hard on the accelerator, Aiden hummed a tune to himself as he made his way back to his last drop. He glanced in the rear mirror at the baby on the back seat. *Seth Wright had taken his brother, so now he'd take his fucking kid.*

• • • •

DAN FELT LIKE HE was part of an exceptionally bad dream as he watched the stand-off between Seth and Jason Miller unfold in front of him.

Even though Miller had caught Seth unaware when he'd barged in brandishing a gun, it had been less than a second before Seth had retrieved his own pistol from its cleverly concealed hiding place under his desk for reasons such as this.

The two men had been locked pointing weapons at each other's heads for several minutes, with no hint of either of them backing down.

Dan eyed the steely resolve apparent in both of the men's eyes, along with the anger and resentment and knew it was only a short amount of time before one of them fired. *This was not good.*

Even though Dan was reluctant to get involved because it was more than feasible that if he uttered a word, one or other of their reactions would be to fire the gun in *his* direction, but he'd reached the decision that someone had to say *something* and it looked like *he* was the only one who could be rational.

Dan took a deep breath. 'Guys, this needs to stop.' He flinched, waiting for his head to depart from his neck, but nothing happened. It seemed neither Seth nor Miller had even heard him they were so fixated upon each other in a silent battle of wills.

'You both have your reasons, but you need to step back and look at it. You've both been played off against each *other*. This is what whoever's been doing this intended.'

Sensing he was getting nowhere, what with the rabid expressions plastered across both of the men's faces, Dan knew he needed to continue talking until they either took on board what he was saying, or shot him dead.

Summoning up courage he'd felt had deserted him, Dan rose from his chair and pushed between Seth and Miller. 'It's *obvious!* Whoever's doing this, *wants* you two to finish each other. Don't you see it's all part of the plan? They've been playing you both off against each other for *months* and it's worked!'

Dan looked at Seth. 'Seth, you've been convinced Jason Miller has been behind these issues for ages and you, Mr Miller, have equally distrusted Seth which has poured fuel on Seth's suspicions of *you* – especially when you publicly pulled your association.'

He sighed deeply. 'For God's sake! You're both clever men, but you've played right into this person's hands! I can see that even if you can't! This person has been manipulating rumours through to involved set ups! Now look at you – you're both pointing your guns at each other for fuck's sake, when you should be pointing them at who's done this – of which isn't either of *you*!'

Dan stomped to the other side of the room. It was all getting ridiculously stupid. He no longer cared if they turned on him. At least he wouldn't have to be party to this bullshit anymore.

'For God's sake, look at yourselves! Seth, your daughter is about to be adopted by some fucking nutter and the guy that's been threatening your family is still out there. Mr Miller, you've been set up more than once, causing you to publicly denounce Seth and act like he's guilty.'

'He killed one of my men!' Jason Miller shouted, suddenly remembering why he was here.

'Everything links back to *you* and your man!' Seth raged.

'But it wasn't Alan Barber,' Dan added quietly.

'Yeah, thanks Dan. I know that now,' Seth muttered.

'You need to be working *together* to sort it out,' Dan continued. *Christ, it was like being at school. Was he actually getting through to either of them?* 'And don't forget Seth that you're about to be framed for that girl's murder as well!'

Dan turned to Jason Miller. 'It's obviously a vendetta aimed at Seth, but you Mr Miller, have been unwittingly brought in to help incriminate him.' *It was true. Whoever this was certainly knew how to work everyone.* 'Think about it rationally. You worked together fine for a couple of years and had a good thing going. Why would either of you choose to change that?'

'Why did you say you thought Alan Barber was the connection?' Miller asked, finally lowering his gun. Dan had some good points even though it all sounded far-fetched that someone would go to such meticulous detail to set Seth Wright up. He liked even less that he'd been used as party to it.

'Because he was ID'd by several people,' Seth said, also putting his gun down. 'He was ID'd as the one who attacked your barmaid and the one who's been seen with my au pair.'

'My barmaid, Billie-Jo?' Jason said incredulously. 'Alan Barber would never have done that.'

Seth nodded. 'He was also shagging my au pair, involved in a prostitute ring for young girls and I think he was also involved in that young girl's disappearance, as well as sending those threatening letters.' He folded his arms. 'Except it *wasn't* him. I took out the wrong man.' He gritted his teeth. *He hated having to admit he'd made a mistake.* 'It appears Barber has a double.'

Jason Miller looked even more confused. 'What do you mean a *double*? None of this makes sense man. This sounds even more ridiculous than the rest of your conspiracy theory!'

'That's why you've been blaming each other because it makes more logical sense!' Dan reasoned. *Were they finally beginning to see the wood through the trees?*

'Somewhere there's a guy wandering around who can answer *all* of these questions and is still very much set on taking me down,' Seth said sternly. 'I don't know whether it's for his own personal reasons, or whether he's working for someone, but whoever it is seems to be cleverer than the pair of us. Either way, he's a spit of Alan Barber.'

Jason frowned. *Could it have been Alan Barber after all?*

'How can you be sure then that it *wasn't* Alan Barber?'

Dan smiled. 'Because Alan Barber hasn't got a tattoo on his neck. That's the difference.'

Jason suddenly felt quite ill. He sat down abruptly and helped himself to a glass of Seth's whisky. *It all made sense.* Taking a sip out of his drink he stared straight at Seth. 'Tattoo on his neck, did you say? I know who it is.'

• • • •

TINA HAD BEEN ABOUT to shoot up when Aiden booted her door in. Walking into her bedroom, he shoved a bundle on the bed and before she could utter a word, jumped astride her and pinned her to the mattress by her throat.

His manic eyes gleamed as he stared into Tina's. 'Where's my money, you cunt?' he snarled.

Tina struggled for breath. She might have known this would happen. She knew he'd come for his share of the insurance pay-out and could only be fobbed off for so long. She'd have probably had a few more weeks to think of a plan if his brother's death hadn't sent him off the rails, but now he'd lost the plot, he was spoiling for a fight with everyone.

This made everything just that little bit worse. He certainly wasn't about to appreciate her mother's life insurance claim had been denied. *Flatly and completely.*

It wasn't even to because she'd been murdered. It was because the old bat had failed to pay the premiums for the last five months and so unbeknownst to her, her mother's life insurance was null and void. *Aiden had done the hit for nothing.*

It was typical. Even after death her bloody mother had got one over on her. Furthermore, she still owed all that money…

'Well?' Aiden snarled. 'Where the fuck is it Tina? Don't try and turn me over, you skanky bitch. I need that money and I need it *now*. I'm out of here.'

'What do you mean? You're leaving?' Tina gasped, attempting to loosen Aiden's grip from around her throat.

'That's exactly what I'm saying, now get me the fucking

cash. I know you've put in for it as it's a cut and dried case, so they'd have paid out by now. Get me the money Tina. I won't ask you again.'

'But…'

'Oh, fuck it!' Aiden raged. Jumping off Tina, he pulled out her drawers one by one, tipping the contents messily on the floor. 'It's in here somewhere, so I'll find it my fucking self! Then I'll be dealing with *you* for trying to turn me over, you horrible junky slag!'

The sudden noise of the crashing drawers startled Toby who'd been deposited on the bed and he started crying.

'What the fuck?' Tina yelled, turning over and trying to focus her drug-addled eyes on where the noise was coming from. 'What the hell is that?'

'What do you think it is Tina? A bloody hamster?' Reaching over, Aiden grabbed Toby by the ankle and picked him up.

'Aiden! Put the kid down!' Tina yelled horrified as the child howled loudly.

'I'll put it down alright! Out of the fucking window!' Aiden yelled, moving across the room with the screaming child.

'NO!' Tina screeched, launching herself off the bed. *She couldn't let this psycho hurt a baby.*

Forty Six

ELIZA HAD JUST ABOUT had it. She'd got more than enough on her plate as it was with the police uncovering Lacey's body. She was shit scared it would lead back to her, without the noise she could hear from upstairs.

She needed to know whether the fibres chucked in with the body would be sufficient to lead the cops straight to Seth without them digging too far and finding a link with the Elipse or Lomond. *And therefore, her and Digger.*

Being as Seth already had more than enough form to last him to the moon and back, all she could hope for was that the police wouldn't feel the need to dig further. That the obvious evidence she'd managed to plant would assure them they'd got their man and no further enquiries would be necessary. But until that happened for sure, she couldn't rest easy.

Eliza wiped her hand across her face, irritated to find a sheen of sweat. *For God's sake.* She'd got so much to be contending with and it was all very much on her right now. Digger's assistance had waned lately and his assistance had been less than minimal. She was beginning to feel very resentful.

Plus, this stuff going on with the kid was taking it out of her. All Digger wanted to do lately was disappear and get drunk –

leaving *her* to handle everything. He could do with remembering that adopting Grace had been a *joint* decision, but now he was forgetting that and she didn't appreciate it.

Hearing the loud commotion continue, Eliza angrily got to her feet. *For Christ's sake*. It was hard trying to keep the little tarts in check without dealing with additional tantrums from the staff. She could detect Tina's voice from a mile away, the bloody stupid junkie. *What the hell was her problem?*

Stomping to the door, Eliza yanked it open. Tina had been useful initially, but now she was a pain in the arse. She'd done her part in what they wanted, so there was no real need for her to still be here. She was causing additional problems that no one needed and there was *no way* she'd be getting the bumper pay out she'd been expecting either.

The ungrateful bitch! She'd got rid of her despised mother free of charge, hadn't she? And she'd be receiving a very nice pay out from that, so what else did she want the greedy cow?

That reminded her. She'd be asking Aiden where *her* percentage of the cut was. Just because he was busy having a paddywack over his brother being bumped off didn't mean he could forget about her money.

He should be bloody glad someone else took the fall for his doings, but he hadn't even taken that on board, the stupid man. *They were all bloody stupid.*

She hurried along the corridor and up the flight of stairs towards Tina's room as fast as her stiletto heels would allow, scowling as the shouting and screaming got louder.

Reaching Tina's door, Eliza barged in. 'What the fuck's all this noi…'

Freezing to the spot seeing Tina's blood-caked face as she grappled with Aiden, Eliza stood astounded. What was that in Aiden's arms? *Oh Christ! Is that a child?*

'What in God's name is going on?' Eliza screeched.

Aiden and Tina paused mid-scuffle and stared at her.

'He's taken the kid. He's taken the fucking kid!' Tina wailed. 'He's going to kill it!'

Eliza looked from Tina to Aiden, seeing the manic look in Aiden's eyes that she hadn't ever seen before. 'Aiden, whose kid is that?'

'Seth Wright's and I'm having it. He killed my brother so I'm having his kid. Eye for an eye...' he spat.

Eliza paled. *Oh God. Seriously? How could this be possible? How could this sort of stuff happen to her? He'd fucked everything up.*

'I got the kid from Anna. She clumped Jane and legged it with the kid. You've been threatening to take the kid for months - so there you go! Except *I'm* dealing with it now, not you,' Aiden growled.

Eliza glanced at Tina clearly seeing the fear in her eyes. Aiden had well and truly lost his mind. *Dear God.* 'What do you mean threatening to take the kid? It's the girl I'm having, not the baby.'

'That was me. I added that into the last few letters,' Tina mumbled through her smashed teeth.

Eliza sat down heavily on the end of the bed. 'You *what*?' *Was she hearing correctly?*

'I wanted to scare the life out of the snotty bitch. The way she spoke to me and looked at me I wa...'

'You stupid bitch!' Eliza roared, backhanding Tina hard around the face. 'For Christ's sake! Are you insane? Oh my God! I didn't want that! That will only give them more clues to link us to *everything*! You stupid, *stupid*... Oh my God!' She was close to hyperventilating, unable to believe the woman could have been so completely and utterly useless.

Eliza began pacing around the room. 'What else did you say in these letters?'

'That you were getting their daughter...' Tina uttered. 'I thought I was doing the right thing...'

'Jesus wept!' Eliza raged. *They were done for.* 'They weren't supposed to find that out until *after* things were finalised! That's not until next week. And I never mentioned anything about the baby.' *Christ. Shit. Christ!*

She began to move warily towards Aiden. By the look in his eyes she didn't trust anything he may have up his sleeve. She'd never seen him behave like this before and it unnerved her.

She forced herself to meet his angry eyes. She needed to get the kid out of his grasp. *All may not be lost. It may be a blessing in disguise after all.* 'Don't even think about attacking me Aiden. I'll kill you stone dead. I suggest you get the fuck away from here. Fast.'

Eliza glanced at the small child staring at her with wide eyes, then looked back up over to Aiden. 'You'd best pray Seth gets banged up before he works out you're the cause of all of this and that this adoption goes through before Jane works out where all of this originated from.' Eliza's eyes narrowed. 'Otherwise we're all fucking dead.'

'You think I'm that stupid?' Aiden sneered. 'That shows how much you underestimate me. How much you've *always* underestimated me. I've had it with you lot. Turning me over all the time, getting me to do your bloody dirty work. Well fuck you! It stops *here*!'

Eliza eyed Aiden warily. He'd definitely turned. For the first time she felt uncomfortable and wary in his presence. *He'd morphed into a loose cannon.*

'It's *you* that's finished Eliza,' Aiden sneered nastily. '*I've* got the bargaining chip now, haven't I?' He held the child up by the scruff of his little top and jiggled him in front of the window. The child's frightened face was clear for all to see.

'What are you talking about?' Eliza asked hastily, trying to keep her voice as level as possible. She refused to show him that unfamiliar tendrils of fear and uncertainty were creeping into her mind.

'I'll be getting what's *mine* this time in return for the child of course,' Aiden grinned. 'And guess what? For once, you'll be getting fuck all! And don't try to threaten me with that 'I'll tell Digger about us' crap. You think that's going to bother me now? It won't work!'

Eliza paled. *Was she that obvious?* She had been thinking

about using that one. Aiden couldn't balls up all of this now. She had too much riding on everything. And why the hell should he be the one to suddenly demand blackmail? This whole thing had been *her* idea from the off. He couldn't jump on the bandwagon now and start calling the shots as and when he saw fit. *She wouldn't have it!* 'Now wait a minute…'

'Wait a minute, *nothing*!' Aiden scowled, his voice loud. 'As I said, I've had enough! Tell Digger about us, go on! He'll know it was *you* instigated it. *Everyone* knows you're a fucking slag!'

Eliza's eyes narrowed angrily and she stepped forward. 'You ungrateful piece of sh…'

Putting his hand up, Aiden smiled. 'Just to piss you off, I'll chuck this kid out of the window. No one will get anything then, will they? *I'm* having his money and then I swear to God, I'll tell the Wright's *everything* you've been doing and there's fuck all you can do about it!'

Eliza stopped in her tracks and paled further. *He wouldn't, would he?*

'Ha ha! It's all sinking in now isn't it? It's all coming back at you!' Aiden jeered.

'Except it's not…' Digger snarled, bursting into the room, his pistol aimed straight at Aiden's head.

• • • •

'WHY HASN'T SHE answered the door Maggie?' Seth asked worriedly as he fumbled with the key in the lock in his rush to get inside the house. He'd tried ringing Jane a while ago to give her the latest on what had gone down with Jason Miller, but she didn't answer. In fact, *no one* had answered, which was what had worried him.

Jane hadn't said she was going out today. He knew she'd been set to deal with Anna, so it was no surprise that she wasn't around, but he'd expected her to be at home.

Out of instinct he'd made the decision to pop back. He'd already arranged for Barry and Martin to reinstate their vigils of keeping an eye on things since he'd taken them off the job again the other day, but they weren't due back out until tomorrow.

Seth had half-presumed Jane had taken Toby round to Maggie's. That was until he'd pulled up on the drive to see Maggie banging fruitlessly on his front door and his unease had tripled. 'There's something wrong,' he muttered, finally jamming the key in the stubborn lock. 'I can taste it.'

Maggie thought so too, but was too petrified to say anything. Everything had escalated so violently out of control she was scared to *move* half of the time lately.

Finally opening the door, Seth raced into the hallway. 'Jane?' he roared, striding quickly along the corridor.

Maggie followed, aware the house was unusually silent. *Something didn't bode well.*

'Oh Jesus!' Seth cried, rushing into the kitchen towards Jane slumped on the floor. 'Jane?' He knelt down over his wife. 'Jane? Can you hear me?'

'Oh my God!' Maggie wailed. 'Is she alright?'

'*Jane*?' Seth shouted, panic rising rapidly in his veins. 'JANE!'

Groaning, Jane's eyes flickered. 'Seth?'

'Oh, thank God!' Seth cried relieved. 'Are you ok?' He eyed the lump on Jane's temple and guessed she'd taken a hard clump from something, most probably courtesy of Anna. His eyes narrowed. 'What happened?'

Jane struggled to push herself up. Groaning as the pain in her head intensified. 'Oh God… No, I'm ok, I'm ok.' She tried to clear her head. Everything was slightly blurry and out of focus. She gingerly felt the swelling on her temple and tried to recall what on earth had occurred.

'I'll get an ambulance,' Seth muttered, getting up.

'No!' Jane cried, grabbing his arm. 'I'm ok really. It's just a bash to the head. I'll be fine in a minute.'

As her memory caught up with her, she paled. 'Shit! Seth, it's Anna. It was Anna. I was going to tie her up in the cellar until she told me who was behind all of this. Who her boyfriend is and where to find him. I'd knocked her out, but she must have come round and bashed me with something.'

Jane looked around for something Anna could have used as a weapon. Her eyes narrowed when her gaze fell on the copper saucepan thrown haphazardly on the side which was most likely the culprit.

Suddenly panic overtook her and she struggled to her feet. 'Toby!' she cried. 'Where's Toby?' *The bitch! The fucking bitch! If Anna had her son...* 'He was upstairs having a nap...'

'Shit!' Maggie cried, dashing out of the room and upstairs. Breathing rapidly, she raced along the corridor and into Toby's nursery. His cot was glaringly empty. *Oh God, no! The baby was gone!*

Hot on Maggie's heels, Seth barged in not two seconds later. His eyes searched wildly around the room. 'Where is he?' he roared, eyes wild.

Maggie didn't know what to say. *What could she say apart from the obvious?* 'I-I don't know Seth...'

Letting out a loud guttural howl, Seth dropped to his knees on the floor. *His son had gone.* 'She's taken my son!' he roared. 'The bitch has taken my son!'

Scrambling to his feet, Seth began trashing the nursery. Picking up Toby's cot, he threw it against the wall where it smashed into pieces.

'SETH!' Maggie cried. 'Control yourself! This won't help!' *Dear God, this was a nightmare.*

'Nothing will help now will it?' Seth raged, swiping items from the top of Toby's chest of drawers to the floor with a loud angry growl.

'What's happening? Where is he?' Jane yelled, rushing into the nursery and staring in horror at the wreckage of Toby's cot. 'Oh my God, TOBY?' She rushed towards the carnage.

Maggie shouted, grabbing Jane's arm. 'Jane! It's ok, he's not under all that. Seth's smashed it up.'

Jane looked around bewildered, her eyes frantically searching. From the expression on Seth's face she knew the truth. Anna Slater had taken her child. She'd now lost both her children, but wasn't quite ready to admit that could possibly be the case. *How could she? It hurt too much.* 'Seth?'

Seth desperately tried to pull himself together and curb his out of control desire to trash the entire contents of this whole massive bloody house. Taking a deep breath to steady his ragged breathing, he walked over to Jane and grabbed her by both shoulders. 'Ok, now you listen to me. We're going to get him back do, you hear me? I'll get him back.'

'You said that about Grace!' Jane spat. 'And look at that!'

Maggie looked down at the floor sadly as Jane crumpled into Seth's arms in a mass of heavy sobs.

• • • •

ANNA CONTINUED HALF-RUNNING, half-walking despite her legs and feet being in agony. Each step she took caused a further jolt of pain to her arm that she suspected was broken when she'd been pushed from the car.

She'd continued walking blindly, unsure whether she was going in the right direction – wherever that was. She had no idea where she was going or even where she *should* go.

Whatever happened, she had to get somewhere to lie low for a while. She knew that even if Aiden didn't return to finish her off to ensure she didn't implicate him in anything, then it wouldn't be long before the Wrights would be gunning for her. She'd bashed Jane over the head and took their child for God's sake. *What had she been thinking*?

Whatever she'd been thinking, she'd been so wrong it was an understatement. She accepted she'd probably get killed for her part in what had occurred and helped engineer, or at the very least, she'd get put in hospital for a very long time, but at this precise moment she needed to get away. Somewhere that she'd be safe and off the radar.

Anna racked her brains. *Where the hell could she go*? She could hardly run to Tina, being as she'd been instrumental in all of this, not that she knew where she was either.

Sweat poured down Anna's back from a combination of

exertion and fear. After the initial heat had died down she *had* to reach Jane and tell her what had happened. That she'd been wrong and most importantly, that she'd been wrong about Toby being better off without her. She'd thought she was doing the right thing. Instead, she'd inadvertently done the opposite. Regardless of anything else, she loved that dear little boy and now she'd unwittingly placed him in the hands of the *one* person who she now knew to be the problem all along.

Tears ran freely down Anna's face as she stumbled along. She didn't care what happened to her anymore. She had nothing left to live for now. *Nothing at all*. It had all been lies. Nothing was real and she'd been stupid enough to think that it was.

Everything had been bullshit from the off and *yet again* she'd fallen for it. *All it this was her fault*. If she hadn't been so desperate to be loved, then none of this would have happened. It had been *her* who had given these people the ability to screw up Jane and Seth's lives. How could she? How could she have done any of it? It was all so clear now.

Oh dear God. She deserved to die. She really did. She'd relish the punishment that would be meted out to her, but even *that* wouldn't lessen her guilt, or deliver the pain she deserved.

Should she go to the police and tell them everything rather than stagger around for miles with no clue where she was heading? Was she causing even *more* harm by not saying what she knew right now? Or was she playing for time and looking for excuses? If she went to the police would she then be arrested for aiding such heinous acts? Oh God, everyone would find out what she'd done. *Everyone*. They'd all know what she was *really* like. What a dreadful, needy pathetic person she was and would always be. *The sad, pathetic gullible bitch that everyone laughed at.*

No. Even putting herself to one side, the right thing to do was to tell Jane and Seth first. They wouldn't want the police involved. She suspected if they were, then Jane and Seth would get into a lot more trouble.

Anna came to the conclusion that she'd already done enough

damage. The least she could do was not to cause any more. She needed to find somewhere to get herself together and work out what do next and exactly *when* to do it.

Her brows furrowed together. *That was it. She'd go to her mother's house.* She'd still got the keys and the house was still empty. Going there would give her the breathing space she so desperately needed.

Anna wiped the tears pouring down her face away with her hand and resolutely continued down the road, pleased to see some recognisable landmarks visible in the distance.

Forty Seven

JASON MILLER WASTED NO time in getting a couple of his men together. He may have come to some unwise assumptions in the past about Seth Wright and knew he'd been wrong. All he could do now to rectify that was to help the man as much as possible.

He screeched to a halt outside of the pub where he'd located Aiden Barber when delivering the news about his brother. Jason scowled. If only he'd known what he knew now. He'd have done more than deliver the news that his brother was dead – he'd have ensured he'd put Aiden in the same place.

The smarmy bastard. Pretending he was distraught when he was the one who'd allowed Alan to take the knock that should have been *his*.

Jason could feel his temper surging in jerky bursts of adrenalin. This twat had disfigured his barmaid and caused all the unrest. He knew he'd find it hard to keep control if he got his hands on the prick first, but he owed it to Seth to have the satisfaction of personally destroying the bastard. Furthermore, this wanker had Seth's son, therefore everything else paled into insignificance.

No, it was Seth's right to have the pleasure of this one and

Jason would be doing everything in his power to serve the sly bastard up.

Seth had been almost rabid with the need to accompany him, but Jason had insisted that it didn't take *two* of them to bring the shithead in. Primarily he needed to check on Jane. He could tell how worried Seth was when she didn't answer the telephone. This worry was well-founded, because too many bad things had happened - several of which he'd unwittingly contributed to… But better late than never to rectify that.

Nodding towards his men, Jason barged through the doors of the broken-down pub and this time wasn't surprised when the place fell into silence at their sudden appearance.

Recognising the barmaid as the one he'd spoken to previously, Jason strode purposefully up to the bar.

'Hello again,' the barmaid purred, a wide smile appearing across her pretty face.

'Cut the niceties,' Jason snarled. 'Aiden Barber? Where is he?'

The barmaid's face fell at Jason Miller's tone of voice and she warily eyed the two unfriendly-looking large men flanking him. 'He's not here…' she muttered.

'I can see that!' Jason snapped irritably. 'Where is he?'

'I-I don't know. I haven't seen him since the night I last saw you,' the barmaid replied nervously, suspecting this would not be the answer the man wanted to hear.

'Where does he live?' Miller snarled, getting impatient. 'Come on girl. This is important, so don't play games. I'm guessing, based on the derogatory comments you made about him last time that you shared more than drinks, so tell me where he fucking lives.'

The barmaid blushed. Grabbing a notepad, she scribbled down an address. 'I've only been there a couple of times, but I think this is right.'

Snatching the scrap of paper from the girl's shaking hands, Jason nodded at her brusquely. 'Thanks.'

Jerking his head towards his men, he strode back out from

the pub.

• • • •

JENNIE HAD MADE her decision. After what she'd heard, she knew Lacey would not be returning to Pegasus Place. Sylvia had been wrong. *Lacey was dead and there was nothing she could do about it.*

She was racked with guilt. If she'd gone to Jane Wright when she was first thought about it then perhaps Lacey could have been saved? *Now she'd never know.*

Either way, she couldn't leave it any longer. She doubted whether anything she had to say would be of use, but she had to at least *try*.

Jennie hurried down the road, knowing she must be nearing the correct place. She gazed at the large houses sitting amidst their immense grounds and pushed down a pang of envy. Now was not the time to be resentful about the hand she'd been dealt in life. What mattered now was doing something that could, even in a small way, help to bring whoever had murdered her friend to justice.

Rounding the corner, she gasped in amazement as the façade of the Wright's house loomed imposingly in front of her. This had to be the right place. *It was like a mansion.*

Taking a deep breath, she walked up the drive, almost having a heart attack when a burly man stepped onto the path, seemingly from nowhere.

'Where do you think you're going?' Martin asked in a loud menacing voice.

Pulling her wits back around her, Jennie found her voice. 'I need to see Mrs Wright.'

'It's not a good time right now, Miss,' Martin said. He hadn't all the details, but the frantic call he'd received from Seth not an hour past, telling him to come around straight away had made it clear something serious had gone down.

Seth himself had left shortly after Martin had arrived, but Jane was still in the house with Maggie and he felt it inopportune to disturb her with whatever this girl wanted.

'*Please*!' Jennie begged. 'It's really important that I see her.' She knew there was no choice in it. If she didn't get to see Jane Wright today, it was unlikely she'd summon up the courage again.

Martin smiled thinly. 'I'm really sorry. It really isn't a good time. I don't thi…'

'I have information on Lacey,' Jennie spluttered. 'Lacey Garner, the girl wh…'

'I know who Lacey Garner is,' Martin interrupted. He also knew the girl's disappearance had caused a lot of upset within the house and raised more than several links to other untoward aspects which had been happening. *Perhaps he should double check to see whether Jane wished to speak to this girl?* 'Wait here. I'll see if she can accommodate you.'

'Thank you,' Jennie replied, buoyed slightly with the prospect of finally being able to tell someone what she knew, however irrelevant it may be.

• • • •

MAGGIE WAS SURPRISED that Martin should even ask for something so absurd under the circumstances. Had Seth not informed him Toby was missing? From her experience, Martin was switched on, so surely if he knew what had happened then he wouldn't be pestering Jane with requests from random passers-by?

Jane was in no fit state to deal with anything right now. She'd wanted to accompany Seth when he'd left earlier, but Maggie had to agree with Seth on this one. When he'd insisted she remained at home in case someone called with news of Toby, Maggie had strongly agreed this was the best thing to do.

Although Maggie would have quite happily remained in the house to take any calls or anything which enabled Jane to accompany Seth, the sad truth was that Jane was a complete and utter mess. As it was, she'd sat stationary in a chair without speaking for the last half an hour, despite Maggie's attempts to keep her spirits up.

She can't say she was surprised. It was bad enough to lose one child, but to then lose a second – and to some kind of vendetta, well – it didn't bear thinking about and she could only *imagine* how Jane must be feeling.

'I don't think it will be possible Martin,' Maggie said. 'You obviously haven't been filled in with what's happened this morning, but Jane's in no fit state to sp…'

'*I'll* be the judge of whether I'm in a fit state or not don't you think Maggie?' Jane said sternly as she appeared in the doorway, resolve back in her shining eyes.

'Oh, erm…' Maggie flustered, colouring slightly. She didn't want Jane to think she was calling her useless. She was just trying to take some of the pressure off. 'I was just sa…'

'Yes, I know. You're just trying to help. It's ok,' Jane said, forcing herself to smile. 'Who is it and what's it about?'

'I'm sorry, Mrs Wright. I'll tell her to come back another time,' Martin said, realising rapidly he was right that something serious had occurred.

Jane held her hand up. '*Who* is it and what's it about?' She was determined to be in control of at least *some* aspects of her life. *Ones that she still had left that was.*

Martin glanced at Maggie apologetically and then turned to Jane. 'A young girl's outside asking for you,' he said. 'She says she has information on Lacey Garner.'

Maggie huffed. 'Oh, for God's sake – Lacey Garner! Hasn't she caused enough problems already? It's probably some silly girl trying to get her hands on that reward money you offered. Tell her to go away! You're got more important things to deal with.'

Jane's eyes narrowed. 'Do you not think I know what's important? You've obviously forgotten Lacey Garner was linked to Anna's boyfriend. You saw him remember? This same guy is also linked to everything else,' she spat. 'So yes Martin. I *will* see her – straight away. Please show her in.'

Maggie stared at her feet contritely. *Maybe it would be*

easier if she said nothing?

She despondently followed Jane back into the sitting room to wait to hear what this girl had to say.

Forty Eight

'YOU'RE GOING TO HAVE to get it out of here,' Digger said, staring at the small child.

Eliza glared at Digger. 'I'm not a fucking retard!' she snapped. 'Don't you think I know that?' His attitude was doing nothing to help her irritation. 'It wasn't like I'd *planned* to get dumped with a random baby was it?' Wincing when Toby yanked down hard on her gold hoop earrings, she swallowed down the urge to snap his pudgy little arm.

Digger scowled sarcastically. 'It's hardly a 'random' baby is it? It's *Seth and Jane's* random baby. That won't draw any more attention to us will it?'

Eliza clenched her teeth. 'This isn't down to *me*!' She glared at Tina sitting dejectedly in the corner, occasionally whimpering from the pain radiating from her smashed teeth.

'I'll get rid of it!' Steve Lomond piped up eagerly, holding his large calloused hands out. 'I've got no problem with chucking it in the river!'

Eliza frowned. *Even she wouldn't stoop that low – although it would solve the immediate issue...* 'That's not going to help is it? I'll get one of the girls to look after it.' She screwed her nose up. 'It's quite an opportune moment for that to happen to be honest. I think it needs its nappy changing.'

She scowled at Tina. 'Make yourself useful, you dumb bitch. Go downstairs and see if any of them are straight enough to cope with looking after a kid for a few hours whilst I work out what to do.'

Quickly scrambling to her feet, Tina avoided Eliza's eyes and left the room. She'd *royally* fucked up, but whatever her faults were, she couldn't see a baby get hurt. *That Aiden was a head case for doing this, as was her sister.*

'And what have you done with that dickhead?' Eliza spat.

Digger knew full well Eliza was referring to Aiden. He couldn't quite believe he'd had quite such a spectacular meltdown. 'I gave him a bit of a slap to calm him down,' he said. 'At the present moment in time he's chained up in Room Six whilst the rest of his anger drains out of him.'

'I want him gone!' Eliza yelled. '*Today,* Digger.'

Digger nodded. He couldn't argue with that. So much for his assurances that Aiden could be trusted. Jesus Christ. He'd lost the plot and was no use to them any longer. He had to go and the sooner the better. The way he was behaving he couldn't be trusted by anyone's standards. He was a Grade A liability. *He'd have to kill him.*

Eliza fixed her gaze on Digger, reading his mind. 'You can't offload him. You've *got* to promise me you won't, however much you want to.' They couldn't risk any more heat brought to their doorstep. Not with being on the cusp of getting the Wright's beloved daughter next week.

She hadn't got this far to lose everything at the last hurdle. *No way!* They'd got away with everything else by the looks of it – bunging an extra risk on top just wasn't worth it.

Digger frowned. 'Hang on a minute. Are you *mad*? What happens if he feels the need to discuss what he knows?'

'Make sure he doesn't. Aiden's *lost* it. Lost it big time. I doubt whether he's even capable of reading from a fucking *kid's* book, let alone cope with having a serious conversation with anyone that could plausibly cause us a problem.' She shook her head. 'Dump him back in his old life and put the fear of God into him. It's the least riskiest option. That way it doesn't give any more leads to trail anything untoward back to us.'

She smiled. 'After all this stuff's wrapped up with the girl next week *then* if you want to offload him, do it - I couldn't care less, but *not* before.' Her eyes narrowed. 'As for the baby – we'll take care of him for now and once we've got custody of the girl, we'll go down the blackmail route.'

Digger nodded in acceptance, hoping Eliza's theory would work. 'At least Aiden's given us an additional option.'

'Oh yeah, great! He's done *real* well…' Eliza quipped sarcastically. 'Still, that's how it is and this is what has to happen now. Promise me?'

Digger sighed. 'Yep, ok I promise you. And don't worry. I'll make sure he gets the message loud and clear.'

'Shall I send Selena down the shop to buy some nappies and stuff?' Tina said, gingerly sticking her head around the office door.

'You what?' Eliza screeched. 'You know none of the girls are allowed out! You really are stupid, aren't you?' *Christ! Did they not have enough problems?*

'All the girls are blotto apart from Selena. I was going to take Toby off your hands and then get Selena to get the nappies so he can be changed. Otherwise you'll have to keep him with you whilst I go to the shops.'

Eliza glanced down at the grizzling child and caught another whiff of the steadily increasing pong emanating from him. 'Oh, just take the kid and send Selena out for the stuff!'

She reached into her pocket and pulled out a five pound note. 'Here! And tell her I want the fucking change!' *Let them get on with it. She couldn't deal with it anymore. She had too much on her plate.*

Quickly taking the money, Tina nodded and lifted Toby from Eliza's arms. 'Come on sweetheart. Let's get you sorted out, shall we?'

Eliza watched Tina play mother to the little brat and

gratefully breathed in a lungful of non-sewage scented air. *That was the reason she'd never wanted kids - non-stop hassle and the constant smell of shit.*

When Tina closed the door, Eliza turned to Digger irritably. 'Now hurry up and get rid of that fucking liability back where he belongs. You go with them too Steve,' she barked. *She needed to be on her own.*

• • • •

'PLEASE MAKE THIS QUICK,' Maggie snapped as Jennie perched uncomfortably on the edge of the sofa, aware for some reason today was obviously not the best day to be paying house calls.

She tried not to stare at the sumptuous furnishings of the room, aware it would be extremely rude, but nevertheless she found it impossible to ignore the multitude of beautiful things.

'Thank you, Maggie,' Jane cut in. She was only trying to help, but it was making things harder than they were already. It was plain to see the girl in front of them was nervous. 'So, Jennie,' she smiled. 'What is it that you need to tell me?'

'I-I'm not after money or anything,' Jennie said quickly, watching Maggie roll her eyes, obviously presuming the *only* reason she was here was because of that. 'No *really*, I don't. I came around before, but chickened out. Maybe if I hadn't, perhaps I could have stopped Lacey from being…'

Jennie's face crumpled as the sad truth that her friend was dead crashed into her mind once again. She quickly pulled herself together. *Now was not the time to appear pathetic.* 'Sorry. I'm sorry.' She frantically wiped at her cheeks.

'That's ok,' Jane said kindly. 'Don't worry. But if you know something, you must tell us. It might be more important than you realise.'

Jane was desperately trying to stop her impatience from overtaking her and was finding it increasingly difficult to concentrate. All she could think of was Toby and whether he was ok. The prospect of what could be happening kept flashing into her mind with vivid and disturbing clarity, which was difficult to ignore.

'I met Lacey at Pegasus Place,' Jennie began.

'Pegasus Place?' Jane asked. 'What's that?'

'It's a hostel for young women. No men allowed!' Jennie managed a weak smile. 'We got on really well from the start. I've never really had a proper friend before and...' Realising she was rambling, Jennie reined herself in. 'I got Lacey a job at a bookshop - she liked it there. Anyway, we didn't talk much about our past but...'

'What did Lacey tell you?' Jane pushed. *She didn't have time for this girl's life story.*

'Not a lot. She said she'd been forced into prostitution and that was about it.'

Jane nodded. 'Did she say where?'

Jennie frowned. 'No. No she didn't. She said nothing apart from that.'

'So, what happened?'

'She didn't come back from work one night. We'd fallen out and I was angry with her, but...' Jennie choked back another sob. 'I felt like it was all my fault because of what happened and what I said to the other girls. I thought she'd run away.'

Jane frowned. 'Why did you fall out?'

Jennie's face crumpled. 'That's just it. I was awful! I believed this other girl and I should have believed Lacey. I know now she was telling the truth.'

When Jane said nothing, Jennie continued. 'A girl started talking to me in a café when I was having a drink before work – I work in the evenings as a cleaner,' she explained. 'The girl showed me a picture of Lacey. Said she was her cousin's friend and that she'd run away. Made out she'd come from a posh family and would lose her scholarship at Sacred Hearts if she didn't return home in time.'

'Sacred Hearts? That's the private college isn't it?' Maggie asked.

'I can tell you now that absolutely *none* of that is true,' Jane said bluntly.

Jennie stared at her chewed fingernails. 'I know, but I believed it at the time. I thought she'd lied about her background and I accused her of being a fake and a liar. I-I told all the other girls and they all turned their backs on her. It's all my fault!' She began openly sobbing.

'It's not your fault Jennie, but what made you realise she was telling the truth?' Jane asked, passing the girl a tissue.

Jennie wiped her eyes. 'I saw the girl from the café again. The one who'd asked the questions about Lacey. She was with some other girls and they were going down an alley. The alley where that dodgy quack deals with all the prostitutes.'

Jane raised her eyebrows. She hadn't heard of this dodgy doctor, but didn't doubt there was one. 'And that's when you realised Lacey had been telling the truth?'

Jennie nodded. 'Yes. That girl must have been one of the prostitutes who'd worked with Lacey.'

Jane's hackles rose. 'And you're *sure* she didn't mention who she worked for?'

Jennie shook her head firmly. 'I'm sure. She was tight-lipped about the whole thing. I think that's why it was easy to believe she'd been making it up.'

'I don't suppose there was a man with this group of girls was there?' Jane asked. 'Young – in his twenties, tall, blond hair?'

'No. No one like that,' Jennie said, then remembered the huge man she'd seen who had given her the creeps. 'I did see a man but he didn't look like that.'

Jane moved to the edge of the sofa. 'What did he look like?'

Jennie frowned. 'Difficult to describe. Big. Tall. Scary-looking. They were all quite far away.'

Jane felt deflated. That description could match a thousand and one people in their circles. 'Oh well. Never mind. Did she mention anyone called Aiden at all?' she pressed. *Surely Lacey must have mentioned him?*

'Sorry, no she didn't,' Jennie said sadly. 'I'd remember if she had.'

'And no one else?'

'No. I'm sorry.' Jennie put her head in her hands. 'Oh, I knew I'd be no use!'

'Don't think like that. What you've said is useful,' Jane said kindly. *Well it was. Just not clear cut unfortunately.*

'The only other thing was one night when we'd had a few pints, she started rambling,' Jennie smiled, remembering that night with fondness. *God she'd felt rough the next day!*

'What was said?'

'Oh, nothing of any use. It was mainly gibberish. We were both quite drunk. It's the only time she really mentioned the prostitution thing and she was banging on about hating digging! I never worked it out!' Jennie laughed.

Jane laughed, then her face fell. 'What do you mean 'digging'?'

'I have no idea. She was talking rubbish. We were both a few sheets to the wind!'

'Digging...' Jane frowned, a tiny spark igniting in the back of her mind. She glanced at Maggie. *It couldn't be could it? Digging? DIGGER?*

FORTY NINE

SETH COULD BARELY KEEP himself from twitching with nervous anticipation as he sat in the van with Jason Miller. The minute he'd received the call from Miller to say he'd got Barber's address, he'd been off like a shot. Leaving Martin watching the house where he'd left Jane with Maggie, he'd raced to the Limelight.

Once Seth had arrived, Jason had broken the news he'd already paid the address a visit, but there had been no answer and he believed Barber may have already done a flit.

Giving his trust back to his instinct, Seth had pushed that they should revisit. His gut was telling him Barber hadn't yet done a runner and that he'd be there. Miller had thought this was a waste of time and instead, they needed to scout the list of locations he'd collected the last time he'd been trying to reach Aiden Barber, but Seth had held his ground.

Seth glanced out of the van window. Even if Barber wasn't there, which he felt in his bones he would be, then they could at least gain access to see if any clues had been left as to his, or Toby's whereabouts.

Seth raked his fingers through his thick hair. He'd got Dan with him and Miller had Tom in the back. *Between them they'd be able to locate this wanker, surely?*

Seth glanced at Dan irritably. 'Get a move on, will you?' he hissed through clenched teeth. He needed to stop this. *He needed to stop all of it.*

• • • •

AIDEN HAD PULLED himself together sufficiently enough to act. He needed to do something rapidly otherwise his chance to get any money was ruined. He couldn't quite believe the moment his brain had chosen to have a belated meltdown was at the vital point where he'd held the leverage in his own arms. Now the kid was in the control of Eliza and Digger, meaning they could reap the rewards of any blackmail and claim what he'd worked for without putting in any effort. *Again.*

He knew his bridges were well and truly burnt whichever way he looked at it. He had no choice now. He wouldn't be welcome back at Elipse and would never be party to any advancement which he'd worked so hard for. It was surely also only a matter of time before Seth Wright caught up with him.

Whilst he'd still had possession of the fucking kid, he had a bargaining chip, but now he no longer had that there was nothing.

Quickly pushing himself up from his bed and out of his stupor, he bent down to retrieve a holdall. Yanking open a drawer, he grabbed a handful of underwear, along with other various items of clothing and shoved them haphazardly into the bag. *Where was his passport? Where the fuck was the bloody passport?*

Blindly he upturned anything which could possibly be housing the important document. *Fuck. Where was it? Quickly. Think, think, THINK!*

Aiden glanced at his watch. He had to clear this place and fast. Dropping to his knees, he pushed the striped rug to one side and gripped at the raised edge of the loose floorboard. Systematically prising it in the way that ensured easy leverage, he lifted the specific board and delved his hand into the exposed hole, retrieving a shoebox.

Grabbing the wads of notes he'd accumulated over the many drug deals he'd had with the girls at Eclipse, he calculated at a rough estimate he'd got around twenty grand. Not an immense amount, but certainly enough to warrant his passage out of here and to find somewhere to start again where no fucker could find him.

But first he needed to locate his bloody passport.

Frantically Aiden tipped out the contents of the rest of his drawers, mindlessly swiping through the mess in the hope of spotting it, but still found nothing.

Oh, it was no use. He couldn't spend any more time on this. He had to go.

He'd got enough cash to get another fake passport put together anyhow and could sort that out the minute he found a base to settle for a few days.

With no time to spare, Aiden hastily crammed the over-spilling items down in his holdall enough to close the zip. He lurched towards the door, just as it was kicked open in his face.

• • • •

SHELL-SHOCKED WOULD BE the only way Jane could describe how she felt. She stared at Maggie, hoping that by some miracle she'd have an epiphany and suggest something that would make all of this alright.

'Is it even *feasible*?' Maggie asked. She'd been gobsmacked after Jennie had left and Jane had suggested perhaps Digger and Eliza were somehow behind all this. This was based on the reference Jennie had referred to. Personally, Maggie thought Jane was clutching at straws.

'I really don't know.' Jane got up and walked to the cabinet where she poured two glasses of vodka. Passing one to Maggie, she sat back on the sofa and raised the drink to her mouth with shaking hands.

The minute Jennie had left, she'd phoned both the Glint and the Limelight to get hold of Seth, but he'd already left. She had no choice now but to let him go off with Miller for what they needed to do and wait until he got back.

Jane didn't know what to think. Her brain felt like it had been fried. Until now it hadn't crossed her mind that Digger and Eliza could be behind this. They hadn't even *fathomed* in any list of possible contenders. Maybe that was where the problem had lay all along.

Too much concentration and emphasis had been placed on every other possible scenario and perpetrator that *none* of them had considered this a possibility. Why would they have? Wasn't that done and dusted? At least that's what they'd believed.

Maggie frowned. 'Don't you think it's a bit unlikely? No one's heard of them for *years*! Surely if they were back on the scene, wouldn't Seth have heard about it?'

Jane sank her teeth into her bottom lip, finding the pain slightly relieved the crushing confusion and stress. 'It depends what they're doing. Just because they weren't on the scene *here* doesn't mean they haven't been working on things elsewhere.'

'But surely they wouldn't be so stupid to pull something like this off? Not after what Seth and Phil did to Digger? Wasn't the proviso that they wouldn't be further harmed, providing they stayed away?'

Jane nodded. 'It was, but I think we've all underestimated their hatred for us. Seth should have kept tabs on them for longer.'

'But they did it all to themselves!' Maggie reasoned.

Jane scowled. 'I know that, but was Eliza *ever* logical? She's also a *lot* cleverer that you think.'

'But Digger was obsessed with you. Why would he want to hurt you?'

'He was quite happy to see me locked up and my daughter taken off me rather than being honest, remember?' Jane spat. 'Whatever the reasoning, it's still a possibility as far as I'm concerned.'

Everyone had been so hell bent on blaming each other and presuming it was a vendetta to do with the club for so long, it hadn't crossed *anyone's* mind that it could be *personal*.

She was trying to contain the rising panic that if her wild theory was correct, then Digger and Eliza had her son and were adopting her daughter.

'And you think they're behind this prostitute thing too? With the young girls?' Maggie cried. 'They wouldn't! They *couldn't* do *that*!'

'I think Eliza would do anything if she stood to benefit. Have you forgotten she sold herself to that foul rapist, Carter?'

Maggie grimaced. She hadn't forgotten anything. She was just horrified this could be even plausible.

'All I know is if they're responsible for this, then they're dead…' Jane muttered. She knocked the contents of her drink down in one. 'Either way we don't know where they are and that's the bit which scares me.'

She put her head in her hands, feeling panic threatening to engulf her. 'I need to find out where they are. Christ, if only I'd kept hold of Anna. Her boyfriend *must* be working for Eliza and Digger!'

Maggie's mouth formed into a perfect 'O' as the implication sank in. 'So everything's been pre-determined and set up from the start?'

Jane nodded. 'I think so yes. Jesus Christ, Maggie, what the fuck am I going to do?'

Maggie stared at Jane despondently. She had no idea. *No idea at all.*

'I need to find Seth. If he's located Anna's boyfriend, then he'll have tortured the whereabouts as to who he's working for and where they're based out of him.'

Maggie seemed less than convinced but didn't want to voice this. Jane's hope very much depended on whether Seth had lost his temper before or *after* he'd extracted the information. 'Or we find Anna in the meantime?'

Jane's eyes narrowed. 'Oh, believe me, I'll be catching up with her the *first* chance I get.' *There was no way she'd be letting what that little bitch had done go on any level.*

• • • •

AIDEN SQUINTED WHEN strip lights came into focus above him as he lay on a concrete floor. He attempted to reach out, but his hands were tightly secured behind his back. He tried to clear his head from its foggy confusion, dimly aware the last thing he recalled was being about to leave his flat.

Suddenly a shape loomed over him.

'Back with us, are you?' Seth said, squatting down on his haunches. 'Start talking…'

Aiden suppressed a giggle. *So Seth Wright had caught up with him, had he? Not that he was surprised.* It was ok. He knew he was finished, but he'd still get the last one over on this cunt. They wouldn't get any information out of him. *Never.*

'Cat got your tongue?' Seth yelled, booting Aiden squarely in the ribs.

Despite the searing pain, Aiden refused to let it show on his face. He wouldn't give the wanker the satisfaction. It was the only way he could piss Seth Wright off now and he was determined to use the ever-present simmering rage about what this tosspot had done to Alan to fuel it and keep it burning.

Seth sensed he'd have problems with this one the moment he'd seen the trace of a smile appear across his face when he'd regained consciousness. Most normal people would have been confused and frightened, but Aiden Barber wasn't. He'd seemed to *relish* what was going to happen to him.

He frowned. It was worrying, but it certainly wouldn't impede him getting the required information from the bastard.

Seth studied the man lying on the floor. The likeness to his brother was uncanny. The only difference, apart from the tattoo of the swallow on his neck, was the determination and defiance evident in this brother's eyes.

Seth grinned. *No matter.* He'd play his game for a while being as it seemed to float his boat. The only thing he had to ensure was that he didn't allow this prick to make him to lose his temper, otherwise it would all be over and he'd be getting no information.

Seth felt secure over this because Jason and Dan had assured him they'd pull him from his rage should he happen to slip into it. That way he could remain focused.

However, the lack of response he was getting from the man who had made his life a misery for the last few months was grating. 'Barber, you'd best start talking. For a start, tell me where my son is,' Seth snarled, his teeth clenching.

A sly grin spread across Aiden's face. 'What makes you think that's anything to do with me?'

'Oh, let's see… Perhaps because you took him? Perhaps because you've been identified so many times I've lost count? Perhaps because you've been fucking around for *months*? You've been in my house, screwed my au pair, been threatening my wife,' Seth's voice was rising dangerously. 'You've slashed up a barmaid and, oh yes, you're involved with some sort of pervy prostitution ring!'

Aiden laughed. It hadn't taken long for the great Seth Wright to start losing his rag. *This would be fun.* 'Right! Well what a well-organised firm you must have! For me to be ID'd so many times and yet I've been still allowed to get away with it all. For so long as well? Yeah, you must be *real* good,' he smirked. 'You must be over the fucking moon about your combined ability?'

Seth's face twisted into a snarl as he slammed his fist into Aiden's face. It was taking all of his power not to pummel the cunt into the concrete. 'Think you're fucking funny, do you? Think you're clever? Tell me where my son is!'

Aiden spat a front tooth out onto the floor and glanced at it dismissively. 'Tell me why I should? So you can get him back?' He laughed loudly. 'I don't think so… I hope your son dies slowly and I hope you suffer immeasurably as a result you bastard! You killed my fucking brother, so you will pay!'

Seeing red, Seth laid into Aiden with his fists, each punch connecting with a stomach-churning crack. 'You piece of *shit*,' he seethed.

Watching Aiden Barber's face rapidly turning into pulp, but

still managing to display the obnoxious smirk, Jason Miller hastily grabbed Seth's arms. 'Remember Seth, we expected this. Don't rise to it,' he hissed quietly. 'Just cool it.'

'Oh yeah,' Aiden mumbled, the broken mess of his mouth making it difficult to speak coherently. 'You need to be kept in line, don't you? Especially what with you going round killing young girls because you fucked them behind your wife's back.'

Seth's face contorted into a manic grimace as he lurched towards Aiden once more, knowing he was referring to Lacey Garner. *He was all but admitting he was behind that too.*

'Hear this, Seth Wright,' Aiden continued. *He'd do anything in his power to ensure he finished this bloke's mental state once and for all. This man killed his brother.* 'You'll go down for that murder Mr Wright. Oh yes you will and your son can be sold on without any hindrance. Likewise with the adoption. As we speak, your daughter's being primed to be the star attraction for men who like little girls. I bet even *you'd* be tempted if you saw her. Very attractive piece she is. We all know you like them young.'

Red mist descended like a curtain in Seth's mind. *He was selling his son and planning on prostituting his six-year old daughter? He'd KILL him, the fucking wanker!* 'Where the fuck are my children?' he screamed, knowing he was about to blow and there was absolutely nothing he could do to stop himself.

Aiden laughed heartily once more. *There was time to get a couple more in perhaps?* 'I'll never tell you that! I want you to fucking suffer!'

'You FREAK!' Seth screamed, throwing himself on top of Aiden Barber.

Before any of the others had even chance to react, Seth had whipped out a screwdriver and slammed it hard into Aiden's ear. It was all over in seconds. Over *far* too quickly.

Pulling the dripping screwdriver out from the man's brain, Seth continued frenziedly stabbing him countless times over Aiden's face, chest and stomach.

By the time he'd been wrestled off the corpse by the other men, they all knew there was nothing to say and that their chance of getting any information had gone - along with the ability to locate either of Seth's children.

FIFTY

JANE LOOKED BETWEEN Seth, Jason and Dan in undisguised panic. 'You must have got the location from that bastard already, so why are you still standing here?' she screamed. 'Get around to wherever he said Eliza and Digger are based and get Toby!'

Quickly recounting what Jennie had said, Jane quickly realised that by the blind rage on Seth's face he also thought it was feasible, but something was wrong. She got the distinct feeling what she'd said was new information judging by the way the men kept glancing at each other.

'Just because you didn't get their names, it doesn't matter. It doesn't even matter if I'm wrong and it's not them! Just get yourselves round to wherever that bastard said he worked.'

Jason cleared his throat uncomfortably. 'Things didn't quite work out as we'd hoped...'

Desolation sank deep in the pit of Jane's stomach and her eyes narrowed. 'What do you mean? Don't tell me he'd done a flit before you got there? He *can't* have – you've been too long!'

Jason Miller glanced at Seth. *Let him tell his wife the news. He didn't want to be the one to break it.*

Seth stepped towards Jane. 'He was there Jane, but the

things he was saying… He wouldn't talk and I lost it…' *He knew she was going to go berserk.* He hadn't meant to lose his rag, but the bastard wasn't talking. Yes, he could have tortured him for ever, but it wouldn't have done any good. When he'd said Grace would be used as a child prostitute… That he, her own *father*, would have a go… *That* was what had done it.

'You *what*?' Jane screeched, hardly able to believe what she'd heard. She jumped her feet with her fists clenched tightly. 'You stupid, *stupid* bastard!' Pummelling her fists against Seth's chest, she felt the rage, pure unadulterated panic and despair merge into one.

Jason stepped forward. 'It's unfortunate, but I was there and Barber wouldn't talk.'

Jane swung towards Jason, her eyes flashing. 'Why didn't you stop him? You said you'd control him! Why the fuck didn't you stop him?' she raged.

'*No one* could have stopped me Jane,' Seth said quietly. 'You didn't hear what he said.'

'I don't give a shit what he said! Finding out who he works for was *far* more important than your fucking ego!'

'Well if your theory's right, we now know who that is,' Jason said, hoping to bring the situation down.

'Yes, but not where they *are*!' Jane spat. Pushing herself away from Seth she slumped down onto the sofa and angrily pushed her hair off her face. 'So *now* what?'

'Find Anna,' Maggie murmured, cringing when everyone turned to look at her. 'She can't have gone too far. She must still be around somewhere.'

Seth looked at Jason and then Dan. 'Let's get on it.'

The men were walking down the hallway when the front door was smashed down. Officers dressed in riot gear stormed into the house. 'POLICE!'

Barely two seconds passed before Seth was surrounded and taken to the floor. Despite his fierce protests and struggles, he was no match for twelve men.

'What the fuck are you doing?' Seth yelled as he was

handcuffed, then dragged him to his feet. 'I haven't got time for this!'

'Seth Wright, I'm arresting you on the suspicion of the murder and rape of Lacey Garner. You do not have to say anything, but it may harm your defence if you do not mention when questioned, something which you later rely on in court. Anything you do say may be given in evidence. Do you understand?'

There were several seconds of stunned silence before anyone moved or spoke.

'What? *Seth*?' Jane said, her face paler than pale.

Seth looked at Jane pleadingly. 'I haven't done this Jane. It's a set up.'

Jane nodded. They'd been half-expecting this, but murder *and* rape? *Jesus Christ*! 'This is ridiculous! He hasn't done this,' she spat.

'That as maybe Mrs Wright, but your husband's DNA has been matched with hair found on the body,' an officer stated clearly.

Seth paled. *How the fuck could his hair be on the body? He hadn't been near the girl. He hadn't murdered her and certainly hadn't raped her.*

Jason Miller stepped forward. 'Surely there must have been some mistake?'

'Aside from the DNA, it was hardly a secret there were rumours about Mr Wright's affair with a younger girl,' an officer declared smugly.

'You've got to be joking! Your defence is some shite that was printed in the local rag?' Seth raged.

'Well, DNA is another matter,' the officer replied. 'You can argue your case in court, Sir. Now you need to accompany us to the station.'

'But you *can't* take him!' Jane cried. *How the hell could this be happening? Now of all times?*

'I'm afraid we have to Mrs Wright,' the officer said, dragging a resisting Seth towards the door.

'Go with them Seth,' Jason said. 'We'll get this sorted. I'll call the lawyer. Don't worry about things here. I'm on it, ok?'

Jane slowly sank to the floor in shock whilst Seth was escorted from the house.

• • • •

'YOU NEED TO CALM yourself down,' Jason Miller said sternly and placed his hands on Jane's shoulders to try and stop her from pacing around the sitting room. He glanced at Maggie pleadingly for support. 'The lawyer's on the way to the station as we speak. You heard me on the phone. We'll get this sorted.'

'Jason's right, Jane. Seth will be fine. The lawyer will deal with it. We all know Seth hasn't done this. He'll be out before you know it,' Maggie said, watching Jane's eyes dart frantically around the room in panic.

'So you say, but they've got evidence on him, so what about *that*?' Jane cried. 'They reckon they've got hair and have matched it with records on the database.' There could be no mistake with that and Lacey had been raped? *Had they evidence of that too*?

As much as she didn't want to admit it, the thought crossed her mind as to whether there could be any grains of truth in it before she just as quickly dismissed it. Whatever Seth was, she knew he'd *never* in a million years do something like *that*.

Jason and Maggie were right. She needed to pull herself together. She wasn't helping anyone like this. She wasn't helping Seth and she *certainly* wasn't helping Grace or Toby. The kids were the priority.

Taking a deep breath, Jane looked squarely at Jason. 'I suggest we find Anna.'

Jason frowned. 'I've been thinking about that. I don't know the first thing about the girl, so I wouldn't know where to start. Do you have any idea where she could have gone? She wasn't at Aiden Barber's place.'

Jane concentrated hard. In a way it was doing her good to channel her speeding mind on something other than what could be befalling her children at the hands of Eliza and Digger.

'She's unlikely to have gone to her sister's,' Jane muttered. 'They didn't get on as far as I know and they had a huge falling out after the mother died. On top of that, the sister – Tina whatever her name is, is also involved from what I've managed to piece together.'

Jason whistled loudly. 'They sure as hell had this all worked out, didn't they?'

'Is there any chance the girl could have gone to her mother's?' Dan asked. He'd been keeping a low profile since he'd got here. He'd sat to one side letting everyone vent what they needed to. He'd never been much good in situations such as these. 'I mean, I know you said the mother's dead, but if it was recent, then the house could still be empty and not sold.'

Jane pursed her lips. 'You might have something there Dan.'

Jason Miller nodded. 'I agree. It's worth checking out. What's the address?'

'I've no idea. I don't know whether I ever had it,' Jane said despondently. Every time it felt like she was getting somewhere, she hit a dead end. Panic resurfaced. *She'd lost her kids and now Seth was gone too...*

'The electoral role?' Maggie suggested quickly, seeing Jane's clarity wavering.

'Ah wait,' Jane cried. 'Anna's job application form! She may have entered her mother as her next of kin, which means the address should be there. I'll go and look.'

Jane raced from the room up to the study to locate the paperwork.

• • • •

STEVE LOMOND SCOWLED watching Tina smile at the infant in her arms and tried not to stare at her saggy boobs visible through her dirty vest top.

Despite his reluctance to look at Tina's chest, his eyes insisted on involuntarily moving back there out of morbid curiosity, purely because they were so hideous. God, she made him feel sick, the junkie whore - sitting there playing Mary-Bloody-Poppins.

This last few weeks had completely done his head in. Everything had gone wrong and he wasn't enjoying himself much these days. Since that unfortunate incident with Lacey, things had taken a nose dive.

As well as not having his favourite girl on tap any longer, everything else had slid south too – including Tina's tits, he thought bitchily.

Even though he was reluctant to, he had to acknowledge this general decline had stemmed partly because of him. It had never been his plan to bump Lacey off. Why would he have wanted to do that? She'd been the *one* thing he'd really enjoyed about this dump and now that was gone.

He'd thought it had been bad enough that she'd gone AWOL in the first place, but to then get her back, only for her to cark it was the ultimate piss-take. In fact, if he didn't know better, he'd have said she'd done it on purpose just to spite him.

Even Digger and Eliza had treated him like an irritating stubborn stain since then. It had been so much more preferable when he'd had leverage. They'd been eating out of his hand and doing everything he'd asked, but not any longer.

Still there wasn't much he could do about it now. He'd have to put up with it and hope things got better once all this disruption had settled down. Either that or make the decision to move on. Lomond sighed loudly. At least no one was suspicious of him being linked to the girl, so that was one thing.

Against his will his eyes moved of their own accord back to Tina's low-cut top. *Christ, she really was a horror...*

'What are *you* looking at?' Tina snapped, glaring at Lomond. She was happy keeping the little boy entertained and giving him his bottle. Well, she would have been if that revolting fat pervert opposite wasn't staring at her like a piece of meat. *Fucking sicko. He made her skin crawl.*

'I'm certainly not looking at *you*!' Lomond growled, even more annoyed that Tina presumed he was looking at her in *that* way. *In her bloody dreams!*

'You'd never be able to afford me anyhow!' Tina spat, wishing he'd just take his pig ugly face and launch himself in front of the next train.

Having Toby to look after was a nice change. She'd utterly surprised herself with how much she'd enjoyed it. She'd never *once* had the urge to become a mother, which was probably a good job, but it was a pleasant distraction from the constant cravings and need for a fix that was getting stronger every hour.

She'd managed to eke out what little heroin she had left, but the rations she'd been forced to limit herself to just weren't touching the sides and she wasn't sure what she was going to do about it.

She could hardly get any more from Aiden, although in some respects that was a blessing in disguise. Now that he was out of the picture, with any luck that meant so was her humongous debt. This was good because now she wasn't getting that insurance pay out, she had no means to clear it. *Ever*.

The downside was she had no one on tap to get a fix from and no money to go elsewhere for it either. Regardless of her lack of gear, Tina hoped beyond anything that Aiden would not be returning. From what she'd gathered, it was unlikely that Tina or Digger would trust him to have anything to do with the place again, so she didn't think she had too much to worry about.

She smiled down at Toby's chubby little face as he slurped down the last of his bottle. Selena had only bought a small packet of formula powder earlier being as she had to get nappies and some other items too, so he'd need some more before long.

Tina looked at Eliza half-watching a soap on the television whilst painting her nails a garish orange colour. 'Eliza, what's the plan with Toby?'

Eliza looked up, an irritated expression plastered across her face. 'That his name is it? Toby?' she sneered. 'I don't know what the plan is - I haven't thought that far ahead. All I know is we'll be taking care of him for a least another week.'

Tina felt strangely happy about that. She'd enjoy looking

after him for a bit longer. It was a nice change from all the crap she usually had to do around here.

'Why do you ask Tina? Broody, are you?' Eliza laughed mockingly. *Tina-bloody-Slater – Mother of the Year...*

'No I'm not!' Tina said defensively. 'I was just thinking he's going to need some more formula tomorrow.'

'What the fuck's that?' Eliza frowned.

'Baby milk powder!' Tina laughed.

'Don't know why you're laughing! How am I supposed to know?' Eliza snapped. *The stupid cow. Taking the piss, was she?* 'What does he need more for? We only got him some earlier. What's the matter with him?'

'Nothing's the matter with him! It's only a tiny packet. They need more than that to last them,' Tina said, trying not to let a smirk appear on her face.

'For God's sake!' Eliza huffed. *This would cost her a fortune at this rate*! 'Selena can go back out tomorrow for some more then. A different shop though. We don't want anyone asking questions.'

Tina nodded. 'I'll make sure of it.'

Eliza huffed and resumed painting her nails. She glanced at Steve Lomond. She wouldn't even bother saying *anything* to that turd. He was the one who'd caused most of this mess in the first place.

At least Digger would be back soon. She'd sent him to check on Aiden and make sure he hadn't done a runner. In a perfect world it would have made more sense to have got rid of him rather than risk him dropping them in it, but as usual, everything was bad timing.

Eliza glanced back at the television just as the local news interrupted her program. Her ears pricked up hearing Lacey's name and a wide smile spread across her face seeing the mugshot of Seth Wright appear on the screen. *Bingo*!

A comfortable warm glow emanated around Eliza's insides as the newsreader spoke:

> *'...a local businessman has today been arrested on the suspicion of the murder and rape of local teenager Lacey Garner. The Police aren't looking for anyone else in relation to this incident at this present time...'*

Eliza blew hard on her bright orange nails to help dry the varnish. Things were taking an upturn. *This was good. Everything was getting nicely back on track.*

FIFTY ONE

ANNA'S STOMACH LURCHED into her mouth when the sound of smashing glass shattered the silence. Jumping to her feet, she threw herself underneath the sideboard at the far end of the lounge, quickly shuffling into the furthest corner near the wall to keep out of obvious view.

It was pointless on the big scale of things, but she had to attempt *something*. If whoever had smashed the window was an opportunistic burglar, then it was highly likely she wouldn't be spotted, but if on the other hand it wasn't, then she knew the house would be turned over with a fine-toothed comb.

Anna's heart was beating so loudly she was convinced it must be audible. She willed herself to stop shaking before the vibrations dislodged the ornaments placed on the sideboard she was hiding beneath.

Her heart sank seeing two pairs of feet rush into the room, one of which donned black stilettoes. *Jane…*

'She's in here,' Jane snarled, spotting Anna's handbag on the coffee table. 'Anna, you may as well come out. We know you're here!' She walked across the room, her eyes scanning from left to right.

'I'll check upstairs,' Jason Miller said, running up the

hallway.

'ANNA!' Jane shouted. 'You're only making things worse for yourself.' *Where was she? She was in here somewhere. She could smell the lies and guilt a mile off.*

Spotting a tiny movement in the far corner of the room, Jane's eyes swung around. She squatted down, clearly able to see someone under the sideboard with their face pressed against the wall in a ridiculous attempt of 'head in the sand' philosophy. *Gotcha!*

Without wasting any time, Jane grabbed Anna by the hair with both hands and roughly dragged her out into the room. 'You fucking bitch!' Jane screamed, enjoying the pain on Anna's face as her hair was half-yanked from her scalp.

Giving Anna a hefty backhander which knocked her flying, Jane jumped on top of her. Gripping her around the neck, it took all of her power not to choke the life out of the girl. *She needed answers to questions first and foremost.* 'Where's my son?' she roared.

Anna looked up with terrified eyes. 'I-I haven't got him. I *swear* I haven't. I'm sorry, I'm *so* sorry!' she wailed.

'Fuck sorry!' Jane spat. 'Sorry won't help. Where is Toby?' She wanted to rip the girl's eyeballs from their sockets. Wanted to knife her clean in the chest and rip her heart out with her bare hands. Maybe then she'd feel the pure agony she'd caused and know the damage she'd done.

'Talk to me!' Jane hissed through gritted teeth. 'If you don't tell me everything you know and I mean *everything,* then I swear to God I'll kill you.'

Anna could barely bring herself to look into Jane's dark eyes which seemed to have the power to stop things in their tracks. She knew she had to talk and talk *now*. It was the least she owed the woman after the grief she'd caused.

Tears of shame and fright poured down Anna's cheeks. 'I'm sorry Jane. I'm so sorry…'

Jane slapped Anna hard around the face once against, her knees pressing deep into Anna's chest. 'I don't want to hear your pathetic grovelling apologies, you little bitch, I need you to tell me what you know. *Now*.'

Hearing the commotion, Jason Miller took the stairs from the top floor three at a time. Jane had located Anna by the sounds of it and he needed to get in there before she lost it like Seth had done, taking Anna out of the equation permanently before they'd got any information.

He rushed into the lounge only to see Jane holding a flick knife against Anna's nose. 'JANE!' he shouted, bolting forwards. 'NO!'

Despite Jane's resistance, he managed to pull her away and held her firmly by the shoulders. He stared into her manic eyes. 'Jane you need to keep it together. We need to hear what she's got to say for herself. Leave this to me.'

'If she doesn't tell me all now, then I swear I'm having her,' Jane spat, too wired to listen to reason.

Jason Miller turned to Anna who had not dared move from her prone position on the carpet. 'Get up, you stupid girl,' he said, watching as she hastily pushed herself up to her knees as best as she could with the arm that wasn't broken.

He dragged her roughly up by her jacket and threw her unceremoniously onto an armchair. 'Now *talk*!'

• • • •

OH SURE, ANNA COULDN'T have been more contrite. She'd spewed out everything she'd done no holds barred and Jason Miller had listened to the endless accounts of how she had consistently betrayed Jane and Seth's trust. He could only commend how Jane managed to keep her temper from exploding. Had it been him he wasn't entirely sure he would honestly have been able to maintain such self-control.

However unpalatable it had been to listen to, it had at least explained a lot of what had occurred. And to think Anna had become embroiled in this purely because of her sister.

Aside from everything else, there were two crucial parts of which the girl had been unable to help with. She'd confirmed

Aiden had taken Toby, but she didn't know where to. Secondly, she had no idea where he worked.

Jason had almost felt sorry for Anna when she'd been forced to recount how Aiden had enjoyed telling her he'd never cared for her. Even *she* had been cruelly set up and used to get information on the Wrights. She was clearly humiliated, but her pain didn't touch the sides compared with the damage the stupid cow had caused Jane and Seth.

They may now have got confirmation as to who was part of this intricate vendetta, but they were still no clearer with where the base of this operation was, or where Toby had been taken. And thanks to Seth, the one person with that knowledge was no longer in the picture.

Jason wiped his sweaty brow. Time was undoubtedly of the essence and that was flying past *far* too quickly.

The way Jane had hovered in the background when he'd grilled Anna had left the girl with no doubt whatsoever that her previous employer was *definitely* in the frame of mind and certainly had both the ability, as well as the motive to kill her at any given time.

Knowing through experience how people tended to react in situations such as these left Jason with little doubt as to the girl's sincerity, so he was confident the girl was telling the truth: she didn't know where Toby was, or who Aiden had been working for. It was very difficult to stage the emotion she had exhibited, especially when shit-scared.

There was one piece of information though which could make a difference – at least in Seth's present predicament. Anna had explained how she'd been tasked by her sister to lift both a blood-stained shirt of Seth's, as well as his hair brush. She hadn't been told what these were required for and she hadn't questioned it.

The hair brush would explain how Seth's hair had been found on Lacey Garner and also confirmed Aiden and whoever he'd been working for had been involved in snatching and killing the girl. It also therefore confirmed they were most likely part of the prostitution ring, so it looked like Jane's theory was right.

But how they were going to find out where the base was as quickly as they needed, eluded him. He knew they had to be careful where they went from here. They had to get the information regarding the hair to the police, but also needed to make sure *they* were the ones to locate these Digger and Eliza people before the cops did.

The only bonus was Anna didn't know these people's names – whereas *they* did. If Anna genuinely didn't know, then she couldn't be tricked into divulging this information when questioned by the police.

• • • •

SETH PACED UP AND down in his cell. He hadn't heard a word off anyone for hours and was starting to lose his rag. He'd had the allotted meeting with his brief who, based on the police evidence he had access to, hadn't any tricks up his sleeve he could use to get Seth released on bail pending charges.

Seth ground his teeth. *He'd kill for a whisky right now. Jesus!* He'd been done up like a kipper and was livid.

Livid that Digger and that slag Eliza had the audacity to pull this off – and so bloody well to boot. He was also livid that it hadn't crossed his mind before now that they could be the ones responsible. He'd hardly given them a second thought since he'd walked away two years ago.

He felt stupid. Stupid, humiliated and *angry*. Digger – his once best mate had betrayed him *so* many times, but Christ, to pull something off like this… Something this big and detailed took a whole lot of planning and attention to detail and it appeared they'd got all bases covered.

And to concentrate on his children? That was just beyond the pale! Anger rose once more. If he'd have heeded Jane's advice and finished Digger before, then this wouldn't have happened. He'd had more than enough reason to do it and he should have. *He didn't think he'd ever forgive himself for that.*

Seth slammed his fist against the thick metal of the cell door and screamed with pent-up rage. He was locked up with – from what he'd gathered from the brief – very little chance of getting out any time soon, if at all whilst that two-faced bastard of an ex-friend and his slag of a wife went ahead and adopted his daughter from under his nose. They'd known what would hurt him the most and they'd bloody well succeeded. Furthermore by the looks of it, they also had his son.

Seth smashed his fist against the cell door once again, grateful for the pain it caused momentarily distracting him from his anguish.

Even on top of all that, he knew he'd have been plastered all over the news as being the *only* suspect in the murder and rape of a teenage! His reputation would be destroyed beyond measure.

In the meantime, he was stuck in a poxy cell when he should be making sure this was rectified and getting his kids back. If any of this could have got any worse, he couldn't guess at how that could be achieved.

Clenching his already blackening knuckles, he slammed his fist one, two, three, *four* times in quick succession back into the cell door in a flurry of red anger and scowled when a pair of eyes appeared through the slit of the cell door hatch.

'Oih!' shouted the police officer staring at him through the slit. 'Keep it down in there Wright!'

'Why the fuck should I?' Seth raged, resisting the temptation of plunging his thumbs into the man's eye sockets. 'I haven't done this and I need to get out of here!'

'Well I suggest you pipe down because your brief's back and wants to see you.'

'What for?' Seth snapped. He'd already said he couldn't get him out on bail because the hair was his, so what was the point of talking? If his brief couldn't get him out so he could go and find his son and put a halt to the bastards adopting his daughter, then he might as well not bother.

'How should I know what for? I don't give a rat's arse personally, but there you go!' the officer quipped.

Seth scowled. *Jumped up prick.* Always clever with being

fly with their gobs and brave with their stupid comments, but only when it was safe to do so. Like now, when he was safely caged the other side of a set of steel bars or a thick cell door. *Fucking cowards.*

Hearing the sound of the metal key turning in the cell door, Seth stood back against the far wall and glared at the brief as he was ushered into the cell before the door was quickly locked once more behind him.

'Well?' Seth barked. 'What is it you've come to tell me?' If he'd just come to tell him he was being moved to prison on remand whilst awaiting trial, then he wouldn't be happy.

'I've some good news,' the brief smiled.

FIFTY TWO

JANE SIGHED HEAVILY, her arms aching with the need to hold her son close, but they were still disturbingly empty. It had been two whole days since Anna had walked voluntarily into the police station, telling them she'd been responsible for passing Seth's brush to her sister.

She'd said she believed this had been given to someone who her sister was in contact with who harboured a very strong vendetta against the Wrights.

It had taken Jane and Jason Miller several hours of instilling into Anna what she could and couldn't say to the police without dropping them all in it or messing up their plans.

It had been a massive gamble. Anna wasn't used to dealing with anything like this and her mental state was so frightfully fragile, it was a *huge* risk to hope she kept her nerve and didn't get coerced into giving away incriminating information. They were trying to get Seth *out*, not dig him in for the foreseeable future.

At least Anna didn't know anything about Digger and Eliza, nor where her sister worked, which although was not good from their side of things, it *did* mean she couldn't let it slip to the cops. It was imperative that they got there before the cops did.

Anna had also been equally confused as to why she wasn't to mention any hint of Toby being taken. It had taken *ages* to get her to see the reasoning behind it. Anna saw things in black and white and couldn't understand how they didn't want the cops to be involved with getting their son back. She was so green she struggled to grasp that giving them this information would only open a massive *barrel* of writhing worms.

They had to do it *their* way, otherwise everything was dead in the water.

The last person Jane would have chosen to be involved in something so complex would have been Anna – whose level of brushes with the law amounted to the road safety talk kids received from the local constabulary at school, but what choice did she have? Anna held the key to discredit and discount the DNA evidence they had on linking Seth to Lacey.

No, it was *far* from ideal and to make matters worse, the press were all but camped out on their doorstep, hounding for information and comments over Seth's arrest. It was getting her down.

Finally, nearly forty-eight hours after Anna had voluntarily walked into the police station it seemed, for now at least, that she'd done what they'd asked and Seth had been released.

Ok, so it wasn't the best news. He hadn't been officially cleared, but due to the new evidence which had come to light, it did mean he was granted bail pending investigation.

Jason Miller had insisted on staying at Jane's house during Seth's absence and had been working around the clock to try to locate Digger and Eliza, but to no avail. Time was running out – both with getting Toby back safely off the record, but also with getting their hands on their treacherous ex-friends before the police did.

Jane stubbed her cigarette out in the ashtray and glanced at the clock. Seth should be back any time now. She'd kept in good contact with the brief and had known before Seth had that there was something in the police evidence that didn't add up.

Although Seth's DNA had matched the hair found on

Lacey's body and the body had been found in the vicinity of one of his lock-ups, it *didn't* match the DNA of the semen found in Lacey's body.

It had been confirmed by the hostel Lacey was living at that she had not worked as a prostitute since arriving several months ago, but also confirmed that she had no boyfriend.

The brief had also managed to get the information from the police that the semen matched someone else on their database, of whom they were trying to trace now. They were not at liberty to release the name of this person, but Jane suspected it must be Digger or Aiden Barber.

Christ, what had happened to Digger to turn him into the monster he'd become?

Seth wasn't off the hook entirely. They needed to run a lot more forensic tests to determine whether there were any other traces of his DNA on Lacey's body or at the scene, but the situation was a thousand times more palatable than it had been this time two days ago.

Hearing a car draw up outside and the clamouring from the groups of gathered reporters, Jane's heart leapt, realising it signified Seth's return. Now they needed to get on the trail of Eliza and Digger.

Jane's eyes narrowed. *When they found them, she'd kill them both with her bare hands.*

• • • •

'IT APPEARS WE'VE MANAGED to get in just in the nick of time,' Carl Mulligan said, glad he'd finally got hold of Seth.

'What's the situation now?' Seth muttered. His head felt like it would burst with everything that was going on. He'd barely been able to catch a breath since being released, but that didn't matter. There was too much to do to worry about that.

'Luckily you gave me the power to act on your behalf and I was able to request the information in your absence the moment the warrant was granted,' Mulligan continued. 'The adoption's due to commence in a few days.'

'A few *days*?' Seth cried, glancing at Jane who loitered next to him, desperate to find out the updates. 'What do I need to do?'

'Nothing,' Mulligan said. 'I've already done it. I've lodged a counter-claim against the final adoption hearing.'

'What does that mean?' Seth barked. 'Is it sorted or what?'

'It had been made known to the court and Social Services that the biological parents have contested the adoption.'

'So, it's finished? Thank fuck for that! When can we get Grace?' Seth asked impatiently.

'It's not quite that simple... What happens now is the adoption process will be put on hold whilst it's investigated.'

'So it could still go through?' Seth raged, astounded.

'I'm not saying that. They have to be informed you're contesting it being as it has got this far down the line without you stepping forward. You'll then need to prove you're who you say you are and all the business we discussed before will have to be gone through.' Mulligan sighed.

He'd known Seth wouldn't like that. 'There has to be reasonable grounds why you don't want your daughter adopted after being off the scene from the start. You need to prove you're in an acceptable position to have legal custody granted.'

'What, so we've still got to prove ourselves?' Seth asked. 'What about all this latest shit?'

'Hmm,' Mulligan mused. 'It doesn't help. You need to hope all the charges are dropped. And dropped, not because of lack of evidence, but from a 'mistake'. Whatever happens do *nothing* further to flag up the authorities.'

Seth frowned. He knew what Mulligan was saying between the lines. *Don't go after the people who have done this. How the hell could he not go after Eliza and Digger for what they'd done?*

He raked his fingers through his hair agitatedly. *He'd have to ensure nothing pointed back to them*. 'I don't suppose you can give me the names of the people who're trying to adopt my daughter?' *Come on. That would make everything so much easier.*

'You know they won't release that, Mr Wright,' Mulligan sighed. 'We've already discussed it several times.'

Seth nodded. 'Yeah, I know. Just hoping.'

The truth was, he supposed even if Mulligan *had* the information it would take a crowbar in his gob to get him to pass it over, so it was back to the drawing board. They needed to shift on this. *Fast.*

• • • •

'YOU'RE NOT GOING to believe this!' Eliza screamed. 'They've only gone and fucking managed it!' She picked up the telephone from the desk and launched it angrily against the wall.

Digger eyed the smashed handset and the dent in the recently painted wall and scowled. 'What are you talking about?' he snapped. *He wasn't in the mood for Eliza's histrionics this morning.*

Eliza swung around, her large bust following after a slight delay. 'What I mean is they've somehow found out about our adoption and have contested it.'

'Who has?'

'Are you thick or something?' Eliza sneered, a trail of spittle spraying from her mouth as she spoke. 'Who do you think? Seth and Jane of course!'

Digger was astounded. 'What? How did that happen? Seth's banged up.'

'That's what I thought too. I need to find out what's going on,' Eliza snapped, picking up the phone from the floor realising she'd rendered it unusable.

Sulkily throwing it down, she stomped over to the cabinet and retrieving another phone, hastily plugged it into the wall port.

'Whoa! How are you going to do that without raising suspicions?' Digger asked. *Sometimes Eliza just didn't think.* 'Do they know it's *us* that put in to adopt?' *If that was the case they were in serious shit.*

Eliza stalked back to the desk. 'I doubt it. The social worker said our names and whereabouts couldn't be released by law. Now go away, will you? I need to try and find out what's going on about Seth's charges.'

Digger stared out of the window, trying to make sense of it. Needing to find out about Seth's charges was an understatement wasn't it? Sod the adoption thing. If Seth had for some unfathomable reason got out, then that could only mean one thing. Someone *else* was in the frame because there was good enough evidence. No one had a brief *that* good who could get them out without an *extremely* compelling argument.

And it that was the case, how long was it before the police knocked on *their* door? Steve Lomond had assured him he'd never been pulled for anything which required giving an DNA sample, so it couldn't be him, so who did that leave? *Apart from him and Eliza…*

Silent fingers of fear slowly gripped around Digger's lungs. He didn't like the sound of this and wondered if they should seriously contemplate how long to give it before they made plans to disappear?

• • • •

'I CAN'T STAY LONG,' Selena said to the man hastily ushering her towards the sitting room where the infamous Seth and Jane Wright were waiting.

She felt like she was in some kind of weird dream. Nothing seemed real. Five times she'd been out to get supplies for the baby and none of those had been the *right* one to cut loose and make a dash to see the Wrights.

This afternoon was different. Eliza and Digger were only what could be described as distracted. Being as she'd shown she could be trusted to go out to get stuff for the kid and return without question there was no suspicion.

Retrieving the well-concealed CCTV tape from under her bed, she'd casually said, after making sure she'd hidden the three-quarters of the last packet, she was popping out for more nappies.

Even though she was convinced Eliza and Digger could hear her thundering heart or see the CCTV shining a fluorescent beam through her handbag, she'd walked from Elipse unquestioned.

Selena had known she would be gone longer than usual, but had tried to cut that down by flagging a taxi the moment she'd reached the main road. She hoped the money Eliza had given her would cover the fare to the area she needed to get to. She'd worry about replacing the money and buying the nappies later.

There had always been the additional chance the Wrights may not have been in but she'd had to risk it. She wouldn't have another chance like that for some time.

Selena hadn't even known the Wright's actual address, but once in the general vicinity she'd only had to wander around for five minutes before she'd learnt which house was theirs. She'd wasted no time in telling the man on security what her visit was concerning, but even then she'd been surprised at the speed in which she'd been whisked up the driveway and into the house.

Selena eyed the couple sat opposite her in the large sitting room, their stares fixed directly on her. They were both extremely intimidating.

'No time for formalities girl. What do you know?' Seth asked abruptly, his hard green eyes drilling into Selena's.

'I used to work with Lacey,' Selena said. *No going back.* 'And I know who murdered her…'

Jane sat forward, her whole body angled like a predator about to pounce. 'Talk,' she said quietly, leaving no doubt over the question of authority in her voice.

'Steve Lomond,' Selena said quickly before she changed her mind about the whole thing.

Seth frowned. 'Who?' He knew most names around here but hadn't heard that one crop up before in any of their circles.

'He's a disgusting bastard!' Selena spat. 'He works as the manager and gets free reign of all the girls. He's a complete toe-rag and everyone *hates* him. He's well known for getting off on hurting us.'

Seth felt his fists clenching. He eyed the young girl in front of him. She looked no more than fifteen. 'How old are you?' he asked, almost scared to hear the answer.

'Sixteen,' Selena answered. 'They like me because I look younger.'

Seth felt sick. 'Who are *they*?' He needed the information as to who was running this sick place.

Jane watched Selena and could see she was faltering with giving up the information. 'Listen, I know you're nervous, but you've done well to come and see us. I can't stress how important it is that you tell us *everything*. Lacey was too scared to speak out and look at what happened to her. You need to help us stop these people.' *That and get our children back.*

'I know and I shall,' Selena wiped her sweaty palms down her jeans and took a deep breath. 'The place is called Elipse.'

'*Elipse*?' Seth hadn't heard of it. Why had he not heard of any of this? 'And who runs it?'

'A couple called Eliza and Digger. Well, I guess that's not his *real* name and I don't know their surnames.' Selena looked worriedly at Jane, hoping that was an acceptable answer. She watched as Seth and Jane exchanged glances. 'You know them?'

'We know *of* them, yes,' Seth snarled. *He knew it. The pair of treacherous bastards. How he was going to enjoy finishing them both*. 'And where is Elipse?'

'Here.' Selena pulled a crumpled piece of paper from her jeans pocket and handed it to Seth. 'The address is on there.'

Seth snatched the piece of paper and studied the hastily scrawled writing. *Right over the other side of town in a crummy area*? Raising his eyebrows, he passed the address to Jane.

'How do you know Lomond killed Lacey?' Seth questioned scrutinising Selena's body language.

'After she ran away to you, they got her back,' Selena hung her head. 'I helped - in as much as I located where she was working.' She cleared her throat. 'They got her back, but Lomond couldn't wait. She was his favourite you see and there were ru…'

'So, it was *rumoured* this Lomond prick killed her?' Seth

barked. *If all this was based on rumours it wouldn't be much good.*

'No, I *know* he killed her!' Selena opened her handbag and fished out a tape. 'Lomond couldn't wait to fuck her even though he'd bust her jaw an…'

'The *bastard*!' Jane cried, bile rising in her throat and anger poured through her veins. *That poor girl.*

Seth gently touched Jane's arm. 'Let her finish Jane,' he said quietly.

'The night Lacey got brought back, we were told a room was out of bounds. I didn't see Lomond kill her, but I overheard them talking. Eliza and Lomond were arguing about it.' Selena cleared her throat. 'I got up that night for a drink, you see and saw them moving a body wrapped in sheets from the room Lomond and Lacey had been in. They were taking it to the basement.'

Seth stared at the tape in Selena's hand. 'And what's on that?'

Selena glanced at the tape and passed it to Seth. 'That's the CCTV footage of that night. I stole it.'

'And it's on there?' Jane asked, astounded.

Selena shook her head. 'Not the murder, but them moving the body is yes.'

Seth smiled. 'You've done really well, Selena. Thank you. Are you happy to talk to the police?'

Selena's eyes went wide. 'The *police*? I thought…'

'I didn't mean now. At some point – regarding Lomond. I reckon he'll have a worse time going to jail as a nonce than giving him the easier way out by death at my hands… Eliza and Digger however will be dealt with by *us*.' His eyes narrowed. 'I'm assuming this conversation will remain between us?'

Selena nodded her head frantically. *Like she'd ever speak out against them. They were the good ones.* They would remove the bastards and she'd do whatever she could to ensure that happened.

'If you'd prefer when this tape is handed to the police it can be done anonymously so you never have to be involved? Either way there'll be no come back on you.'

Selena breathed a sigh of relief. 'I'd much prefer it to be anonymous if you don't mind?'

Jane smiled. 'No problem. That's all settled then.'

Seth glanced at Jane and then back to Selena. 'There's just a couple more things we need to know…'

Selena didn't need to wait to hear the question. 'I know what you're going to ask. Yes, they have your son. That's where I'm supposed to be right now – buying nappies.'

Jane felt tears fill her eyes. 'I-Is he ok?'

Selena nodded. 'He's fine. Tina's looking after him.'

Jane grimaced in horror. 'Tina? That junky? Anna's sister! *She's* looking after him?'

'He's absolutely fine Mrs Wright, honestly. He's being well looked after.' There was no doubt about that. The way Tina was caring for the kid had surprised them all.

'Have you seen another child?' Seth needed to know this too. 'A girl? About six?'

Selena's eyebrows knitted together. 'I saw a kid once a couple of weeks ago. I don't know who it was, but rumour has it they're adopting her. Can't imagine why – they do nothing but shout at the poor kid.'

Jane's teeth clenched in rage. The thought of Grace being yelled at by Digger and Eliza in a fucking brothel made her blood boil. Her sadness quickly morphed into rage.

Sensing Jane's erratic emotions, Seth knew he needed to bring this to a close. 'Thank you, Selena. You've been *more* than helpful. Martin will drop you back where you need to get to and we'll be in touch.'

Seth got to his feet and walked over to an antique cabinet. Pulling open one of the drawers, he retrieved a mobile phone and charger. 'Take this,' he said, handing the phone to Selena.

'I want you to call me when Eliza and Digger leave for the night. The number to reach me is programmed into this phone. I also need you to fix it so Steve Lomond is otherwise engaged. I need this done as soon as possible and we'll be on standby.'

He fixed his steely gaze on the girl. 'Don't use this phone for anything other than to receive or make calls to me, unless I tell you otherwise.'

Selena gingerly got to her feet and took the phone and charger from Seth's hand, aware that whether she liked it or not she was now entwined in all of this.

'Remember, not a word eh?' Seth reminded Selena, the glint in his eye that he meant business, clear to see.

Nodding quickly, Selena hastily followed the large man who was to drop her off out into the hallway

Fifty Three

'WHO'S THAT FROM?' Digger asked, watching Eliza rip open an envelope and scan the contents of the letter whilst she took a bite from her toast.

Eliza glared at Digger angrily. 'It's from Social Services. We need to attend an appointment to discuss where we go from here in light of the adoption being contested.'

'What does that mean?' Digger asked, even though he wasn't interested. This adoption had seemed like a good idea at the time but it had caused so much extra hassle. Although it would have been the *ultimate* way to piss the Wrights off, there were several other major issues in play at the moment which he felt needed preference.

Eliza rolled her eyes at Digger's obvious lack of knowledge. 'It means if we don't turn up to discuss why the biological parents have appeared out of the woodwork and that we want to fight it in court, then the Wrights automatically win the right to go to court to get legal custody.'

'Oh, for God's sake, Eliza! How can we possibly fight this?' Digger sighed. 'You know as well as I do, the minute they find out it's *us*, then all hell will break loose!'

'But we've come this far,' Eliza whined. 'I won't give it up now. I want that kid!'

Digger bit back a snotty retort he was itching to voice. Eliza was conveniently blind to the fact that things weren't going well. He had an extremely strong feeling something was brewing and was close to exploding in their faces and he felt they needed to take that seriously and put things in motion before it was too late.

The problem was he doubted whether Eliza would accept that. He just wished he knew what was going on with the police. If he could get some inside information as to why Seth had been released then things would be a lot clearer.

If the press were correct then it looked like charges against Seth had been dropped because the police had issued a statement:

> *'...the arrest had been an unfortunate mistake and all charges against Mr Wright were unfounded...'*

It had been when he'd read something about an unnamed woman being held in police custody awaiting trial for aiding and abetting that the alarm bells had really begun to ring. If someone such as Tina's sister had opened her gob, the Police would know it had been a set up and they'd definitely be looking for another suspect to 'help them with their enquiries...' He didn't want it to be *them*.

Digger watched Eliza reading the letter for the fourth time. 'I think we need to make plans to disappear for a while,' he muttered.

Eliza's head snapped up and she looked at Digger with disbelief. 'You what? What are you talking about?' The *last* thing she needed was Digger getting cold feet on her. 'Are you suggesting we do a runner?'

Digger shook his head. 'No, I'm suggesting we go on an extended *holiday* for a while. Just until this has died down.' He frowned. 'Something's not right Eliza, I can feel it. Something's going to happen and it won't be good.'

Eliza rolled her eyes and slapped the letter down on the desk. 'Do you realise how ridiculous you sound? You been on the gear or something? Why are you so paranoid? If the cops had anything on us, they'd have come for us by now!'

Digger shook his head. 'Not necessarily. We did a very good job of not having much to trace back to us where this business is concerned or where we live if you remember?'

Eliza stood up from her chair. 'I haven't got time for this. You sound like a bleating hormonal woman! Who exactly has got anything on us then, I'd like to know? Aiden is dead, Lomond is here, Tina is fucked and so busy playing mummy to that brat she won't say anything, so pray tell me who else there is?'

'Tina's sister?' Digger suggested. 'I think it must be her they've got in custody and who got Seth off with the evidence thing.'

Eliza narrowed her eyes. 'Tina's sister is as green as a leaf! She knows zilch anyhow. She never knew who Aiden worked for and she doesn't know where Tina lives or works either, so what could she say even if she wanted to?' she exclaimed.

'Well, I just feel something's going to happen,' Digger pushed. 'I think we should go.'

'So you want to give up our business along with everything we've worked for because you've got a *feeling*? What would we do then huh?' Eliza barked. 'You going to get a job as a fucking psychic, are you?' She sneered contemptuously. 'Did Seth Wright cut off your balls, as well as the other bits?'

Digger rose from his seat and caught Eliza by surprise when he backhanded her around the face with his good hand, quickly knocking her to the floor. 'Shut your fucking mouth Eliza! You think you know it all do you? You with your stupid hair-brained schemes! You're a bloody joke!'

Eliza raised her hand to her stinging face and glared at Digger. *Like that was it?* He could run away if he saw fit, but she'd worked *far* too hard to let the chance of finishing that pair of psychos who'd ruined her life slip through her fingers again.

She was continuing with this whether Digger liked it or not.

'If you want to do a runner Digger, then go for it!' she spat. 'I'm finishing what we started.'

• • • •

SETH REPLACED THE PHONE into its cradle and smiled. 'That was Mulligan. He's sourced Eliza and Digger's home address like I suspected he would.'

Dan stared across the table at Seth. 'Ok, so what's the plan?'

Seth turned his cigarette packet around methodically on the desk. 'First and foremost, we get Toby. Then we pay Eliza and Digger a visit at their house.' He glanced at the clock. 'Miller and a couple of his men will be here soon, as will Barry and Martin. I need to keep everyone assembled in the event I get the call tonight.'

Dan nodded. He knew things weren't necessarily going to happen tonight. It all very much depended when this Selena girl called. He'd already silently questioned Seth's decision to put power in the hands of a slip of a girl whom he'd never met until today, but also acknowledged he had little choice but to hope she delivered without any conditions.

He knew full well time was of the essence, especially where the safe return of Toby was concerned. If he'd been in Seth's shoes, then he'd probably have made the very same choice.

'Where's Maggie?' Seth asked. Maggie had been tasked, once they'd lifted Toby, with taking him back to the house, accompanied by Barry for protection whilst they dealt with the rest of the problems.

'She's sorting out things with Jane upstairs,' Dan replied. Jane was getting things ready for when Toby got back. She wanted to make sure he'd got everything he needed on tap. Maggie was concerned about what would happen if they *didn't* succeed in getting him, but Dan suspected Jane would not consider that as being a viable option. *How could she?* Jane and Seth needed their child back and there was no time to lose.

Dan studied Seth's strong-jawed face, set in an expression of intense concentration. *What a bloody mess all of this had become.*

Seth fixed his gaze back to Dan. 'Before you ask, no we're not taking Lomond out,' he smiled savagely. 'You might think that strange, given what he's done and his big part in this...'

'Well, I do a bit, yes.'

Seth folded his arms and grinned. 'I'll be giving him a pasting, but I won't finish him. I figured given with what he'll be going down for, I don't want to give him the benefit of being dead when there are so many blokes in prison just *itching* to rip people like him apart. I'll personally make sure several influential residents at Her Majesty's Pleasure will know to expect him.'

Dan had to smile. Seth's attitude to all of this took some beating when all was said and done.

'In a way it would be nice to give Eliza and Digger that experience too,' Seth mused. 'However, what *they've* done is far too personal to warrant anything other than obliteration. Jane would divorce me if I suggested we let them walk away from this.' He frowned. 'Don't forget, I let them go last time – a *huge* oversight on my part with what's happened, as you can probably appreciate.'

Dan nodded. 'Understood.' He did. It made sense. He just hoped Seth wouldn't disappoint himself again by losing his temper at Lomond. It would defeat the object.

Seth sparked up a cigarette. 'When all this is over, we can concentrate on getting Grace back. We've managed to place it on hold for the time being, so at least we have a bit of breathing space.'

Dan thought Seth made everything sound so straightforward, when with everything considered it was anything but, however he wisely chose to keep that point to himself.

• • • •

DIGGER FORCED A SMILE across his scarred face as he grabbed Eliza around her waist from behind and pulled her close against him.

Feeling her stiffen and start to shrug him off in one of her usual petulant tantrums, Digger kept hold and trailed kisses down the side of her neck. If he could get her mind off all this business that she'd got her knickers in a twist over, he stood a *very* good chance of talking her into doing a flit with him whilst they still had the bloody chance.

'Digger, get off me, will you? I'm not in the mood,' Eliza snapped, twisting her body in an attempt to get out of his grip.

Not in the mood? She usually was with everybody else... Digger persisted with his advances. 'Come on babe!' he murmured in her ear, pulling her even closer knowing she'd feel his hardness pressing against the small of her back.

'We've been so stressed out lately, what with all the crap that's been going on.' Digger's tongue flicked teasingly in Eliza's ear. 'What do you say to knocking off early tonight? Let's go home and spend some time together.'

Eliza paused. *She could do with a bit of release if she was honest...* 'But what ab…'

'Forget about everything,' Digger said, remembering to keep his voice calm. He turned her around to face him. 'Forget all of this – all the grief, the kid thing, Lomond. Forget Seth and Jane. Let's just ditch it all off for one night.'

Digger's good hand inched underneath Eliza's short skirt. 'I know I haven't been giving you enough attention lately and I'm sorry…' *He wasn't. He wasn't at all. She pissed him off and he was fed up of it.*

Hearing Eliza let out a small moan as his fingers slipped inside her knickers, Digger smiled to himself. 'Let's crack open a bottle of champers at home and have a bit of fun. It's been too long and we've both been *far* too distracted recently. You'll see - after a bit of fun, things will be a lot clearer and we can work out what to do.'

Eliza pulled back slightly and looked up at Digger accusingly. 'I'm not running away and leaving this,' she stated. 'That won't change Digger, whatever you think.'

Digger smiled and gently moved one of Eliza's loose hair extensions off her face. 'It was only an idea, babe. Besides, do you really think I'd go if you weren't? It's me and you babe. Me and you. Always.' *Yeah right. If she wanted to wait to be lynched, then fair play, but he had no intention of doing that. Tonight however, she could think what she wanted just as long as she got off his case.*

Eliza grinned and palmed her hand over Digger's crotch. 'Glad to hear it. Come on then, let's go and drink that champagne. You can show me just how much you love me as well.'

Eliza snatched up her handbag from the desk and quickly left the office with Digger following behind.

At the end of the corridor, Selena slunk back further into the shadows and pulled her mobile phone Seth had handed her from her pocket.

Fifty Four

JANE'S HEART WAS BEATING like a drum as they drove along the road. Bile had been lurking ready to creep into her throat ever since Toby has been snatched, but even more so since Seth's mobile had rung three-quarters of an hour ago.

She hadn't expected for him to get the call so quickly and just hoped this wasn't yet another set up. The prospect that Selena could be part of a ruse was first and foremost in Jane's mind, but like Seth had pointed out, they had little choice but the trust the girl. Correction. They had *no* choice but to trust her. *They were out of all other options.*

Jane's nerves were completely shredded. She grasped pointlessly at the side of the car door purely for something to do to quiet her fidgety hands. If Toby wasn't there after all this, she didn't know what she'd do. Her heart already felt like it had been ripped clean out of her chest since the moment he'd gone and her mind was lurching between angst and anger. She was unable to quieten either of these overwhelming emotions.

Sweat trickled between her shoulder blades and whether she wanted it to or not, the images of Toby's dismembered corpse in the corner of a room flitted in and out of her mind. She shut her eyes and shook her head in a vague attempt to dislodge the reoccurring images, but to no avail.

She glanced in the wing mirror double-checking for the tenth time the white van containing the men was still following, along with Barry's car bringing up the rear and carrying Maggie. Satisfied they were all still there, Jane glanced at Seth, his green eyes fixed on the road ahead and his knuckles white from gripping the steering wheel.

'What if he's not there?' she asked, watching the nerve in Seth's neck twitching rapidly.

'He will be,' Seth muttered, still looking straight ahead.

'But what if he's *not*?' Jane cried. She had to try and prime herself for all eventualities, but she was struggling. She might die if her son wasn't within the confines of this dump of a building they were driving towards or *worse* – they'd done the unthinkable and killed him.

Tears burnt at the back of her eyes and Jane angrily blinked them away.

'He'll be there Jane,' Seth replied. 'Selena confirmed he's with Tina when she called.'

'I'm going to kill that bitch!' Jane spat, her jaw aching from clenching her teeth.

'No point in that,' Seth said. 'By all means give her a slap but save your wrath for your mate.'

'She's not my mate!' Jane snorted, not appreciating Seth's sarcasm. Oh yes, she'd definitely be catching up with Eliza, but she needed Toby back safe and sound first. Then and only *then* could she concentrate.

'I think this is it,' Seth pulled up alongside the kerb outside a row of large terraced houses.

Jane stared at the houses to the right. 'What, here?'

Seth nodded. 'This is the address.'

Jane eyed the tall row of houses backing onto an old industrial estate, full of disused factories. 'This doesn't look like a *brothel*!'

'I don't think it's *supposed* to look like a brothel! Isn't that the point?' Seth barked.

Jane shrugged and clambered out of the car.

• • • •

TINA WAS CRADLING TOBY on her lap, softly singing a song when the door to her bedroom burst open. 'What the…'

Her eyes widened with fear seeing Seth and Jane Wright crash into the room, closely followed by several other unsavoury looking characters.

'Thank God!' Jane cried, spotting Toby and rushed towards Tina as Seth grabbed a handful of the woman's hair, pinning her firmly into her chair.

'Give me my child,' Jane spat, snatching Toby effortlessly from Tina's arms.

'I'm sorry!' Tina garbled, her face contorting into a grimace when Seth's hand tugged harder at the remaining hair left attached to her scalp.

'Don't be telling me you're sorry!' Jane spat, before turning to Toby and smothering him in kisses.

Seth let go of Tina's hair and threw her roughly back in her chair. 'Maggie, take Toby and go with Barry,' he instructed, still watching Tina to ensure she didn't make any rash movements.

Jane reluctantly allowed Maggie to take Toby from her arms. At this precise moment she'd quite happily bin off all the other things they needed to do and go home with her son, but she knew that Maggie and Barry needed to get him out of here as quickly as possible.

There was a very real risk the noise could have disturbed and alerted Lomond from his distraction and they needed Toby as far away as possible if that had happened.

'Mummy will see you later baby,' Jane whispered to Toby as Maggie smiled, then scurried from the room with Barry in tow.

Now her son was no longer a distraction, Jane's eyes narrowed as she glared at Tina.

'It wasn't my fault!' Tina bleated, sensing correctly that something was undoubtedly about to happen. 'Lomond will hear you!' Even as she said it, she realised how ridiculous it sounded.

She glanced back at the people crammed into her small bedroom. *Like he'd be able to do anything to this lot!*

'Lomond eh?' Seth muttered. He nodded towards the men to follow Selena who waited in the hallway outside to show them which room he was in. 'Wait for us there. We won't be long.'

Tina's eyes flicked between Seth and Jane in panic when they resumed staring at her and she swallowed the lump of dread lodged firmly in the back of her throat. *How did they know where to come? Who had sold her out? Anna or Aiden?*

Anna didn't know where she worked, so she couldn't have been the one to send them here. *Which only left Aiden…*

'I've looked after Toby well, I promise you,' Tina blathered. 'I've enjoyed it actually,' she smiled.

Jane grabbed Tina around the throat. 'And I'm supposed to be pleased about that am I? Are you crazy?' she screamed.

'I didn't take him! It was Aiden and my sister. They're nuts. They were the ones, not me!' Tina pleaded, staring into Jane's dark eyes that were drilling holes into her brain. '*He* told you where Toby was, so you know it was him.'

'Aiden didn't say a fucking word, you junky whore,' Jane spat. 'You lot obviously have a lot more enemies than you realise.' *Enough of the talking.*

Jane began laying into Tina good and proper, raining her fists down into the woman's face. Tina was no match for Jane's speed and animal-like aggression and she raised her hands over her face to try and shield herself from the punishing blows.

Jane continued smashing her fist into Tina's face, sneering as her nose exploded and more of her teeth became dislodged. As Tina toppled from her chair, Jane started smashing her head into the floor.

Seeing the woman start to lose consciousness, Seth stepped forward. 'Think that'll do for now, Jane.'

Jane glanced at Tina's battered face and the blood pouring from her nose and mouth. 'I haven't come here for you anyway Tina,' she spat even though the woman was now out cold. With one last smash to the head, Jane spat in her face as she pushed herself up. 'Don't you *ever* touch my son again!'

• • • •

STEVE LOMOND WAS quite happily enjoying himself watching the girl in front of him slowly remove her clothing. Ok, so she wasn't a patch on Lacey Garner, but she was the best out of the rest of the bunch.

He'd been pleasantly surprised when she'd unexpectedly offered him her services tonight because he'd tried to get a session in with her previously, but she'd always managed to be 'otherwise engaged'.

He'd been beginning to take it personally but now it seemed he'd been wrong in his assumptions. He was very glad about that as she was a tasty piece.

Lomond eyed her pert young breasts greedily and ran his tongue along his fat bottom lip in anticipation watching her slip her pink knickers off. He'd get his money's worth out of this little slapper tonight. Not that he had to pay her, but that wasn't the point.

He tugged at the zip of his trousers. 'Firstly, girl, you can get your mouth round this!' he leered, pulling his rock hard erection free.

As the girl sank to her knees in front of him, Steve Lomond closed his eyes and awaited the feel of her lips around him. That was until the moment was ruined by the door being noisily kicked in. 'I said I was fucking busy ton…'

In a state of utter confusion, he stared as men stormed into the room, his eyes widening with shock when he realised who whey were.

'Steve Lomond?' Seth said, his voice betraying the utter contempt he held for this pitiful excuse of a man sitting in front of him.

Unable to articulate any coherent words, Lomond continued staring wildly around him and fruitlessly attempted to shove his now limp cock back into his trousers.

'Yeah, that's Lomond,' the girl muttered.

'You little bitch!' Lomond hissed at the girl, having finally found his voice.

Jane Wright stepped forward, grabbed the girl and pulled her out of the room to where Selena was waiting. 'Get your stuff and get packed. Selena will tell you what you need to do next.'

The girl nodded and ran off up the corridor, whilst Jane returned to the room, seeing Seth had the man pinned up against the wall.

'What's the meaning of this?' Lomond barked, attempting to play his bravado.

'Lomond,' Seth snarled, tempted to smile at the arrogance of the man before him. 'Or should I say *Carl Mulligan*... How are you, mate?'

Seth watched Lomond scowl, making his fat, pig-like face even more grotesque. 'Hear you've got a good thing going at this place, what with your penchant for young girls?'

Lomond squared up to Seth and sneered. 'Don't know what you mean. All the girls here are legal and over-age. There's jack shit untoward in this gaff *mate*.'

Seth's mouth twisted into a snarl. 'Over-age? Barely! You think that's ok, do you? Holding young girls against their will?'

Lomond laughed. 'Against their will? You joking? They want it. They all do. They don't *have* to be here!'

Jane felt her fists clenching. The need to claw this man's squinty little eyes from his sarcastic face was strong, but she'd let Seth have his time. Judging by the expressions of the other men's faces she could tell they were finding it equally difficult not to pummel the fat bastard into the floor.

'What's with all the set-ups then?' Seth barked, tightening his grip around Lomond's throat.

Lomond snorted derisively. 'Nothing to do with me. That's down to Eliza and Digger. I'm merely the messenger.'

'Then you need to take responsibility for that don't you! Your part in everything is your choice!' Seth raged.

'Why have you been setting us up against each other?' Jason Miller raged, stepping forward. *He wanted to rip the bastard apart.*

'And what about Lacey Garner, you perverted bastard?' Jane added, unable to help herself.

Lomond grinned. Let them do whatever they wanted. He didn't care. He was happy for them to finish him if they wanted to, but either way they wouldn't be receiving any form of apology. *Not now. Not ever.*

'Think this is funny, do you?' Seth raged. *The man was lighting his touch paper. He needed to keep cool.* 'Where's my daughter?'

Lomond laughed openly and heartily. 'Pretty thing she is. She'll do just fine here, don't you worry about that. Not sure if she's been broken in yet or not though,' he smirked. *That comment would push the baboon over the edge.*

Seth snarled as he laid into Lomond with the speed of light, but as his fist pounded the man's face into a mush, Jason Miller pulled at his arm.

'Seth,' he hissed. *He couldn't blow it now.* 'Remember the plan.'

Jane stepped forward and knelt down where Lomond was lying breathing heavily. He still retained a smug smile across his face. 'He's enjoying this, the twisted freak,' she spat.

Repositioning herself so she was looking directly into Lomond's repulsive face, she smiled nastily. 'It would suit you to be finished wouldn't it?' she said quietly. 'You're a bit fucked now really, so you're past caring, right?' She hated this man more than she thought physically possible.

Having reined his temper back in, Seth picked up Jane's threat. He knew where she was going with this. He placed his foot on Lomond's windpipe and exerted a slight amount of pressure. 'There's not much more than we'd like to do, other than rip you to pieces. It's exactly what you deserve.'

He pushed down a little harder with his foot and smiled when Lomond gagged. 'The thing is, after much discussion we've come to the conclusion you're such a fucking head-case, you'd get some satisfaction from that. Not to mention, the easy way out.'

Lomond forced himself to look up at the man who was slowly choking him. 'Nah, you're wrong. Whatever you do to me you're still fucked, Mr Wright. *You're* the one in the frame for the girl's rape and murder after all,' he grinned. 'And there's *nothing* you can do about it.'

Seth grinned widely, exposing his straight white teeth. 'Except there is. I can almost guarantee you've left your 'calling card' in that poor girl, you filthy piece of shit,' he snarled. 'Although I'd love to finish you, it will be much worse for you to go down for this…'

Realisation seeped into Lomond's brain. The first sign of fear flickered across his face when what could happen focused in his mind. He quickly shook it off. *They were playing him*. 'And how do you plan to pull that off?' he sneered. 'Unlikely you'll involve the police in all this. You won't be able to help yourself from killing me. I've heard all about you.'

Seth ground his boot a little harder into Lomond's throat. It was true. He'd have finished this prick if it had been up to him. His temper played right into some people's hands. *Not this time though.*

'Got to say you're wrong on that one. I'm not quite as predictable as some people like to think… You're right on one thing though – we're not going to the police...' Seth watched the sneer creep back across Lomond's face.

'That's right Lomond, *we're* not going to the police, but that's not to say *you* won't be served up by anyone else does it?'

Jane quickly injected Lomond's thigh. 'You'll be staying right here until the cops arrive.' She glanced at the clock on the wall. 'And I'd say that will be in about forty-five minutes from now.'

'What was that? What have you just done?' Lomond screamed, feeling the stab of the needle.

'Nothing dangerous. It'll just bliss you out for a couple of hours until you get picked up. The cops will be here soon and will be more than happy to find your DNA matches the sample they're waiting to put a name to,' Jane sneered.

'Now hang on,' Lomond babbled, attempting to push himself up, then realising the boot was no longer against his neck. Instead, his arms and legs were going fluffy and his head was beginning to spin. 'Wh-what you…'

'Hang on nothing, you cunt!' Seth roared. 'You're done! Furthermore, there's a very good associate of mine who's more than happy to spread the word of your deeds once you get sent down. That way you'll be dealt with accordingly.'

Real fear spread across Lomond's face. If he got sent down it would be for a good stretch. If the other inmates knew what he'd done, then he'd get grief for *years*. 'Wait, that won't… oh Christ…' His mind was spinning faster and faster and he knew he was beginning to lose consciousness.

This wasn't part of the plan. He hadn't expected them to pull this off. *He couldn't go to jail. Fuck no!* 'You bastards,' Lomond slurred.

Seth brushed himself down and smiled, watching Lomond's eyes rolling. 'We'll leave you to it now. Enjoy the next few years. Don't forget, I'll be waiting for you when you come out too – that's if you last that long…'

'You can't do this,' Lomond mumbled, desperately losing his fight against the strong sedative coursing through his veins.

'We just did, didn't we?' Seth laughed. 'Now shut the fuck up.'

Grabbing Jane's arm, Seth walked out of the room. 'Let's get on the road. Selena can put the call in to the cops as soon as we go.'

Jane nodded as they all hurriedly made their way down the stairs. 'The drug will last him about an hour. I've already given Selena the address of Pegasus Place. I've squared it away with that Sylvia that Jenny told us about. She's expecting all of the girls from here.'

'What about the junky?' Jason Miller asked. *When she came round would she attempt to help Lomond before the cops got hold of him?*

'Tina will be doing a runner the minute she can, I don't doubt,' Jane said. It was guaranteed that woman wouldn't be helping Steve Lomond with anything – that much was clear. 'Let's get a move on.'

Fifty Five

THEY'D WANTED TO DRAG it out and turn it into several hours of prolonged torture and misery, but it hadn't quite worked out like that.

Jane had got as far as individually breaking each of Eliza's fingers whilst she'd lay screaming and writhing on the floor, but she hadn't been able to bear looking at the woman using up oxygen any longer. Without warning, she'd slit her throat in one fail swoop.

Even Jason Miller had been surprised at how rapidly Jane had meted out the final payback.

The only thing she held in her mind was the terrified expression across Eliza's face when the knife had sliced through her neck. *It was done.*

Jane was still slightly in shock as to how her once good friend had turned into such a monster. Despite everything, she still felt a slight pang of guilt that it had come to this. *It should never have come to this.*

However, things couldn't be changed. Eliza couldn't take back what she'd done and nor could she. *And she didn't want to.*

She'd had no choice but to finish it. Even if she'd somehow found it in her power to forgive Eliza for the pain and damage she'd personally caused, it wouldn't have brought justice for Lacey or for any of the girls she'd used so despicably for a few quid. It *certainly* wouldn't have been justice over what she'd had planned for Grace either. *Her beautiful daughter*.

Jane scowled down at Eliza's inert body lying crumpled on the floor and shivered involuntarily with the creeping knowledge of what might have happened to Grace if Eliza and Digger had had their way.

The fact that the pair hated her and Seth so much that they were using their child as means to try and destroy them – an innocent child – in their quest for payback wasn't remotely acceptable in *anyone's* logic. Neither was what they had done to Lacey or what they had allowed to happen at the hands of that beast, Lomond.

Jane shuddered again and a mix of hatred and sadness washed over her, which was a strange combination. She blankly turned her gaze to the body of Digger who laid slumped on the floor the other side of the room.

Seth hadn't fared much better than her with keeping a lid on his temper. He'd rapidly dispatched Digger after spending a few minutes enjoying the man's agony during the removal of both his kneecaps.

Like Jane, Seth's combined hurt and anger had been his downfall and stopped him from dragging out the punishment they'd both agreed should be used. He'd finished Digger with a single clean shot to the temple.

Seth pulled himself up from the blood-splattered chair where he'd been sitting, staring vacantly as Jason and Dan started moving both the bodies into the centre of the room.

He ran the back of his hand across his mouth. 'Think that's us done then,' he muttered, placing his hand gently on Jane's arm.

Nodding, Jane stepped aside to let Seth begin setting up what was needed to ensure the evidence of their presence was removed.

Epilogue

'SO HOW ARE YOU feeling about it all now it's final?' Seth studied Jason Miller sitting in one of the leather armchairs in their living room.

'Relieved!' Jason answered. *It was true. Divorcing Linda was the only option he'd had.* Apart from the stirring she'd previously been responsible for, she'd also been publicly outed as manufacturing stories to the press. It had become obvious to all and sundry, especially Jason. Her aim had been to expose his dealings and then divorce *him* to get her hands on his assets.

Due to this, Jason had been able to cleanly remove his association with her, along with his marriage - without her receiving a penny. Not only had she lost her affluent lifestyle, but she'd also lost her standing with her beloved cliques. This was payback enough – at least for someone like *her*.

He couldn't even say he was upset. He just felt embarrassed and stupid for allowing her to get as far as she had. However, everything had worked out for the best in the end because his and Seth's joint venture was going from strength to strength.

The collateral they'd generated by merging their businesses into one joint holding company had been huge. Wright-Miller Clubs were now more on the map than ever. So much so that they'd recently purchased two further clubs in another city. It was all going well, however he was in no rush to get involved with another woman after getting his fingers burnt with Linda.

Jason Miller smiled warmly at Jane as she moved awkwardly across the room to sit next to Seth on the sofa. The expensive cream dress she wore clung to her heavily pregnant figure. 'How are you feeling, Jane?'

'Four days overdue is how I'm feeling,' Jane grumbled, wincing uncomfortably as she eased herself onto the seat.

Seth stared transfixed watching Jane's belly distinctly rippled from a flurry of kicks visible through her skin-tight dress. He was unable to stop himself from placing his hands on her and feel the miraculous movements.

'I wish they'd hurry up! I've been waiting *ages* as it is!' Seth smiled, picking up Toby's car which had slammed into his foot. He passed it back to his son, who took it and giggling, ran back across to the other side of the room to attempt to steer the car at his father once more.

'*You've* been waiting ages?' Jane squealed. She'd been shocked to discover she was pregnant again a couple of weeks after the Eliza and Digger incident. Another baby hadn't been on the cards until everything was sorted and they'd got Grace back, but nature had other plans it seemed.

She'd been even more shocked to discover she was expecting twins. Even Seth had been gobsmacked, but Seth being Seth, was doubly elated.

Shortly after this revelation, Seth had been officially cleared and exonerated from all charges or suspicions over the Lacey Garner case and a well-timed payment to someone in the right place ensured nothing else was being looked into by the police. *It couldn't have gone better.*

The sickening set-up Eliza and Digger had been operating had been nationally reported and cited their involvement in Lacey Garner's death, as well as the housing of the perpetrator – Steve Lomond.

Lomond had been duly charged for both murder and rape

when the DNA samples inevitably matched and he'd been sentenced to fifteen years. It had also not been sad news for anyone to learn the charred remains, only identified by dental records in the burnt-out shell of a plush suburban residence, had belonged to Eliza and Digger. *Freak electrical fire by all accounts.*

Had they not been already dead it was likely they'd have been lynched.

Jane winced once again as a barrage of kicks pounded inside her from the two tiny pairs of feet. Enjoying the feel of Seth's fingers trailing absentmindedly up and down her arm as he chatted to Dan and Jason, Jane closed her eyes momentarily in satisfaction.

Toby had not suffered for his kidnapping ordeal and it had been true that Tina had looked after him surprisingly well. Jane had no idea what had happened to that woman since that night in Elipse and quite frankly, she didn't care.

Anna however had been charged with aiding and abetting and had been sentenced to three years. The authorities however had, after a complete breakdown in police custody, deemed her mentally unfit and she was seeing her time out in a secure unit.

The girl had written several times apologising and asking for forgiveness. She'd even had the cheek to ask how Toby was. Jane had not replied. She would *never* forgive Anna for what she'd put them all through. Even though she hadn't breathed a word about anything that could have incriminated them, that girl had done too much to hurt her family to *ever* warrant any forgiveness in her opinion. No – it was done and she would not dwell on Anna Slater a moment longer.

Seth had also finally taken a back seat. The Wright-Miller holdings were all but running themselves and Dan had taken over the majority of the day to day running – not that there was much to do. They had so many staff between their businesses they were fast becoming one of the city's biggest employers.

There had been some further satisfying news when word had reached Seth that Lomond had been refused the protection of isolation. Seth had managed to ensure Lomond had been chucked into general population inside, thanks to his contacts. Lomond, the twisted bastard, had endured five months of consistent torture, degradation, humiliation and pain before he'd been finally found dead in his cell. *Shame...*

Things were definitely good.

'Look who's got something to show you,' Maggie exclaimed, entering the living room, quickly followed by Grace who darted past her like a little whirlwind.

'Mum, look at my hair!' Grace cried, her exquisite heart-shaped face alight with excitement and her dark green eyes bright. She tossed her curly raven hair from side to side and smiled widely when Jane admired the collection of tiny butterfly clips Maggie had placed in her hair.

'Auntie Maggie's done it. Do you like it? Do I look pretty?' Grace asked.

Seth scooped his daughter up onto his lap and kissed her on the forehead. 'You look beautiful Princess – as always,' he smiled.

Jane squeezed Seth's hand. The icing on the cake that had completed Jane's world had occurred when she was five months' pregnant and they had won custody back.

They both knew they still had some way to go with their daughter, because the last six years couldn't be erased just like that. At first, Grace had retreated deep inside her shell, but after a couple of weeks, she'd begun to tentatively shine through.

It had been heart-breaking when Grace had consistently asked when she'd be sent back or how long she'd be staying for. It had taken several further weeks for it to sink in that she wouldn't have to leave *ever* again. Now, apart from the occasional hiccup and nightmare, things were settling down.

They hadn't asked Grace to call them Mum and Dad – accepting that would take time – if ever, to happen, but one day it had sunk into the little girl's mind that the most recent strangers she'd been sent to live with were in fact her *real* parents.

It had been one of the sweetest things Jane thought she'd ever heard when her lost daughter called her 'Mum' for the first time.

'Are the twins still in there, Mummy?' Grace asked, pointing at Jane's massive belly.

'They're most definitely still in there sweetheart,' Jane smiled as Grace rested her head gently against the huge mound. 'I don't think they'll be too long now though.'

'I want to call them Angela and Belinda,' Grace chirped.

Seth laughed. 'One's a *boy* silly! You can't give a boy a girl's name!'

'Why not? My dolls are called Angela and Belinda and they're not even real. They're plastic! I want the babies to be my *real* dolls,' Grace insisted, her rosebud mouth pouting in frustration.

'I'd best get off,' Jason said, getting up from the armchair. 'Before Grace renames *me* Lilly or something.'

'That's a nice name too!' Grace said. 'Can you have *three* babies instead, Mummy?'

'I don't think so,' Jane laughed, struggling to get up. 'There's barely enough room for these two in here as it is!' Hefting herself to her feet with the help of Seth, Jane kissed Jason on the cheek.

Shaking Jason's hand, Seth put his arm firmly around Jane's shoulders, resisting the impulse to run his hands over her belly once more. 'I'll catch up with you soon, Jason, ok? And don't sweat over your divorce!'

'I certainly won't be!' Jason smiled, glancing worriedly at Jane when her face screwed up with pain. 'Jane, are you ok?'

Jane clutched at her belly and doubled over as a sudden and massive contraction racked through her. 'Oh!' she cried. 'Oh God!'

Seth held Jane as she lurched forward to make sure she didn't topple to the floor. 'Jane?'

A second strong contraction immediately followed the first. *These babies were coming and they were coming now.* 'Shit

Seth! It's happening!'

'What's happening?' Grace cried, darting back around the sofa, her big eyes wide.

Jane sucked in a large breath as she rode another excruciating wave of pain. 'OWWWW!'

Seth attempted to steer Jane to a chair. 'Come and sit down.'

'Can't!' Jane panted. 'Can't sit down. They're coming… Coming *now*!'

Seth paled. *He could do most things, but deliver a baby? Two babies? Oh shit.*

'I'll call the hospital,' Dan said, moving quickly into the hall.

'Come on you two!' Maggie said brightly, grabbing Grace's hand and beckoning Toby out from behind the curtain where he'd built a den.

'You won't have to wait long to meet your brother and sister,' Jane smiled at her children between waves of pain.

'Really?' Grace beamed. 'Can I watch?'

'NO!' Maggie laughed. 'Come on. Let's go and play a game.'

As Maggie herded the children out of the room and upstairs, Seth helped lower Jane onto the floor where she knelt on all fours, panting heavily.

'The ambulance is on its way,' Dan said edging back into the living room.

'No time,' Jane cried. 'I need to push!'

'Fuck!' Seth exclaimed, glancing at Dan and Jason as an unfamiliar wave of panic washed over him.

'Get her knickers off Seth – we won't look,' Jason said calmly. 'Dan, go and grab some towels.'

• • • •

THERE WAS BARELY ENOUGH space for everyone in the small hospital room. When the ambulance arrived ten minutes after the first contraction, the first of the twins had already been delivered into Seth's waiting hands. The ambulance man delivered the second twin seven minutes later.

After giving Jane several stitches caused by the speed of the delivery, the hospital confirmed everyone was fine and in good health. She and the twins could go home the next day.

'I love you Jane,' Seth murmured, kissing Jane gently on the lips. She was glowing with happiness and he watched a tear roll down her flushed cheek as she cradled the new-borns in her arms. 'I'm so very proud of you.'

'You didn't do too badly yourself,' Jane smiled.

Seth grinned. He wasn't about to tell her he'd thought he might pass out with fear when he'd realised he would have to deliver the first child. It had all happened so fast and they were beautiful. *Absolutely beautiful.*

He took in the twins' tiny matching faces and little fingers and his heart swelled once again with all-encompassing love. Finally, their life was complete and everything was perfect. *Everything.*

Thank you!

Thank you for reading *Vengeful Payback*. I hope you enjoyed reading it as much as I did writing it!

If so, would you please consider leaving a review on Amazon and/or Goodreads.

Reviews from readers are SOOOO helpful and especially important to us authors and without you we would have nobody to write for!

Thank you once again and hope you enjoy the rest of my books.

Edie xx

More From this Series

#1 - UNTIL THE END OF TIME

'Brutal, vicious, shocking... A cataclysmic novel of life in its most raw form...' *– 5 stars – Picky B*tches Book Blog*

Dive into Seth and Jane's train wreck life, where drugs, alcohol and obsessional love means this downright dangerous pair will do *anything* to ensure nothing gets in their way.

They do bad things. *Very* bad things and their promise to love each until the end of time turns into a war against each other.

A war neither of them can win.

'...I couldn't help but think of Seth and Jane like the couple in the movie Natural Born Killers. Which, at the time was a pretty controversial movie, much like what I think this story is as well... I love how the author did not hold anything back. The story is in your face, every messed up thing you can think of is probably written in the pages... ' *-5 stars - Sinfully Wicked Book Reviews*

#2 – ESCAPING THE PAST

'Dark and impossible to put down...' *- 5 stars*

Things have changed and Jane has got on with her life.

Well, not *entirely...*

Embroiled in a bitter feud between two rival firms, it is clear that not everyone is who they proclaim to be.

The net is closing in and some things just can't be changed.

'Totally addictive...' *- 5 stars*

'...a well-written, fast-paced, gripping, edge of your seat kind of tale... This story is strongly recommended...' *- 5 stars*

'...I am very impressed by this author and their ability to write a book that was like a mobster movie...The characters were real, believable and raw... Shocking twists and turns...' *- 5 stars*

*** These are Downfall Series books, but can be read as standalones. They contain written depictions of graphic violence, sex and strong language and also contain some themes that may be uncomfortable for certain readers.***

MORE FROM THIS AUTHOR

RETRIBUTION SERIES:

#1: AN OLD SCORE

Three families... One prize...

Teagan Fraser had no idea what she was getting herself into when she took on an assignment as a live-in carer for Dulcie Adams – a retired dancer from a Soho club. Dulcie has waited forty years for a time that never came and left looking after something important, which Jonah Powell and his firm want back.

In addition to the notorious Powell firm, there are others wanting to claim what they believe is rightfully theirs and they'll do anything to get it back.

A lot can happen in the space of two weeks and Teagan might wish she'd never become involved.

#2: FINDERS KEEPERS

The race is on...

When Saul Powell is released early from prison, it causes mayhem for the family firm. His brother, Jonah, has enough problems trying to keep semblance amidst the chaos, not to mention his fast approaching unwanted marriage.

Even Jonah's problems pale into insignificance compared to what Robert Adams is discovering about his mother, Dulcie – the woman he's always put on a pedestal.

Can anyone come out of this nightmare unscathed?

#3: THE FINAL TAKE

The time is now...

Even knowing Ron O'Hara is somewhere in the vicinity, Jonah Powell feels it's time to finally get rid of the diamonds which have haunted his family for decades and caused so much trouble.

However, other problems start to arrive from unexpected and additional sources, some of which Jonah didn't expect.

But what does it all mean? It may be apt to call time on the curse plaguing his family and of those around him, but how can this be achieved while so many other things are at stake?

More From this Author

HUNTED SERIES:

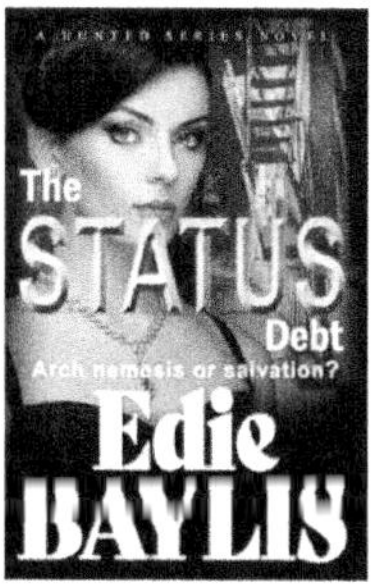

#1: THE STATUS DEBT

Lillian Morgan would do anything to regain the status she lost by marrying beneath her and to cover the sordid details of her husband's death. This includes blackmail and the hand of marriage of her own daughter.

Tori thought her life couldn't get much worse, but someone is not being honest and secrets have the power to rip everyone to shreds.

Especially when life is built on lies.

#2: THE FAMILY LEGACY

Unsure of whether Matt or Hunter has fathered the child growing inside her, Tori's unwanted wedding to Matt grows closer, but is there light at the end of the tunnel? Unfortunately, Tori hasn't counted on another man present in her life. One who is more instrumental in her misery than she realises.

Sometimes the truth is too late in coming and makes bad things happen and sometimes a hidden legacy can cause the most horrific thing of all…

#3: THE TARGET OF LIES

Neil Sparks has a score to settle. In fact, he has several… His first port of call when returning from France after a five year exile is to catch up with his estranged wife. Secondly, Neil wants to even a score with the people instrumental in his departure and thirdly, he wants an explanation from the man who promised his marriage would be free from hassle. The trouble is, he's not the only one with an agenda…

There are too many people about to become caught in the crossfire and everyone could become a target.

MORE FROM THIS AUTHOR

ALLEGIANCE SERIES:

#1: TAKEOVER

Samantha Reynold hadn't bargained on unexpectedly needing to step into her father's shoes and take over the family casino business and known nothing about the rules of this glamorous but deadly new world. But she won't let her family down, especially when it looks like they could lose everything to their biggest rivals – the Stoker family.

Eldest son Sebastian hasn't got time to pander to pretty girl Samantha as she plays at being boss. Rumours are swirling around the streets of Birmingham that have the power to rip the Stoker family apart and destroy everything they've built.

#2: FALLOUT

With the odds stacked against her, Samantha Reynold is determined to prove she's tough enough to be the boss. But when a secret from the past threatens to ruin Sam's reputation, she suddenly feels very alone in this dark new world. There's only one man she can turn to – rival club owner, Sebastian Stoker.

Seb knows first-hand how secrets and lies can tear a family apart. He wants to protect Sam at all costs, but siding with her could threaten his own position as head of the Stoker family and risk accusations of betrayal.
With loyalties divided and two families at war – the fallout could be deadly.

About The Author

Over the years Edie has worked all over the UK as well as in several other countries and has met a lot of interesting people - several of whom have supplied ideas for some of the characters in her books! She has now settled back in central England with her partner and children, where she is pursuing her writing.

Edie writes gritty gangland fiction, using a combination of thrillers, suspense and romance.

She is currently signed to Boldwood Books for a 5-book gangland fiction series set in Birmingham. The first in the *Allegiance* series, *Takeover* was released in January 2022 and the second, *Fallout*, will be released in May 2022.

Edie's other series are the *Retribution* series, the *Hunted* series and the *Downfall* series - all trilogies.

When she isn't writing, Edie enjoys reading and is a self-confessed book hoarder. She also enjoys crochet and music as well as loving anything quirky or unusual.

Visit www.ediebaylis.co.uk for the latest news, information about new releases, giveaways and to subscribe to her mailing list.

ACKNOWLEDGEMENTS

Thanks to the people that kindly read my drafts of *Vengeful Payback* – you know who you are and I appreciate your time and feedback.

Printed in Great Britain
by Amazon

60814387R00262